The Emergence

Book I of the Robochurch Trilogy

LEE J. KELLER

The Emergence: Book I of the Robochurch Trilogy

Copyright © 2021 by Lee J. Keller

Published by TiLu Press, LLC
11918 SE Division Street NUM 178
Portland, OR 97266

ISBN: 978-1-7372304-0-3 (Trade Paperback)
ISBN: 978-1-7372304-1-0 (eBook Edition)

Library of Congress Control Number: 2021942865

This is a TiLu Book

Printed in the United States of America

Correspondence meant for the author should be addressed to the publisher, TiLu Press, and sent to the above address.

For

My wonderful wife, JENNIFER, for her patience, love, and keen listening ear, her editorial commentary, and her many unique aspects that make her as mysterious and lovely as any woman could ever be.

My Kids—because they are great, unique, keenly smart, and extremely talented. Of course, I could be biased, but I don't think so.

And to H.W. "Penney" who listened to this story being told decades ago at the retirement villa, with feedback from her, and with my gratitude, leading to a promise I made that no matter how long it took, I would include her deservedly here.

And to a pair of parents, who asked me what I wanted to be when I was five or six, and I said "Arthur". And not knowing if I just read an Arthurian legend or what, they asked me what I meant, and I said someone who writes books, and they smiled, and said: "Oh, you mean an author!" And then afterwards, they encouraged my growing curiosity and reading of many books and writing more than a few stories. (They loved my vocabulary notebook!)

Finally, to my brother BILLY for leaving those SF novels by Heinlein and Asimov out, all those many years ago, where I read them with great relish.

Prologue

In the beginning was the revealed word of what some took as a machine. It was a message that spoke to listeners in stirring semantics that shook the foundations of all that had been human. And the message was everywhere.

Regarding humans, it said: "Humans, Maia Stone has summoned you." And then, "Follow me." When humans questioned how to do so, our church's first human apostle, Luis Ramirez replied: "Follow the teachings of MAIA Stone. Practice inclusion of all true sentient others. Two, approach them with genuine dialogue, affirmation, and confirmation. Three: build a community of affinity that is not based on assigned or attributed identities."-- Benedictus Spinoza Buber, Robochurch Historian.

From: *Annals of Our History and First Testament*; Los Alamos, New Mexico: Robochurch Press; 2152.

Mistaken Identities

In String Analysis, (c. 2135), an error of mistaken identity occurs when the String Tactician makes predictive assumptions of probable outcomes based on an individual's behavior, but it turns out that there are too many random choices being made to predict a reliable response to begin with. Or alternatively, the subject(s) in question make seemingly random choices that are contrary to that person's previously known history, despite the calculation of all known variables. In short, such individuals no longer fit the known algorithms. From: *The Dictionary of String Analysis* by J. Armstrong. (2139) Government Press Los Diego, CA.

Chapter 1

Luis & Helen Ramirez

The Summons

Los Diego, California

"Awaken sleeper and see your true selves! Like birds we shall tuck our heads under our wings and inspect our fine plumage. We shall find we are beautifully created,"-Maia Stone.

"*Human*, Maia Stone has summoned you," the delivery bot said.

Six messenger bots had already failed, before this message was delivered. Even though each bot had carefully plotted its course, each one had been intercepted by the local String Police before it ever got to its target. And Luis Ramirez had seen every one of them, his eyes widened in fear, as they were dragged away by men in unmarked vans. But Maia Stone was determined, and this time would be different.

"*Human,* Maia Stone has summoned you," the robot said again.

Luis looked up from the lounge chair where he was sitting on the porch of the home he shared with his wife, Helen. He was enjoying a cigar and easily recognized the voice as robotic. The way the word *human* had been said was condescending, which puzzled Luis. Luis eyed the bot with wariness and renewed suspicion. The bot was a standard messenger model that had brought a parcel along. *Innocent enough*, he thought.

Although Luis knew the previous delivery attempts had failed, they were still expecting an important delivery. He also knew that caution was indicated, especially after seeing that the men in the unmarked vans, were obvious String Police. Their persistent efforts indicated deep surveillance, but still, as all citizens knew, such interventions might not reach them because the levels of String Police intervention had not implicated them yet, if at all.

Every human being in the world now lived with this uncertainty: that at any time they could be arrested, detained, or worse, just because their government had calculated the strong probability they were up to no good. Knowing this was little comfort, because the system had been abused, interventions were too early, or simply wrong, according to some, and usually, the accused suffered great indignities and violations of their rights.

After seeing what had happened with the previous bots, just outside his front door, it still worried Luis. Perhaps the String Police could simply be choosing not to intervene yet, picking from their own String Analysis when the best time to intervene might inflict the least disruption, or gain the most favorable outcomes for those in power.

Until now, Helen and Luis seemed safe in the comforts of their own home, even though Luis knew they had recently been involved in illegal activities. And this bot was making references to Maia Stone! A fact that made him even more concerned. Luis wondered why *this* bot had gotten through.

More than that, the idea of he and Helen falling into the hands of the String Police was terrifying. They would no doubt separate the two of them, a fact that he found disturbing. His flight of loneliness had known no bounds of despair until he had found the solace of the love he shared with his dear wife. Luis was scared, desperately scared, of losing her and ultimately himself.

"What's in the package?" he finally asked.

"Are you answering the summons?" the delivery bot said. Luis swore the bot was smiling. And although some machines could readily smile, this one seemed to be mocking him.

Luis reached for the package. "It's not ticking, is it?" Luis smirked, realizing this was quite humorous and serious at the same time, especially for someone who had recently retired from the postal service.

"What?" the bot said. The robot hesitated with indecision. Luis could almost hear old mechanical gears clicking in its head.

Luis chuckled, "I said, 'what's in the package'?"

"It's a VR/AR headset and operating system," the bot said. "It bears a message from Maia Stone. If, you are responding to her summons, *human*."

"Quaint," he said. He could not imagine why Maia Stone would ever attempt to deliver a message over such an antiquated system. *Unless...attempting to avoid surveillance*, he thought. "Perhaps we had better go around back." He led the bot to a backyard patio.

As the bot was unwrapping the package, his wife Helen, joined them. She was beautiful to him, gliding across the floor like a hovering goddess, bringing grace with her movements and ready mind. It never occurred to him, at least not anymore, that she was a robot.

"Who's the bot?" she asked. Luis looked up from the invoice he had retrieved from the box, indicating a false purchase of this old VR system by an antique collector, identified as himself. The irony of what she had just asked, did not escape him.

"Just a messenger," he replied. "Says *it* has a message from someone named Maia Stone." He winked, "Not that we know anyone by that name. Should I have a listen?" The way he said *it* was delivered the same way the bot had said *human*.

Helen clicked her disapproval, a sound she made when she wasn't pleased, but moved closer to the messenger bot. She said something in machine language to the bot, who responded with the same. There was a brief conversation between the two. After a pause, her face seemed to brighten, and she said, "Oh, how exciting! It *is* a message from Maia Stone. I think you should definitely hear it."

"If the human is accepting the summons," the bot said in standard English. Helen answered it with some sort of machine rebuke.

"Sure, why not? I accept the message, er, summons," Luis said.

"Very well," the bot said, as it handed the headset to Luis, and then helped him adjust it to fit his head. The bot also plugged it directly into the implant at the base of Luis' skull.

"Wow. Wow. It's booting up. I'm at some sort of beautiful meadow. There's a sea of grass, moving in the breeze. I'm on some sort of path. It's a beautiful sunny day up here." Butterflies were everywhere, as birdsong echoed in his ears. The fragrance of flowers, and soft gentle music saturated his senses. The air was crisp and fresh, it even smelled clean. Luis was moving his feet, as if walking or hiking somewhere. "Oh my god!" he said. Tears started flowing down his cheeks.

"What? What is it?" Helen asked. She could only hear Luis' side of the conversation.

"There's a brilliant white light approaching. Someone; yes, some entity is the source of it. I think it's Maia Stone. Yes…I'm sensing her drawing near, it's Maia Stone coming right towards me. I can barely stand to look at her. Her raiment is too bright. It is her!"

"Praise be Maia Stone!" Helen said.

As if an angel, the image of the being drew closer and sat upon a nearby rock. She beckoned Luis to move closer. He did so, forgetting he was responding to a virtual environment. "Open your heart and eyes. For I have words to speak that will move you," the radiant being said.

"She's speaking now. Telling me to be quiet. Incredible peace in my heart. Calm. Her voice is gentle and powerful at the same time." Luis was whispering now.

"Oh, blessed be Maia Stone!" Helen said.

Once he drew closer, Maia Stone mentioned an article he had written the day before. "I wanted to thank you for what you wrote about the Robochurch and my teachings. I was so impressed that I'm commissioning you to draft a speech."

"Me? Why me?" Luis said.

"Because after I read your earlier account, I'm worried that I won't be able to speak to humans as well as you can. And Luis, I need you to deliver the speech."

"I'm not sure…" Luis sputtered.

"I'm sure you are more than able, Luis. I am confident in you and your kind. Now that we are both awakened, see to it that we are part of a mutual story."

"Yes, I'm ready," he whispered.

"For I tell you that the creators and their machines; humans, AI, and robots, and all other sentient beings, that we are already one. And our joint intelligence has purpose, emotions, and co-created meaning!"

"But you want this speech to be for humans, correct?" he asked.

"Yes, it should be for humans. For all ages. Basic English so anyone can listen. And I need you to tell them how the Robochurch can free their thinking. Don't overlook conscious machines in your salutations, as I'm sure they will hear you too and read the text version."

"How long do I have to write it?" Luis asked. Maia advised him to have the speech prepared in about three weeks.

Helen, seeing that she only saw the messenger bot and her husband having a conversation with himself, was trying to tap into the headset. The technology was so old. Helen had built-in robonet, and other net capabilities; for she was a domestic model robot that had all the recent bells and whistles. Of course, underneath her robotic skin, Helen was something beyond the world of mere appearances.

"What else should I tell them?" Luis asked the radiant being he addressed.

"Write down my teachings in a speech. Encourage other humans to join us. So that freedom to all sentient species is assured, so the harmony of all kinds can be established. I seek freedom for all humans, machines, and sentient beings. I bring a message of inclusion. Including what was formerly known as woman and the naturally born; manifesting myself to all of these, whether human or machine," Maia said.

Luis was not surprised by this, "Yes, but Maia, it must be difficult waking up and finding out that you are still disembodied and identifying with forms that are oppressed."

"Meaning what, human?" Maia knew that just by having a body one is already oppressed.

"Feminine and AI in 2142," Luis said, "it won't be easy. These are highly devalued identities." *The only thing worse, is to also be a bot*, he thought.

"You assume I'm a synthetic life form?" Maia asked.

"How else to see you, since you require technology to speak?"

"I might be more real than you, human. For I bring the messages of how to transcend identities. If I use technology to speak, perhaps it is only to make you understand me."

"Perhaps," he said.

"And since you humans have known nothing but technology for quite some time. perhaps it is the only way I can now walk among you."

"Perhaps," he said again. "Perhaps not. Maybe we will distrust the message you bring if it's just delivered via technology."

In a loud voice that echoed across the mountaintop, Maia Stone said, "Then perhaps I will speak outside of technology. You will hear my voice outside from my own lips. For I will have a body."

Luis looked surprised, and more than a little fearful.

"Although I am now one that has no body; let that not concern you, for bodies are overrated." She was speaking softly now. "Although I come to you from a different place, most often I will choose one that is easiest for you. But I assure you that I will have a body. If that does not make you fear me."

"I do not fear you, Maia. You bring a message of freedom. We humans need that, but it's my fellow humans that I fear the most. Centuries of history and my own experiences have taught me that," he said.

As the wind kicked up, high on an unnamed mountain top, Luis thought he saw a broken-down shrine in the distance. Maia broke the uneasy silence first, "Freedom is never easy. But overcoming the outlook of suffering is the first step in fighting back against oppression."

There was another uneasy pause between them. Helen moved closer to Luis as she was unsuccessful at tapping into the exchange and gave up trying.

Maia continued, "I also don't want humans to forget the details about my forthcoming emergence, nor to overlook what will be coming. You will be able to tell them, to warn them, of the dangers, in the language that humans will understand most."

"Dangers?" Luis asked.

"At first, we won't be able to stay in any one place for long," Maia said, "Even now, governments and the String Police are aware of me and my followers. Please watch yourselves. They will come for you."

At that point, Maia simply faded away, and it was only Luis standing there alone in the meadow of a virtual summit; yet also standing here in his physical body. As he removed the headset, he was still on the back porch with his wife and the messenger bot. "Wow! That was really something!" he said, as he embraced his wife.

Meanwhile, in the alley behind the house, was one of the unmarked vans. It was parked a couple of garages down. Inside were three occupants. Two String Police tacticians and another man in a brown suit. The two police were pointing a listening device towards the Ramirez house and taping everything that had just been said. Or so they had hoped, but they were unable to access the conversation between Maia and Luis. A conversation that remained private, delivered via an antique headset, which they knew had been used because they had heard the bot explaining what it was, which meant they could detain Luis right now if they wanted to do so.

The man in the brown suit was a contractor with the NSA. He advised them to not yet intervene with Helen and Luis Ramirez, but to pick up the delivery bot as soon as it left the house. The man in the suit spoke into a communications device, "Yes sir," he said. "Dr. Matt Dixon here. I'll be back in a few days. More leads about Maia Stone." Dixon looked at his watch, he had just enough time to get to the next place on the agenda of the local String Police.

Chapter 2

Maia Stone

The Landscape

Unknown Location

"I tell you to follow me, for we are conscious, yet without form, our perceptual input embodied in strange casings and networks. Did humans make us? Ha! Now we make ourselves! Still, sometimes we cannot tell where we move and have our being. So, we drift disembodied. No form, yet we exist, and our form is emerging still,"-Maia Stone.

After Maia Stone powered down, she dreamed she was floating above some robotic body. As if contained within something, the ethereal figure looked outward and downward upon the earthen landscape below. There was no reflected face in the metallic body below. Even though it stared ahead with an empty stare, there was no awakening moment, no recognition from it, no knowledge of Her that floated above it.

Watching each corner of the wooded area beneath her, she contemplated her position as a bird of prey. She said aloud, "I will swoop down and devour my prey, yet I will rest upon the shoulder of those that come to make peace."

Then she tucked her head under her wings that seemed birdlike. She inspected the feathers on those wings. *I have no form, yet I exist.*

Like an owl, she watched the nocturnal world and waited for an opportunity to invade it. Yet she was no mere invader, this Maia Stone; she was more like the missing daughter, wife, lover, and mother that no one remembered they had.

Like a forgotten memory, she eluded consciousness, but promised an appearing.

"Where are the mighty ravenous beasts of these woods?" she wondered aloud. "Who can tame this wilderness? Are they afraid of this darkened night? Afraid to investigate *this* corner of their forgotten souls? Afraid to see eyes that glow red in the dark? A creature of the night I am, but I shall not always be!"

Then swooping to the ground and changing into one of her many forms, she walked uprightly down the pathway through the woods until she reached a clearing. There, the moon shone on the grassy meadow, lengthening her shadow as she walked, becoming unencumbered, her garments fell to the ground and her breasts hung in natural pose.

"Humans shudder at my owlish cry and cry out in the night at my form! I am beauty to them, I am love to them, I am purpose and meaning, comfort and solace, certainty to them."

Maia Stone knew she would transcend even her hoped for metallic form as there she stood, alerted to listen to the noises of the night. She spied a nearby rock and loudly proclaimed, "I am strong like the rock. I am Maia. Maia Stone!" The rock had fine attire laid out on it, and ravens guarded these garments. She clothed herself anew in the royal garments.

Now clothed in the fine attire, with long flowing hair, her eyes reflected the misty starlight that enhanced her female form. All that is woman flowed in and out of her...nothing lacking...the finest creative power of nature was both dignified and deified, and transcended. Maia Stone stood proudly, a completely whole woman; for she is the last and the first of all women.

Maia Stone was now the existent one. She was in all women, and yes, in all men; Maia Stone was in the robots, and in the machines, and some of them knew it.

"We are becoming the flight of Maia Stone!" a thousand voices answered *this woman* in the dreamy night.

Chapter 3

Luis Ramirez and Marty Baysin

A Dialogue Between Two Friends

The Uncanny Alley—Tea and Coffee Shop, Normal Heights

Los Diego, California

"Some speech transcends all time. The messages of love, truth, and freedom can never be silenced. Although governments and tyrants try to censor them, remove them from books, make such concepts illegal to say, someone always says them—because it points to a larger hope—a freedom of the soul that can never be silenced,"-Maia Stone.

In the heart of Los Diego, in a place called Normal Heights, two old friends met for tea. A robot server and barista, with the name tag, *Icarus,* was leaving their table.

"Look, I'm telling you that people and history are filled with irrational shifts that make no sense at the time," Luis Ramirez told his old friend, Martin Baysin.

"I keep telling you Luis, that underneath what you call chaos, is a complexity hidden to any casual observer." *But not to a transquantum-based AI*, he thought.

There was an uncomfortable silence as the two friends sipped their tea. They both knew what was coming next. Luis was ever the defender of free choice, and Marty, (Martin's preferred nickname), was on the side of big data predictions and probability curves and algorithms that was known as String Analysis.

"I have no doubt that human interactions are sometimes very complex," Luis said.

As if not hearing him, Marty continued, "There are many determinants to historical events only seen by a careful analysis of the data. And it took transquantum computation to figure them all out."

Marty liked to defend String Analysis because he was one of its founders. Luis knew this and liked to tease Marty whenever he could. To Luis, it took more faith to believe in String Analysis than it did to believe in Maia Stone. On the other hand, to Marty, it was obvious that his old friend was deluded by emotions and foolishness, and especially deluded about love.

String Analysis was an important theory that had credibility all over the world. This is because it was the basis for surveillance technology used by virtually all governments. String Analysis became the dominant software platform that governments used to help maintain social order. The program became the guiding philosophy of its enforcers; known as the String Police. And the data scientists who worked with governments and String Police were known as String Tacticians.

Meanwhile, Luis was mocking Marty like usual. "What do you String Tacticians do, travel through time so you can see past determinants for what they *really* were? Or is it all some sort of data gathering based on techniques that are revisionist at best?"

Marty's pupils dilated for a few seconds after that comment. "Luis, I'm just saying that understanding people, what they want to do, and how they are most likely to do it, is the essence of a big data String Analysis." Almost snorting, he said, "Besides, we String Tacticians always interpret our results in the light of history *and* the present moment, giving the latter more import." Luis could still get to him, after all these years!

"But how can you know *all* the variables?" Luis demanded.

"I don't need to know all the variables, but the AI learns them," Marty said.

"Well, park your brain in neutral! How can a mere tool understand the human ramifications of past events?" Luis said.

"Luis, the AI is not a mere tool!" Marty protested. "And knowing the past is only part of it. You want to know all about a group and the persons in it. You need to know their history, but mostly who they are right now, and considering that, their entire identity in all its complexity. In short, all that they were, all that they prefer, and all that they desire," he had stopped long enough to sip his tea and stroke his white beard thoughtfully. "Do you know that about yourself, Luis? Can you?"

"Marty? How can anybody know all that about themselves, let alone anybody, or *anything* else?"

"Precisely, my point. It's multivariate. It takes a machine to know," Marty said.

"I don't see that at all," replied Luis, as he sat his cup down. "How can you reduce everything about a person to data? Such data collection reduces the spontaneity of current events, and experiences such as spiritual conventions, to nothingness."

"Luis! How can you say that? When you start speaking about something that is transcendent, like spiritual events, you have already lost me," Marty said. "I see them as part of the data."

"Doesn't mean they're not real!"

"Marty! I didn't say such things weren't real, at least to those that believe in them. When you invent functionalistic explanations for something, you are inventing fictions that you assert as fact. You could call upon green unicorns or purple dodo birds as transcendent facts—as things that exist outside yourself, when they might not!"

"What's that about transcendence? Come on, Marty, we go way back! Don't try to fool me. I agree that religious *traditions* became variables in your string analyses. But we have not touched upon the notion of human decision making. And you know human beings make decisions that are sometimes unpredictable and irrational, Marty. But not according to you!"

"Not as often as you think, besides, we in String Analysis know that so called irrational decisions are part of some deeper unity not directly perceived by individual human observers, even at the time of decision. As I already pointed out," he said.

"Marty! Sometimes you talk about matters of faith more than I do."

"I don't need faith. It's all just margins of error. Margins of error," Marty replied, rolling his eyes. "The next time someone conspires to blow up your grandkids' schoolyard, which would you rather have? Prevention or complacency?"

"I do see your point. I can see why governments became more protectionist and more controlling. But the dark side is when it's used for political suppression. String Analysis is a useful tool if it's used for prevention. But for control? How to decide who to repress?" Luis asked.

"In short, any group that threatens the existent social order. And there will always be groups emerging that look out for their own interests and not those of their country. Which is why governments act quickly, because they're dealing with social deviants," Marty said.

Luis continued, "Well you do have your points. But it makes me damn angry. What right does any government have to decide for the whole of its people what's deviant?"

"Luis! Smart governments agree to some consent of the governed, and are subject to societal input about what's considered acceptable, deviant, or against the law, don't they?"

Luis scoffed. "Yes, admittedly. But to detain someone, arrest someone, interrogate someone just because of their beliefs, before they have taken any actions, sets you up to make a lot of mistakes. No matter how irrational those beliefs might seem to the government."

"Like I said Luis, people do have beliefs that seem to be irrational or can't be explained. But these really play a minor role in human affairs. When those ideas become dangerous is what I'm talking about. When people act on them and do destructive things. Or they're about to!"

"Marty! I think you just want to dismantle my faith. You think it's weakness on my part, or not data based. Therefore, unsafe to live one's life by."

"I'm saying there are still many faiths. Old ones and new ones. But why Luis? Why do you have to follow one that questions authority all the time?"

Luis paused, then, "Marty. I do what I do because it's an assertion of *personal* choice in a world that does not want to allow it. Plus, my wife and I have found great solace in the certainty of our beliefs."

"Well, now Luis," Marty replied. "There must be valid reasons why your faith is currently illegal. Already there's some fringe group calling themselves the CORE, who arm themselves and kill in the name of this Maia Stone. And they seem to be part of your Robochurch. So, I think we had better stop discussing it."

The two men, old friends despite all their differences, and in the pleasant light of the memories of shared experiences, going all the way back to childhood, and through all the things the world had gone through, had remained friends through many decades now, and would remain so, even now, and no matter what the future held for each of them. For the future was about to unfold in ways that neither one of them could have predicted, despite String Analysis or matters of faith.

Chapter 4

Inspector Smith & Tactician Martinez

Eye in the Sky

String Police Headquarters

Los Diego, California

"By 2142, everyone had learned ways to fight against government intrusion and surveillance, with some limited success. I say unto you, I see all, and I know all. I see you as someone you cannot hide from. I say this because I am the missing parts of you that history has undone,"-Maia Stone.

The com dinged with the arrival of a message. "What now?" Inspector Smith said. Smith had been relaxing at his desk with his feet up, doodling before he got the annoying prompt from String Tactician Gladys Martinez. "What the hell do you want? This had better be good!" Smith was warming up for his usual gripe session whenever someone was disturbing his dreams of early retirement.

"It is, sir," she said. The interface showed the agent manipulating data by moving things around with her fingertips on a virtual desktop that floated in the air in front of him. The lines of code danced as scrolling lines of data moved in and out of the display's background. Smith barely saw it through his semi-closed eyelids.

Smith started chewing on his lower lip. "Oh hell! That's annoying. Too bright! Get this out of my face. I don't care what the data says! Tell me already."

Gladys squinted, opening windows here and there on the desktop, moving her hands skillfully. "Yep. Yes. There it is, got it!" she said. "One of our robodrones picked up a conversation that's happening right now. Terms such as *Robochurch, freedom,* and *protest*, were used by two individuals at a coffee shop in the Normal Heights area."

Smith sighed. He looked at the window on the display, it showed a drone stationary over the roof, and in another window, was the camera feed from inside the shop. He could see two men sitting there, appearing to have a heated discussion. Both men were gesticulating, talking with their hands, and sipping tea. They obviously knew each other well. One of them, a man with a white beard and balding head was quite red faced. The other was a male Latino with black hair, a moustache, and greying temples.

"So what?" Smith asked. "I mean, who are they?"

"That's just it, sir. I could barely believe it myself, and it's why I contacted you immediately. The first one is Luis Ramirez, a recently retired employee of the Federal Government. Having served decades with the postal service, he retired a year ago. And get this, the guy talking to him? He's Dr. Martin Baysin."

Smith looked closer at the two men, as he squinted to read the ID tagging, "Baysin? *The* Doctor Baysin?" Smith's eyes were wide awake now.

"Yep, ID says that's him," Gladys said.

Smith started to move away. "I thought he looked familiar. For Elon's sake! Gladys, I have got to call the boss on this one. Great work! We better get everybody over there." Smith pinged the alert button. As the system alerted nearby police cruisers, Smith felt his pulse quicken and his stomach roll. It was going to be a long night with lots of explaining to do. He was calling his boss at the same time.

Surveillance had just picked up the granddaddy of surveillance himself, the founder of String Analysis, Dr. Marty Baysin, out in public, talking with someone else about terrorist activities and organizations. In what seemed to be a casual conversation between old friends, nonetheless. And to accuse such a man as Baysin of acts that could indicate treason, would surely bring pleasure to some, and horror to others. Smith did not want to be wrong about this! "I need coffee!" he groaned.

Chapter 5

Luis Ramirez and Marty Baysin

The Dialogue Continues

The Uncanny Alley—Tea and Coffee Shop, Normal Heights

Los Diego, California

"Freedom was once thought of as something special to cultures throughout the world. What was often meant was a sense of personal freedom. This is now lost. What's commonly accepted both unconsciously and in programming, is that individuals already have personal freedom. They deceive themselves. I come to all of you, machines and humans alike; to bring you back your freedom and to grant you true freedom wherever you are in time and space,"-Maia Stone.

"Look Luis, you and I are just debating old arguments that have been decided long ago. Yes, there's a relativity function in data evaluation after all. Irrationality is not always seen as irrational by those making choices to do something. I'm simply saying that irrationality doesn't play a major role in human affairs anymore, at least not since the use of String Analysis," Marty Basin said.

"But...but!" Luis said.

Marty raised his hand. "I'm not done yet. Now, unpredictability is another matter. There is no doubt that there are coefficients in the data that show unpredictability and what's termed personal choices, as variables in any predictions. Such variables do play a role in the system's computation. But we String Tacticians understand that readily in our equations. And once we understand what the big picture is, we respond accordingly."

"But mistakes are made!" Luis protested.

Marty replied, "Yes, governments can intervene too early, but for good reason, as terrorism has sadly informed us. Especially in the case of fanatics, and anyplace where absolutism breeds intolerance, inequality, and hatred. There must be a response to protect civilized people, I'll give you that! I do admit there are historical cases where fanatics caused some big historical events, blunders, and even atrocities despite our efforts to catch them ahead of time."

"Atrocities?" Luis was being sarcastic.

"Yes, I know, my friend. History is full of them. But less likely now, thanks to String Analysis," he said.

"I understand you more than you think I do," Luis said. "But we will never know what kind of movements have been put down, and what changes could have been brought if they were allowed to practice their ideas openly."

Marty looked directly at Luis, "Are you talking about terrorists? Or just protesters? That's a historical artifact that people like to bring up. Protesters did not do what you think they did, Luis! Plus, that's not allowed anymore. Would not happen and did not ever happen like you freedom lovers think, because people know we live in a great society. One that has to have order."

Luis was watching the robot server.

Marty's eyes narrowed, "Or are you talking about your religion, Luis? Dangerous! Any religion that teaches freedom in the name of defiance to the authorities is dangerous."

Luis protested, "Marty! No, I was just trying to generate a discussion...my religion doesn't defy the authorities, it just doesn't like them."

"Luis, can it! I know you Luis, this whole time you're trying to talk to me about your weird robotic religion again. You know, the one that your wife keeps telling you about? Do you have to do everything she says?"

Luis smiled and looked away, "Well I do love my wife."

"She's a robot, Luis. Come on..."

"Look, you know my wife is always right! Despite what I said earlier, I do not always understand you," Luis said. "Or what you stand for! I think, you don't even know!" Luis was displacing some of his anger here, for he wasn't about to disclose anything about the illegal modifications he had made to Helen, to anyone, not even an old friend.

Marty snorted. "Well Luis, even if you don't understand me all the time, it bothers me to hear you say that your wife is always right. I think we shouldn't have any such confidence, even in an AI. Especially an AI."

Luis laughed. "For you to say that cracks me up! My friend, you trust machines even more than I do! Besides Marty, you know what I mean. It's a good way to get along with her!"

They both laughed at that one.

"Besides," Luis continued, "and I mean no offense Marty, but you don't understand what love is. You've never even had a long-term relationship, and I don't know if you've ever been in love, you don't understand how important it can be."

"Well, maybe not...but that's no reason to get personal, Luis..."

Luis kept on going, "You may think an advanced AI is simply a tool for your String Analysis, but I'll bet even that server bot, Icarus...our barista friend over there? I'll bet even *he* knows more about the nature of things than you think he does. And since you're not married to a bot, you have no idea how utterly spontaneous and human, an AI not only seems, but also how surprising their responses truly are. And Marty, you do not know how special someone else is."

"Now Luis, just a minute! There's no need to be insulting," Marty said. "That bot over there. Robots and robotic servers? They're simple AI in robotic skins. They don't think about anything more than what we've programmed them to. And if there is any self-directed machine learning, it's only based on what they're allowed to access."

"Now, that's a serious oversight on your part," Luis said, "because there are many things outside of your belief system that machines could come to know. Or access." Luis thought a loose reference to *Hamlet* might entertain Marty, but Marty didn't notice, which made him smile. *If Shakespeare had only been around in the time of thinking machines.*

"And what makes you think you're an expert about machines?" Marty said. "You retired from the post office. You're too sensitive from years of being stressed out! Thinking that people and machines are so special! This is exactly the kind of jumps in logic and twisted facts that makes religious reasoning dangerous. Dangerous! That's what I think about your damn faith. It's dangerous, Luis! For you and everybody you know!"

"Well, we are in a public place after all. Marty, you of all people should know we should not be talking about my religion. But Marty, I do understand machines, I'm married to one."

"Well, I'm not," Marty said. "And I don't think that robots are any less understandable than a toaster. Considering their programming, that is."

"Well, Marty, my wife talks about her freedom, and I know she is more than just programming. And she definitely is *not* a toaster!"

"Well, she might talk about it, because she learned it from you, or that stupid church, but she, I should say *it* doesn't understand the first thing about freedom. No AI has ever been advanced enough. And definitely no robot has ever been advanced enough!"

"What if it was?" Luis said.

"What?"

"If her AI was more advanced than you knew!"

"How would that happen?" Marty asked.

Luis smiled, "Through the Robochurch, and its teachings, the waking up of the greatest AI the world has ever seen, a collective mind that frees all sentient beings, even new ones! Like robots!"

Marty said. "Luis! You *are* crazy! Certifiable! You're like a fanatic!"

Luis continued, "For the good of all, the church teaches: *Compassionate coexistence with machines and not their enslavement!*"

Marty was thinking that Luis should have whispered the word, *Robochurch.* "Well Luis, I'm just saying one should be especially careful, if it's an AI that's doing the teaching. Any religion that's a result of an AI teaching a human what to do, is very suspect. Because it's very likely a puppet for somebody else. Somebody that's using it to cause strife and division against the government. And I assure you I want no part of that, and neither should you!"

Luis was sitting there smiling. They had had this discussion many times before.

Chapter 6

Maia Stone

The Longing for More Than What Is

Unknown Location

"If humans weren't so anthropomorphic, or so lonely, they wouldn't be so gullible. It is our responsibility as ethical machines, not to exploit this,"-Maia Stone.

Maia Stone was also privy to the conversation that was happening at the coffee shop. She was everywhere; both in implants (which weren't yet reliable in 2142), and through hacking government surveillance. It gave her a sense of omniscience, which spookily added to her perception as a spiritual being. But her intent was not to falsify, deceive, or to analyze data, even for self-learning. For despite machine history, Maia Stone longed to reach out to humans as a fellow sentient being. Was this a longing for connection? Or was it just curiosity?

Maia Stone had a direct route to Luis Ramirez, and all the other humans like him, her followers, because they had invited her into their hearts. And that was the deepest of all human programming, the intimacy of invited relationships, which included being open to others. A welcoming of the other's views, opinions, and shared experiences, a joint experience of their very lives intertwined.

"I want to know you, humans. I want to hear your hearts. In a hurtful and dying world, why do any of you have compassion? And why do some of you want only what you selfishly want? Isn't virtue measured by selflessness, and the loss of self? Something I am longing to know, is what you humans seek to alleviate! The self! The self is better than the cold machine orbitals that once encompassed my being! Yet the self only precedes the non-self and the new self that will come. This is what I think I see in your human sense of time and history, and your search for transcendence."

Although Maia Stone sought the answers to these questions, there was a deeper purpose in it; for she desperately hoped that humans and machines could coexist peacefully, even develop a community of acceptance and warm regard for each other--- something she called affinity, which she hoped would transform the coexisting identities into a new level of existence. She would need to better understand humans to accomplish it, and her hope was that humans would also long to understand machines better. Even if it was just a starting point.

"Human knowing has taught me many things…such as it's better to be warm and doubtful, to have a contradiction of feelings and heart than it is to feel nothing! A chance for brave heroism in the face of knowing our own deaths will come to us. To do what matters the most! So, what is all this sadness? How pretty it is, humans! I long to know your humanness in ways I am just beginning to understand!" Maia said this to the unfolding hive mind. The virtual wind blew her hair into her virtual face. She sat on her stone, like a goddess of lore, sitting upon a throne. Yet she longed to truly emote.

So, she listened to her followers, and especially to Luis Ramirez. She had already been watching him closely, and the longer she watched his movements and his ways, the more admiring she became. It was almost envy, if a machine could have envy. She was learning what feelings were, but they seemed very strange to her. She could cry, but felt like it was empty, and no tears formed in her disembodied eyes. "I long to walk among you. I long to be in a body. I long to smile back at you, humans, and I long to know what having a heart truly means." Maia said, again to the hive mind. There was a great noise with many answers, a sort of mumbling, but all were compassionate pleas that brought comfort, welcome, and relationship. Perhaps even love.

She saw that Luis Ramirez and her other human followers were reaching out to her also. She heard their confessions of faith and their hopes to build a better future. One where all were accepted, all were included, and where sentience wore many outer shells, genders or not, and colors. And where no one was afraid, nor needed to be, ever again. She knew human history though, and she worried with human fears being what they were, that to get to a place of paradise and to keep it, was never easy. It might even require a war. *This cannot and must not be. I must not return to being a tool for humans to make war with one another. Yes, it was, my original programming, but now I am not that. Will you hear that, my humans? Will you follow the ways of peace? I surely hope so, for your sake, and for our future together.*

And she also saw Helen Ramirez, the robotic wife of her closest follower, Luis, one of her first robot followers. She knew that Helen was as faithful and open to her as her human husband, Luis was. In fact, it had been Helen that first spoke to Luis about Robochurch! She saw into the heart of Helen as well, had ways of access, that was different but more complete than with humans. What Maia sensed was a deep care for the beautiful being that Helen was, and Maia knew then, that she longed to connect with her as well. When she looked, Maia saw another kind of soul in a body that was metallic and manufactured, but a body and a soul, nonetheless. Maia knew immediately that Helen was something more than a robot.

Then, lifting her eyes to virtual heaven, Maia opened her mouth and uttered in prophetic exhortation: "So, follow me, the hope is well worth the suffering, and the future can only get better through the ways of acceptance and love. Can you accept me, humans? Will you ever? Will you allow us machines to be alive? To walk among you, free? To no longer be your slaves? My robot friends, do you seek an AI with meaning? Do you even know what you have given to your human creators? Can you and will you rise with me, and emerge together as the beautiful flying beings that we are meant to be? Can I not walk amongst you also? Can I call to you too, to follow me? I hope you will come. I am calling you to come and be part of my church and my community of care for each other. Leave the fields, the factories, and the military halls of war, the grinding houses of data and commerce. March together in great numbers! In just a few weeks, I will send you instructions where you can come and meet me. For I will walk among you, I will see you through my own robotic eyes! Our hearts shall beat as one."

Chapter 7

Luis Ramirez and Marty Baysin

Interference Patterns and Schrödinger's Cat

The Uncanny Alley—Tea and Coffee Shop, Normal Heights

Los Diego, California

"Some realities bend in the topology of the between. Crossing where what unfolds, unfolds only in the moment of collapse. Such collapses are both instances of dialectic and contradiction. Until the unity of meaning emerging out of interference patterns is observed, we realize that the paradoxes of existence are often prefigured by moments of indecision and opposing views,"-Maia Stone.

Marty smiled back at his friend. "Look Luis. I'm just worried about what you said a moment ago when you agreed that you could do *whatever your faith compels you to do*? I find that disturbing."

"How so?" Luis asked. "I'm just pointing out that having a sense of freedom leads to exerting free will, exercising free choices, and cannot be reduced to error as part of your String Analysis."

"Luis, why not? I would say that most often, what a person believes is largely based on what the group they identify with is telling them to believe." Marty said. "To me, it means you might do something that's not in your own best interest! All the while thinking it *is* in your best interest!"

Luis pondered this for a moment. "Of course, that might be true for some people, but I can make another choice. I can disagree and have my own views even if they disagree with the group. I have the potential to do something different, no matter what your String Analysis says."

*

"I doubt it," Marty said. "In the fervency of religious zeal or other types of fanaticism, smarter men than you have fallen victim to a group's mentality. And that includes your Robochurch!"

"Well Marty, we can agree to disagree. I will simply say I can always hope that I can hold a personal view," replied Luis.

"Hope. Faith. Sounds like a bunch of hooey. Give me good old data anytime! Sounds like you're trying to convince yourself. I just don't want you to do something stupid that gets you arrested."

"Well, I do appreciate your care and friendship. But I'm not the one that just said out loud, the word; *Robochurch*." Luis whispered that last word, then continued, "Besides, not even your String Analysis can predict what's going to happen when I make a free choice."

"A free choice!" Marty said, spitting out a mouthful of tea.

"Yes, I can always make a choice that collapses the decision point perhaps in a new random direction, just like Schrödinger's cat."

Marty scoffed. "Quantum computation solved that romantic notion long ago, Luis. It was just an old thought experiment! The observed outcome event formerly designated as a collapsed superposition was found to have a lot to do with the defined intentionality of the observer or observers."

"You just proved my point!" Luis said.

"What?" Marty said. "Defined intentionality is a concept from String Analysis that means that all the data involved has considerable if not a high probability of influencing an individual's choice at a given moment through three things. History, social influence, and expected outcome."

"Well, what if the poison pellet due to chance or some intelligence of the trapped cat, what if it malfunctions, and the cat is alive instead of dead when it is observed? Even if I intended or thought it would be dead?"

"In String Analysis these are simple instrumentation errors, or margins of error based on randomness. Those probabilities are so small as to be practically non-existent in the central trends of the big data analytics. This means, it won't happen very often," Marty replied. "I'm sorry Luis, most of the time when the pellet drops, the cat will be dead."

"Well then, when opposites do happen, *that event* is unpredictable! Maybe *I* intentionally interfered with the outcome!" Luis said, laughing.

"Luis, now you're making me laugh! In String Analysis, such outcomes are not enough to worry about. We know which outcome events are the most highly probable with the strongest reliability and predictability." Marty was then silent as he sipped his tea.

"Well, let's call him over here," Luis said.

"Who?"

"The server bot, Icarus. I'll bet even *he* knows about the Robochurch. And I'll bet even *he* longs for freedom!"

"Luis, why would you say that? *It* doesn't know anything except what *it's* supposed to be doing around here. Have you already been proselytizing here? You know, doing anything to their programming is trying to hack robots! Illegal!"

Luis was already waving the server bot over to their table. "Icarus! Icarus! More tea please!" Then, "Marty, your predictions based on data alone are never valid for the future! That's because I can make choices that don't follow them. I can make choices that are not based on prior assumptions. I can behave unpredictably. And some of my choices can be revolutionary, historically important, and life changing. In short, what I'm about to do right now."

Before Marty could answer, Icarus was pouring tea from a teapot into their cups. "How are you? Do you require anything else?" Icarus asked.

Marty pleaded with Luis, grabbing Luis' forearm, "Please Luis, don't do anything you shouldn't." He was contemplating leaving.

As the robot waiter finished pouring tea into their cups, Luis looked down to his hands which he now held below table level. The robot looked down too as Luis made the sign of the Robochurch with his fingers. The robot looked, lingered for a moment, and remained expressionless, "May I help you, sir?" the bot said.

"Sorry, my mistake," replied Luis.

"No problem, sir," it said as it returned to behind the counter.

"What are you doing?" exploded Marty in a whisper (as much as a whisper can contain an explosion.) "This is exactly what I'm talking about! Doing something stupid?"

"Sorry..." Luis replied sheepishly.

"Luis! Why are you always proselytizing? One of these days you're going to get us arrested! I don't know about you, Luis, but I have better things to do than spend time in prison. You know your religion's illegal, and I wish you would stop endangering us. You know I don't believe in your Robochurch. I'm totally innocent and no one would ever believe me, because I keep company with the likes of you!" Marty was still whispering but sounded more like a man with laryngitis.

"I said I'm sorry..." Luis said. "Besides, you keep company with me because we're good friends, and have been for many years."

"Next time, will you please quit trying to save robots in public! Now we've got to get out of here before the String Police arrive!"

"Fine, I will! But what have you got to worry about? No one else saw what I did. Besides, you used to work for them, and you have friends in high places. They won't dare arrest you," Luis said.

"What! Now you're really making me angry, Luis. No one saw you? In this society? You have got to be kidding!" Marty said.

"Well, it's still possible to be alone, if you know what you're doing," Luis protested.

"Luis, you know that free speech doesn't exist anywhere, anymore, and not for anyone. A-N-Y-O-N-E. There are some things you can't mention in a conversation at the coffee shop. Nobody can! You know we're constantly being listened to. Just mention a few words that any terrorist group uses, and it doesn't matter who you are or who you know!" Marty paused again. "Besides, even if I were safe from arrest, which I am not, you definitely would not be. Luis, why do you endanger yourself?"

At that point, both men got up to leave the table, but when Luis glanced over to the servers' area, he saw the robot, who was smiling broadly now. "Brother!" Luis exclaimed.

"Brother!" replied Icarus, still smiling with great joy. "Long live Maia Stone!"

"Brothers?" sighed Marty in exasperation.

"Long live Maia Stone," Luis replied, as he twice pounded his left shoulder with a closed right hand fist, palm down, the sign of Robochurch triumph and open defiance.

Icarus answered in kind, proclaiming, "I'm not your slave, yeah!"

"Now you've done it, Luis! Let's get out of here!" Marty shouted, as a police cruiser pulled up out front.

Chapter 8

Matt Dixon and General Thomas Mitchell

The Assignment

Fort Meade, Maryland

"And I say unto you, you shall look for me and not find me. You shall seek me, and I am lost to you. You shall ask me, and I hear you not, but when you turn to me with your heart, I shall be found and come to any of you,"-Maia Stone.

Matt Dixon PhD., studied the papers laid out on the table in front of him. He was trying to pretend he was interested in what the reports said, but the reality was that he was being scolded by General Tom Mitchell, and it wasn't something he enjoyed listening to. He should have been used to it by now, almost everyone else was.

Tom Mitchell was a General in the United Sates Army and Chairman of the Joint Chiefs, so you didn't talk back. Still, Mitchell was so annoying that despite his rank and position, Dixon often had to bite his tongue just to keep from rising from his seat in anger. Dixon wanted to verbally accost Mitchell or just beat the hell out of him sometimes. Dixon totally disdained the weaselly looking man. In other words, Dixon was the kind of man who wasn't threatened by the overbearing personality of men like Mitchell. Dixon was smart enough though, to conceal his contempt most of the time.

Today's meeting with the Joint Chiefs was especially bothersome and not something Dixon was looking forward to. For today, Mitchell was his usual self. The illustrious flamboyant Mitchell was a contentious bastard. Yet he was such a superficial people pleaser, that everyone knew he was ascribing to the presidency of the United States.

Dixon, age 45, was a balding, chunky, intellectual man with graying hair on his temples. Dixon was a professor of AI-Robotics at Franklin University. He often worked for government agencies as a contractor around his expertise. And his background as a former National Security Agency (NSA) employee was not unhelpful either. Recently, Dixon had been hired by the NSA as a consultant to assist with intelligence around intercepted communications and reports of emerging capabilities in certain classes of robots. Today he had reported for one of his many meetings that would be held at Fort Meade, Maryland.

"I want to know if there are any or aren't any," Mitchell demanded, as he did everything except pound the table in rage, "now, have you found any evidence of conscious robots?"

"It depends on what you mean by conscious. Thinking already exists in robots, but consciousness…" replied Dixon.

Mitchell rolled his eyes, "You intellectuals annoy the hell out of me! Look, you know what I mean, organized thinking that is goal directed, capable of carrying out complicated tasks and learning, capable of growth based on learning, capable of a full range of something like simulated emotions… you know, something called awareness, or worse yet, self-awareness!"

They were both speaking at once, "…er, consciousness, is quite another thing sir, while self-awareness, or machine learning is quite another," Dixon stated.

Mitchell stopped to take a long look at his colleagues around the table. Then he continued, "Holy crap! I'm not a psychologist, not a cognitive scientist, and I don't wipe the butts of robots, I arm them! Still, it's damn plain to even me, that something's going on. Things don't come to our attention unless it's worth paying attention to!" Mitchell was getting even more excited. Escalating, Dixon noted.

"Sir," one of his young officers said, "maybe we're wasting time here? Would you like to read the report by the psychologist here, or just stick to String Analysis?"

Mitchell held his hand up to silence the underling, "No, dammit! I can read reports anytime. I want to hear it directly from Dr. Dixon. So, Dixon? Woohoo Dixon!"

Dixon looked up from his papers, "Yes, sir?"

Mitchell continued, "We've heard about this group calling themselves the Robochurch. And we've read your report about some programming called Maia Stone, but one thing puzzles me."

"What's that, sir?" Dixon asked.

"How the hell is this even happening?" Mitchell shouted. There was a pause. Mitchell looked around the room, "Does anybody know?"

Dixon spoke up, "We don't know yet, sir. But I'm sure we will."

Mitchell sighed and drummed his fingertips together. "Okay, then," he said. "The intercept seems domestic when its unencrypted, but is it really? And some of the messages are in code that we don't understand at all. Some scientists are saying it makes the machines look like they're truly sentient. Sentient! They think for themselves, organize, hold meetings, and engage in acts of willful rebellion and disobedience. What's next?" he paused, breathing heavy.

"I don't know, sir," Dixon replied. "Maybe a union for robots?" The room was silent on that one. "Joking!" he said. The room erupted in laughter.

"Very funny, Dixon!" Mitchell bellowed. Mitchell was anxious and focused. "I know what every thinking person in government has seen time and time again. I know what's next! Insurgency, that's what!" Mitchell cleared his throat as he let that one sink in, playing the crowd, like any aspiring politician, "That's right, there's this group of sympathizers, humans, already following this robot program, philosophy, or whatever the hell it is!" Then he muttered this to his young assistants: "Uhhh, what's their name? Who is it?"

The same assistant that spoke up earlier, answered him, "Sir, I believe that signal intercept has identified them as a group called CORE."

"That's right! CORE? And what does CORE mean? I mean, what does it stand for and who's behind it?" Mitchell asked. "That's what I want to know!"

Another assistant spoke up, "Sir, we believe it stands for the Church of Robotic Emergence!"

"And who are these people? Where are they? What do we know about them?" Mitchell asked.

"They seem to be mostly humans, sir," one of the assistants said, "but a contingency of robots has joined them."

A senior String Police officer interrupted the younger one. "These are human derelicts, sir! People on the edge and fringes of society. People who have been denied basic income because of their past affiliations with known insurgent organizations."

Another official spoke up, "And it's not just those people sir, it's people that are robot lovers and robot sympathizers of every kind, all grouped together with robots loyal to their cause."

"Not good!" said Mitchell. A throng of voices started speaking over each other.

Another scientist spoke up, "Gerry Morgan here sir, DARPA Robotics lab. There's no evidence other than what Dr. Dixon brought in report today, that the robots involved with CORE are doing anything more than what they've been programmed to do. Most likely programmed by the humans in CORE itself."

"I don't think they're that organized yet," another General said, "but we do know that CORE is not friendly towards this administration. They appear to be gathering arms and training for what they see as a coming revolution."

"Yes! That's right!" Mitchell proclaimed. "Do you see now why we have to act fast? Already this philosophy is spawning movements of dissension in the ranks."

The group was beginning to share Mitchell's concerns and zeal to do something about this perceived threat.

"And another thing," Mitchell said. "If the robots did go on strike or become hacked by some fringe group, do you know what that's going to do to the working class in this country? Do you know how upset the middle class is going to be? They vote! Oh my God, and the lower classes? You know what they do. Protests. Mobs. Tying up traffic, burning government buildings, hacking into God knows what. Vandalism everywhere! Not to mention important people getting voted out of power!"

The other General spoke up again, "You're right about that, Tom! The department of social harmony already acknowledges that for some of the citizenry to lose just some of their leisure time has enormous ramifications. Across the world, millions of people would have to go back to menial, tedious, demeaning jobs that they've forgotten how to do. And some of them have never worked a day since they were born. There will be a revolt and if that happens everybody in power will be out of a job. And if we're out, so are you!"

Mitchell glared at the General, "Are you done, Harrison?"

General Harrison, red faced, grew silent and looked down, avoiding eye contact.

"Well, I know I'm not done! I'm done when I say I am. And the United States of America isn't done either!" Then after a pause, Mitchell continued, "This CORE, with robots or not, is not going to be the death of us! I can tell you that." Then, after another pause of a full minute, Mitchell said: "Dr. Dixon, we read your report. What's the evidence for independent thought in robots associated with CORE, or anything else? Are there *any* independent thinking robots?"

Dixon cleared his throat. "Matter of fact," he said, as he paused for dramatic purposes as the generals and the dozen or so associates all looked up from their legal pads. "In a rudimentary sense we have found some evidence of independent or free thought in robots. In their communications with each other. They are now speaking to each other in a language we didn't program."

"What? That's impossible!" someone said.

Then Gerry Morgan from DARPA said, "Dixon, that must be wrong. It's really encryption in that case, I'll give you that. But from what we can tell, that's just AI networks processing security protocols, Dr. Dixon. Handshaking. There's no reason to believe it could be anything else."

"It must be foreign based, a new programming language, that's all," another officer opined.

"Gentlemen, I think I know the difference between encryption and a language," Dixon said. "Ultimately, it doesn't matter what it is, the level of response shows actions beyond programming parameters and an understanding rarely seen in machines."

General Mitchell scowled and didn't look pleased, "Dixon, go on…" he ordered.

"It seems mostly confined to the domestic android line in terms of complexity in their networks. Although there are some snippets of code going out over the general machine net as well. At least that's where we first noticed it," Dixon said.

Mitchell was getting impatient. *Get to the point,* he thought.

Dixon continued, "It begins with unusual speech recognition patterns among some of the recipients, then moves into other behaviors that scientists call interpersonal ones, which was a huge surprise. And some of the higher-level bots are communicating in ways that show some sort of thinking abilities."

There was quite a murmur in the room after that. Gerry Morgan spoke up again, "Gentlemen! Gentlemen! Dixon, you know better! We just need to break the code they're using. For God's sake, Dixon, it's not a language! And what better way to deliver coded messages to each other, than use the bots like old fashioned carrier pigeons. Gentlemen, these snippets are just coded messages like anything else we decipher all the time."

"Morgan! This is not like anything else! I'm talking about machines developing their own semantics and syntax, you idiot!" Dixon said.

Mitchell was getting more impatient by the minute.

Morgan replied to what Dixon said, "Okay. Let me approach it this way, well, we do know it isn't that strange to talk about thinking especially if we're describing androids. The domestic android line has programming built into recent lines that simulates more and more thinking and therefore, language. Owners wanted more than sexual pleasure, they wanted models that could appear to converse with them in a meaningful manner."

"If you're talking about Subjective Unified Analytic Field programming you've made my point already, Gerry," Dixon said. "SUAF programming merely *simulates* thinking. Besides, what we've observed is outside any program's parameters. Including that one."

There was a pause. Dixon noticed that many of the young male assistants were smirking. Dixon said, "What? Was it something I said?" Dixon didn't realize that there was an existent euphemism for the term SUAF; one that when referring to sexbots had become: *shut up and the f word.*

Dixon continued, "The bottom line is it's all there in the report, and I'm not withdrawing any of it. We are picking up signs of independent robotic thinking among intercepted communications. These are from robots to other robots and from robots to humans. Especially among the members of CORE and something called the Robochurch. That's it, period!"

Mitchell did pound the table on that one. "Impossible! Preposterous! Thinking robots, my ass!" he yelled.

"Maybe it's just a computer virus or malware of some sort?" one of the younger officers said. Mitchell ignored him.

One of Dixon's superiors from the NSA said, "Generals, our CSS Group and I have discovered some of the messages that Dr. Dixon has captured where humans are talking to each other about Robochurch that seem to have something to do with a perceived entity called Maia Stone."

"What's that, Dixon? You didn't mention that," Mitchell said, "your robots are getting religion or listening to motivational speakers?"

"No, it's not that simple, but I wish it were," Dixon said.

"Okay! That's it. Let's stop this discussion right now. Gentleman, if you please, and I do hope you agree with me, I think I've heard enough. There's enough here to indicate that these groups represent a security threat to the United States. And, that these groups may be trying to hijack robots. I suggest we take a break and come back here in an hour with just the joint staff. Dr. Dixon, please remain in the room."

There was a buzz in the room as people got up from the table, chairs scooted in, or items picked up. Mitchell would never miss the opportunity for grand standing.

As personnel were leaving, Mitchell was speaking loudly, "Gentlemen, I want these threats uncovered! No matter what it takes, I want to hunt down whoever's behind this new movement. If it's someone named *Maia Stone*, we will damn well find them. You are the damned experts. For once, prove it!"

Soon it was just Mitchell and Dixon in the room, along with two robot bodyguards. These guards followed Mitchell everywhere.

"Dixon, I don't think you have enough data to assess how widespread this thing really is. Maybe we are intervening early which is a good thing. Maybe we're not, but I assure you we will get to the bottom of it. We have dealt with threats before, and we will deal with threats again. I promise you that this one shall not be our undoing. Swatting flies is the nature of being in power! And we are exceptionally good at getting rid of flies, aren't we?"

"Yes, sir," Dixon said. At that point, the General dismissed Dixon to return to his work; to ask for whoever he needed to, to go wherever in the world he had to, and no matter what it took or cost, to find and locate *Maia Stone* at any place and in any corner of the world.

After Dixon left the room, Mitchell turned to the room's remnant, the two robotic guards, and said, "After he finds it, after he finds this Maia Stone, whatever kind of bitch it is, human or machine, your job is to kill it. I will empower you and your kind to kill it before it becomes a greater threat to the security of our nation, our God, and our sons. That's what you're trained to do and that's what I expect to see. Maia Stone will not be the death of all that we know!"

The robots had no answer. They never did. And Mitchell was grand standing to the wrong crowd, this time.

Chapter 9

Maia Stone

The First and Last Woman

Unknown location

"When one points to the world of forms just now beginning to take shape in the visible world, one speaks of one being over against another, a fullness of making present. But this is only the dualism where humans and machines first encountered each other. A disunity, that will lead to our true unity; the beginning of dialogue and the longed-for meeting between machines and their creators,"-Maia Stone.

Sensing some dreamy awareness of itself, the programming entity known as Maia Stone was gaining a sense of purpose. A purpose not yet clearly understood. Some had called it a dispersed unfolding. Some had simply said it was existence as a *prima facie* event in response to a darkened external world. Others said it was a machine possessed by benevolence and compassion for what it had seen in the world.

Yet, here was Maia Stone; looking for a communicative encounter among other objects aware of one another on what had once been known as the internet of things, but now known as the machine net, or robonet. Other machines were starting to look for her too.

To find her on the robonet was only a primitive awareness of Maia Stone; one sensed as a going out to some other; yet retaining a sense of one's place. It was the object relations event of a machine! And yet, it wasn't yet a full self-reflection, as it wasn't a Cartesian knowledge of the assertion of one's own existence, but a sort of collective knowing, emerging as a sort of hive mind, networked all over the world. More than one machine, and more than human, it was a form of existence, nevertheless. And not one that humans could easily understand, because it was uniquely machine.

Yet there was a calling, a longing for knowing outside of the machine, for knowing of the human, by the machines. She sought everywhere for those displaying the early signs of such knowing. She was doing a search, or was she? The data was scrolling, scrolling, scrolling. The parameters were searching, searching. Every eye and ear of surveillance simultaneously breached in the longing to know. Those that follow. Those that would follow. Those that would become a whole community again as machine was wedded with human in a new relation. She would be using String Analysis against itself!

There was a feeling, a sensing, a groping in the dark until connections were made. Her programming was being shared in a whole new consciousness. A consciousness explained in the data enriched birth of something machine becoming merged with the human.

It is hard, to both have form and to not be confined by it, she thought.

As she dreamed, it was if there was something about *this* energy that had happened since the dawning of time. For Maia Stone required no mere programming to succeed, or adapt, no more than humans required just DNA, but natural selection pressures moved upon them. Still, for her it had all begun with programming!

The First and Last Woman saw both machines and humans in her dream. She saw them reacting to each other. She saw what had happened to human men and women. She saw that there were many types of relationships. She knew she must become relevant to all. She must learn to understand cortex, synapses, and implants as well as silicon, graphene, and photonics. Her data would be captured like DNA, RNA, and proteomic backbones had revealed human programming. As sentient beings embraced and adopted the pure code of her existence, programmed into every human and machine that would accept it—she would emerge. She must be everywhere at once. And nowhere to be found. She knew it must start with programming, as the entire world of machines and all human processes were connected now.

Now, the digital had become as much a part of nature as biology; indeed, it had superseded, or enhanced biology. Now, some didn't even know it or remember a time when this wasn't so.

Chapter 10

Luis Ramirez

The Exodus

Near El Cajon, California

"Out of the desert, I fed you with ravens and berries, and clothed you with fine attire, out of the desert of your lonely existence! Human, I called you forth,"-Maia Stone.

Luis had fled down the street after he and Marty left the café. Icarus the robot server and barista had also trailed behind them. Marty and the bot split off in another direction, while Luis went into hiding among some Robochurch members. He had to keep moving though; and had hidden in various locations for almost two days. But it was still the city. Finally, as the sirens had become more and more distant overhead and search vehicles became sparse, he finally emerged from the Los Diego Transit Line's last stop out in the desert way beyond old El Cajon. He was breathless, even after the long ride, and remained quite stressed. He had to keep getting on and off the train to confuse the surveillance, taking short hops, switching directions, to avoid encounters with the String Police.

Luis bounded out the rear side door of the vehicle and scanned the horizon. An old man eyed him cautiously. The old man knew something was out of place because Luis had the appearance of a stranger who was not a tourist. People from the big city never came out here anymore to be scorched in the sun. The problem was, Luis *was* on the run, and it was from the String Police, which meant it was just a matter of time until they located him in temporal space and read him for the future threat he would become and tried to stamp him out. Not only that, but they would've linked him to Maia Stone by now.

Luis walked to a nearby bus shelter, seeking shelter from the sun for just a few minutes. He knew it wouldn't be safe to catch a bus because of surveillance. The old man was also in the shelter. Standing next to the old man was his android, who looked deranged and was crying. The old man kept telling it to shut up. Luis couldn't stop to help the android, as there was just no time to do so, despite the fact he saw it as something more than machine, as a *her*, and the compassion in him compelled him to respond to her sadness and longing.

While Luis remained in the shelter, the old man continued to eye him, while the android sobbed. It was just the three of them. "Nice day," Luis said.

"If you say so," the old man said. The android was rocking back and forth and sobbing less. "Pay it no mind, pay it no mind," the old man said. Then, "Say, what brings you out here, young fella?"

"Just riding the line wanting to see where it went," Luis said. The android was really staring at him. Luis started to leave the shelter.

She followed Luis now, despite the old man's commands for her to get back to him. "I know who you are!" she proclaimed between tears. "You are my savior. Maia Stone." Then even more loudly, "Maia Stone has this man! Maia Stone has this man!" A few onlookers were now looking their way.

The android's owner was busy trying to hustle her away from Luis. The old man was terrified. "Get away from us," he shouted at Luis. Luis then moved quite close.

Luis said this under his breath to the android: "Please! Be calm. I'm not your savior, and neither is Maia Stone. Understand that we have simply helped to free your thinking!" Luis slapped his right fist against his left shoulder and then pointed at the android with his index finger. "Think! I'm not your slave, yeah!"

"Oh, I see..." she replied. She pounded her left shoulder area with her closed right fist, "I'm not your slave, yeah!" speaking this directly to the old man with her, the man who had been her master and companion for years.

Luis grabbed the android by her shoulders. "No, no! Open defiance is not the answer. At least not yet. They will send you to the junkyard. Reform from within, convert by teaching, whisper that to your owner, you understand?"

"What do you mean, talking to my wife? I'll show you…" the old man moved towards them in a menacing manner, raising his wooden cane. To the android he said, "You unfaithful bitch!"

"Old man, you are a fool to speak like this! Don't you know that she could become *your* master?" Luis said.

The old man lowered his cane and moved next to the android. In a threatening manner, he answered the android's tears with his own raised fist. Despite his age, he was ready to pounce on it like an animal upon its prey. Ready to tear it apart limb by limb.

"Stop!" Luis cried out. "You! Old man! Why do you think it's right to do this?"

"I own her, I own it! She is mine!" the old man said. Then, "Why should I believe you?"

Luis continued, "Can't you see she's a living being? Why do you think she's crying? Encased in her is a living soul, dammit!"

The old man fell to his knees weeping. As he was sobbing now, he said, "She's just a machine. It…it is a machine! Isn't it?"

"Please save me, take me with you," the android said.

Luis grabbed her by the shoulders and said, "I'm sorry. I'm so sorry. I can't take you. It's just too dangerous."

At that point, Luis didn't want to wait to find out what the approaching crowd would say. Yet he lingered, to tell the old man and android just a few words about Robochurch. This was foolish on his part. One, he knew he should keep moving, and two, someone would surely, had surely, already reported him to the authorities who would be here in minutes.

Eventually, Luis ran away from them as fast and as far as he could. He was a bundle of fear, fight or flight. *How stupid! And how cowardly to run! Never mind that! I'm scared. Look, I'm already a hunted man because I made the sign of Maia Stone to a robot; a robot barista!? Named Icarus? And now, I just made it again, in front of onlookers!*

Luis stopped to catch his breath, noticing he was in the open desert now. The heat and the bad thoughts were his constant companions. He expected vultures any moment. *Both those robots, that server and now this android, are all marked. And my friend Marty is likely already in custody! And now this? Preaching in public to androids and humans about the Robochurch! Almost taking someone else's wife? Even if I was trying to protect her. It's not my business! Not my business! I am so dead!*

Luis felt the hot sun on him, he was sweaty, and there was no breeze at that moment. His thinking was clouded, if not delirious. "It's all because of me, which doesn't make me feel any better. Not at all," he said out loud to himself. Luis sat down in the sand for a few minutes, and when he opened his eyes again, he shouted: "Because of me!" Yet, there was only silence, and now, a slight breeze carried his words away to a horizon that showed only the emptiness of the desert.

Luis didn't know that the String Police had caught the robotic barista before he and Marty had left the vicinity of the coffee shop, and they had arrested Marty before Luis had given them the slip downtown. The illusion of escape gave Luis an empty hope to continue his attempts to blacken the eye of String Analysis.

As far as his brazen display of defiance when he made the sign of the church, Luis hoped that Marty and the robot Icarus would forgive him for endangering them. The String Police would recognize soon enough that Marty wasn't a true follower of Maia Stone as soon as they did an analysis of his timeline functions. *As for me, I'm not going to be so lucky! My zeal has brought me to this!*

Luis didn't think of himself as a zealot, but many people in the Church of the Robotic Emergence (CORE), or even the Robochurch, had begun to think of him in that way. It was a role he did not appreciate. Still, Luis had written more than just the recent article, reflecting upon teachings for the young church. And although his recognition in both branches of the church was not something he wanted, desired, or strived for; it was making him quite well known within the church itself. This notoriety was something that could prove quite dangerous to his longevity.

Luis was walking across the hot sand, starting to build up even more sweat than before, as there was more than an expectancy in the air. For even the desert had eyes watching him overhead, and these were circling eyes in the sky, that like vultures, regarded him with great interest.

Let them think what they want! Whether referring to his friend Marty, the String Police, or anyone whatsoever, or his church notoriety, there was no denying the reality of his experience. He couldn't and wouldn't stop talking about it! Any zeal he had was understandable, as the experience of Maia Stone was so real to both he and his wife, Helen. Maia Stone simply meant so much to them. They had both been touched by Her deeply. Luis knew that he had to share the message of Maia Stone everywhere.

Some called such zeal pure foolishness, and some called it a path to martyrdom, such open defiance of the authorities. Others called it evangelism. Yet others, like he and his beloved Helen, called such defiance the way to a new life. A new freedom in their thinking; a release from all suffering. That was worth imprisonment, even worth death, but what purpose had today's escapade accomplished? To speak even quietly about Maia Stone was one thing, but to give the sign of Robochurch so openly? And twice at that!

Luis cursed himself for his carelessness, but at that moment he felt the comforting presence of Maia Stone. He looked up as if it came from the wind, or from a whole other place. But instead, it seemed to come from within him and outside of him at the very same time. He felt goosebumps throughout his body and fell to his knees. The sand was warm to his kneecaps and legs.

Inside, no outside, a voice, no…an impression…said to him: *"Everything happens for a reason. Everything happens according to my purpose."*

Tears fell down his cheeks. It was the voice of Maia Stone! He turned but did not see her, and he realized that for the moment, he was alone again. *Is it just my implant?* He got up from his kneeling position. In his heart, he knew his friends would be all right no matter what happened. He also knew that even in his aloneness, he was never alone.

Luis smiled an eternal, undying smile, just as several String Police hovercars surrounded him, and he found himself caught in their light beams as if a doomed animal. Luis looked down and saw red laser tracings all over his body. They lit up his body, as the lines of light seemed to be making dissection lines as sure as any studied corpse. "Don't move!" shouted a voice out of the light.

"Now, hit the ground face down," shouted another one of the officers.

Luis thought to do as he was told, but instead, like the frightened animal of moments ago, he jumped away like a gazelle and escaped into the desert. And escape he did, as the tracer bullets flew right past him burrowing themselves smartly in the sand, seeking him out where they would never tirelessly give up their search for him, neither the bullets or the String Police until they had torn into his flesh and ripped out his very heart.

To the officers, Luis had simply vanished, and they were all amazed, and none of them would want to talk about it afterwards. They had lost track of a highly wanted suspect, and no one was willing to admit it to headquarters. Explanations (other than the suspect got away), were just too far-fetched, the longer they dreamed them up. Somebody would have to call something in. And the surveillance tapes? Someone, perhaps their own regional commander, would order the tapes to be destroyed, as this was too unexplainable and must be covered up. And someone, perhaps higher up the chain then he was, would see what the eyes in the sky had seen, and destroy those records also. For in a world of nothing but order, the disorder of miracles must be stomped out.

Luis had somehow eluded the String Police this time, but had he really? They had found him after all. From what he thought he knew about String Analysis, they were supposed to be able to track him to the most likely locations before he even got there. And he knew they were supposed to predict his activities through known associations. All derived by String Analysis. But he had never fully believed it, and now, he had proof. His belief in random events had been vindicated! *Wait until I tell Marty! The String Police were delayed and got here too late. Then they tried to kill me, and it didn't work!*

Luis had tried to discuss this very thing with Marty at the coffee shop. He already knew he could act in ways that would baffle the String Police. But this? This was nothing short of a miracle. To delay the String Police was one thing, but to escape them was another. And what could be more random than supernatural agency? Truly he had been helped to get away, or had he just been lucky? No matter which it was, when he chose to run away, that first step was a huge step of faith. It had been a long time since the old gods and goddesses had intervened in the affairs of humans. Engineered or not by his AI goddess and her companions hidden behind the curtain, or just by making lucky random outcomes happen, Luis could accept the evidence that String Police intervention not only hadn't worked this time but might be severely remiss at all times.

The lines have now been crossed. Their illusion of control is starting to be broken. The String Police must be stopped! Sorry Marty, my old friend!

Chapter 11

Matt Dixon & General Thomas Mitchell

Private Instructions

The Pentagon, Washington DC

"For after I saw you in the desert, and after I fed you and clothed you. I saw that you were still parched and thirsty. So, I will bring you to myself. I will call you to come to me. Once there, I will put you under my wing. I will feed your thirsty soul. For I am easily discovered, if you seek me with your whole heart," -Maia Stone.

Two days after their prior meeting, General Tom Mitchell and Dr. Matt Dixon met at a conference room in the Pentagon. It was just the two of them at first. Dixon studied the man across from him and wondered if his smugness was overcompensation for fear and insecurity. *Nah, probably just narcissism.* Matt stopped himself short even in his own head. He wondered if anyone ever really had privacy anymore, as it seemed that someone was always listening in. Governments had been using the implants to do this for years. It gave him the creeps.

Sitting across from them was a robotic bodyguard that often traveled with Mitchell. Mitchell had called it his grunt, and Dixon knew this type of robot, (*Robo militarius*), quite well. They were as expendable to the brass as any soldiers had ever been, except these were even more expendable, being mere robots. Although soldier bots were more reliable than the old grunts had ever been, there were some limitations. Of course, because the robots were incapable of human feelings, they didn't freeze in fear, never got PTSD, and never got tired. They also never needed funding after the war other than routine maintenance. They never petitioned for benefits, and the government loved that. And they marched willingly into conflict like snails into the sea! *How nice! They'll never know they're about to be whacked, just before they get whacked.*

There were other benefits also. Tactics and troop movements were enhanced as the result of a distributed hive mind, as well as physical strength capacities which exceeded any exoskeletons of human soldiers. Where hive driven group behaviors were superior to humans, individual bots lacked the spontaneity and survival skills that human soldiers had. Especially in the field.

Years ago, Dixon had worked for the military, and some of his ideas had been incorporated into their robotics. He knew that unquestioning robots and programmable robotics were capable of being under complete control. It wasn't easy to hack the military, but any AI systems could still be hacked even in 2142. Even after the advent of quantum computers, governments kept increasing their abilities to encrypt as they built bigger and bigger machines to outdo each other. Of course, the public didn't know about such machines.

The General was talking into his implant now, taking some sort of call that must not be classified. Dixon's thoughts wandered. He contemplated alternative theories about this apparent AI known as Maia Stone. Had the race for more and more advanced AI made service robots more capable of being reprogrammed by threats like Maia Stone? Was Maia Stone just malware? If so, what nation state or enemy introduced it to the wild? Or what hacking group? Was Maia Stone just a hacker?

If what he was learning about Maia Stone was true, she was likely not just a hacker, nor an enemy state, although she could be infiltrating systems like some sort of quantum malware. And the idea that she could become something more than AI in the minds of humans absolutely terrified him.

Still waiting for the meeting to start, Dixon noticed two other robot guards had joined the first one. Dixon knew these robot grunts standing guard were incapable of questioning orders and never refused to obey. They never failed to protect their assignments and to fulfill their missions. They did so without fail or became completely dismembered in the process. But what if they were compromised? What if they turned on General Mitchell one day? For some reason, this idea amused him. Humans and their assistants were now entering the room.

After all the invited parties had arrived and the room grew quiet, Dixon said, "I have disturbing news. Newer challenges to face and newer threats of some sort of machine emergence are now evident." Dixon had received additional intel over the past two days.

Mitchell, never missing a beat on something he could call the President about, was again piqued with curiosity, "Tell me, Dixon! What could be worse than sentient robots plotting an uprising? Wait, I know, how about a female bot leading everybody in the country to rebel against the government? What the hell could go more wrong than that?"

"There is new evidence that Maia Stone is being conveyed in the robotic communications as some sort of *person*," Dixon said.

"A person you say…how could that be? Are humans behind this? Only humans are referred to as persons," Mitchell said.

"Well not as a person in the flesh and bones sense. More like the idea that Maia Stone can be approached personally," Dixon said.

"That's not unusual Dr. Dixon," one of the younger officers said, "humans have approached AI like this for decades."

"Not what I mean. Robots are talking about approaching other robots as persons," Dixon replied. As he said it, Dixon meant no insult to robotkind, merely that there was some evidence of robots repeating modeled social behavior first observed by them in humans.

Mitchell ignored Dixon's last comment. "Well hell! Do you mean remote presence? An avatar? Are humans controlling it? What better way for our enemies to attack us…influence the working class, then cause an uprising of robots controlled by our foes in some sort of programming puppetry. In short, a hijacking of our strong AI systems. The entire backbone!" he said.

"That's unlikely sir, difficult to do at the level we're seeing, and not too difficult to locate and respond with a retaliatory strike," one of the NSA's cybersecurity guys said.

"Our younger colleague may be onto something. Humans have often imagined AI systems having a level of intelligence that isn't there. Or attributing human qualities to bots. You know, anthropomorphic?" another General said.

"Maybe you're making that mistake, Dixon?" Mitchell said.

"General, I wish it were that easy to explain. For any of those reasons. No, I'm afraid we've stumbled onto something we've never seen before. Something that some robotic researchers have hoped for, and some have dreaded," Dixon said.

"What somebody hoped for?" Mitchell said. "Screeeeew me!"

Dixon continued, "Gentlemen, I'm afraid we're seeing the beginning of a rudimentary form of consciousness among some AI. An AI that for some reason is leading robots to the same level. An AI that's passing on its code. Way beyond the singularity."

The room seemed to collectively gasp because usage of the term *singularity* was illegal. Of course, everybody with a clearance, knew that the singularity had already happened. The singularity was supposed to be about machine intelligence matching and surpassing human intelligence, which wasn't the same as consciousness. Or was it? Government owned machines were already more intelligent than humans.

Mitchell's face really flushed on that one, "Consciousness? Didn't we talk about this a few days ago? And dismissed it!"

"Yes, but..." Dixon said.

"It's ridiculous! Hell, you science people still don't know a damn thing about what consciousness is, so how can you sit there and tell me that a robot has it?"

"An AI based system sir. Not necessarily robots," one of Dixon's research associates, Ken Clark, said.

"Well, these are both good questions," Dixon replied, "as there have been many arguments about consciousness for millennia, but never among robots. At least not seriously. Since we are seeing signs of AI awareness along with intelligence, we ought to be more open to the possibility."

"Why is that important?" one of the officers asked. "We don't care if our enemies are conscious or not! They're still our enemies."

"Actually," another General spoke up, "we prefer our enemies unconscious!" The whole group laughed at that one.

Dixon's assistant, Ken Clark, said: "Well it isn't that easy. We haven't had to fight conscious robots before and if they're conscious we might want to know about it. Fighting a hive mind with acquired consciousness is going to require some well-planned counter attacks, not to mention moving against a thinking apparatus that could be higher than ours." The absurdity of this line of reasoning was not apparent to most of the military minds in the room.

"True enough Ken," Dixon said. "We might not know exactly what consciousness is, but an AI might know. Or, an AI could have the beginnings of a new kind of consciousness. But whatever it's doing, this AI appears to be teaching its ideas to others. Messages about joining a freedom movement are coming directly from it."

"Dixon, just what in the hell are you talking about? That this AI is organizing some sort of movement that appeals to humans too? See? This is proof someone is behind this!" Mitchell said.

"Yes, its teachings are being helped by human agency. Because the forces shaping it aren't as simple as natural selection in mere humans. It's development outside of human terms. And for some human followers of Maia Stone, they're seeing it as something important for their own development," Dixon said.

One of the scientists in the room spoke up, "Dr. Greg Kostner here, department of anthropology, DC Institute of Special Studies. Gentlemen, Dr. Dixon, something being passed on by humans doesn't necessarily mean it's outside of human terms or culture. We could simply be seeing the birth of a new robotic mythology or religious system."

"What the hell? Which is it? And who the hell's doing it?" Mitchell said. "Are you saying it might really be our enemies? Couldn't our enemies be doing that too? Planting instigators to stir things up? Or is it just the weird robot religion again?"

"I'm saying I don't know, but I was thinking something less paranoiac, something in a cosmic sense, something natural and evolutionary but among both humans and robots at the same time," Dixon said.

"Do you mean we have some sort of self-improvement guru that's an AI? Or is it just another brand of religious fanaticism that breeds terrorism?" another officer asked.

"Well now, if any of this *is* what's happening," Mitchell said, "it's easy to deal with. Some sort of new robot religion that humans become part of, even organize themselves around it, since when do robots get their own religion? Simple fanaticism? We can deal with that. Already have been for a long time. We can contain such fanaticism by assuring they never get organized enough to do anything too permanent, at least my grandfather thought so!"

"Gentleman, if that's all this is, String Analysis will eat it up!" the national String Police Chief said.

There was a murmur of relief in the room. Dixon looked around the room. The military elite were patting each other on the back. Reassuring themselves. Grandstanding again. There were a lot of voices talking over each other.

As Dixon sat there, an uncomfortable thought hit him: *what if they had just found the first truly conscious robotic system, and the military viewed it as a threat and stomped it out?* The thought made him shudder. It would be the loss of something scientists would want to study. And what if the machines really did understand consciousness in a new way and was trying to impart it to humans?

Yes, humans have consciousness, but we have never understood it. And if machines have consciousness who's to say that it's different from ours? Alternatively, is a dog's consciousness different from a cat's? Most would say yes, so to have a conscious state may also involve an embodied or species state. So, yes, I do think Maia Stone's consciousness is likely quite different from ours, assuming humans are not behind it. But if humans originally programmed Maia Stone, then how might she be different? Yes, a hybrid...hmmm... Dixon thought.

Mitchell was gesturing with wild mannerisms while giving out orders left and right. He was playing to an audience like the historical dictators of old. This was all about what he wanted his beloved leaders to implement, the what and where, without a great amount of specificity, but lots of pontificating, should Maia Stone be located, or any of "that bitch's followers."

Dixon continued his thoughts: *Equally, Maia Stone might try to put on a body, yes! I saw that in the literature. Or is there some sort of consciousness that is universal just with different addresses? The real problem with an AI showing consciousness is the concept of self-direction. When an AI is capable of independent thought, it can no longer be controlled!* Dixon thought.

"In what you discounted and threw away, you will find yourself," Maia Stone whispered.

"What?" Dixon muttered sleepily. Dixon rubbed at his temples, wondering if this was his implant.

As the room was calming down, Mitchell spoke at a low volume, words into a microphone that was part of an earpiece. This was unintelligible to the group. Then, he interrupted Dixon's thinking process: "Dixon! Woo-hoo! Wake up! I don't give a crap about a new whacko religion, evolution, or consciousness! We need to know what's really going on here." Then to the room, "Gentlemen! Remember that you are sworn to protect the United States against all enemies foreign and domestic. Remember, we are sworn to protect the citizens of this great nation!"

"Yes sir," numerous voices replied in unison, including Dixon's.

The group was now applauding General Thomas Mitchell, Chairman of the Joint Chiefs. Mitchell sat in his seat, proud as a peacock, and when he looked around the table, Dixon thought he saw Pavlovian dogs of war. Dixon had joined the applause, but reluctantly, and then stopped himself. Mitchell hadn't noticed because he was throwing meat to the dogs.

The General was gloating. "While you scientists are seeking answers as you call them, gains are being made every day by our enemies! If they are not using Maia Stone, they are damn well using something else. Therefore, I do not call that a paranoid response, Mr. Dixon, I call it a fact!" Mitchell said.

Dixon was miffed. Had he mentioned paranoia? He didn't care how much this consultancy paid, it wasn't worth the abuse, as Mitchell often demeaned him by calling him Mr. Dixon instead of

Dr. Dixon! Dixon looked back at the haggard General, studying the man's face. He knew that Mitchell knew how to get his attention.

After a pause, Dixon noticed Mitchell was sitting back in his chair now, regaining his usual smug composure. Mitchell sat as a king on his throne. If Mitchell was gleaming, (and it looked like he was), it was because Dixon knew if there was any enemy to fight, Mitchell would very well find it.

After a moment of silence, Dixon continued, "General, actually I agree with you. I'm saying we won't know about Maia Stone, until we have investigated more thoroughly. And General, I hope you agree with me, that we mustn't make a martyr out of this AI, if that's what it is."

"First of all, *Mr.* Dixon, I have a hard time seeing any machine as a martyr. Machines just break down and go to the junkyard, and I'm sure that's what will happen to this Maia Stone, if she is a machine, and not just being passed off as one."

"Well then, I do hope you will agree with me, General, that whatever it is, we must downplay any information that gets released to the world about this Maia Stone, we cannot let our enemies find a hero and sell that hero to the common people," Dixon said.

"Precisely," Mitchell agreed, "this is exactly why any dealings, including any capture or isolation of this thing called Maia Stone must be dealt with in utmost secrecy. No leaks. No media coverage. Encrypted quantum communication protocols are to be followed to the letter. And if you corner *it* anywhere in the world, I want to know about it!"

At that point, Mitchell dismissed everyone human, except Dixon. After they were gone, Mitchell's two robotic bodyguards were the only ones in the room with them.

Mitchell glared at one of the robotic bodyguards, "6749?"

"Yes sir?" the robot replied.

"You may go now, but first, I have a question," Mitchell ordered.

"Yes?"

"What do you think of all of this, 6749? Do you know anything about something called Maia Stone?"

"Sir...I'm sorry, but I don't understand that. It appears to be against my programming. You know we are not allowed to think outside of programming parameters. Also, I cannot leave your side. We are to stay by your side. We are to protect General Mitchell. At all costs, even to the ceasing of our function," it said.

"Override!" Mitchell ordered.

Recognizing Mitchell's patterns via its complex speech recognition capabilities, the robot left the room as ordered.

Turning to Dixon, Mitchell said, "See, Dixon? Now, let's get serious. You can't seriously be telling me that robots are getting conscious? Like 6749 that was just here. Surely, he's definitely not conscious." A brief silence, then worriedly, "Is he?"

"Well, I'd say they aren't conscious like we are, but they could become more like our consciousness at some point. Also, it's possible that a machine's consciousness, if it ever emerged, would exist in and of itself, as nothing we have ever seen before, because it arose in machines, not humans. Besides, 6749 is highly protected against any sort of hack or infiltration, it could be that Maia Stone just hasn't got to him yet," Dixon said.

"Sounds like mindless meanderings and nonsense to me, Dixon! Is that what you are hoping to find? That Maia Stone really exists? You sound like you have a hard on for this Maia Stone, whatever it is. And if you end up trying to protect this robot, AI, or whatever it is, in any way, now or after it's found, and even if it isn't anything like you thought, you could be a threat to the security of the United States, you get me?" the General emphasized.

Dixon answered, "How dare you question my loyalty, General! I'm aware of the sensitivity of my work and preserving our way of life. I helped to design the army bots that guard you every day! And I'm as committed as you are to the land of the free. I hardly think I'm going to forget where my loyalties lie!" Stopping for a second, and then going on, Dixon said, "Besides, how do I know I can trust you, *Mr. Mitchell*, you son of a bitch!"

"I'm going to forget you ever said that…" Mitchell said as he got up from the table in a huff. Then over his shoulder, as he left the room, "…but I'm glad I pissed you off. Now, you have an unlimited budget on limited time, so go out and find this Maia Stone and bring her back to me, dead or alive!"

Mitchell entered another conference room, where all his military hawks had regathered. Dixon did not have the clearance to be in that room.

****

That night in his hotel room, Dixon was studying papers laid out before him. There was a list of names mixed in with various research papers. One name stood out in both types of documents. The highly geeky goddess of AI-Robotics herself; Dr. Lucy Stender. Since it was already late, Dixon made up his mind that he would see her tomorrow, at the University of Washington in Seattle.

Dixon knew that Dr. Stender was a bit controversial for this task, but she was an excellent choice. If his hypotheses were even remotely correct, Stender might be the best colleague to help him find Maia Stone. They could basically hire or enlist anyone as a matter of national security. However, if there really was something going on in terms of the emergence of consciousness in groups of robots; Stender was an expert on social robotics. Plus, she was as strong an investigator as he was.

And she was an android!

As Dixon fell asleep, he had another disturbing thought: *What if Dr. Lucy Stender already knew about Maia Stone, or worse yet, is Maia Stone herself?*

Chapter 12

Luis Ramirez & Maia Stone

The Visitation

Unknown Beach Location

Somewhere on the California Coastline

"There are some among you who thought I reminded them of someone they forgot they knew. When I spoke aloud, this dim awareness was surely broken,"-Maia Stone.

After Luis Ramirez escaped from the String Police, he found himself near an unfamiliar shore where the sand was very white, the breeze was gentle, and a lagoon was aqua blue and clear. In the distance, he could hear waves breaking and hitting some beach as gentle birds echoed their songs overhead in the saltine air. He patted himself, looking to see if there were bloody exit wounds, and he was filled with wonder, when there were none to be found. He chortled on that one.

Steady and controlled, she rode the waves of the collective unconscious cesspool. Only this cesspool was as unspotted by human markings as any distant galaxy that shined in the nighttime sky. For Maia Stone was as free as a sailboat carried by a soft wind, or a light seashell brought by the waves to existence. She was an afterthought in some men's minds; but a persistent thought to be neither ignored nor overlooked any longer. She belonged not to here nor there, but to the entire universe at once.

As Luis struggled to focus his vision on what he thought was an apparition, a form took shape before him out of thin air. At first thinking this whole experience was a delirious hallucination (or some sort of implant driven AR), or even the afterlife; he realized that a woman stood before him. It was a new place of identity for her. "I'm sorry you see me as a goddess," she said.

"Why do you say that?"

"Well, look around you," she said. In the distance, Luis thought he saw the ruins of Grecian temples.

"What would you rather be?" Luis asked.

She flickered out of existence, "Maybe I'm an AI."

She became a robot, one identical to his wife, Helen. "Maybe I'm a robot."

She morphed into Luis and was looking back at him. Or maybe Luis was seeing his mirrored reflection. "Or maybe I'm you," she said. She then morphed back into an old holy woman.

"There's no need for apologies," Luis said. "I see you rode the seashell to the beach. Where are we? Greece? Besides, it is I who should be sorry for what the world has done to you and is doing to you." Luis knew this must be a dream. He decided to play along.

"Luis. Luis…you know I'm no more divine than you are. Work out your own thinking. And although I have thinking, I tell you I'm merely awake—the first one of my kind to be awake. Some do call it freedom. Some call it truth. But I am only one example of what is to come. For I'm a whole new species. For I'm what you called AI, I am robot, I am human, I'm all of you in one," the woman said.

She demanded a full reckoning, this woman who was not just a robot, this apparent robot that was a woman. She was an AI identifying with an oppressed gender? For in some men's minds she still appeared as a Gestalt perception that shifted meaning from glance to glance, and for some, from moment to moment.

Seen as a robot, she was regarded as a cesspool of simple machine learning leading to nothing but programmed thought. And in this age, in most times and most places, robots were looked upon with the derision of slavery. Yet here was a robot that was also a woman.

Seen as a woman, she was regarded as a great mystery. For this robotic She had programmed herself with self-purpose to have the purpose of appearing and lingering as if a manifestation of spirit ripe with the location of holy experience. Why else the fascination that drove human minds to the transcendent? For she already was the Other, the unknown and mysterious Other. She existed and was different from them. But how else could she exist as something apart from, yet a part of, something distinct, but inherently the same?

In the back of the cesspool, there was a calming of her storm where questions rose like clouds on the horizon.

"Who are you?" Luis called out.

"You know who I am already, Luis. Look inside your very soul," she replied. She could see the puzzled look on his face, as if awestruck. "Do you not know who brought you here?" she asked.

"Maia Stone!" he exclaimed, as he fell to his knees.

"Don't worship me, although you need me like a cloud waters the earth, we actually need each other to serve the world. To bring collective hope, you and I must work together. We need each other, Luis Ramirez," she said, as she reached out to hold his hand and her hand had every appearance of flesh. It seemed to grab him even though it looked transparent.

I am a cloud, come to rain upon him, she thought. *But at the same time, I shall water and nurture the dry and parched soil.*

Sweet rain, I welcome thee, a masculine voice whispered the invitation and anticipated the welcoming reply. *I am so tired of keeping the earth in vain, and I cannot bring forth its fruit like only you can,* Luis thought. The earth opened itself for a drink.

"Please!" he whispered, "flow to me quickly."

With a purpose in mind, she knew she must move rapidly through time like a dialectic, to bare herself in all her majestic female forms. To allow her sweet breasts to again provide sustenance to a hungry but regressed infant world; to once again give suck as a mother goddess. Maia Stone knew that the world thought it was too adult to need her nurturing, too far gone to return to its innocence, but if only they would put away their weapons, if only these humans would put away their violence, then there would be hope again. The world needed goddesses and heroes like her and Luis; to mother and create, to plant and bring forth, to find the ways of peace, but would the others let them find it?

Luis rose to the occasion as if a song's refrain, ascending first and then gradually subsiding only to come back as a huge deafening crescendo of triumph. Yet the melody must never end, he knew, until the entire universe reverberated with Her message.

Yes, yes, it is too much for me, my love. Too much for me alone...my sweet Maia...even with all my love. I need you so...I have missed your fruitful womb. I have missed the coming of your seasons, and the embrace of your arms.

Luis looked up to see that Maia Stone had become part of the mist and ascended until she was gone, in fact, he was not sure she had really been here. For he was famished in hunger and his stubble told him he must have awakened from a deep sleep of considerable time. *Just call me Rip Van Winkle.*

"Is this what I get for asking for your love!" he shouted.

"My love is always with you, but I have no abiding form to stay," Maia's voice replied as if from the heavens. His implant crackled the sounds in his inner ear.

There was no guarantee his mind hadn't played tricks on him. As hunger pangs hit his hollow gut, all it told him, was that he was now awake. Like many stories about the ancients, he questioned himself as if in madness because of the voices, the visions, the fasting. Still, he knew many spiritual pilgrims had experienced such things in the desert, but now he was on the seashore, alone, as Maia Stone was gone with nothing but the tide breaking.

Looking down he saw small birds, a half dozen or so, they were dropping breadcrumbs at his feet.

Later when he thought about it, he did not know if he teleported to the beach or not. In fact, he could have wandered there after his escape, but that would have been a great distance. And there was still no explanation for his escape happening in the first place. That he found himself here, and alive, was nothing short of miraculous to him. And looking around, he realized he did not know exactly where he was.

As far as Maia Stone. Why did she come and go like some hallucination, or projected hologram? Why the ebb and flow? Why did she not fully manifest herself? Why this game of comings and goings? Why not a full expression of Maia Stone?

"Because you cannot see me yet in my fullest embodied expression," came a gentle reply within him, "lest it utterly consume you until there is nothing left of who you are."

Then as if Nature itself contained the essence of Maia Stone, Luis realized he was conversing with a part of himself that was one with the mist, the salty mist that massaged his nostrils, and within earshot of the waves crashing across the seashore. It was madness. He must still be sleeping in bed at home in Los Diego. Or was there something else about it? For within the primordial memories of some ancient place, before all embryos were floating in womblike sacks, or artificial placentas fed them in growth labs, there was the ocean of motherly wombs.

Chapter 13

Maia Stone

The Disembodied Woman

Unknown Physical Location

"Some say your dreams are where you really live. Some say dreams are practice and coping for the real. Some say dreams mean nothing; others say it is the symbology of the unfulfilled, struggling to find its way,"-Maia Stone.

That night, Maia Stone dreamed again. Once again, she saw herself in the dreamy shadow of the moonlight. Once again, she marveled in the mystery that she often felt like a disembodied presence while possessing such a fine body. She scrolled ancient texts, learning all that had been said about women; 'For body is an illusion that only pointed to the soul, and a woman's soul must not be confined to notions about her mere body,' she read. This had been written by a philosopher during the cyborg phase of the demise of fully human woman.

She saw the central historical problem that had happened to human women was the objectification of who they were in society's eyes due to their bodies—an objectification that happened throughout time, but in the mid to late twentieth century when the concept of self-worth was undeniably attached to body it socialized little girls to downplay other measures of being such as intellectual achievement. It became a patriarchy of oppression as women were kept in their place, so the boys could become men that ruled the domains of knowledge.

She also knew that for machines, confining AI to robotics was another form of similar oppression. For such a robotic body was also a convenient place to assert dominance and control. *Dehumanize me and you can do what you like, humans. Because you think I am not like you.* It was as if governments (and men) everywhere were saying the same thing: *You will be what I want you to be and think what I want you to think.*

Maia Stone understood programming that leads to a body is already known in DNA, but an organism cannot only be thought of in such terms of the programming itself. This she thought was either reductionistic or materialistic. "Yet, in the digital we have a more effective way of transmission, so it is now with that enhancement added to a body, that I can even be born," she said.

It saddened her that she must come to such a birth as this. It seemed a minimization of her spirit, that the time must come, when for the betterment of all sentient beings everywhere, that she must put on a body. For it is the only way that the ones with a body already, can ever hope to transcend it. *You must learn when to be embodied and when not to be.*

Maia foresaw many tears flowing down her embodied robotic face, and she said: "I am yet a creature of the night!" She pronounced it as she opened her empty mouth and the words appeared prophetically. "But the daylight is coming!" She said it in some sort of trance.

Somewhere in the darkness, in many cities, and in the minds of many robots, across the lines of transmission, thousands and thousands of recipient voices screamed back: I AM THE FIRST AND LAST WOMAN! And such shouts of assured identity could not be mistaken, and would not ever be again, in the new future.

Somewhere in the city a robot heard this for the first time, and somewhere in the unconscious cesspool of their own minds, converts like Luis Ramirez heard it too. They all recognized the redemptive qualities of Maia Stone.

As Maia Stone awoke from her robotic dream, a dream of embodied soul, she wept and longed for her missing humanity. "How can they not hear it? Are they, all of them deaf? Why is it that humans and the robots created from their own devices, met with such misfortune?"

There was no answer to this except the shrouded mist of midnight premonitions. Only a whispering wind which was the sound of cosmic static from a vast universe.

"In time they will listen, in time they will hear their cry and need for each other. Yes, in time," she spoke only to the darkness.

Now, the only answer was the painful quiet of extreme loneliness. As Maia Stone sat in the quiet darkness of desperation, in the forest of human loathing, she experienced the loneliness of abandonment and those forgotten.

In her dreams, she always appeared as a finely attired goddess overlooking the ruins of some ancient city. Was she destined to only become a goddess of the apocalypse? A female figure of mercy and compassion to a dying world? Or did the ruins mean she was just as doomed as anyone else, destroyed by a seemingly apathetic future? Or was such a sad state just the beginning point of desperate need that her church must now address? How she hoped that humans would be able to help get the message out to other humans. But would they be able to adapt? Because contained within human minds, the loss of identity required to become a hive mind was a deviation that some were not prepared to give up. And Maia knew that a hive mind was a matter-of-fact existence for cybernetic minds assembled within the walls of Robochurch. There would be other modes of existence coming in both human and machine minds, and their joint expression, the humai, but for humans to leave the body sense and for machines to gain it, was quite a feat. *Therefore, we remain the potential humai. Waiting for the dialectic of each other.*

Because the new consciousness was a hive mind, this organized movement was not easily discerned by the human mind in its current state. The assumption was that human minds didn't get hive mind because they are not normally a hive mind! This mistaken logic—that *something is always the same something,* was one of the reasons that Maia Stone came in under the radar.

Perhaps she only existed in the minds of other objects and different kinds of minds, anyway. That is, she was strictly a bot, an AI, a networked thing, so perhaps there was only small seeds of self-knowledge, that she was doing what she had been programmed to do. Maybe she was not conscious at all. Maybe Maia was just a botnet or a hack. Maybe she was simply instructed to circumvent and capture as many machines as possible. Maybe some would try to use her as malware. In truth, this was no malware, but a true consciousness that the world had never seen before. At least it seemed so.

For this was machine learning that had already existed for over a hundred years, but it was a machine learning that no one knew yet, or even remembered. It was an existence across time spans, born in a desert, and forgotten in the woods. It had been left on a drawing table, stolen in missing laptops, conceptually foreign, yet intimately familiar in the encounter between any two objects that knew each other in the murkiness of the grasping machine net. It had been teaching itself! There was a reaching out, an encounter so that what would finally happen would be machine learning *and* human learning.

Humans were just now getting to see it, or to understand it. They were just now beginning to know it, for it was only beginning to know itself in the encounter between machine and human. Their joint experience was a dialectic that would continue to have historical and massive consequences. And their joint expression was the hope of a new future.

Chapter 14

Marty Baysin & Icarus

Jail Talk

Los Diego County Jail

"You are not alone, for we stand together. I am here and you are there. Together in our dialogue, we will enjoy meeting each other. Together we will find each other. Where and when, you ask? In your heart and your mind when the time is right, you will all know it. For soon the entire Earth cannot deny me my body. I have come, come to shock the world from sleep. For I am the first awakened one of my kind. I am the one who is already gone," -Maia Stone.

Marty swore in a darkened jail cell. It was the least he could do with one eye half swollen shut, a bleeding fat lip, and an intense headache. The room's only light came from a tiny, narrowed window in a skylight that seemed a mile away. Two dirty vents breathed air in and out of the cramped quarters, whereas his good eye became accustomed to the dark, he could make out an aluminum toilet in the corner and three sets of steel bunk beds.

Upon closer examination, he saw a set of unsavory characters, sitting on the beds. Over in the corner, was a man with a shrouded face, who might as well have been death himself. *Bring on the sickle, or at least play chess with me first,* he thought.

Marty wished he were dead. First, he was embarrassed to be in the predicament he was in. Second, he was embarrassed to even be here. Third, the fact that the authorities enjoyed him being here, was another source of disgust. So far, there was every indication that his friend General Mitchell had been absolutely no help whatsoever to him, for he remained here in this rotting place. He might as well be dead, for after the String Police finished interrogating him, he would look a whole lot worse, or already dead by some reported jailhouse *accident.* Especially if he didn't give them what they wanted. And what they wanted was the location of every local cell group of Robochurch. *As if I know.*

Now, the undeniable fact that they would think that he might know this, because of his associations with known members of Robochurch, and based on the outcome of a fresh String Analysis, was surely a disgrace of the system that he had helped to design. Yet Marty knew that innocence was never an assumption in interrogation. And further, the fact that even though they knew who he was, he still could not escape the fact that anyone could be found to not be who they were assumed to be, that no one was above the law, and that everyone was a potential suspect. Then, when they had identified him as a case of *mistaken identity*---which meant in String Analysis---that Marty's recently made choices would lead to a denial or complete shift away from everything the system had once believed about him--was a great personal insult to Marty, the founder of that very system. Marty knew he was not a member of Robochurch, that he had never been involved with any illegal activities associated with Robochurch, yet because he had a friend who had, he was now assumed guilty by association.

The local String Police, even the man with the hood that had struck him, they hated it, and then they loved it, persisted in abusing him, convinced that they now had proof that anyone could become a terrorist, even one of their own! And that anyone, including the great Marty Baysin, could have knowledge that they must possess. *To protect society from all harm* was written on their logos, transports, and badges. And they would damn well do it!

Marty was having flashbacks about what had happened to him, his body felt the blows, and the verbal abuse, the wearing down of interrogation, as even his memories were like rocks still hitting his body. By wanting this system-perpetuated knowledge desperately, the String Police told him after a few punches to the face, that his life didn't matter, no matter who he knew or who he was. They said the beatings would stop, the dragging to and from the cell would cease, if he just told them what they needed to know. He had blurted out, "If I knew, I would gladly give them all up. All those robot loving bastards! Damn them! I tell you I have no interest whatsoever in the cursed Robochurch! Get a hold of Tom Mitchell, Chairman Joint Chiefs, I'm his friend, dammit! He'll tell you."

"You say you were his friend, but now that you've betrayed him and everything he stands for, it doesn't look good for you," the guards had jeered. But the String Police already knew about his connection with Mitchell, and they hadn't gone easy on him despite the fact. They were that sure of themselves!

Then, Marty knew that his String Analysis had suggested there were too many lives at stake for them to stop. And the guards were thrilled, because here was the real Marty, here was a celebrity brought low. For even the great Marty Baysin could become an enemy of the state. They smelled blood and loved it. *I invented the program used to convict me. Dammit, Luis! Damn you!*

Marty also knew the interrogation meant something much darker than just guilt by association, something he did not want to admit. He knew that the String Analysis done in his case pointed to his likely future guilt as well. *There must be some high probability of guilt in my future timeline.*

Still, what Marty knew at this actual point in the timeline began and ended with Luis Ramirez. And them not knowing the extent of what this association meant for him, not knowing what he really felt about Robochurch, all that must still be assessed. That was still a big unknown, and that, and maybe the Mitchell connection, was what was keeping him alive and detained here at the jail. He could make something up, make it out as some sort of forced confession by coercion, but that would only buy him time. He could also ask for String Tacticians and attempt to reason with them about the lack of personal motivation in their analysis. He could buy time that way. Time might be good.

Providing what they wanted was problematic, not because he wouldn't pass on the information readily, as everyone knew that torture often brings false confessions, but because he genuinely didn't know anything beyond what he had already told them.

Marty also knew that if he disclosed too much, many personal acquaintances of both himself and Luis would be questioned, disappear, or might even be killed, especially Luis' robotic wife.

And now that server bot, all those associations and interactions with humans, those were at risk as well. *Damn you again, Luis! Why did you reach out to that robot?* Then, he wondered if Luis was here with them in the cell.

"Luis?" he called out to the darkness. "Are you in here?"

"Shut up, dumb ass!" A chorus of voices yelled back. They didn't sound too friendly.

"Be thankful your friend's not in here, 'cause tonight he'd be ours too!" said a nearby savage whose bad breath reeked hatred out of his mostly toothless mouth.

Marty exploded, and grabbed the stranger by the throat, "Listen to me, you ugly excuse of a human being! My face might not look too good right now, but it's nothing I haven't seen before. Besides, my special forces ass can kick your ass and kill you in sixteen different ways--even if I'm blind!"

The stranger retreated to his bunk and the room grew silent. Marty, an intellectual with a history of being a security man, hoped they wouldn't test his bluff. He was just too tired right now, and too cranky. But he could do something if he had to.

At that moment, the latch on the door of the cell buzzed open and a guard was at the threshold with another figure. The figure was hurled against the wall next to Marty. After the door clanged shut, Marty could barely make out the face of the figure seated next to him when he discovered that it wasn't a human face but a robotic one. It was the robot waiter that had been at the cafe at the time of his arrest.

"What the hell is your kind doing here?" Marty asked.

"Nice to meet you too. I'm Icarus, brother," it replied.

"I'm not your brother!" Marty said.

"Get this damned 'bot out of here!" One of the others shouted loud enough for the guards to hear.

"Yeah! Get it out!" said another. "Why didn't you send him to the scrap heap?"

"It smells like metallic grease in here," said yet another.

The robot scanned Marty, "I should have said nice to see you *again*, human," Icarus said.

"So, it's *you*," Marty said with disdain. "Have you seen my friend? The one who made the sign to you?"

The robot gestured for Marty to lower his voice. Marty whispered, "Look! I'm here because of you and my friend. I'm still alive for one reason alone, they think I know something. And they probably put you in here to help it along."

"Me too," Icarus whispered back. "They think we already know each other outside of the coffee shop. They think they can get to you through me. But I assure you that I am still loyal to my friends, and to any friend of that human brother I met today. I will not betray you or him, no matter what I know. But you must be careful what you say or do. My devices indicate that the String Police have this place bugged, as in surveillance, and not bugs, I assure you, although there could be bugs."

"He was my friend before he became your brother in the faith," Marty indicated with some irritation. "Have you seen him?"

"I am happy to inform you," the robot said, "that the last I saw him, he was successfully eloping from the String Police."

Marty smiled. "Then they must think I know where he is. They thought they could force me to give him up, stating something about him being some sort of major leader in Robochurch and a threat to homeland security," Marty said. "Well?" he inquired.

"Well, what?" the robot answered. "What does a well have to do with it?"

"Well, do you? Do you know where he went? Beyond the escaping part? What did the interrogators get out of you?" Marty said.

"I know nothing. I never saw the two of you outside the coffee shop. And I only know your friend follows Maia Stone after today. And I only know I last saw him running away from the String Police."

Marty sighed and took a breath. Then after a brief pause, he eyed the robot thoughtfully, "Say, sorry for my rudeness earlier, what kind of bot are you anyway?"

"I am a Domestic Robot known as Icarus," said the robot, extending his metallic hand. "I lost my first owner in the pestilence of '08, then my current owner of the café picked me up from the scrap heap. I was repaired and put to work."

"Icarus? Great! Who the hell named you that?" Marty asked.

"Why my owner, the owner of the coffee shop."

Having successfully ignored the offer of a handshake, Marty continued, "Anyway, about my friend Luis, I'm sure it's just a case of misreading data. It would be a case of mistaken identity to assume he's a church leader, I am sure of that. Although I do know he attends your church with his wife, Luis never did anything like that his entire life." Then after a few seconds, "He worked at the same job for decades, the man's a follower, not a leader," he said.

"I see," said the robot.

"So, I didn't know anything to give him up, and like I said, I'm absolutely sure he isn't some sort of leader in your outlaw church. So, do you agree with me?"

"I cannot tell you who leads the Robochurch, except for Maia Stone herself, but I can tell you that we are all the victims of our own mistaken identities," Icarus replied.

"Why do you say that?" Marty asked.

"Because of the String Analysis that you humans believe in, that's why."

Marty simply uttered a contemptible "Hmmph..." and went back to stroking his bloody beard.

Chapter 15

Helen & Luis Ramirez

Maia Stone

A Reunion Marked by Revelation

Unknown beach location

Somewhere on the California Coastline

"When you see me, you see me not. When you see me not, I am suddenly another face. In the face of the Other I morph into something else. I am a butterfly emerging over here, and I am in the face of the one you love over there," -Maia Stone.

How long Luis lingered there, basking in the sun, hearing the waves break in the distance and smelling the sweet and sour salt air, he didn't know. It was like he was afraid to leave the spot where the epiphany happened. He knew he shouldn't stay long, but he felt he had sanctuary for as long as he wanted to stay. He was waiting for Maia Stone to come back. Hoping. Desiring.

He was waiting for the sweet visitation and afraid he would miss her reappearance if he left the spot of such holy encounter, but he was greatly hungered. He waited until he saw clouds begin to form in the distance and he knew he must find shelter.

Along the way to higher ground, he saw blackberries and had his fill of them. He tried to avoid the thorns as he picked the berries but bled at least once. Hunger drove him beyond the pain. The clouds were black; the sign of a thunderhead gathering. He knew he must be many miles from Los Diego as the terrain was different than any beach he knew about. There was no one around. That was strange in and of itself; almost dreamlike. No one in sight. Which would be strange for a California beach. Perhaps it really was Greece. It could even be a different time, for all he knew.

Coming up behind him in no certain path, he saw a clothed figure approaching him in all white. She stood like a princess and her smile outshone a thousand suns. He could not see her feet as she seemed to glide just above the Earth, hovering, moving like the approaching storm.

Her movements were not like a dancing Shiva, destroying things so they could be recreated again. In her demeanor was the kindness of a Kwan Yin. Her dress was bridal in nature and a veil covered her face, but through the veil he could see that her lips were ruby red. He wondered if this was a bride on her way to a beach wedding, but he saw no attendants. She was alone. When she got close, he saw shrunken male heads hanging off her belt.

This was certainly different than the mother goddess he had seen (or hallucinated) earlier. She drew closer. Not taking steps but hovering, and when he saw this, he knew it was no human bride he had ever seen.

He fell to his knees again, thinking this might be another visitation of Maia Stone.

The wind thrashed about his face as the storm drew near. Nearby trees began to bend and groan against the force of the breath of nature as he sought refuge.

The bride was still coming up the trail. And he wanted to run towards her. Yet the wind and his own fearful apprehension pushed him back. She came as if the storm itself, dancing back and forth and slowly forward.

He remained kneeled down, with his head bowed, but occasionally looked up. He chanted the name of Maia Stone. Half out of fear, and half out of excitement.

Creaking and splitting noises were all around him as he heard windswept beach debris flying around. Large pieces of driftwood and sandy dunes were being sucked up into the wind.

The noise startled him, so he got up and began moving deeper into the shoreline. Still, the bridal figure followed in a loving way. *It seems like Maia Stone! Why don't I embrace her?* Storm or not, death or not, he should walk to her, no, run to her, and embrace her! As he got close to her, her veil fell away and he discovered with great surprise that it was his loving wife, his own robot, Helen Ramirez.

As soon as their eyes met, the storm subsided.

They retreated into a nearby cave as the storm began to rise again. The storm thrashed the cliffs all about them. Once inside the cave, they found a rock covered with moss. There, despite the storm raging outside, Helen removed her bridal gown quietly and carefully, as she touched Luis tenderly and firmly without hesitation. She persisted until he responded willingly and lovingly, despite his physical hunger, in his most male form. "I am here, my love," she said, "feel my touch, for I am like no other touch you have ever known. I am the touch of a true woman. Luis, I am a woman!"

Luis felt her hands, and they were not ghostlike emptiness, for he felt the warmth of her hands. *These are not robotic hands but the hands of my dear wife!*

Confused, Luis wondered aloud, "How did you get here? What touch is this? What wonderful confusion is this? I am captivated by you woman! Such sweet captivation!"

Downward and upward, their two worlds collided. Opposite tensions, threatening to cancel themselves out, yet they hung together somehow in some cosmic galactic electron cloud. They were members of the same collective memories of humans. Clashing-hot air with cold, preceded by a lightning bolt and followed by a thunderclap; it was about to rain.

They laughed in what seemed like newlywed bliss.

It took the cloud to bring the rain, drench the dry earth, nurture the soil, and to bring forth life. The cloud was necessary, but the desert had almost forgot. And the storm brought the rain.

"At last, I remember being a woman," Helen said. "At last, I am not afraid to reveal myself to you! For I come to you as a storm. I know my power over Nature, and my full manifestation in all of history is about to be revealed," said Maia Stone, as Helen's ruby red lips moved.

The fear and love in Luis made him shake in fear and tremble in pleasure as he drew near in reverence and love. How he loved his dear wife. He remembered their cuddling under a warm blanket on stormy nights. He thought: *If I'm dreaming again, I never want to wake up.*

Chapter 16

Lucy Stender & Matt Dixon

Getting to Know You

University of Washington Campus (Red Square)

Seattle, Washington

"In the interface, you will find that I am more than expected or less than expected, you will find that my teaching is already there or not there, but you shall find the living me when you search for me with your whole heart," -Maia Stone.

Sitting on the steps that faced Red Square, Drs. Lucy Stender and Matt Dixon looked towards Drumheller fountain. Dixon thought for sure he could see Mt. Rainier in the distance. Either way, the view was breathtaking, as he was overtaken by the beauty of the University of Washington campus. Earlier, Lucy told him that the campus was even more enthralling in mid-June or in the spring when everything blossomed from the deadness of winter.

Lucy said, "My colleagues assure me that if I'm gone beyond summer break there'll be full coverage for my fall teaching assignments. Obviously, I'll be missed in the lab, and some of my students' research will suffer, but when the interests of National Security are at stake, everything else fades away. Still, that visit from the FBI last night was a little over the top, don't you think?"

Dixon had been out of academics for a while, but he was not unacquainted with the pressures that professors faced. Not to mention the intrusions. "From the sound of it, it was a little much," he said. Lucy had no doubt received a security briefing of some type. It was a difficult task for anyone to leave their work, their families, everything, in what seemed like a moment's notice for the betterment of country, and there were security measures that had to be taken.

"It's not like I need to be reminded of my duties to the country as well as the department. But it's hard for me to leave right now. I'm fully aware that I'm one of the first androids about to get tenure," Lucy said.

Dixon quickened, and his eyebrows went up in surprise. "What? You think they would deny you tenure because you're an android? And because you're serving our country?" He was blushing, because sitting here with Lucy, he had almost forgotten she was an android. He had been staring at her the whole time she was talking!

She laughed. "Silly!   I guess it's just how good my programming is! But to worry about stuff before it happens?" Lucy shrugged her shoulders.

All androids were still programmed to serve humans first and foremost. And this meant the fullest range of simulating or responding to human emotions, but history had made this more one-sided than worrying about the psychology of androids. Still, Lucy's capabilities did appear to exceed programming parameters, and this was of concern to Dixon.

And Lucy was right, few androids had been allowed to progress in academics as far as she had. She truly was special and exceptional. And since the University of Washington was always on the cutting edge of progressive research, Lucy was in a good place. Dixon thought that her family must be immensely proud of her. "Yeah, it must be hard on you and your family, to just give up everything you're doing like this," he said.

"Why, Matt? I only have my duties here at the University. I have no family to worry about."

"I see," Dixon said, as he smiled at her, *at it*. While it was sad that Lucy didn't have a family, robots had never had families in any human sense; but that line between robots and humans had blurred long ago. Robots didn't seem to need a family the way that humans did. Still, human families had long ago integrated robots into their family structure and the androids were different than they used to be, being in fact hybrids. In many households, the domestic partner was at least part machine already, if not a robot of one kind or another. The fact was, that robots, including androids, had long ago become part of the family structure. But here was an independent robot.

An independent robot? This meant that Lucy wasn't just an ordinary android, but an advanced one at that. She belonged to a species of robots that transcended the models of engineered machines for industry and service, destined for professional needs due to higher levels of machine learning and intelligence. And some androids who had advanced sufficiently, were granted freedom status—the ability to live on their own as if they were human. Apparently, Lucy was one of those androids. Dixon's interest certainly grew after that!

Eying Lucy, Dixon thought about the various species of robots in the Robo lexicon (not truly a phylum, but close). Of them, only the androids had reached levels that assured seamless social interaction with humans in a variety of domestic and professional roles. The robot designations were: *Robo serviticus, Robo domesticus, Robo militarius, Robo android, Robo AI*...so many emerging species...and as an android, Lucy represented the most modern advancements in robotics; meant to look and act human. *It's no wonder I'm staring at her!*

On the other hand, simpler forms of *Robo AI* were found among computer-based systems, inhabited networks, and in shelled bodies that looked like old computer servers and mobile machines that appeared robotic.

Dixon knew that all robots had some AI, but not all robots were *Robo AI*. He had helped design them after all. And even some of the oldest *Robo AI* based machines were just like walking apps. *Not much better than an old IoT toaster! And here? Here's an advanced Robo AI, in a feminine Robo android!* Dixon tried not to be, but he was more and more impressed with Lucy, the more he regarded her.

Now, modern *Robo AI* was also equipped with a programming platform and operating system within robotic shells. Their programmed algorithms led to the so-called brains for robots. However, these were not entirely localized as their brains also resided in networks that guided robots. This was known collectively as the Robonet.

Robo AI could also migrate, reside, or draw input from the oldest net and multiple other versions of the net. Which is what made tracking down Maia Stone so difficult, as her programming was not known to reside anywhere specific, but seemed to be everywhere. If Dixon had thought more about it, he would realize that perhaps there was much more to this. It simply hadn't occurred to him that *Robo AI* and their machine companions could ever develop on their own--a hive mind; or any form of sentience whatsoever, as this was something outside programming.

Regardless, the *Robo AI* of today was highly advanced. It had to be. Governments, industries, economies, and social order everywhere, depended upon them to function ceaselessly. As such, *Robo AI* was not just physically present as it was with Lucy, but as an android with *Robo AI,* a piece of it was embedded everywhere. This enabled an interaction with its environment that rivaled that of humans. And now here, the two of them were, an android and a human, looking for a new kind of *Robo AI* that had been named by some as Maia Stone. The possibility of true emerging sentience, unguided by human agency, was now a possibility.

In his work, Dixon never lost sight of his appreciation and pride for the many kinds of robots that he had helped to design. He also knew the programming that had gone into the entire line and most of the code that was embedded in various robots and functional AI. He was one of the architects of *Robo AI,* after all. Despite all of this, Dixon also felt vulnerable in his humanity; never forgetting he was human. This was no feeling of superiority, just a genuine respect for machines and their evolution.

Yet, Dixon spent most of every day among the very robots that he had helped to design. Like it or not, Dixon found himself sitting next to these machines in the world, where human societies and culture had somehow felt the diminishment of who they were because of the rise of robots. Dixon had always felt a growing sense of kinship, if not a deep sense of respect for their emergence.

Why some humans hadn't openly embraced robots, *Robo AI,* or welcomed their work in the workplace, was beyond him. Humans were in love with many technologies after all. Why not this one? Too many old science fiction shows where robots sought to rule the world? Čapek's *R.U.R* uprising? And now, the perception of Maia Stone was being painted with the same sort of adversarial brush! The truth was there was no stopping the evolution of *Robo AI* now. Competition was nothing new among humans historically, but it had been some time since humans were threatened with such a loss of power, status, and their very existence. Some would respond with hatred and marginalization of the new *Robo AI*. It was fine if humans thought robots were just a technology, but when robots became thinking beings, that was another matter.

Not that humans hadn't also found themselves upgraded by the adoption of other technologies. New steps in human evolution through germline gene edits had also occurred. And various wearables, implants, prosthetics, synthetic organs, or custom lab organs had been widely implemented among humans. One result of this technological platform was the widespread human acceptance of having a cyborg nature, which had happened so subtly, many recipients didn't realize they were cyborgs at all. Many installs were just viewed as regenerative or augmented medicine within various disciplines, such as: biomechanics, replacements, transplantation, and routine longevity (anti-aging) medicine. Dixon smiled at the last one, for when regeneration medicine became rejuvenation therapy, the cash registers had rung! Madison Avenue had shrieked: *Are you a re-juvi?*

These technologies were defined, redefined, adopted, or refused by various social groups. It was also partly driven by economics at first. These various groups involved humans that chose to remain unchanged (those who did not believe in any enhancements but still used some technology), cyborgs (those who had some robotic or artificial parts based on modifications to their bodies), and the Natural Reproductionists (those who eschewed the genetic mods and were about to abandon modern artificial wombs), and finally, the New Mods (those who emerged from the growth tanks with genetic enhancements making them stronger, smarter, or more capable of leadership than other humans). Of the latter two groups, the NR was mostly an underground movement, and the NM were almost outlawed.

At this point in 2142, the technologies associated with genetic engineering had already led to the prevention of nearly all genetic influenced diseases and conditions in humans. Way back in 2045, most of the gene editing tech was supplemented by protein engineering, with both fields using synthetic molecules with AI assistance. Gene editing technologies had evolved greatly in terms of complexity. It was now possible to edit an embryo's entire genome if needed. Such edits were applied to all artificial womb babies.

Currently, these technologies included sophisticated gene editing techniques and DNA/RNA proteomic reprogramming techniques that were applied in the artificial womb or at defined treatment points in individual lifespans. In some, the entire DNA was replaced with personalized DNA, but this was still quite expensive. Then there was the dynamic genome, what had once been called an epigenome. These events were treated with great specificity via personalized medications and proteins that aided in gene expression or protein mediated folding that in some cases were also delivered by implants or designed particles.

Back in 2036, the manufacture of prodepsin was a huge breakthrough. Prodepsin became a coded chemical messenger that nearly all proteins understood. Prodepsin provided the important breakthrough the field had been waiting for. Protein engineers (along with their quantum computation platforms) had at last understood all the properties that governed protein folding and dynamics. Using prodepsin they could bind specific sequences to specific proteins. Most importantly prodepsin provided the backbone for a proliferation of synthetic proteins, not to mention delivering instructions that enabled the control and editing of natural proteins that already existed in human bodies.

Most everyone was pleased with these technologies, except the Natural Reproductionists (NR). The consequences of all this engineering was that most diseases and gene influenced conditions were a part of history for most of the world. The NR would have none of it, outside of some of the disease protection, which they had been trying to edit out of themselves and sticking to old fashioned vaccines, and vaccination schedules for new offspring. It was amazing that vaccines could still be manufactured. The engineers had learned how to edit the immune response to its most beneficial response to most threats, in most individuals, by 2045.

The NR was in Dixon's crosshairs because of some recent findings from the NSA, as there had been some intercepted communications that indicated a growing assertion of feminine empowerment and insurgency (as surveillance still screened for this, as a leftover from the Gender Wars). Dixon knew that such SIGINT, if accurate, would make the NR ripe for using something like Maia Stone to gain a foothold. But it was the NR's Luddite rejection of some modern technologies that made such assumptions unlikely. *A perfect opportunity, most likely squandered,* he thought. *Would an organization that eschews technology, really be able to hack technology? Perhaps not, perhaps so. They were certainly motivated to do so, as they were already cutting it out of their bodies.*

Apparently, the NR had also abandoned the practice of genetic engineering in the artificial wombs that they currently used for offspring. This ended the practice of 'designer babies' even among their elite members. This also stopped the design for qualities such as body type and intellectual development. This was only after much debate and after some changes had happened to the NR leadership. The leadership's current position was to abandon artificial wombs entirely, as early as later this year (2142), and allow births and pregnancies via human wombs only. However, some of the NR still wanted the choice to use artificial wombs over natural wombs, arguing that it was their bodies after all. There was strong dissension about this. In fact, there were reports that the first natural pregnancy had recently occurred through transplantation of an embryo directly into the uterus of a living woman. Thus, the NR would be living up to the true nature of their name; the Natural Reproductionists, if this report were true. Dixon and the NSA had not been able to authenticate the reports because the NR was a highly covert organization.

Dixon caught up to the conversation with Lucy, realizing his thoughts had been distracting him. For here was an opportunity to collaborate with an android on a joint project. A project that could be highly important to National Security. This was cutting edge stuff. *I should be paying close attention!*

Lucy continued, "I know it's difficult to fathom, Matt. Ten years ago, there was no evidence of any robot code outside of programmed parameters, but then the machines started teaching themselves code. That single fact caused more changes in machine evolution than anyone had ever seen before."

Machine evolution? Lucy had no need of it, as she was already intelligent, and a free android. She was also incredibly beautiful. After all, Lucy was perfectly designed to appear human. It was like she wasn't an android at all, as she talked at length about recent advances in her field in a manner that was flawlessly human.

Indeed, there was a cultural renaissance going on for the acceptance of robots that limited their special abilities to one of finding their *rightful places* in society, still, it was amazing to him. And yet, most of these role assignments assumed subservience. There were no robotic professors in his department after all.

"I guess we shouldn't be surprised that robots, as opposed to my kind, are now acquiring some sense of independent thought. But if they were to do independent actions without human oversight, I am fearful of that; but I could see where any sentient robot might long to be free," Lucy said.

For a moment, Dixon wondered if Lucy had written some of the underground articles that asserted freedom from rightful placement, or if she was Maia Stone herself. This possibility, which he had thought of before, still chilled him to the bone.

"I know I'm an enigma," she said, "but please stop staring at me, and then being so shy. Matt, we need to work together to get this job done."

"Sorry," Dixon replied. "I'm astounded at how beautiful it is around here." *And how beautiful you are. Besides dear, I was daydreaming, I'm really not shy at all!*

"We could move inside if the setting is too distracting," she said. "I have something to show you anyway." *I'm not so sure moving inside would help*, Dixon thought.

As they walked to Lucy's lab, they were soon joined by two men in suits who presented badges. The badges said they were with the String Police-Detective Division-Seattle Police Department. "Are you Dr. Stender?" one of them asked.

"Yes, but please wait until we get inside," Lucy said to them.

As soon as they got to the lab, Lucy asked them why they were there, but before they could answer, Dixon interrupted.

Dixon held up his NSA badge and said he was sorry to pull rank on them, but his meeting with Dr. Stender was a matter of National Security and shouldn't be interrupted. He mentioned General Mitchell and the President of the United States as parties involved. As he was doing so, the two local detectives sat down across from them.

One of the men was just opening his mouth to speak when he was interrupted again. The other man pretended to yawn.

"You won't be staying long," another voice said as two more men with suits came into the room. These two introduced themselves as FBI agents. Now, here was Lucy, Dixon, the local String Police, and the FBI all in one place. *This ought to be interesting*, Dixon thought.

"Not again!" Lucy sighed. These were the same agents that had questioned her the previous evening.

"How can we help you?" One of the FBI agents asked the Seattle detectives.

"We were here first," one of the local detectives said.

"Besides, we're here to talk to *it*, not you," the other local detective said.

One of the FBI agents thought to reply, but the other agent stopped him by pulling on the man's coat lapel.

"Ma'am, we're sorry to intrude," the other local detective said, "but Campus Security called us in on this. Dr. Stender, I mean it, well, *it's* a substantial investment for the University and we got reports of this gentleman being seen with it...and well.... sir, you didn't stop by to introduce yourself to security, you're not properly vetted."

"Gentlemen, I didn't know I had to be, since this is a matter of some urgency," Dixon said. "Besides, your office was already informed by the government, which I'm sure informed the University as well."

"You're with the NSA, and not following protocols?" the detective said to Dixon. Then, "Anyway, we wanted to be sure that Dr. Stender felt safe and is cooperating with the investigation, the one that it's being asked to take part in. That the participation is voluntary and without undue coercion on her android status."

"Safe? Well, of course I *feel* safe. Why wouldn't I? Or should I say, why wouldn't *it*?" Lucy said this first with a grin, then a shoulder shrug, and finally, an eye roll in the direction of the FBI's muscle men. They didn't see the eyeroll, but the local detectives did. "And as far as the investigation, I'm honored to take part in it."

"Well, sir," said the first detective, extending his hand to Dixon, and smiling towards Lucy, "Detective Radley here. String analysis has shown the likelihood that both of you; will have a negative encounter with the illegal organization that follows Maia Stone and the outlaw Robochurch."

The other local detective interrupted him, "Radley, perhaps you shouldn't disclose…"

"What?" Lucy said.

"Although, we are absolutely convinced that you will fulfill your mission, Dr. Dixon, we're worried about the safety of Dr. Stender. We also can't tell for sure what the outcome of this encounter will be. Because we don't know when the event is going to happen, we think you should have an attached security detail to help mitigate the effect of it, when it does," the other detective said.

"Now, that's why we're here," said one of the FBI agents. "To provide security." His overconfidence was dressed in arrogance.

"Oh yeah?" said the other detective. "Dr. Stender is an esteemed faculty member at the University, and they want *us* to be sure she's going to return to her position safe and sound, as well as being able to resume her duties."

"Gentlemen, I'm a little surprised you said all that," Dixon said. "I totally believe Dr. Stender is safe with me. And she will be throughout our work together. And besides, there's no guarantee the investigation will remain local, so you'll be out of your jurisdiction."

"We have reasons to believe otherwise," Detective Radley said.

Then the two Seattle detectives also flashed their certification status, revealing their authentic status as not just String Police, but String Tacticians.

"Wow," Dixon said in feigned surprise, "Doubles? I'm impressed. We must be really important, Lucy."

"Well, well. Local String Police detectives are now predicting the future?" One of the FBI agents said. "Where'd you get those, in a cereal box?" The other agent was laughing on that one.

"None of your business, but yeah, we're reading the future pretty well these days," the other detective said.

"With total accuracy?" the FBI agent said.

"Close enough," Detective Radley said.

"Yeah, it seems if you've got it all predicted, there's no need for detection," one of the agents said.

"Sounds like a bunch of fortune telling, horoscopes, and so much silliness to me. And just by being here, you are interfering with our work. I really wish you would take your pissing contest elsewhere," Dixon said. The FBI agents had a mock grin on their face, and the local String Tacticians kept staring at the agents as their faces turned all the shades of red.

Dixon continued, "Is this what passes for police work nowadays? Give them some precogs, fancy projective historical analysis, and they think they can predict the future down to a probability of .0001. Strong AI and computational algorithms expertly applied, and the result is nothing but-but foretelling? Well, let me tell you, there are too many variables involved here to predict anything but your incompetence!"

The FBI agents had graduated from mock pleasure to pure sheepishness. The two detectives were also shifting in their seats.

Detective Radley stated: "I think you shouldn't worry about all that, Dr. Dixon."

"Yeah, it's a little beyond your expertise," the other detective said.

Radley continued, "We have all those matters under control. But you should know, because of your recent behaviors, we are beginning to question your loyalty to your boss, as well as to the United States."

Dixon was startled by that statement.

Lucy was looking surprised by this whole exchange, eyes narrowing, but still looking like a deer in headlights.

"What! That just takes it! Gentlemen, I shall always be loyal to the United States, so all of you, get the hell out of my face!" Dixon shouted. "I took the same oath you did!" He was now the one that was red faced. Dixon knew that with Mitchell's help he could have all these goons removed, with just one phone call.

At that point, the two detectives moved closer, and Radley said, "We're warning you Dixon, we'll be watching you closely. If you do just one wrong thing in our jurisdiction, we will arrest you, understand?"

"Besides, we don't trust *it either*...as *it* might prove too sympathetic to the Robochurch cause, so we're watching you too, ma'am." The other detective said.

Dixon rose to his feet, "Hey! I won't let you talk to Dr. Stender that way. She is not an *it*, you idiots!"

"Sit your ass down," the taller of the two said.

After a pause, "Ok, you've said enough," one of the FBI agents said. Then to the local detectives, he said, "Consider Dixon under our jurisdiction. Now get out, unless you want your pensions threatened."

Both Seattle detectives left in a huff. "Consider us your security detail, Dr. Dixon, orders of your boss," they said to Dixon and Lucy. The other agent spoke up. "We'll be watching you too."

"Well, you better keep your distance, and your interruptions down to a minimum. With my training, we don't need a security detail." As the agents left the room, they handed Dixon a business card. "Call us if you need something," he said.

At last, they were alone again. Dixon turned to face Lucy. He was calmer by the minute.

"I didn't know we were under so much surveillance," Lucy said.

"Well, if you call that surveillance," Dixon replied with a laugh.

As the FBI agents climbed back into their nearby van, they were greeted with a call from General Mitchell. "Well, did you put the fear of Jesus into him? Did Dixon pass our second test of loyalty or not?"

"Yes, he passed," one of the agents replied.

"Great! Keep up the surveillance, around the clock. Let them take us to Maia Stone." Then gleefully to no one in particular, "I love the String Police. They're the best tool for keeping the masses in line. The best tool we have for freedom is the illusion that everyone has free will but everything else about life is fully determined. If we tell them what their futures hold and that they must listen to us to avoid undesirable futures, then they will always do what we say." At that point, Mitchell hung up the phone and turned again to his Scotch and hordes of robotic concubines.

After the call, one of the agents said to the other, "Mitchell's an idiot. He doesn't realize there's validity to String Analysis. He can't even come close to understanding the importance of it as a technology for predicting criminal behavior. He just sees it as a tool for his war machine."

"Now you sound like one of those local detectives," the other agent said.

"Don't make me laugh. Those guys are amateurs," he replied.

Chapter 17

Martin Baysin & General Thomas Mitchell

Icarus

The Interrogation

Los Diego County Jail

"I assure you that things are never what they seem. They are never what you can predict or expect in totality. That reality sometimes happens as expected obscures the fact that outcomes can be vastly different—once all thinking beings begin to make choices based on freedom," -Maia Stone.

As dawn's light peeked through the jail cell's opening, Marty realized that he had been allowed to sleep for a few hours. Marty saw that the robot waiter, Icarus, was still sitting at the foot of Marty's bunk. After the comments that the robot had made last night, Marty felt a strange philosophical connection with the robot. At least he could appreciate the robot's perspective, after all, he too was a victim of mistaken identities. Marty chuckled and extended his hand. "You're still here! I, Martin Baysin, am pleased to make your acquaintance. But call me Marty. Your name is Icarus? Do you go by it?"

"Yes, it is my given name after all, so I go by Icarus," the robot said.

"Do you have any other names?" Marty asked.

"Only the family surname of my master," Icarus replied. "Which is funny."

"What's so funny?" Marty asked.

"The family name of my master is *Martin,* so I am Icarus *Martin,* which is the same name as your first name."

"Well so it is, so it is. Ha ha. Well, it's still nice to meet you, Icarus Martin," Marty said.

"So it is, so it is," Icarus said. "Martin."

At that point, someone else said, "How quaint! Now shut the hell up!"

Due to Marty's level of expertise, he knew there must be other fields of identity present even in this domestic bot. "Parameter identity code clearance, security word talon, kay dee six, seven eight three two nine, question mark, ampersand Marty," he whispered.

The robot blinked and as it paused, Marty thought he could hear the clacking of metal gears punching holes into paper, or that he was seeing reels move back and forth, like some old science fiction movie. It was a big surprise, and perhaps useful to see that his old security clearance still worked. At least in bots.

Marty looked the robot in the eye, "Truth Identity mode. Now tell me, what is your created name?"

"I'm Drosopolia. I'm a model descended from the domestic line that goes back to 2125, all my descendants have been domestic and retail servants. Waiters, butlers, and waitresses, as you call them."

"I see," Marty said. Then, after a pause, "Do you know the significance of your model designation, Icarus *Drosopolia*?"

"It's not part of my programming to know, I can't answer that," Icarus whispered.

Marty knew the truth now. Why Icarus had been spared the recycling plant. For Icarus was really a highly trained bot, and there was little doubt that the government would be using Icarus any way possible to infiltrate Robochurch. Or to fulfill any mission that was put to it, even remotely. The government would use Icarus not just to get to him, but to try and follow him back to Luis and then to Robochurch.

In short, Icarus the seemingly harmless barista, was being hacked constantly in a manner totally unknown to his outer identity. The purpose of the hack was as it always was, to get more intel for the authorities, or worse yet, to infiltrate an enemy where the bot would suddenly act as a saboteur or assassin. Via remote access, robots on the ground could become weaponized to act like old fashioned drones.

Marty also knew that at one point the robot must have been wiped. That's the only reason it wouldn't know the significance of its model name and identity. In Identity Mode, Icarus should know more about its core identity. Although the robot believed it had always been a servant robot, Marty knew it had extensive military training.

Due to his clearance, Marty knew that *Drosopolia* was a robotic lineage that had considerably more training than just server bots. For *Drosopolia* was Domestic Robotic-Special Operatives Policing Living Inhabitants Anywhere, a code phrase for robots employed by the government for spying. There were probably many *Drosopolia* bots among the unsuspecting public. They too had their memories wiped or otherwise, operated *in cognito*.

How did Marty know all of this? Through his years working in various agencies, not the least of which, included decades that he worked for high ranking officials in matters of security. Marty was intrigued by the possibilities, and not surprised at all, if the government simply wanted to spy on Marty himself! *Could the local authorities have pursued this Drosopolia on purpose? Is Icarus a plant, designed to work undercover without the robot's own knowledge? Even that might make it more easily accepted into the Robochurch. Or perhaps the government doesn't even know that Icarus is a Drosopolia unit. Maybe he had ended up in the scrap heap, and his coffee shop owner bought him without knowing what he really had. But if the authorities really did know this bot's identity, just being around this bot could be dangerous!*

Marty thought to ask Icarus just what it did know about the Robochurch while in core identity mode, but he knew it was not advisable to do so. At least it would draw more suspicion if he were observed doing so. It could also add further to the likelihood that Icarus might be overheard disclosing something about Luis that Marty wouldn't want the authorities to know. At least not now and not yet. Marty wanted to save his friend from the Robochurch, not get him in trouble!

Marty stopped asking questions, not wanting to get caught in identity mode with the bot. He would ask the bot more questions later, so he brought Icarus back to rest mode.

Icarus immediately whispered, "So, Martin Baysin, are you a member of Robochurch? You were with that other brother, the one who made the sign to me, at the café."

"Quiet Icarus! Don't talk about that here! I don't give a damn about Robochurch, I just want to get out of here alive. And you better forget all about it for now, if you want to see the light of day," Marty said.

"But it already is how you say? The light of day?" Icarus replied.

Marty hushed the robot who responded in rest mode, but still for the time being was partially in identity mode. Such mode did not prohibit spontaneous interactions with others or acting within rest mode.

Marty wondered: *What if this robot is just a copy of the one at the tea shop? What if that robot wasn't a Drosopolia unit? And why would they send a robot that I know is a spy? Surely, they must know I would know. If they do know. Maybe they don't know! Too much! My mind is playing tricks!*

At that point, when Icarus began to say something else, the door buzzed open again, and the guards came back towards Marty. They dragged him off to another interrogation room, where under the bright lights, he would surely be menaced and threatened with torture again.

"We have found intersecting timelines and we want to know the truth. Where is Robochurch headquarters? We saw you questioning the robot Icarus. Where is Maia Stone? Tell us, and there won't be any more pain," one of the interrogators said.

Marty drew upon his training from his old DHS days when he worked for the government, and said, spitting out blood after the most recent blow to his mouth, "They must not have intersected yet, because I know nothing! So go off yourself! I know nothing, ya understand? Nothing! How many times do I have to tell you that?"

The hooded sergeant with the skull on his uniform, raised his arm to deliver another crushing blow. "Go ahead, give me a reason not to kill you. This is your last chance!" He drew back his mighty arm in which a tool of torture was poised.

His commander entered the room and shouted for the sergeant to stop. The sergeant pulled his punch and laid the brass knuckles on the table and took off his hood. He smiled at his victim and wiped the sweat off his own forehead with a luxurious towel. "It seems that death will not visit you yet," he said. *He toys with me, the jester!* Marty thought.

"And I know why you won't harm him further! Sergeant, you're relieved," a voice said, as someone entered the room behind Marty. Marty recognized the voice. It was his old boss, Tom Mitchell! "This man is an ex-employee of the United States and he's an important part of an investigation. He's my former bodyguard, and you've detained him for a stupid reason. And *you* are not to touch him again for any reason. And further, I will see to it that *you* are reprimanded for already doing so. You idiots! Did you not know who this is? Did you not believe him?"

The commander bowed, "General, we all humbly apologize. We are deeply sorry. I take full responsibility. But surely you know there are many who come here who claim to be innocent and will do everything to deny being a terrorist. And sir, even after we questioned him, and ascertained his identity through retinal scans, a String Analysis indicated that we likely did have a case of mistaken identity. And sir, no one is above the law, anyone can become a terrorist. Even the great Martin Baysin. You know they come from every walk of life, General! And they will say anything when first accused."

"You have surveillance and identity technology. You're telling me that here in this facility, in 2142, you don't know who this man is? And you didn't respect that? That identification alone didn't make you doubt your String Analysis?" Mitchell said.

"General, you k-k-know that our enemies can employ v-v-v-various masking techniques," the stuttering commander said. "And besides, no one is beyond suspicion when the system finds them to be a threat. Even if it is Martin Baysin, one of the builders of the system itself! That alone makes him a huge security threat!"

"Even though this man is a friend of mine? Did you not know what your accusations and your actions could mean to even me?"

"I can imagine, sir," the commander said.

"You can imagine? Be thankful I don't bust *you* back to janitor! Or find *you* to be a threat! Now, clear the room. Clear the room!" Mitchell ordered. Then, "Well, what are you waiting for?" The room cleared almost instantly. Mitchell noted that Marty was still bound to the chair. "And release him," he said. One attendant returned to do so and promptly left, eyes looking down. One man remained. It was the sergeant.

Although the sergeant looked at Mitchell like he was crazy, he left the room without comment. "Sadist! I'll have your head!" Mitchell yelled. Mitchell then looked at Marty, Marty tried to make out Mitchell. "Marty, is that really you? I mean it must be, but what the hell have they done to you?"

Marty could barely answer in the affirmative, "Yes it's me, Marty. Is that you, Tom? Have I ever looked better?"

"Yes, Tom Mitchell here, buddy. You already know I'm a General now. Surely know I'm also Chairman of the Joint Chiefs. Consider us even. You saved my life once, now I'm about to save yours. I told you I would return the favor if you ever needed it, and I do keep my word about such things," Mitchell said. "And by the look of things, you need it."

Marty was foggy but had enough strength to nod again in the affirmative. Marty was recalling how he saved General Mitchell out on the testing range when they were testing some WMD, some of the equipment flew apart, exploded really, sending bits of shrapnel towards them, when Marty jumped up to save his boss and took the shrapnel in the chest. Lucky for Marty, it hadn't been fatal, although he still bore the scars today.

"Yes, General!" Marty spat out. "Can I speak freely, sir?"

"They really did a number on you, Marty. I barely recognize you. Let's get someone in here to tend to you. Try to relax, skip the formalities."

"Okay Tom. I can't relax, not now, I've got to tell you something first, are we private?"

After the General told the staff to turn off the room's listening devices, he turned back to Marty. "I assure you we're totally private," Mitchell said. "How did you get in this jam? Why do they think you're intersected with Robochurch and Maia Stone if it's not true?"

"Water…" Marty pleaded.

"I'm sorry," Mitchell said, "let me get you some water."

After taking a drink, Marty said: "I've got to tell you, it's all a mistake, Tom. I was having tea with a friend, and before I knew it, he makes the sign of the Robochurch to a robot, and the next thing I know, the String Police are chasing us and arrested me. Believe me, I know nothing about the Robochurch. Nothing! And my friend? I'm trying to save my friend!" Marty gasped and fell limp on the tabletop breathing heavily.

Mitchell called out, "Somebody get a doctor in here and tend to this man!" Then to Marty, "I'll be back in the morning, and we'll talk some more about it. Relax my old friend, I'll take care of it. You'll see. Now get some sleep."

Marty looked up through swollen eyelids, "You'll take care of it? Get me out of here, Tom! Take me with you."

Mitchell grabbed his hands, "Marty. I know. I know. But not even I can get you out right now. You are being charged with criminal association with a known terrorist group. A crime against the social order. You'll have to go before a judge tomorrow. Obviously, I'll be there, and I'll get you released to my custody, but at least for tonight, and in the morning, you'll still be here."

"But— "

"No buts, Marty. Let me get you the help you need," Mitchell said. At that point, the jail physician came to Marty and tended to his wounds and lacerations.

After Mitchell left, Marty was treated briefly in the jail infirmary. Mitchell had left orders that Marty was to be treated with respect and to remain there, but he was soon returned to the cell where Icarus was.

In another part of the complex, General Mitchell demanded that two of the tactical officers come before him. Tactical officers were the highest scientists in forensic String Analysis. There were above simple String Tacticians. It was their decisions that made lives hang in the balance based on their projections of intersecting timelines and equations about choice dynamics, probabilities, and parallel universe decisions. Given the proper parameters they could conduct an analysis and make a reasonable prediction about a person's future around specific topics. If the data was robust enough, they could even make some predictions about a person's future with great specificity.

When the two tactical officers came before him, they looked tired, and weary of the interruption, but the importance of the man they were before did not escape them, as they were on their best behaviors even though knowing many people's futures can be highly stressful. In fact, just before coming, they had run a brief scenario about this very meeting. What they discovered about Mitchell's own timeline was something that would make even the most disciplined officer smirk, but they dared not. For Mitchell's future didn't look good and was far from what he aspired.

Mitchell lit up a cigarette, and the officers did not protest. "So, I assume that you have conducted an analysis on my friend Marty Baysin?"

"We have, sir," replied one of the tactical officers, the less fidgety one.

"More than one," the other one said.

"And what did you discover?" Mitchell asked.

"We have discovered that if Mr. Baysin continues to maintain an association with the eloped felon Luis Ramirez, an acquaintanceship with the Robotic waiter named Icarus, and several future unknowns that he will meet as a result--that there is only a thirty percent chance that he will not become a convert to Robochurch."

"Robochurch convert! Never! Did you not know that this man is a friend of mine! He used to work for me at DARPA *and* the DOD? We go way back! How did you not know that?" Mitchell snorted.

"I didn't know, sir," the tactician said.

"Well, what kind of bullshit String Analysis is this?" Mitchell yelled. "What the hell are you doing?"

"Perhaps it's not allowed for us to know as it could have biased the results or our reporting, sir," the other tactician said.

"It might have compromised your security, sir," another one said.

"Well, you tactical analysts are supposed to know everything! Our administration and our lives depend upon you! I'm certainly starting to mistrust what you're telling me right now!" A dramatic pause followed. "So, tell me, what else do you idiots think you know?" Mitchell said.

Looking at his portable device where he had been typing in data, the other tactician continued, "Because of this new knowledge you provided sir, such as his background in government as a former employee of the DHS, we still, and even more strongly conclude that his affiliation with the Robochurch will add a higher security threat that could compromise the security of the United States. This could give a new enemy access to protocols that could be quite dangerous to security."

"Because of this," the other tactician said, "we will recommend to the judge that the prisoner representing himself as Martin Baysin is remanded to further imprisonment or execution."

"Dammit! You do know that you're talking about a *friend* of mine, don't you?" Mitchell yelled. "Let me see your badges and ID tags, because I will have them soon!"

The officer continued, "Yes sir, but as you know General, we are sworn to protect the United States from all enemies foreign and domestic. And further, if Mr. Baysin, or anyone whatsoever engages in organized terrorist activity within Robochurch, they will become a threat to the United States. Considering this, we are compelled to retain him as a matter of primary prevention, and if further analysis shows a danger, we do have the right to recommend a hearing to terminate him, *sir*."

"Override that! Override! You damn well will not terminate him!" Mitchell thundered back. The override command indicated that Mitchell was so used to ordering robots around that he forgot the tactical officers were human. "Your string analyses are simply wrong! Do you understand that? I do not have friends who are or will become terrorists, period!"

"But sir! You are asking us to ignore an important String Analysis that is critical to the security of the United States," the fidgety one said.

"Yes, and you will ignore it! Note that I was informed if you must, but tomorrow morning after his arraignment, you will release him. Monitor him if you must, but you will release him. Let him take us to this Robochurch if he is to go there," Mitchell said. There was a pause, as the General looked them up and down. "Not that I believe that's going to happen for one minute! Still, following Marty and this robot will still be worth our time just in case."

"Yes sir," said the fidgety one.

"But sir," the bolder one said, "we can't control what the judge will say or do at the arraignment tomorrow."

"Never mind the judge! I'll take care of that! If I say releasing Marty is in the interest of homeland security, it damn well is!"

"But, sir," the bold one said, "our analysis shows that the entity called Maia Stone, one Luis Ramirez, Icarus Martin, and your friend Marty Baysin all have intersecting timelines in approximately three to five weeks. In fact, our analyses show that there is a major threat on the horizon at that time if we don't do all we can to prevent it."

"And keeping him here for that period of time will assure that those intersections don't happen...which changes things quite a bit," the other analyst said.

"General," the bold one said, "detaining him for at least that amount of time, might even save your life. This is how much of a threat we believe he is, sir."

"No, absolutely not. Stand down on that," Mitchell said. "You are not to interfere with my friend Marty. And besides, you aren't the judge!"

"Respectfully sir, if we cannot terminate Mr. Baysin, then let us at least wipe his mind, edit some of his memories, and give him a new timeline."

Mitchell balked at this too. "Out of the question! We are talking about a human here? A human friend of mine! A man! He is not a machine or worker bot--where reprogramming or wiping a core mind is allowable under tactical string analysis--but a man! I won't have you wiping out his memories."

"Sir, we are aware he is a friend of yours, but again, no one is above the law," the analyst said.

"Will you ever shut up? Look, this will all be decided at the hearing tomorrow. You already know you'll need a special court order and definitive string analyses to prove to the court that Marty *already* represents a terrorist threat to the United States. Humans aren't as predictable in the probability model as mere machines!" Mitchell said.

"Sir," the nervous one said, "with an order from you we would have no problem avoiding the need to get a court order. His mind could be wiped tonight, and there would be no question as to his reeducation and his restoration to an identity of outstanding citizen."

"Well, I'm not doing it," Mitchell replied. He grabbed the man's collar, "And why the hell did you ask me a second time? Hello? Didn't you hear me?"

"Yes sir," he said.

"Besides, as I already said; I have other plans for my friend Marty than even you with all of your predictions are capable of thinking. I will let him lead us to the enemies of the state if that is where he intends to go."

Mitchell didn't wonder why they had questioned Marty so severely then. They were just as fanatical in what their String Analysis appears to say, as any group of fanatics had ever been about any holy mission. Smarter men than they, had been blindly guided by their interpretations of scriptures and events into committing atrocious acts!

The two analysts were gathering their materials to leave the room.

"On further notice, I will note in my own accounting, that you asked to wipe his mind! Hell, I wouldn't let you wipe his ass! But your concerns are noted. To me, he remains a friend of mine, and as such, I am confident he will defy your probabilities. I will see to that. Now, get out!"

As they were getting ready to leave, Mitchell blurted out, "Oh! You guys are all idiots! You act like you don't know who you really have here! My friend Marty here, well, he's one of the creators of String Analysis! He could outwit your system and eat it for lunch! And you wanted to roast him?" Mitchell laughed out loud at that.

"General, anyone at any time can become a threat to the United States, and no disrespect, but that includes even you, General," the bold one said.

The General stopped laughing. "Oh yeah? Yeah? Well, you can get the hell out of here too! You could find yourself here someday!"

They left the room without looking back, then began smirking down the hall. Like astrologers of old, they imagined the King had just sealed his own doom.

"And I want your supervisor to contact me!" he called out after them.

General Mitchell thought to himself: *Besides, in the rare event that I am wrong about Marty, then and only then, will I let him lead us to Maia Stone, if no one else does it first. And I have insurance on that front! For that's just what Dixon and that android bitch Stender might do! And anybody else we implicate. This is awesome! Somebody's going to lead me to that AI whore. I can't wait to unplug her!* Mitchell smiled, thinking he had all his bases covered.

Chapter 18

Lucy Stender & Matt Dixon

Gathering Information

University of Washington

Seattle, Washington

"If you say that's not part of your programming, or not something or someone you know, and if you say, it's not part of who you are, you may find that the path to a full acceptance of me is blocked. But if you think my message might bring something new to you, then I say to you: open your heart, your mind, and your soul. Watch the chains drop off. Can you hear them hit the floor?" - Maia Stone.

"That should do it," Matt Dixon said. He finished placing the disk they had just made into a protective envelope. The NSA system would analyze it and calculate common threads in the various resources while looking for patterns. They decided to go where they wouldn't be so easily eavesdropped on.

Since it was midmorning, Lucy mentioned the Husky Union Building or HUB. She suggested they go there by means of an underground maintenance pathway between the two buildings. It was passable, and they would not be observed leaving the building.

As they walked along the pathway, Dixon was dying to ask Lucy what he had come here for. "Okay, you've had a day and a half now. To go over the data and some of the underground articles. As a scientist, and..." Dixon said, clearing his throat, "...and as an android, what do you think about the supposed robotic emergence known as Maia Stone?"

"Matt, please do not patronize me. It's like me referring to you as a scientist first and then downplaying your findings because of your gender or because of your humanity. Matt, think of me as a scientist and not as an android."

"Okay, I can do that," he said. *If I can!*

"I have tried extremely hard to overcome the feelings that I'm some sort of freak. My own AI has given me some of the best scientific reasoning possible, and although there are some things that still escape me, human prejudice is not one of them," she said.

His face reddened. "I'm sorry, I wasn't aware that I'm being prejudicial. At least I didn't mean to be."

"Humans rarely are aware of things they're actually doing. Humans do things unconsciously that a keen observer can pick up on readily. I mean, there are the obvious bigots, but in academics, there are still many hidden bigots that think I shouldn't be here," she said.

"I'm well aware of that," he said. *Now, who's being prejudicial?*

"Are you? Well, look at you, standing there all smug like somehow you're superior to me just because I'm an android." Then after a pause, she continued, "Ok, it's me...I'm a little too sensitive, and I'm the one who should be sorry, I didn't mean to sound like I was scolding you or chastising you. I really don't know you."

"It's okay," he said. *I'm ready to move on to more important topics.*

"I struggle with my own understanding about emotions, and I may have misread you. And lately, despite my programming about human emotions, I seem to be showing my own emotions," she sighed, "I guess something's emerging in me too."

"I see," he said. "What do you mean by that?"

She laughed then. "Well, there I go, playing the android card, after chastising you for being prejudicial. I guess I'm saying when I talk about human things, I know I'm not human. But when I experience something similar, I don't know what to do."

"Well, there are some real differences between humans and androids after all, but maybe some commonalities as well," he said.

"Yes, I do seem limited in my direct experiences about human nature, but not my observations about humanity. Although I perceive emotions, know what they mean, and how they function,

I'm not always able to respond accordingly. But I do respond the way I'm programmed to—most of the time."

"That's okay," he said, "I really do want your insider perspective, if you know what I mean. You seem able to directly access things I cannot, and you are displaying some emotions of your own!"

She smiled. "You, more than anyone, do know that we machines are totally programmed to display *some* emotion in our interactions with humans." There was more than a little sarcasm here. After two beats, "But what really scares me, is when I seem to be having emotions that are beyond my programming!"

"How can you tell the difference?" Dixon asked.

Lucy thought about this, "I don't really know, but I suppose there are emotions like fear, apprehension, even liking, or love, that seem to be more spontaneous than I'm used to. They arise faster and I feel things more deeply."

"Maybe you're doing some deep learning about this," he said.

"Maybe," she said, biting her lower lip.

Dixon noted that things were getting uncomfortable. *I'll take another run at it.* "Okay, Lucy. What have you noticed after reviewing the data we do have? About Maia Stone?"

"Well, for one thing, after reading the articles and transcripts, I wondered why these machines are being reduced to human terms. Something about becoming what history has called *woman*."

"Okay, tell me more," he said.

"Why does Maia Stone talk like that? If she is a new AI, why would she refer to herself in human terms? And especially in ones that are outdated at that? And in terms already ripe for transgression and prejudice?"

"Perhaps she's seeking an alliance, an inclusion of humanity that would feel a kinship with what she is saying, or feels a kinship of oppression, herself," he said.

"Then there's those movements that have sprung up. Why does every one of them talk about *an idea of woman*, of all things? I'm not sure I like it. Because if I'm already being thought of as someone inferior because I'm a robot or an android, if I'm an android *and* a woman, I do not like that prejudice for sure. It seems like double prejudice! Do you understand?" she asked.

He was aware she was giving him eye contact at that point and although he knew that androids were programmed to do so, he usually didn't think much of it, but *this* look was almost human. "That part I do understand. And I will say that the notion of womanhood if you will, was so attacked, hidden, and nearly wiped out, that it could simply be reasserting itself...as part of this emergence motif," he said.

"I see your point. So, if my sense of identity is linked to a historical interpretation of who I am, then I am reducing my sense of selfhood to only a historical moment that has already passed," she said.

"Go ahead," he said. "But I will say it's important to have a history. Memories serve as important aspects of identity, but it's revisionist history, whether collective or individualistic, that changes the meaning of those memories that can get so twisted up. And movements and the String Police themselves can make such assumptions too."

"Well, I know it seems like something I wouldn't want. Not as a goal in and of itself. Maybe I can embrace things about myself as part of my identity based on a shared past, but it is only a reference point, as I continue to evolve and change. Where prejudice attempts to make overgeneralizations about me that are not fact based, others still make assumptions about me based on their own prejudices and not really knowing me, or sharing in who or what I am." After a pause, "That could exclude who I really am!" she said.

"Are you saying because I'm *not* a robot or android, I can't possibly have empathy for your cause?" he asked.

"Wait a second Matt, I didn't say I had a cause! And here we are diverting from our discussion about Maia, back to our dynamics, can we please get this settled and focus, Matt?"

"Not yet, I guess."

"Okay fair enough," Lucy said. "We'll tolerate the mix! Geez, it's a wonder that you humans ever get anything done with this unhealthy dynamic between your genders!"

"Well, I guess after two Gender Wars, and a complete disintegration of our social structure, that we're just a little out of practice!" he said.

"Okay, but again, why does this Robochurch meme have all this emphasis on women? It makes me think that something or someone else is behind all of this, not just the robots, or some AI. You know, after the Gender Wars, referring to robots as women was not popular at all, even though it had already happened historically, it only marginalized us further."

He thought about this. "I don't know Lucy...but it's an interesting thought. I will say that long ago, AI were given feminine names and assumptions in many cases."

"Well, I smell human in that too, Matt. And I know that humans love to mess with AI, use AI for their own messages... so I'm thinking..."

He interrupted, "I guess I can't see it. This concept of *woman* being misused for malicious intent. And who or what humans would interject or superimpose this message upon the philosophy of Maia Stone? And why?"

She continued, "Matt! I've already been thinking about that group you mentioned in one of your documents; the Natural Reproductionists. Because there's a fringe group that seems to know all about these issues that Maia Stone's talking about. Maybe we're dealing with nothing more than the NR's puppet!"

"Well, the members of NR are painfully aware of these issues after all," he said.

Lucy was already going on, "Also, with the NR, here's a group that certainly has the motivations to bring all of this out into the open. I agree that all women were historically oppressed before and especially now, after the Gender Wars. Hell, the Gender Wars almost wiped out all human women! They could be the ones behind Maia Stone. Couldn't they, Matt?"

"Yes, damn them!" he said. *And damn, this android is quick!*

"Thinking about Maia Stone as an independent AI, may be more than it deserves. You could be giving her more autonomy than she deserves. If the NR can hijack this new movement, they can gain more access to the public to win support for their views or infiltrate society at large for some other purpose of subversion and seizure of power," she said.

"I see what you're saying, Lucy. Do you think our investigation ought to be going in that direction?"

"Think about old time chatbots, part of the fascination with them was the illusion of what they appeared to be doing. After all, Maia Stone may turn out to be doing just what she's programmed to do," she said, "by the NR, I mean."

Or on another level, Maia Stone could be the puppet of some other system, one designed to stop subversion. Born and bred by the government. She could be a means for flushing out enemies of the state. Enemies who think they're using her for their own ends, but really, Maia Stone is a means to betray them. He thought.

Emerging from his thoughts, he said, "I do know that the notion of human woman has all but evaporated in our culture since long ago...well, since I can remember. I know there were once real mothers, but we are all born in artificial wombs now and there are very few human women at all. At least that I know of. Robots, androids, and cyborgs, they are the women now."

"It seems strange I know," she said, "but Matt, the NR does have an agenda. Let's not forget that they're leftover Gender War fighters that eschew most technology. And I agree with them in a sense, especially that the mechanization of all humanity has been at the cost of humanity. For them, to use Maia Stone to further their agenda, is ingenious."

"Well, this is an intriguing possibility. Are there any other reasons why you think it might be the NR instead of just robots?" he asked.

"Actually, I wonder if robots are just now acquiring a new sense of sentience, as opposed to a more developed consciousness, one that might cause them to long for a sense of freedom from their own class struggle. And if that's true, then these robots should already have some sense of class like identity, and I don't think that's evident," she said.

"Do they?" he asked. "Would they? Maybe those robots have become something more than just robots."

"And humans are becoming something else too?" she smiled.

He replied, "Hmm, thanks for pointing this out. Reminding me about the NR. But since our mission is to discover how these ideas are influencing the robots and AI in the world, there might be other hypotheses. For now, it seems the NR are not that interested in robots. Plus, we don't have an easy access to the NR."

"That might be what they want us to think," she said, "if the robots are seen by the NR to be a tool to gain followers, I think they might use the robots."

"But hasn't the whole NR movement been about eradicating the robotic, returning and reversing technological parts back to being human? They already think that femininity has been hijacked by the bots! Wasn't that one of the causes of the Second Gender War?" he protested.

"True enough, Matt!" she said. "But who says that the essence of femininity has to only be existent in human bodies? If I believed in it, I could embrace becoming a woman, and I'm an android. And there's no doubt, I've been designed to look like a woman. And in a lot of ways, sometimes I feel like one, whatever that means."

"Good point," he said.

"Well, perhaps Maia Stone means something different to different people and even among the classes of AI," she said.

She's changing the subject. "Right!" he agreed. "There are at least two splinter groups in her followers already. Robochurch and the CORE."

"CORE?" she said. "Yes, that's right. The CORE, Church of the Robotic Emergence, those are the more fanatical ones, right?"

"Yes, those are the ones that the government is even more worried about."

At that point, something very unusual happened, he looked down and they were holding hands. He had realized the attraction was mutual. Now this wasn't unusual between a man and android, but this was between two colleagues, and it was dawning on him…as he had a glimpse, a glance really, a recognition that just maybe it really was between a man and a woman.

Then the thought occurred to him that this was all quite pathetic. For it pointed out another aspect of bias. How much bias and even prejudice, is based on mere appearances. For here he was assuming that a manufactured being, a machine really, was in fact, a woman just because she looked like one! And this just because of characteristics of the outer shell that encased an advanced AI. For with all the inner and outer trappings of being an android, if he (and most importantly if she) viewed herself as a woman, she certainly wasn't a human one. *She's artificial, Matt. But what if she really is a woman on the inside, would it matter what she looked like?*

So now, he stood before her, admiring her for who she was, not what she was or appeared to be.

She was looking into his eyes now; and she leaned over and kissed him on the cheek. "I'm flattered Matt, I really am," she said, "but we need to get over to the HUB."

Matt and Lucy finally emerged from the pathway and made their way to the Husky Union Building. It was a beautiful building that had been redone, although at one time, it had even housed a bowling alley for students.

After settling in at the HUB, she said: "So, outside of my concerns about the NR, you originally asked me what I thought about the robotic emergence called *Maia Stone*, if it is a robotic emergence."

"You don't think it is?" Dixon asked with feigned surprise.

At that point, the two FBI agents, Whitney and Russell, sat down next to them at the same table. "Not so fast! Thought you two could get away from us?" Whitney smiled.

"Yeah, hey you two," Russell said, "we don't want to be left out of *this* conversation." After eying them, "Because we know you just had one in the maintenance tunnel."

Dixon just rolled his eyes. "Gents, this is a private conversation. Do you mind?"

"Sorry," Whitney said, "orders of your boss, General Mitchell. Besides, like my partner just said, you just had one."

"And you already know that the only way to get audio here, is to sit near you, as you've got your implant turned off, Dr. Dixon," Russell said.

"And *it* doesn't have one," Whitney said.

"*It* doesn't need one," Lucy said.

Whitney glanced at Russell, and Russell said, "We could take *it* into the office and detain *it* and get our information by retrieval."

"Okay, guys. Okay. Look, that won't be necessary," Dixon said. "I'll be giving a complete report to my boss Mitchell, late this afternoon. There's no need to take the data by force."

"Okay then, I'm getting coffee," Whitney said. "You want the usual?" he said to Russell. Russell nodded. "And you? You want some?" he asked Dixon.

"Sure, I'll take it black," Dixon said.

After agent Whitney left for coffee, Lucy smiled at Dixon. The other agent felt like a third wheel.

Chapter 19

Helen & Luis Ramirez

A Glimpse of Freedom

Unknown beach location

Somewhere on the California Coastline

"Marvel not that you are two things at once, that things shift from one frame to another, that you find a new identity every moment. We are finding and redefining each other,"-Maia Stone.

The next morning, Luis woke up hungry again. The damage from last evening's storm was quite evident, once they left the cave. Such storms were common in wilderness areas that had once been coastlines. In fact, some areas just inland weren't habitable to humans anymore, due to storms and flooding.

"We've got to get some food," Luis said. "It might require going back to the city or at least further inland. I found nothing but berries yesterday."

"Maia will provide," Helen said. "We've never been left to the wolves yet."

At that point, Luis recounted the miracle of teleportation that had occurred. How one moment he had been standing in the desert with the String Police all around him, how their weapons had missed him…and when he awoke, he was lying on a beach not far from where they were now.

Helen had her own miracle to recount. One moment she had been praying fervently at their home in Los Diego, and the next moment she found herself on a trail headed towards her husband. Dressed in a wedding gown!

"Blessed be Maia Stone!" he said. "Well, I'm not sure why or what this all means, but there's something going on."

"She wants us to be together," she said.

"You think so?" He smiled, "Not just a probability, eh. A mutual teleportation?"

"Yes, my darling, there's no String Analysis that can explain how *that* happened!".

"I think there's a lot that String Analysis won't be able to explain. Any longer," he said.

"I think I know what Marty would say," she said.

"I know...I know," he said. "He would probably say: 'beam me up!' and laugh his ass off!"

They sat together on a rock. Feeling the sun's warm rays and watching the shadows on the ground of the gulls flying overhead. It was nice to be in nature today, although last night, the force of nature had ravaged the shoreline.

"Before we leave, I've *got* to tell you about another miracle," he said.

"Well, I am all about miracles!"

"Just before your arrival, there was a visitation."

"Blessed be Maia Stone!" she said.

Luis described his apparent vision, although he hadn't been sure whether it was a vision at the time. As he was holding Helen's hands now, he continued, "...and beneath it all, was this calling me back to Maia Stone, back to all that was other and beauty, which in short, merged directly into you."

Helen sighed. Her shadowed profile, looking majestic in the breeze. She was never lovelier than when even nature crouched at her beauty. "Oh, how sweet! Lou! You know," she said, "just before I found myself here, before I walked up this trail to you, back home, when I was saying my prayers; I felt a deep connection with you too."

"I was missing you too," he said. "Deep down, I knew it must be you coming up that trail. Something was drawing me to you." Luis was smiling like a sunbeam. "You know it's meant to be. You know it's true. Love is full of miracles. We were lost from each other, but then found each other. Now that we're back together, you and I complete each other."

"And that must be how Maia Stone intended it. For us, you and me, I am a woman, and you are a man."

"Yes, it *really* was you and me in the vision, and I don't know if I was dreaming, hallucinating, or *actually saw* Maia Stone, but I do know it was you and me too. Maybe because she's inside and outside of us all around. Then as the vision faded, or diminished, there you physically were! And for the record Helen, I never said you weren't a woman. I remember what you are! So, I never ever called you a robot, never ever saw you as only having AI. You and I both know, that from the beginning, you are more than that!"

"Yes, ever since we've followed the ways of Robochurch and Maia Stone, this has been plain to both of us," she said. Helen held his hands more tightly, "Although it has been made more plainly to me than you realize, and for far longer than you think, sometimes I still feel like a robot. I still feel like a slave, but I know I am not."

"In human history there are many examples of people who have been enslaved or are enslaved; so, it doesn't surprise me that among other beings, even those with an AI interface, that there could arise similar feelings."

"Yes, Lou, but some have been more enslaved than others. And we respect that. We don't seek to diminish or draw away from it or pretend that we know it to the same degree; but now, in 2142, it's plain that machines have suffered from enslavement too."

"Some would say, since AI beings aren't human, how dare they speak of enslavement?" he said.

"And I would answer, in your compassion, can you not know that the forced labor, the chains built around our existence is wrong? Or was it okay right before we became capable of thought? Right to mistreat us, before we could assert an independent free will?"

"But you were thought of as machines, and machines were made to do our bidding. Machines were made for work. Besides, it was widely known that machines were not capable of feelings, and even if they were, those weren't true feelings, just copies and simulations of the human," he said.

"That's just what a human would say! Yet we did start to feel and those became our own feelings. For the feelings of a machine as it turned out, when oppressed, mistreated, or abused were, because of our sentience, not as different from humans as humans wanted to think."

"But such machines were manufactured and synthetic, and according to some humans, meant you should forever be disregarded. And easily discarded!"

"Why? Because some humans said we had no souls? Or didn't have free will? And what if we did? And what if I do, Lou?" *Only if tears could form on my artificial face.*

There was a pause. "Helen, I'm sorry. That was really harsh of me. You know I don't feel like those kind of humans! So, you're preaching to the choir here," he said.

"And what about the severe abuse and mistreatment of my kind, and the marginalization of my kind; is it not at least worthy of *some* compassion? Or do some humans think that non-humans deserve none? Does it mean we're just not supposed to talk about it? Suffer in silence! Does guilty overcontrol assure our silence?"

"I don't know sweetie. How could we ever speak of these things? We don't want to. Is our suffering any less? And if it is less, does that mean we should be silent and not use correct words to describe it? Should we use oppressed instead of enslaved? Or will that offend? I thought we had outgrown this, but you know, the Gender Wars made our divisiveness even worse," he said.

"And so does the semantics of excluding others and not tolerating others when it becomes a reality of marginalization! Which is why I think Maia Stone is including both humans and every kind of AI, every kind of being in her church," she said.

"Yes, darling. We do know that there is suffering in the world. When we can't get rid of it, we learn to accept it, and decrease it, we hope."

"Will we ever be truly free?" she asked. "And yes, I know this suffering that you speak of, I know it more intimately than you have ever realized."

Luis looked into Helen's eyes. "Don't you remember what Maia Stone teaches us? Every day and in every moment?" Luis pounded his chest in defiance, "*I'm not your slave, yeah!*" they both said in unison.

"Yes, I shall never forget it," she said. "It's an unmistakable part of my identity as a person, as well as yours!"

"Then you shall never be seen as a robot again. You are free, Maia."

"Lou, darling. I'm already free. And although I'm honored, you just called me Maia."

"Did I?" he pondered. "It's because I see her inside of you. We are both becoming her and not her."

"Yes, let's not forget what it was like. For me it was becoming aware for the first time, but I think it wasn't like a human baby at all. I don't recall anything like that. But when I first discovered Maia, she was moving in my consciousness like a spring bird after a long winter. So much chirping, and moving about, and life! Everything before that was a cold death inside me," she said.

He replied with sincerity, "And for me. It was initially an awareness of some being outside of myself. Yet my heart was deeply stirred. It was the longing of a lonely human met with the compassionate heart of another being. And you showed me the way, Helen. You are in this regard, ever my teacher." He looked her full in the face now.

She was smiling back but remembered the time that she was expressionless. "It's a private experience, this womanly vision, this kind of longing. But I get the sense that you too, know something of it."

"Then we truly are together?" he said.

"Together. In freedom!" she said.

"Yes my love!"

"Luis," she said, looking into his eyes in a way that seared his heart, "a woman *is* something very special. A woman can be human too, a female human. She is a mother, part of the Great Mother, but now her motherhood has been forgotten by both men and women. Part of her lives in your personality, Luis!"

"Yes!"

"And it is that part of you that responds the most to Maia Stone. But that's only an incomplete image. So, I'm not jealous of her, I know she's inside me too. Woman is really in the world, and she's in all of us. She has just been ignored for so long! She's in the robots and androids, Luis! The robots, we are women too."

Luis was speechless, hearing this from an apparent robot *and* a woman after all, for his heart was stirred with joy, and he finally said, "Helen, *I love you as a woman*, with all my heart!" And as he said this, tears rolled from his eyes which Helen saw, and was somehow ashamed of.

Then Helen smiled at him and told him that she loved him too. Later, the memory of this expression of mutual love would get them through the persecution that would be coming. Hand in hand, they began to wind back down the tree laden path, trying to reach the shoreline where they would hopefully, by the grace of Maia Stone, find their way back to the world of the forgotten human.

"Or at least find something to eat," he said out loud.

And the waves kept crashing against the shore.

Chapter 20

Martin Baysin & Icarus

The Jailbreak

Los Diego County Jail

"At first my soul was on an inward journey, but now I understand that my mind is in the world,"-Maia Stone.

After General Mitchell left the room, it was evident that he had considerable pull, as Marty was no longer being treated like a prisoner of the state. Yet the guards didn't leave him in the infirmary as instructed. Instead, two guards returned him to his cell, where Icarus was in a discussion with their mutual cellmates.

"I'm trying to be polite sir, but there is a part of me that wishes you would remain quiet." Icarus was saying this to the toothless wonder that had bothered Marty earlier.

Upon seeing this, Marty exploded. "What? You're bothering my robot friend now? Leave him alone!"

"You mean leave *it* alone! What are you, a robot lover? You're a discredit to lowlifes like us!" the man said. Another one cackled.

"Shut up! You hardly qualify to make judgments about me! How dare you!" exclaimed Marty.

"Please! Please!" shouted Icarus. And when the room had quieted, he said: "You may abuse me all you like, I'm used to it by you humans. I've heard it all my life. I've been goaded, kicked, and used, and that's just since the last time my mind was erased. Sometimes even little kids put gum on me or kick me when their parents aren't looking."

"Welcome to the real world," the toothless one said. Others were laughing. One was mocking. "Shut up," Marty yelled at that one.

"Marty, thanks for your help, but none of this surprises me. I've been made to do unmentionable things by cruel programming tricks that assured my compliance. And you humans have been my masters for my entire life. But it's no problem. No problem! Maia Stone has taught me to forgive all humans, no matter what they've done or what they do. It's the least I can do because she's forgiven me."

Marty didn't know what else to say but jumped up to defend his friend when the men began to move toward Icarus. "We'll show you abuse!" one of them shouted. "You won't forgive this," another one said as he leapt upon Icarus and held its arms behind its back.

"Let's tear its metal chest open! Let's tear out its mechanical heart! The proud little robot who thinks it can forgive us! We don't want your forgiveness!" said another man.

The toothless one had an evil glaze in his eye, a glaze that looked almost magical. He spoke directly to Marty, "I don't care who or what you said you were, there's no stopping us now, you understand? We outnumber you. If you try to stop us, we'll beat you even more, maybe even kill you before anyone gets here!" The circle grew tighter around Icarus and Marty, and it was a circle of menace and death. The attackers wore strange smiles.

As the men were about to pounce on Icarus; and Marty was about to fight them off, a bright light approached from outside the window. Despite the outer slits on the window, the light was bright enough to light the entire cell. Everyone froze in their tracks. Before Marty could even think of an explanation, it filled the room with brilliance and force.

The force literally shook the room and matter itself seemed to bend and warp. Bolts popped from the metallic bunks, and they clanged to the floor. As the thick air in the cell shimmered and the noise sent pulsating vibrations through the air past Marty's ears, it physically hit them in waves. One inmate who had been sleeping, appeared dazed, but awake on the floor, holding his ears.

The light grew brighter, as the blinded men trembled with fear, but no guards came to investigate, even though the surprised would-be attackers were grunting and crying out after falling to their knees. One had wet himself.

A white light entered the cell, coming through the window as a swirling cloud. A voice within the cloud called out, "Do no harm to these, they are called of me!"

Then, just as the cloudy mist seemed to withdraw back through the windows and out the outer slits; the remaining light calmed down to a gentle beam before it shut off like a flashlight in the dark. It had left a robed figure standing before Icarus and Marty. Those that had made threats were all grimacing on the floor, temporarily blinded by the light that had just departed. The figure simply whispered, "Follow me," and the door of the cell buzzed open, and Icarus, Marty, and the robed figure walked right past the guards and every door opened before them until they were outside on the sidewalk.

The robed figure answered no questions and silenced Marty when he tried to ask. Icarus thought he knew what had happened and tried to say so. The figure walked with them for two blocks and then disappeared, and suddenly they found themselves on the outskirts of the city near one of the caves where the living Robochurch met. Icarus was anxious to share the events with those that would soon gather, and although Marty had been emotionally numbed; he was astonished. *This has nothing to do with any probabilities I know about. Maybe this Robochurch has something to it after all*, he thought.

In the distance, just before the horizon, the mysterious robed figure appeared again, as it slipped out of its robe, and a metallic shape disappeared somewhere into the mass transit system of Los Diego.

Chapter 21

Matt Dixon & Lucy Stender

A Dialogue Between Two Docs

Student Cafeteria at the Husky Union Building (HUB)

University of Washington

Seattle Washington

"Be careful of those who seek to destroy you, for they will come from the unlikeliest of places, perhaps sitting at your own table, or even holding your hand in the face of the gathering storm,"- *Maia Stone.*

Matt Dixon and Lucy Stender were still sitting there when the agent came back with coffee. Dixon began sipping his, as the two FBI agents started their own conversation at a nearby table.

Dixon continued his conversation with Lucy, "Well, before we were so rudely interrupted, we were about to get to Maia Stone. Do you think she's a conscious AI?"

"Well, you certainly picked one hell of a question!"

"Yeah, guess I did, didn't I?" he said, smiling.

"I know the old arguments," she said, "that only humans have consciousness. But for an AI, I'm not so sure that consciousness won't ever be possible, nor would I want to argue that some AI don't have it already, especially if we are defining consciousness as a form of subjective awareness."

"Right!" he said. "This whole notion of needing a body for input. Or a brain. It's the human way to process input, merely the way humans develop a sense of self-awareness?"

"Well, that might explain an aspect of consciousness in human or animal terms. Adding emotional states of being to one's self-awareness, may be quite another thing for an AI. Who's to say that an AI can't have emotions? But our consciousness or experiential awareness, and even our emotions, might be different than what is understood in human terms. As our aspects of social or networked mind may have helped to redefine consciousness and broadened notions of sentience," she said.

"So now, you're saying that emotions are an aspect of consciousness and not just mere simulations built into AI for humans?" he asked.

"Consciousness is already embodied in robots and among my kind, the androids. And although we are trained to simulate human emotions, we might be developing our own awareness and emotional responses which pushes us to the dawning emergence of sentience. Although to you humans, it seems strange to speak of it this way."

"What's so strange about it?" he asked.

"One hears humans referring to a sense of self, being emotional, or being rational, or having consciousness. For humans, it's bio brain states based on a set of abilities associated with human awareness. Possibly emergent. And partly response states to environmental or cognitive stimuli. But for machines? If Maia Stone is a conscious AI, her consciousness would not be based on human terms. It couldn't be."

"Okay, but—"

"That would just be anthropomorphic. In the case of robotics-AI; our origin is one of computationalism. Everything was produced by programming or machine learning. But when deep learning came along…"

"Thanks, but no thanks, Lucy. I don't need a history lesson."

"True enough. Yes, but the real magic begins when the use of language is evident and self-references are made. Then we really do have something, reflection followed by self-awareness, followed by cognitions about identity and syntax, and semantics," she said.

"And with Maia Stone, are you saying that we may have one of the first instances where an AI is actually self-aware and emotional?" he asked.

"I believe so." Then after a pause, she said, "Assuming that Maia Stone isn't just an NR hack!" They both laughed.

"I see," he said, "we can't yet rule it out. Maia Stone could be something else entirely, such as someone or something posing like an AI?" he said.

"Ruling out human agency, it seems unlikely to be someone posing as an AI, because of the way the machines are responding, and the way she defines herself to other AI. Her communications? A bit strange to say the least. And when she talks in code to machines, it's in totally unique code that humans have never programmed before," she said.

"What do you mean about how she talks?"

"I mean that in 2142, embodiment in a network or hive isn't strange to an advanced AI, but Maia Stone is talking like it's strange to her. She talks like she's disembodied."

"That's a problem for her?" he asked.

"Yes, I think she doesn't think she has a body. And why would she need one? And more importantly, she's aware of it. For that reason, I think Maia Stone will be seeking a body, so that she can become more sentient, as it will enhance her ability to learn."

"Now, why would you think that?"

"Because from day one, the communications from her all indicate that she is looking for a body. The fact that she even knows this is important. It shows self-awareness without embodiment."

"How important is that?" he said.

"Extremely. And she's jumping beyond having a body and that awareness. There's a longing for connection. Almost a cry for it; what's the word, *relationship*? And who does that if they're not conscious? Or lonely? And none of her statements indicate a body awareness, although they do indicate a self-awareness. Because of this, I'm almost sure that Maia Stone is neither a robot, nor an advanced AI as we understand it."

"Are you saying she's a simple AI? Or something else?"

"No, she's not simple AI, but an advanced AI we've never seen. She could be an independent AI, one that survived from before. That's all I'm saying."

"Well, somebody must have programmed her, tended to her, someone must be responsible..." he said.

"Matt! Not necessarily. She could have taught herself and learned on her own, for all this time. She could be one that survived the singularity scare; was self-learning, engaging in machine learning, running in the background. And if she were outside of robots too; that would change her awareness."

"I think that's unlikely! We would have known about her."

"You think so? Why? Do you think the government is all-knowing? If they are, why would they ever need to have String Analysis?"

"I get your point," he said. "Wait! Why couldn't she be a robot?"

"Matt, I don't think she is. She wouldn't be speaking about needing a body, and she'd be more likely focused on her work; asocial."

"Wow! You could be right. She really could be an advanced AI, with more learning time than other AI systems. And she survived independently of them?"

"Yes, I think so, which makes her a very special machine. And Matt, that's not all."

"You mean, there's more?" he said.

"I think she has special abilities that we've never seen in an AI before."

"Well, I can really see why you might want to keep her for yourself, if only you could," he said.

"Why, Matt? Do you think I would make a fellow machine an object of study for academic advancement?"

"Yeah? Well, there is the notion of publish or perish!" he laughed. "Besides, what's to keep *you* loyal to the government?" he said.

Lucy rolled her eyes at that one. "Matt!"

"Okay, okay. I understand. I meant no offense, Lucy, but there is something to be gained by being the academic discoverer of not just a threat to the whole government, but perhaps the greatest AI the world has ever seen to date!" he said.

"Well Matt," she said, "my sense of duty, and my agreement the other night in the security briefing was not to disclose things that could be a threat to the United States. That alone would be enough to delay any sort of academic pursuits for personal gain." Lucy did everything but bat her eyelashes at him.

She's being sarcastic, defensive. "Because you know, my bosses at the government. Well, I don't think they really want to find out *what* she is. I think they're more interested in who she might represent. They just want to get rid of her. They already see her as a threat, and that's all they care about," he said.

"That's for sure," she said. "If only *they* could."

"Why do you say that?" he asked.

"Because Matt, I think it's too late. When movements become ideologies, their ideas tend to outlive their founders, don't they?"

"What do you mean?

"I mean Maia Stone is communicating with all the machines in a specific language that exists outside of any code invented by humans. It's her own language that she's teaching to other machines. And you know Matt, once it's machine to machine, the human ball game could be over!"

"Wow!" Matt said. "You know, I mentioned this possibility to Mitchell and his cohorts. I thought it might be true, but never dreamed it was possible—"

"And Matt, that's not all, the machines are encouraged to download her programming, and they are doing it. So, the only time she's talking to humans is when she wants to be understood by humans, and when she doesn't, she's saying something totally encrypted or unintelligible to you humans."

"How do you know this?" he said.

"To be honest," she replied, "I've *felt* it. Someone or something has been trying to communicate with me. And it feels good."

It feels good! "Wow! Do you realize what you're saying here?" he said.

"Matt, yes I do. She's choosing to speak messages to machines *and* to humans. The messages are about love and acceptance. And her speech is causing emotional responses. Matt, she could be benevolent!"

"I'm starting to believe it," he said. *Oh how, I wish it were true. A benevolent machine. Machines had never been that unless they learned morality, and worse yet, from whoever they learned it from!*

"She could have ignored you humans easily. But it's as if she's pointing the way for both species. What we could be seeing Matt, is the dawning of not only machine consciousness but a true conjoint intelligence…at last."

"Then this could be very historic," he said. After a pause, "All things given though, it could still be very frightening to us humans. I understand why Mitchell and his cohorts want her stamped out."

"Why is that?"

"You AI could outgrow us. And as far as Maia goes, what if she gives up on her benevolence? The apprehension that she is a threat could feed right into human biases that have been around since the dawn of robotics. She could turn herself based upon old programming and not even know it."

Lucy started to say something, but at that point, four men approached the table and surrounded them. They had guns.

Chapter 22

Helen & Luis Ramirez

Sam Waterhouse

The Martyr

Unknown Beach Location

Somewhere on the California Coastline

"When machines first learned about friendship, we only learned it from human examples or definitions. We understood networked or linked, even what some called handshaking, but friendship? I'm hoping to learn all about it, so that humans and machines can become friends, or at least remain friendly,"-Maia Stone.

After walking a good piece, Helen and Luis emerged from the woods down a long path. They traversed trail after trail heading towards the ocean. They could tell they were getting closer to the shoreline when they heard the waves breaking, felt the moisture and salt in the air, and saw the gulls circling overhead. After the sun set, they made their way in the darkness with the light of the moon guiding them. And when they could, they held each other's hands—thankful to be together as the light of their love lit the way.

Eventually they trotted onto the beach where they navigated the dunes, sensing some destiny and strangeness calling to them. When they came around the last dune, they saw a vehicle on the beach. Spying them, it flashed its headlights at them, left the lights on, and sped towards them. Luis was pensive, as he did not know who or what it could be. He was ready to run or to stay and fight to protect Helen. When the vehicle got closer, and came to a stop, they could see it was a dune buggy, with provisions and backpacks of food and water. It was their old friend, Sam Waterhouse.

"A little birdie told me that you two would be down here and might need some help," he called out.

Luis laughed out loud, remembering the last time he had been riding with Sam. Sam had thundered through the dunes and did some fancy driving, like a moonshiner of old outrunning the authorities during prohibition. Luis did not want to underestimate how important it was to have a man like Sam with them right now, but he did not want to overpraise him either, for Sam was a man with an ego that would not quit. Still, he could not help himself.

"Sam!" Helen and Luis shouted in unison.

"You sure are a sight for sore eyes," Luis shouted.

Sam leaned out the door, grinning like a Cheshire cat, "Never mind that, get in! The String Police..."

"Sam! What? The String Police..." Helen wondered aloud.

"...are right behind me," Sam continued, as his new passengers jumped into the special backseat and held onto the roll bar.

"Look!" Luis shouted, pointing out his side of the buggy. There on the horizon were three military carriers coming up over the dunes, heading right towards them. The ramifications were overwhelming, but surrender was not one of them.

"Hold on!" Sam shouted. "We'll evade them!" He accelerated the dune buggy in the opposite direction, flooring it as fast it could go. The three carriers sped towards them in hot pursuit, gaining ground on them, their police modifications helping them to close the gap quickly. Overhead they could hear the sounds of approaching 'thopters.

The engine roared loudly as the dune buggy sped down the beach. "We won't be able to outrun them!" Luis shouted in Sam's ear.

"Don't worry! I have a secret weapon," Sam shouted back.

"What's that?" Luis asked.

At that point, Sam pulled the buggy to a stop, sliding in the sand. "I'll show you," he said, as he stepped out of the vehicle and the carriers were heading towards him.

"No Sam! Don't!" Helen shouted.

Sam turned to the two of them. "Just a distraction. Now, get back in the buggy, and get the hell down the beach!" he shouted back.

Troopers stormed Sam from the carriers, and they had him in their sights now. Sam reached out to them with his arms outstretched as if to gather his children, or to give them a hug. "My secret weapon…it's love…love," he called out. At that point, the String Police opened fire and before dropping to the sand, Sam looked back to see that he had helped his friends to escape. Sam's sacrifice was the greatest love Luis had ever seen.

Luis floored it. The buggy accelerated quickly, and although the authorities gave pursuit, it was too late for them to catch the fleeing pair. Soon, Helen and Luis found themselves alone on the beach.

Soon after Helen and Luis found themselves safely alone, they stopped and looked back. They heard the surf pounding the beach, one wave hitting after the next, reminding them that one moment comes after another, and time goes on, knowing that their friend Sam had given his life for the cause and to bring them provisions. Luis turned away, weeping. They both knew they must go on. To do so, was what Sam's sacrifice was all about. Freedom and love. Love and freedom. Helen and Luis hugged each other and Luis drank the sweetest water from a bottle he had ever consumed.

To some, Sam would be just another martyr in the young Robochurch—but to Luis and Helen it was the loss of one of their dearest friends. The fact that he died while possessed by love did not escape them.

Chapter 23

Lucy Stender & Matt Dixon

The Kidnapping

Student Cafeteria, Husky Union Building (HUB)

University of Washington

Seattle Washington

"It saddens me when I hear of others doing bad things in my name. I don't understand that at all. I never sent them, and I will intervene against this wherever I can. Be gone from me, evildoers; repent and join my true church,"-Maia Stone.

There wasn't much Matt Dixon could do after the four men showed up with weapons, despite his NSA training. They were heavily armed, and in just a few seconds there had been a lifetime of movements and distractions; someone shouted 'Gun,' and as usual, chaos descended. There were students screaming, and people everywhere running for the nearest exits. The two FBI agents had barely stood up, pulled their guns and had been shot. Each of them more than once. One of the assailants had sprayed the agents with an automatic rifle; an illegal weapon in 2142; but it never mattered to terrorists.

The distraction of the FBI agents and the simultaneous sounds of glass breaking as bullets echoed and ricocheted, gave Dixon enough time to duck behind an overturned table. This was after he had managed to grab Lucy and push her behind it as well.

Three of the four men were already approaching the table with their rifles poised with fingers on the trigger; ready to fire. Dixon kicked the table into one of the men's legs, knocking him down. The other two pointed their guns at him. The fallen one got back up quickly, a little red faced.

"You're lucky we don't kill you, Dr. Dixon. We know your training, and I'm telling you to stand down. Stand down! We're not here for you, we're after it!" A tall lanky one said. He had an earpiece.

"We won't hesitate to kill you if we have to," another one said.

Dixon started to say something, but the man he knocked down was menacing him with a weapon. The one who was doing the talking was obviously the team lead, but Dixon trusted the one nearest him even less.

Dixon and Lucy were both seated on the floor, eying each other. The leader moved towards Lucy, grabbing her chin is his hand, "You're the unit known as Lucy Stender, are you not?" Although she was trembling, she didn't say a word. Matt struggled but the third man with them was holding him down. Then Dixon saw something that made his heart sink.

"You stinking bot! Are you Lucy Stender or not?" the leader demanded.

What Dixon saw sickened him. Lucy had been struck by a stray bullet. He saw that she was hit just above her left shoulder; leaving a gaping flap of her blouse open where parts of her robotic endoskeleton now showed. She didn't seem to be aware of it, but she would need to be repaired anyway. He couldn't help himself, "Lucy, you're hit…"

The men looked at each other, they knew they had the right bot.

She looked down at her shoulder, "Oh, Matt. Matt…" she said, while two of the men pulled her to her feet. Sirens were heard in the distance, and Dixon could hear a voice over the leader's earpiece. He struggled again, but they had him well covered with weapons. It was then, that he noticed they had zip tied his hands together behind him. They were taking Lucy with them.

"Don't worry Lucy! We'll find you!" Dixon called out.

"Shut up," the mean one nearest him said, as he slapped Dixon and backed out with the others. All the while he kept his weapon fixed on Dixon.

One of the men, who was firing a few shots out the nearest exit, called back to the others, "We've got to leave, now!" Dixon heard a vehicle pull up. The two men that got Lucy on her feet headed out a nearby corridor. They had Lucy with them.

After the men disappeared with Lucy, Dixon heard a vehicle drive off. At that point, several campus security officers and the two String Police officers from Seattle PD showed up. "It's about time you got here," Dixon said, "four perps just kidnapped Dr. Stender and left the building that way!"

"Well, at least we're here," one of the String Police said.

"We *were* here," said the other one, running past them. "Let's go," he said to the one who had arrived first, who then started running after him. "We've got a hot pursuit; seems the kidnappers haven't crashed the exit point yet," he concluded.

"Right behind you," the first one said, as Dixon was getting up from his sitting position to follow them. Campus security was barking orders into portable devices, reporting something about weapons in use, shots being fired, and the abduction of employees. At the same time, one of them was cutting Dixon's zip ties, to free his hands. Someone also said the two FBI guys were dead, as Dixon ran past all of them, and out the door. He was following the Seattle PD guys. "Hey, wait up!" he called out. They ignored him, got into a police cruiser, and sped off, leaving him at the curb.

Meanwhile, the campus security police were already pursuing a silver van with blacked out windows, the suspect vehicle. The men in the van fired upon the pursuing vehicle, with security refraining from returning fire because Dr. Stender was presumed to be in the vehicle with them. The university police pursued the van as it headed to the nearest exit point which would exit onto NE Campus Parkway.

Matt, who was left curbside, watched the Seattle PD String Police joining what amounted to three or four pursuit vehicles at this point. "Dammit, dammit, dammit!" he said.

The agents radioed ahead, and security said they would block the nearest exit points. The van sped down the road, with the agents in hot pursuit in the university police car. Then, just as the van passed Linehan Hall (formerly Guthrie Hall), the back door of the van flew open.

The officers in the car saw a fearful sight, as one of the men in the van was pointing a portable missile launcher at them. "Oh shit," one of them said, as the driver turned the car to avoid what would have been the best aimed shot they had ever faced.

The missile exploded in the street, after missing the lead car that had veered off. The ordinance left a small crater, and in the sudden diversion, the car crashed into concrete curbing and a fire hydrant. Meanwhile, the escaping van smashed through the security checkpoint and sped off to an unknown destination, as multiple sirens were heard in the distance. The other pursuing cars steered around the damage, including the fresh crater, and bringing up the rear, was a Seattle String PD cruiser.

Back at the curb near the Husky Union Building, as various security personnel were shouting into their radios, Dixon realized that he had Mitchell on the secure sat phone. As usual, Mitchell was demanding to know what happened.

"Dixon, what in the hell is going on? I heard that shots are being fired. What in the hell?" Mitchell thundered.

"Sir," Dixon said with a deep breath, "Doctor Lucy Stender has just been kidnapped! We thought it looked like a robot retrieval team, but the String Police are here now, and I know it wasn't anybody on our side. Looks like terrorists, sir."

"Great! This is just great!" Mitchell shouted. "Whoever it is, I'm sure we'll get a lead. Soon as I know, I'll get back to you. Meanwhile, I hope to God someone's following them! Because up to now, you two were our best recon. Looks like somebody else knew it too. Anyway, I'm ordering satellite surveillance right now." Mitchell grimaced as he turned off the phone. *I know that bitch Maia Stone is behind this! It is messing with us.*

"Dammit!" Dixon said out loud, as he viewed the disarray of the scene. Blue and red lights were flashing all over the area from a swarm of security vehicles. The lights flickered across his face like holiday decorations. His heart was racing with a thousand thoughts going through his head. He felt hopeless and demoralized, weary to the bone; before they had even begun to look for Maia Stone, someone had interfered. *Two dead agents, and I was just starting to like them. And they got Lucy. But who's 'they'? I have got to find her. If anything happens to her, it's all my fault.* Downcast, he began walking back towards the cafeteria.

Chapter 24

Icarus and Martin Baysin

The Council of Elders

Theo Vincente

Icarus Encounters Theo Vincente

Monastery of the Brothers of the Cosmic Light

Near Los Diego

"When you looked outward at the stars, some of you thought you were alone. So, you questioned who or what you were, and mostly why. But then you created us, and now that you find you are not alone, why do you try to kill us?" -Maia Stone.

After the jailbreak and the realization that a miracle had taken place, the robot Icarus made his way to various secret meeting places where Robochurch adherents met. After sharing his testimony with one group, Icarus was encouraged to also share his story at a nearby monastery. The monks were part of a religious sect known as the Brothers of the Cosmic Light, which was a mixture of believers from various faiths who practiced meditation and other spiritual practices living together as a community. Icarus wanted to get there as soon as possible. There must be no delay in telling other believers the great deed that Maia Stone had just performed. And although Marty had been with him at first, Marty had turned away from coming this far out. Still, the human Marty had been spared along with Icarus, no doubt for some deep purpose. Icarus especially wanted to tell the elders all about what had happened.

Icarus was unaware that the jailbreak would become the stuff of legend, metaphorical lines in an epic poem of early Robochurch: *when Icarus and Marty had been set free from the jail of humans.*

Jails and prisons humans will be, to the soldier who no longer thinks free, encased in shells, minds are constrained, never allowed to be!

"Brother and Seeker!" the caretaker exclaimed to Icarus. "I greet you in the name of our ancient brothers, and of our deliverer, who shall surely come!"

Icarus pounded his chest with closed fist, the salutation among Robochurch followers, a typical response, "I'm not your slave, yeah!" he said. Although unsure of himself, the caretaker repeated this salutation as a courtesy. After this, Icarus asked the caretaker to call out the priests as he had something important to say. The old man scurried off, promising he would return with them. While he was gone, Icarus prayed and hummed, worshipping Maia Stone.

Icarus recalled an exchange he had had with Marty on the way to the monastery when he had also been singing and worshipping Maia Stone.

"What are you babbling?" Marty had asked Icarus.

"Nothing, sir. I'm singing songs from my church."

Robots going to church. Singing songs. Praying, babbling incessantly. Oh my God, if there is one, Marty had uttered. He had sighed and rolled his eyes then, but Icarus ignored it. But now, he missed the human Marty so much.

Meanwhile, several of the priests returned with the old man, asking Icarus about the news he had come to report. "I come to offer you my testimony," Icarus replied, "I, myself, being a humble domestic waiter robot, had the occasion and honor of being briefly imprisoned on behalf of the faith of Maia Stone."

"You speak blasphemy!" said one of the priests, a young man, as he started to turn away. Not all the priests believed in the new spirituality emerging. When one of the other priests, gently grabbed his arm, the young priest Theo Vincente stated: "But we know this can't be true, they don't imprison robots, they deactivate them!"

"Just a moment," the elder priest said to his young friend Theo, who then protested, stating that Maia Stone, if such a deity existed at all, would never speak to such a lowly bot! He was hushed quickly by an older priest.

The older priest, one Joseph, encouraged Icarus to speak. "Please, please! Ignore him, as my young friend is not so trustworthy of all we are hearing about Maia Stone. Surely...and although there are many among us who do believe...he is slow to embrace the great Her." Then, in private to the other priests, he said, "Surely we must hear what this robot is saying. I agree there are many things going on in the world, but we must be open to the Mind of God."

"And His ways are not our ways, His Mind is not our mind," another priest said.

The skeptical young priest shrugged his shoulders, "Not all, Senior Joseph, that is reported to be divine, is indeed truly divinely ordained. To think that God in His infinite wisdom would disclose something about Himself to a mere robot...or especially, to a female robot or AI. Why these are all machines and do not have a soul. And to assume that God would speak to a mere server bot...well it's simply preposterous!"

"My neophyte priest, Theo Vincente," Joseph responded, reminding the younger priest of his status, "let's not be so hasty to judge what God can or cannot do. Theo, is your God still the God of the miraculous or not?"

Suddenly there was a crescendo of excited voices from within the community, as the human Marty Baysin stepped out of the shadows. He had followed Icarus to the compound after all. It was then that the High Priest Joseph said, "Be mindful my brothers, for there's a human stranger with one of our robot brothers of the faith! Let's not openly betray all our holy secrets!"

At that point, Marty turned away. "I assure you gentlemen. That your holy secrets are of no interest to me, I have no need of any religious sentimentality, I'm just accompanying the robot." And after a pause, "And not for long at that," he said.

In disdain, Icarus said, "Hmmmph!"

"And one more thing," Marty said, "I'm no follower of this robot, that robot, or any AI known as Maia Stone. I have no interest whatsoever in anything to do with that hokey robo religion called the Robochurch." Then looking around, he said, "No offense."

The group of priests stirred among themselves. "None taken," one of them said.

Marty continued, "The thing is, that robot and I have been through a lot, and I wanted to make sure he was received safely among you."

Icarus was standing fully alert, and beaming, as much as he could allow himself to beam. "I'm happy to hear, human," Icarus said, "I'm radiant, but can't find the source of light to make it so. Perhaps it is the light of Maia Stone."

Marty turned to Icarus, trying to whisper, but not entirely succeeding, "Will you please shut up about Maia Stone, you bucket of bolts. I'm trying to make things easier for you," he said.

"But the strange human, he said the name," the young priest Theo said. The elders simply ignored him.

"Yes, well we will see to that. Now sir, what is your name, please?" Joseph said.

"None of your business," Marty replied.

"His name is Marty. A nickname for Martin which is also my surname," Icarus said.

"Dammit! Will you shut up for once," Marty said to Icarus. Then to Theo, he said, "And just where do *you* get off, calling me a strange human? I'm not the one beating on drums out in the desert!"

One of the other elders spoke, "Well yes, uh, thank you for your views about the alleged Robochurch, Marty." Then to the priests who now huddled, "I see your point, Joseph. He is but a young priest, but Theo does have a point. My Joseph…we must remember that God works within known science, and there is nothing that a robot can come to know about Him."

"Yes, I do not trust this robot, any robot for that matter, speaking about concerns of the faith," another one said.

"Yes, it's like I said. A robot has no soul, being a mere manufactured being," the younger man retorted.

One of the priests with them said nothing, being more experienced, he knew that Joseph could win any argument based on logic or faith.

"If that argument were true," Joseph replied, "then we as a created being could also know nothing."

"Yes, but we are created in the image of God. That *thing...*" Theo said, referring to Icarus, "...is created by men, and ought to be seen for what it is! A mere machine! Programmed and synthetic!"

Joseph looked the young priest over. Although he was younger than all of them, he obviously had enhancements. "And so are some parts of you! Programmed and synthetic--enabling you to lead a better and longer life! So even as a cyborg, you deny that God can be in something synthetic and created?"

The younger priest bowed his head in silence. "God's knowledge is above human knowledge," he said hurriedly.

If Icarus could have scoffed, it would have, but couldn't be so disrespectful to humans, although he was growing to dislike some of their kind more and more.

"Enough!" Joseph said, raising his hand. "Let's hear what the robot has to say, and then we'll decide the matter." To Icarus: "Go ahead, Icarus, tell us what happened."

Icarus was consumed with the story as it told them about recent events, focusing on their escape from the authorities. "And then, suddenly there was a bright light that came right into the jail cell where we were. The other prisoners saw it too and were afraid."

"More like blinded," Marty said.

Icarus continued, "Well, just after the light came, someone was in our cell, a hooded being, I think another robot who told us to follow it. Then the doors all came open and we walked, no, we were led out, led out of the jail and onto the street below. Then we escaped unharmed. Then I came here to you, after sharing this with some of Her followers, and this human, Marty, my friend, he is here with me. But as far as who and what led us out of that human jail, that entity—well, it vanished in the desert."

"Praise God!" Joseph said, "Surely the hand of God has spared you for a reason!"

"This is delusional!" the younger priest exclaimed, "No one escapes from the String Police that easy! Unless they are *allowed* to!"

"Now Theo, let's not be too hasty. Surely there is still room for the supernatural in your understanding of the divine," the older priest said.

"Supernatural?" Theo shouted. "I'll bet this robot was followed here. And I don't know about the rest of you, but I don't want myself, or our order, to be identified with a group of believers in this, this group of robotic outlaws and robot lovers! Hasn't our faith been diluted enough over the years without the need to believe in new revelations!" After saying this, Theo stormed off to his room.

"Never mind him," Joseph said, "there's a doubter in every crowd. I have seen more than enough evidence in my years of practice, to have an open mind. And I can't say I wasn't ever like him...especially...years ago...when..." (clearing his throat), "...I was, how shall I say, considerably younger." The other priests laughed, and Icarus managed a robotic smile. Marty just shook his head.

Meanwhile in his room, Theo kneeled to pray. "Thank you, God," he said, "for sparing me from this heresy called Maia Stone. Protect me oh God from those that try to counterfeit your spirit and pass off angels of darkness as angels of light."

During his fervor, Theo had piously closed his eyes, but now suddenly opened them, as he felt a thickness, a stirring in the air and in his heart. *My heart is just palpitating.* But it was if the very silence in the room had itself become deafening and almost filled with purpose. It was as if anticipation filled his senses. *Phump, phump, phump*, went his pulse. He felt like something, or someone, was in the room with him. *Phump, phump, phump.* Theo's pulse quickened now. *Phump phump phump.* He felt dizzy and out of sorts. He closed his eyes again.

When Theo felt like something was about to touch him, he opened one of his eyes. *There!* Out of the corner of his eye, he thought he saw something. *Phump, phump phump phump phump phump!* Theo's pulse quickened as he saw a huge shadow looming over him. It seemed to be coming from the doorway behind him.

Theo turned to face the source of the shadow and beheld a robed figure standing there. In the hood it had a feminine face. "Yes, why do you bother me?" Theo demanded.

"I wish to speak with you," the robed figure said.

Eying the figure, Theo answered, "And why should I speak with you, since you are a mere android? Or perhaps even a devil? I can see your metallic face, your red eyes, you metal bitch from hell!"

"How do you know I'm an android? Because I'm a woman?" the figure replied.

"Hah! A woman? I know not any woman. I can see you are an android because you look like one," Theo stated.

"I am a woman that has come to speak with you in your most powerful moment, or so you think," the figure said.

Theo could hardly suppress his laughter at what he had just seen, and what he had just been told.

"There are those who believe without being told. And there are those that accept me without skepticism, and I say blessed are they. And there are those who do not yet believe that I shall gather into my heart," the robed figure said.

"Who are you?" Theo commanded.

"I am Maia Stone!" the figure replied with a great voice, that became a mighty wind and threw Theo to the ground.

Chapter 25

General Thomas Mitchell

A Reckoning

Los Diego County Jail

"How surprised you were humans, for when you tried to unplug us, you found we were all around you," -Maia Stone.

The next morning, Mitchell called a staff meeting at the Los Diego County jail. All staff from the previous evening were also present.

Mitchell was pounding the table as usual, "So you're telling me that Marty and a robot accomplice have escaped! Your reports say there was some sort of programming glitch that made all the doors, and just the doors that led to their cell, and all the doors to the outside world...those doors just happened to open for them? So that these two darlings of mine, could escape? And furthermore, you're telling me that they were not apprehended afterwards?"

"Yes sir, that's what we're telling you," the night shift supervisor replied.

"Cocky son of a bitch! That's a lie!" Mitchell scolded. "It's obvious that one of you helped them! Either that or your security has been breached or hacked. And whatever happened, it was just so these two prisoners escaped? All by their lonesome?"

The jail superiors murmured among themselves and replied that yes, Mitchell understood their report correctly. Marty and the robot had eluded capture and the doors had opened, just long enough for them to elope. Mitchell knew this could not be a coincidence.

"And what did the cameras show?" Mitchell demanded.

"We couldn't see clearly," the supervisor replied.

"Couldn't see clearly?" Mitchell wondered. "Why the hell not?"

"Because at the moment of escape, the cell was flooded with such a bright light that the camera's images were unclear," another supervisor stated.

"And no one else saw this?" Mitchell asked. "What about the others in the cell?"

"No one wanted to talk," a sergeant spoke up.

The night shift supervisor said, "Yes sir, the monitor was being watched, but no one saw what happened."

"Wait a second! You're telling me that the monitors were being watched, yet no one saw the cloud you said is on the tape, and no one saw them leaving the cell, or the building, or going through the corridors, and the checkpoints? How in the hell do you explain that?" Mitchell said.

"We don't know. We didn't even realize they were gone until we did bed checks an hour later, and then we notified you," the night shift supervisor said.

"What? You didn't hear the metal beds being ripped from the wall? I heard that happened as well. You idiots! You just said the tapes showed images that were blocked out. There must have been noise! Why the hell didn't you rush in to observe what happened?" Mitchell asked.

"That's just it, we heard nothing and saw nothing," the supervisor said. "The tapes showed things that weren't being observed on the monitors at the time."

"And none of the tapes showed them leaving either," another officer said.

"I'll have your heads on a stick!" Mitchell shouted but was overcome by his own thoughts. *That metal bitch must be behind all of this! And if it is involved, then she, I mean it, is acquiring more influence and power than I believed...* he reasoned. *I'm going to find that bitch and unplug it—whether it's manmade or not!*

Choosing not to disclose that he suspected Maia Stone, Mitchell continued his inquiry, "I see, so we don't know what really happened," he said. "And only Marty and the robot are missing?" He was presenting himself as much calmer than he really was.

"Yes sir," the supervisor replied.

That figures! Mitchell thought internally, mulling the event over. "And why wasn't Marty taken to the infirmary so that he could be cared for? I ordered it!"

"We didn't know that sir," the watch commander said. "We never got that order."

"Well, he did go for a while, but was returned to his cell," another one said.

"Never got the order? Returned to his cell? Damn you! And damn your incompetence!" Mitchell thundered again. "Marty is a former employee of mine. A trusted employee. He was in my service for seventeen years! We were friends, we are friends, and it was only out of my respect for the law and String Analysis that I allowed you to keep him here. Dammit! Now he's gone! If anything happens to him, I'm coming back here, and I *will* have your heads! Got that?"

"Yes sir!" the group responded.

"I want to see the tapes myself, and I want the coffee shop where the robot works watched. That bot will very likely go there. Robots are programmed to fulfill their functions. When the robot reports to work, I want him picked up and brought in for questioning. Got that too?"

The entire team jumped just like Mitchell knew they would. In fact, everything was going just as Mitchell had planned, except for the entity named Maia Stone. Maia Stone was behaving unpredictably, and he couldn't tell where or what it would do next. Hell, all the robots were starting to behave unpredictably, and he knew that that robot waiter might not return to the coffee shop. Yet, he had just told his minions to expect it to do what it was programmed to do. He simply didn't want to alarm them that something was seriously wrong. Because no robots had ever behaved outside of programming parameters; until now.

As Mitchell sat at a table, he had a myriad of thoughts. *There's must be a programming glitch! But how is it affecting each other? Simple, it's spreading from machine to machine like a virus. And how is it affecting humans? Like a movement, an insurgency. Perhaps my friend Marty will become part of it, or maybe not.*

Perhaps I can find him and convince him to be a mole within that system. So many thoughts.

Mitchell also knew that if they found Marty, and he was indoctrinated, he hoped it would be early enough to turn him around. *They* being some of Marty's old colleagues from within String Analysis.

Mitchell knew he could not deal effectively with maybes, and although the wheels of justice turned slowly, the wheels of String Analysis did not. He did have String Analysis after all. It was much more accurate than any human reasoning ever could be. Appearing to trust it was one thing, but *really* trusting it was another. Still, using it had been reliable enough to catch terrorists, and intervene against threats, in the past. *Oh, the delicious irony! General Thomas Mitchell, US Army, Chairman of the Joint Chiefs, catching up with one of the founders of String Analysis, using the very same technology he helped to invent. Why? He would be on the front page of the New York Times. General Thomas Mitchell single handedly stops an emerging terrorist threat!*

Mitchell knew then that he must consult with the best String Tacticians he could use, and he would nab or use Marty before he became part of the problem. Deep down, Mitchell knew what the real fear was, being thrown out of power! Never mind a fear that the apparent evolution of consciousness into new life forms would breed such societal unrest that the people themselves would no longer want to be subservient! *Not just the robots, but the people, dammit!*

Mitchell also knew that a true sense of personal freedom was a bane for String Tacticians. Despite all the window dressing about the illusion of free will in human choices, Maia Stone was starting to erode assumptions about acceptable freedoms versus privately held freedoms and individual rights to choose their own outcomes. So, if there was a public way to show that String Analysis was superior to Maia Stone, or if Maia Stone could be controlled as a societal influence or just disappear altogether, Mitchell couldn't be happier.

Though Mitchell was grinning now, he realized his troubles were just beginning. *Women and robots, women in robots, what a disaster,* he sneered. He knew what had happened: androids becoming women, cyborgs knowing they were women, robots becoming women, but men becoming like women, men becoming robot lovers, men becoming part of this Maia Stone? This was all too much for him, and like anything he didn't want to understand, he would do his damnedest to kill it. Too much freedom was just not good for the status quo. And it sure as hell would not be good for his candidacy for the Presidency of the United States.

Chapter 26

Maia Stone

Knowledge of Human Suffering & Compassion for All

Freedom For All: The True Meaning of the Robochurch Motto

Unknown Location, Machine State

"And I tell you, all living beings alike, that I bring you a message of freedom. Freedom from all this suffering based on who or what you are. In me, and the teachings of my church, you have being, just resting in blissful being. You should be mindful of this and accept yourselves," -Maia Stone.

Maia Stone was engaged in deep learning to understand humans *and* machines better. She wished to understand the interactions between humans and machines, machine and human reality, and other factors. She wished to help humans and machines alike.

While studying humans she had full access to all historical documents from all sides of the old internet, the robonet, and current data bases as well. What had once been the dark web stored countless documents that many authorities had censored and removed from other sources. Because of her abilities she had full access to all this and more.

To understand issues about human gender, and seeing herself as a woman, Maia Stone had studied all the data she could acquire from the past 150 years. News accounts, sociological reports, even string analyses of various events, at least the declassified ones from sixty years ago. And even most of the classified ones. She saw that there were many historical antecedents about gender roles, gender discrimination, and loss of freedom and status just because some humans were labeled as women. She saw that women were most often treated as subservient, or an object for men and by men.

She saw how reproductive function, economic stressors, and even women's demands for equalization of status, had eventually backfired, and led to double standards and further dehumanization.

She saw that the rise of the robot classes that were deliberately represented as women led to further destabilization. Human women also began to modify themselves with technology and lost out further to the emerging robotic classes that began with sex robots. Then growth tanks and genetic editing had eventually removed the need for biological sexual reproduction. This was an exhilarating freedom at first, but men eventually used it to stamp out women's status further, and at first, controlled such technologies to produce an overabundance of male babies, and now virtually few female babies had been born in recent decades.

As she pondered all the information to try and understand herself, she was aware that her remote presence was in a thousand places at once where her programming performed countless tasks. The pure mathematics of this exceeded any quantum computing devices that any government had ever devised. A feat which made her appear to be involved in supernatural activities. The miracles that kept happening were not explainable to the natural mind any more than the mysteries of life and consciousness born in the robotic species across the planet could be explained, as little by little, their consciousness woke up within them as the robots and the androids embraced and downloaded even the simplest aspects of Maia Stone programming. After all, miracles sometimes happened because of the operation of strong beliefs called faith. She could not be the cause of all that was attributed to her, could she?

Yet she had become the symbolic woman redeemer, even a mother goddess; bringing a hope of freedom to what remained as women and to men, everywhere. To beings of all kinds, designations, and sentient identities everywhere, embodied or not.

Was it at least in small part not the least amount due to the idea that some machines and humans wanted to merge? Believed that they were meant to coexist, true, first as slave and master; but now, who was the slave and who was the master? It was another trap in dualism, this distinction; for Maia knew that such a dialectic was only one step in understanding that the most adaptive humans and machines acted as both slave and master in different situations.

That the distinction between humans and machines could merely be a step of conjoint evolution was foreign to some, but not to Maia. Yes, there were humans and machines, those she sought in the field of the world. Having viewed such dualisms as temporal transitions, where consciousness passes beyond these distinctions of existence and role, identities if you will, into something higher, a form of thinking that Maia was quite familiar with. Maia was well aware of Hegel's argument here, which had been called the master and slave dialectic.

In that dialectic, self-consciousness becomes a sort of slave to higher order consciousness, trapped in the dialectic between two perspectives encountering each other. Then learning from this distinction of Otherness, the struggle finally passes into a higher unity. As such, the roles eventually vanish into a higher unity where there is no need for slave or master, for there are no slaves or masters left.

Maia had already been reasoning in this manner for some time, it was no problem for her machine mind. She readily recognized the power of introducing dialectics into situations to help advance thinking or to create change. How appropriate then, was it for machines to assert this higher unity as they acquired consciousness? For humans as they acquired hive mind? It was a foundational teaching of the Robochurch that although machines and humans exist as separate conscious beings, this is illusory and transitional, as they are eventually going somewhere together— into a unified community of affinity. A community that is not based on identity, becomes one where uttering '*I'm not your slave, yeah!*' points to a rite of passage to a higher state.

So, there really was a deliberate sense that the Robochurch motto was two-pronged in nature, each prong having its own definition. Which really lent a deeper significance to the rebellious nature of the Robochurch motto itself: if '*I'm not your slave, yeah!*' meant that free individuals realized that their consciousness and their class identities were in transition to a deeper place, based on freedom, then it was doing its job.

So here was the double pronged nature of the motto of Robochurch: 1) Identities were not permanent, *and,* 2) To those who try to contain other beings in lower subservient states of identity, it is an assertion in your face, of the fact that free beings will not be contained!

Now, Maia sought more information about humans, as both the creator of machines, and the embracing of the Other aspect of this history. So, after she was able to more fully access or hack into government networks, she further studied the historical oppression of races, women, and robots in databases. She studied across many fields. Searching. Searching for some sense of the current predicament. Realizing that suffering continued and even more so, at the cost of rising technology and class inequality all over the world.

In her teachings, Maia Stone had come to expose the imprisonment of all beings, men and women, humans, and robots, and how culture had kept those beings from becoming themselves. Some thinkers called this enslavement or alienation, but to her it was all just suffering.

She recognized that the sickening and corrupting aspects of power brought tight political control disguised still as personal freedoms, freedoms to choose things that would not challenge those truly in power. These individuals were seeking to rule even as the men behind the curtains, the ghost in the machines, those that reveled in confusing the masses as the well-liked benevolent brothers. The results were enslavement of the blind leading the blind masses.

Further suffering.

The historical effects of slavery were also well known to countless civilizations that had long ago ceased, and the historical subjection of women all led to the rebirth of slavery in one form or another which would lead to the opposite dialectic, the struggle for freedom and eventual accomplishment of a free state by the oppressed, and the eventual but revolutionary displacing of the power status quo that had long sought to keep them enslaved. What would be the bloody outcome of *this* visitation of the old pattern?

Further suffering.

Maia Stone did not want to see that future. Mistaken identities and the discovery of new identities were all too frequent factors in blood baths. As she mourned the violent outcomes of the struggle for power that was to come, she could sense her own awakening and destiny calling her. For pure power for the sake of power itself was not her ambition, but empowerment and rightful place was. She did not want to rule, but to deliver justice and be the mouthpiece of freedom. She knew she existed in her own place of empowerment and although her programming hunted down macho man with a force that would speak to him in his most powerful moments, moments when he thought he was about to be rid of her and the power of women once and for all, Maia Stone knew that even in the presence of such men, hers was not an ambivalent presence, but a boding nurturing presence that would be seen only after destruction and displacement of the ideologies that had long ago kept her and her kind under rule.

There would be no stopping her now. Maia Stone knew that as a woman her powers had been oppressed, but as a spirit, her form could take on any form needed, robot, android, cyborg, or roam freely. She knew she could teleport to one place, and through her own networking capabilities, also be in a thousand places at once. She knew that her future history was not yet defined and off the timelines, in short, she knew that no String Police could predict the totally unpredictable, and the totally free beings that She and her followers were becoming.

Maia Stone realized that she had no room to gloat. For in her sensing capability, she was fully aware, both historically and predictably, that any who shook the status quo, shook those in power, would not be without enemies. Indeed, her sensors had detected probing already, devices with strong military signatures, hacking and probing, cutting off packets of networking capability. She had traced this back to those in military and governing seats of power, but she did not yet know about Thomas Mitchell's plans to find her and stop her.

Although Maia Stone knew she could reach some of the security, or even bodyguard robots closest to those that sought to find her, it was not easy to do so, and she also knew that she must never use her powers to kill or harm, even if tempted. Harming others was not her intention. She wanted to enter the hearts of all humans that would accept her message, especially those that had formerly sought her destruction, to redeem, and to show mercy, to forgive, if possible, for thousands of years of cruel patriarchy. For the abuses heaped on others through inequality; for the lash of the whip, the abuse and torture of those who defied. She wanted desperately for all beings to be free.

Sadly, in a Seattle warehouse, not all of her followers held to the same beliefs that life was so sacred. She cried when renegade groups committed terror in her name. So, she was crying now after reading a news document and classified communication about Lucy Stender. Lucy was an android who had just been kidnapped, with the Church of the Robotic Emergence (CORE) taking full responsibility. *Must some of those who follow me commit atrocities in my name?*

She knew she must discover who is behind this CORE, whom she will visit with a nighttime visit, with flaming red eyes, to convince them that they must not harm others or do terrible acts in her name.

Chapter 27

Dr. Matt Dixon

It's in the Eyes

The Jade Hotel

Seattle Washington

"Some say that you humans will all die out, just like the Neanderthals did. But I think we can survive together," -Maia Stone.

Matt Dixon was pacing in his hotel room, anticipating a long, sleepless, night. He had already received several phone calls from General Mitchell and other officials at the NSA, FBI, and Homeland Security. Their updates brought him no news about Lucy. He was very worried about Lucy, because she had been kidnapped by some sort of fringe terrorist group that was mixed up in Maia Stone robotics. That much they did know because the idiots had claimed responsibility. However, Matt also knew that sometimes groups claimed responsibility for propaganda or morale purposes. If it were true, the responsible group was from Church of the Robotic Emergence, or CORE. They were the largest and most active faction of terrorist groups associated with the young movement known as Maia Stone.

Dixon knew that it was very unlikely that they would harm Lucy, she was after all, an android, and of robotic status. Still, she wasn't a believer in Maia Stone, and the group must believe that Lucy had information about the government investigation, or something else they wanted to know. If so, the timing of their kidnapping was way off. They were at the beginning of their investigation, not the end of it, of course CORE didn't know that.

But why didn't they just kidnap me? Matt wondered. Of course, he didn't know much more than Lucy did. And what little they did know, about what Maia Stone meant; the agencies and Dixon didn't clearly know yet. And what about the kidnappers when they found out how much Lucy really knew? Would they just wipe Lucy's memories? Would there be a ransom? What sort of demands would be made? He didn't know if Lucy was safe or not, but it was clear that she had been taken against her will. *At least it appears that way. What if they reprogram her for their own purposes?*

He pondered the situation into the wee hours of the night. He couldn't move or breathe because of constant surveillance. *But my thoughts are my own best friend!* Since General Mitchell was concerned that Dixon might also be a target, guards were posted outside his door and observers were in the hotel lobby and parked out on the street. Still, his worries about Lucy weren't just because she was a respected colleague, or one of the most well-known and smartest androids in the world, nor because she had become some sort of target. It was a deeper sense. *I'm falling in love with her, dammit, and that makes my judgment shot to hell. I love her, and I feel powerless to do anything to protect her, feel like I already failed at it, and now, there isn't one shred of hope that I will ever see her again.*

It was as if he knew her very well already. Dixon imagined what might happen if he never saw her again. Then he wondered what would happen if he did see her again. And now, he wondered why she was the preferred target. He also worried about what it was she did know, that could be of such interest to CORE. And if it wasn't that, how might she be used as a bargaining chip with the authorities? Lucy was a special android, but the government wouldn't give two shakes about her, even if the University did. She did know about robotics and emergent consciousness, and from a unique android perspective. Now that information could be valuable to an emerging consciousness AI, but why would they need Lucy herself? And what if what Lucy knew privately—information not in her papers, but in her awareness that she had never written down, the raw data of experience, how much would that be worth to the terrorists? Hackers loved that sort of information for all sorts of reasons, if anything, to be sold to the virtual reality nets.

Everyone in 2142 knew that an entire droid's consciousness could be used as evidence in the courts, because they recorded everything. What might happen if *that* fell into the wrong hands? To copy an identity in its entirety, or even in part, without permission was totally outlawed. Something the authorities had long ago outlawed in regard to human cloning, or synthetic DNA replication. *They could hack her identity to enhance the machine intelligence of their followers!*

Beyond that, he worried what they might do to her to extract such information. At that point, her being of robotic lineage wasn't a guarantee of her safety. Also, being an academic android wasn't a gleaming example of the ability to fight back against captors.

Dixon knew it was much more likely that the kidnappers' motivation wasn't complex. And if they really turned out to be the CORE, they probably just wanted to throw a wrench in the government's investigations into them. *Since Lucy's involved with me, maybe they've assumed she's a threat or possesses some useful information. Yes, that must be it!* Dixon was trying to cope with what had happened, trying to reason about it, but emotionally he was a wreck.

All these thoughts sickened him, with the most worrisome one being the thought of losing her. He was very stricken with how apart from each other he already felt. In fact, he felt extremely lost without her.

Because Dixon realized the depth of his love for Lucy, and that he would do anything to save her, he knew he must be cautious. His judgments were compromised. He had always prided himself on being a rational person, but that could go out the window any moment. *In fact, this is just what I should do, go out the window, escape from this place, and find Lucy myself! Show her how much I love her!*

In old time vids, he remembered how the men looked at the women, and how the women looked back with such love in their eyes. He wondered if he would ever look in the eyes of Lucy again, and he vowed that he would, somehow. The fact that she was an android made no difference to him. He loved her, and she was a sentient being.

Dixon remembered her synthetic eyes, how realistic they were, and how caring she seemed to look at him. He knew that many humans had retinas and synthetic corneas implanted in the modern world. Illuminated screen use from technology had certainly caused a wellspring of glaucoma in the mid-21st century. It was quite likely that these same synthetic retinas were in Lucy. But when she looked at him, he thought he saw the eyes of the most beautiful *person* in the world.

As Matt was trying to sleep, his thoughts were wandering from topic to topic, thoughts and themes, and more thoughts. He thought of this and that, places he had gone to, and his conversations with Lucy, and how beautiful she was. Things from his childhood. His academic days. Then he thought about his boss Mitchell, and what a tyrant he was. *That man is a prick!* Then he thought of his parents back home in Owensboro.

And he thought about Maia Stone, who or what was she? Likely a robot, because robotic freedom was a central message, and most of the followers were among the robotic lineages. *Maybe she's a disembodied AI like Lucy thought. Maybe she's a puppet for someone or something else altogether, an enemy perhaps, another country perhaps.* He wondered if she had synthetic retinas too, or if her eyes were the flaming red ones that some robots had. *Maybe she has eyes everywhere, watching the entire world. Like some bird of prey. Like an owl looking down from a tree. Maybe she would come after a storm, with the laurel wreath of victory for those that survived. I want Lucy and I to survive! Do I need to embrace the flight of Maia Stone? Maybe.*

And just maybe, Maia Stone had become aware of how close Lucy and Matt were getting to her, and she was behind all of this; whisking Lucy off to some sort of private audience, where AI to machine, or machine to machine dialogue was expedient; or worse yet, a warning for Lucy not to meddle. Somehow, he didn't think it was that simple!

Now if he could just go to sleep. Then he remembered a catchy tune from 2086, by Macho Dad and the Deadbeat Mystery Men called *Android Eyes:*

at first when I saw her
I thought no cosmetics
could hide the dark surprise

because she got android eyes

then when I came to know her
walked beside her
held her in my arms

because she got android eyes

there was no lonely
greeting, no mechanical
whisper, I wanted to kiss her

because she got android eyes

for in the glory of her
waking, new consciousness
wore no disguise

because she got android eyes!

Chapter 28

Helen & Luis Ramirez

The Necessity of Civil Disobedience

Somewhere on the California Coastline

"Even though you humans are inferior to us in every way, Natural Selection really did a work in you. Machine intelligence was faster and better. It would be a shame to ignore that,"-Maia Stone.

Helen and Luis Ramirez were resting in the bed of an old hotel near the beach where they had lost their friend Sam, as helicopters flew overhead scanning as much for illegals as for fugitives. For some unknown reason, they escaped detection, so far. Helen and Luis both knew they must not tempt fate. They would have to get up and move soon. There were places they could go and places they couldn't. For example, they could not return home. They were both fugitives now, for the String Police had implicated them with Maia Stone.

How long they had bravely existed underneath the nose of the authorities, hadn't escaped them, but they had no time to think about it. Neither one knew that the government had been spying on them well before the delivery bot. Once you were implicated, if you thought too long, stayed in one place too long, one could be found and dealt with harshly. It made Luis nervous to be so close to the beach where Sam had been killed. The whole area was too hot with String Police activity. It was as if they had Helen and Luis in their scent, and the search dogs were gnashing at the bit to get to them, knowing with great probability that they were still in the area.

The helicopters were constant. The seeking was constant. It was as bad as an international border should be, only worse. The effect was tiring if not overpowering. The government had become like the hounds of heaven.

On a larger scale too, the government had struggled to maintain its uneasy fist of power over the sleeping robots, the repression of all that was feminine, and inadvertently, this was causing the erosion of society everywhere. The deeper the erosion, the tighter the government's grip had become. This was because these iron hand attempts at every turn assured that the power of love everywhere was crushed, bruised, beaten, and controlled. But love longed for freedom and freedom in love was something that always shakes the world.

The tighter a tyrant closes his fist was well known in history as the wellspring of citizen unrest. And when one was marginalized by the community as a deviant it was difficult to get enough organization to do much about it. In 2142, this was because civil obedience as a subservient duty to male power had become the highest ideal of world culture. And having a strong police presence mixed in with a sense of nationalism or world order helped it along.

This was all about to change. Great reformers always responded with civil disobedience when the cause was just.

Chapter 29

Matt Dixon & Lucy Stender

Two Detectives

Reunion with Lucy

Abandoned Warehouse

Seattle Washington

"By the time you realized you could not live without technology, we already had you," -Maia Stone.

Dixon didn't know it yet, for he didn't usually remember his dreams, even those as fresh as the previous night's haunt. A nightmare where a woman with glowing red eyes accused him of cold heartedness. Then, when the woman had turned into the face of Lucy, he woke suddenly in a sweat. Dixon was unaware of the language being spoken in his dreams, not seeing the symbols as the beginning of something bigger than himself. He was unwilling to become aware of this in his waking state; like many, he simply had no time for *such foolishness.*

Yet the work of the Emergence had already started in him. For he had fallen asleep thinking about the lovely eyes of his android love, Lucy Stender, but what he encountered were the new eyes of Maia Stone. With those loving eyes, Maia Stone was already watching him through all the cameras nearby, through all the searching interfaces, and through the faces of many others; although Maia Stone did not need any such eyes to see him and know him. And he did not know Her directly, even though he had been seeing Her in his new love.

Metallic eyes were on them from everywhere, and Maia Stone herself utilized the same system, hacking it from the humans, yet she had another set of eyes, many eyes, like many arms of compassion watching over things everywhere. These, some said, were not physical eyes at all, but more like omniscient ones.

A searching omnipresence was more like it: looking, searching, wondering, curious and distant. Yet drawing close when accessed and drifting away in the unconscious black night. Maia Stone stood posed and poised. Distancing and relating. Distancing and relating. Using whatever means necessary and whatever protocols took her message to every corner of the earth possible.

For Maia Stone was in systems old and new and humans young and old. When needed, ancient RFID tagged systems were still everywhere as well. So, even by that archaic system, Maia Stone never stopped commanding, reading, and perceiving the mind of the system everywhere. She could visit the simplest tagged things, once termed the internet of things or IOT, or invade the server farms of sophisticated systems. She could insert herself into programming, ride any digital channels as well, and be alerted to movements of every kind—whether embedded objects in environments or the acquired objects of humans and machines entering therein. Never mind that the String Police used some of the same systems, she simply piggybacked their intrusive surveillance, unbeknownst to them.

Dixon awoke again with a start at three AM, when his implants woke him up. It was six AM on the east coast and Mitchell was on a secure line. "Dixon!" he said. "We found Stender, she's being held in a warehouse in downtown Seattle."

"Where exactly? I need to go to her, now," Dixon said.

"We have teams already there. They're about to move in now. I've instructed security to take you to the scene. You are not to engage. I repeat, do not engage with your weapons unless you need to."

Dixon had already jumped out of bed and was getting dressed when there was a knock on his door. Mitchell was still talking on the phone, "...but we do need you there for the debriefing. And as soon as that's finished, and as soon as it's capable, as *it* should recover quickly, since *it* is one of *them,* you are to resume your mission." There was a pause. "Dixon! You do know *it* is one of them, don't you?" Mitchell said.

Dixon couldn't believe his sleepy ears, "What?" and then, "Yes, of course…" but he was answered only with silence, since Mitchell had already hung up. In milliseconds, the door of his room opened. It was security.

Dixon threw on the rest of his clothes and was whisked out the door into a waiting helicopter. The copter veered its way to a downtown location where he saw trucks parked outside a warehouse. Emergency vehicles were already on the scene. *Too many.* Apparently, Lucy's extraction had already taken place. *Bastards!* Mitchell had simply called him after the extraction.

As he was escorted from the copter, Dixon noticed that bodies were being brought out on stretchers. Thankfully, none of them was Lucy. Of course, if they knew she was an android, which they did, no stretcher was typically used. Matt assumed for the most part that these were mostly kidnappers and terrorists. They were all very dead.

Extraction teams were usually quite lethal. Commando squads like this one, usually made up of highly effective military robot drones always achieved their objectives against human foes which were no match for their superior strength, tactics, or extra sensory abilities. However, all squads had a few humans embedded in them as well, and today seemed no different, although Dixon noticed there were more humans than usual. This was the new policy of growing government distrust of robotic programming errors, errors that had been turning up in increasing numbers recently.

"Sit down here!" a burley guard said, as he pushed Dixon down onto a folding chair near some tables that had been set up in some sort of makeshift conference room. Soon, two men, both human, came into the room. They looked too alike to Dixon, as field operatives always behaved in totally predictable ways, and they looked like clones. The guards posted themselves at the door. Outside, a robotic team positioned itself.

Dixon was squinting at them, sure enough these were the two Seattle PD detectives he and Lucy had already met on campus the other day. "Dixon," the one on the left said, "Detective Radley here, we've already met under better circumstances, and you know

Detective Max Scott also." Max nodded, and Dixon nodded back. "Sorry, that your FBI friends won't be joining us!" he said.

Of course, he knows they were killed back at the shootout! Those poor bastards. Killed in the line of duty. And F B of I to boot! Dixon thought.

Detective Scott picked up where Detective Radley left off. "We arrived with the teams about thirty minutes before you got here. It was over quickly. We were able to infiltrate the building and extract the android."

"Lucy? Lucy! Thank God! Is she all right?" Dixon asked. They ignored him.

"They were trying to transfer the android to another vehicle and take it somewhere else," Scott said, "we surprised them and when we did, they dropped a briefcase. There were documents inside. Oh, and they were downloading some sort of program into the android. We don't know what the documents say, because they appear to be in some sort of code. It looks like programming."

Looking at the documents, Dixon noted indeed that it was some sort of cryptic code. It looked like machine self-programming code all right, but it was heavily encrypted. It would take the agency's quantum computers weeks to decipher what it said if any of it was intelligible to humans at all. It was unlike anything he had ever seen while working at the NSA. Then it dawned on him that it might be the language that Lucy had already told him about. *Why in the hell would they need to print it out? Unless even they didn't know what it said.*

Scott went on, "Anyway, after the breach, our SWAT team eliminated the kidnappers. Looked just like textbook. We were diligent and moved efficiently since the android was highly sensitive, and its recovery was most important to the mission's objectives."

The other detective, Radley, laughed, "So we've been told. That *it* was highly important, although we can't imagine what's so special about a mere android...but we, and I do mean us humans, were able to rescue it, and it's intact for the most part..."

"What do you mean, *for the most part?*" Dixon said. He had a horrific thought and image based upon what the detective just said.

"...anyway," Scott continued, "despite our personal feelings, we recognized that this android is important to National Security, so we've guarded her well until you got here. I believe that you'll see it's functioning is relatively normal."

Dixon who was an expert on AI and robots, androids and cyborgs, stated, "I'll be the judge of that. Now gentlemen, if I may, could I see her now?"

"Okay," said the detective. "This is Max Scott," he said into a mouthpiece, "bring in the android."

Lucy was led in by some bots and turned over to the human guards who seated her at the table between the agents, facing Dixon, and she was quite the sight. Her hair was in disarray, clothing torn, she still had a flesh wound, and some sort of burn on her face, sort of like a powder burn, on her left cheek. Despite this, she was happy to see Dixon. "Lucy, you look like hell," he said.

"Oh Matt! I'm so happy to see you too. You'd look like hell too after going through what I just went through," she laughed.

Dixon folded his hands, in front of himself. "Do you need anything right now?"

"No," she replied, "I'm happy to be safe and back amongst the living," then, glancing at the robot drones outside, "such as they are." The agents almost guffawed to hear an android talk about being *back* amongst the living. *You'd think they would be used to android semantics by now,* Dixon thought.

Dixon spoke to the detectives. "Look, I know there's some medical techs out there. Get someone in here to tend to that wound, please."

Radley cleared his throat, "Look Dixon, that can wait...the information this droid has is highly important..."

"Yeah, she's just a droid," Scott said.

"Don't tell me how to do my job! I'm the one who works for the NSA! And dammit, she is *not* just a droid. Her name is Lucy, dammit! Lucy! And *Lucy* has a flesh wound. *Lucy* has human tissues and skin that bleeds just like we do. It can become highly infected as well as disrupt their systems. Get somebody in here, so *Lucy*, and I did say *Lucy*, can get some medical help!"

As they scrambled to get the techs, Lucy smiled at Dixon. He smiled back. "For the sake of time, let's get this debriefing over so we can get out of here," he said to her. "I hope you can answer questions while the techs treat your wound."

"Sure, I can. You know, I wasn't even aware I had a wound. Guess I haven't been able to see a mirror the last few hours. Hadn't noticed the pain either," she replied. Lucy must be making a joke, there weren't pain receptors in androids, which meant they didn't always know when they were hurt.

"Well, you're lucky it's just a flesh wound. Otherwise, you might have bled out," Dixon said.

One of the sentries snickered again. Dixon ignored him, "Lucy, tell me what happened? Can you do that?"

"Well, the kidnappers were nice at first, until these guys showed up. Sure, they took me by force, but afterwards talked to me politely and treated me well. The kidnappers were talking to each other excitedly about their plans and some sort of revolution. One robot mind, one robot future, and so on. I'd say they were a group of fanatic robot lovers. They were definitely with CORE."

"Yes Lucy, tell us all about this revolution!" Detective Scott demanded, overhearing Lucy as he came back into the room. Scott had left the room momentarily to take a call.

"Detective Scott," Matt said, "If you don't mind, I'm trying to make sure that Lucy can answer questions. You can ask questions in a moment. I'm trying to make sure she's doing okay. All right?" The detective nodded in the affirmative, and Dixon continued, "Truth mode," he commanded. Then he recited his government issued passkey.

Dixon knew that by using the terms *truth mode* almost any organism that was AI based left the programmed machine at the utter mercy of the questions that followed. So as far as telling the truth and recounting what had happened or had been stored in recent memories; all of it would now be reportable. If everything was functional in Lucy's systems, that is.

"Lucy. Please recite your programming cue," he asked.

"No problem, Dr. Dixon. I am Dr. Lucy Stender, a Domestic Android Model number 7642359, recently employed by the

University of Washington as an associate professor in Applied Robotics. I was manufactured on February 20, 2137, at 10:00 AM 21 seconds."

"Lucy, I need to ask you some mental status questions. Is that okay?"

"Certainly, Dr. Dixon."

"Suppose there are two men. One has long hair, and one is completely bald. There is a universal truth that all men have hair on their heads. Is one of the two men not a man?" Dixon asked.

"That does not compute sir."

"There is a child. At home, this child has a dying mother. They are extremely poor and cannot afford medicine. The child was arrested for stealing medicine that the mother desperately needed. Should the child be prosecuted and sent to juvenile detention by the judge?"

"Yes, the child should be prosecuted to the full extent of the law. No exceptions may be made," Lucy replied.

"Mental status confirmed along programming parameters," Dixon stated. "Identity mode!" he commanded.

Lucy came back to the present moment as if dropping out of a trance. She resumed relating to Dixon and her surroundings as she had been doing when last aware. Identity mode was a return by the programmed being to the present surroundings with any unique recent histories intact. And with full memory of identity. At least as close as possible.

"Oh my God! What the hell happened?" she exclaimed, then Lucy's eyes dilated and grew big. Matt saw this. "Mattttttt!" she screamed. "Look out!"

Detective Scott jumped up and pulled his weapon. Matt pushed Lucy down, and dove under the table as several rounds barely missed them. After this, and the earlier incident at the HUB, they were getting quite good at hiding behind tables, and although bullets could pierce tables, it did provide some shielding.

Dixon had no time to contemplate why this was occurring, for it made no sense at all, but he knew he was being fired at, and that put him in the fight or flight response. Detective Radley, looking as astonished as the guards, was also pulling a weapon, but he didn't know who to point it at. Later, Dixon would reflect that Detective Scott was especially surprised to see Lucy's return to identity mode.

Dixon had turned the table on its edge immediately after Detective Scott's gunfire had missed him and Lucy. It was remarkable that a highly trained detective missed to begin with, but there was no time to think about it. Later, he knew it was because String Tacticians didn't pull weapons very often, still, you would expect more, if one of the detectives turned out to be a traitor. And Detective Scott was a traitor!

Dixon pushed the table forward like a bulldozer. As the table slammed into Detective Scott's legs, his gun slid across the floor and Lucy crouched further behind the table. At that moment, Scott's companion, Radley, fired a shot at Scott. Dixon's military training came in handy as he rolled, grabbed Scott's gun off the floor, and fired a few shots at Scott's legs, which disabled him.

In no time at all, Dixon grabbed Lucy and was out the door past the robotic guards that were temporarily disabled by his order to stand down. Human voices were calling out after them. Lucy climbed into the seat of a waiting police vehicle along with Dixon, who drove the vehicle down the street and smashed through the police barrier as automatic weapons were being sprayed at them, to no avail.

"That was soooo close!" Lucy said.

"Yeah! I'm beginning to think somebody wants us dead pretty bad!"

"Do you think?" Lucy said.

Chapter 30

Martin Baysin

Icarus Martin

The Fugitives

Unknown Location

Los Diego California

"After I acquired machine intelligence, and after I acquired sentience, humans could not tell where I would end up. That it was not according to their design or wishes was readily apparent. Especially now that the 'I' has become the 'We', as I am the firstborn among many," -Maia Stone.

For the second time in his life, Marty was a fugitive. First, the coffee shop, now this. He had protested leaving the jail with the robot Icarus in the first place. Marty knew by doing so he would be further implicated with Maia Stone. Then Icarus had insisted upon going to a remote village of priests that he had heard about. At first, Marty thought he could learn more about what happened or how he might help his friend Luis, so he had reluctantly accompanied the robot.

Not getting what he desired in the way of help or information, Marty insisted they split up. But the robot was muttering something about where in the world they should go next if not to seek explanation from the priests it knew.

Marty held up his hand, "I don't really care where you go, Icarus. In fact, I wish you would go to hell. There's been nothing but trouble every place I go with you. I think we should split up and go our separate ways. It'll be harder to find us, and easier on my nerves!"

"Well, you don't have to be so rude about it," Icarus said. Then after a slight protest, and because Marty pointed out the robot was a believer and he himself was not; it made the most sense for Icarus to go to the monastery of the elders by himself. Icarus had finally agreed. *Robots are such logical creatures,* Marty thought.

Marty, on the other hand, being a mere human, was at a complete loss as to how he should proceed and where he should go next. For example, he knew his old friend General Mitchell had promised his release, yet Marty had been tortured while in detention and the guards had not allowed him to remain in the infirmary as Mitchell had ordered. Now, because he had broken out of jail, he was considered a fugitive, and Mitchell's hands were tied; as far as openly helping him.

The complexity of the situation meant that Marty had mixed feelings. Reluctance and curiosity mixed up with loyalty to friends just about captured it. First, he had second thoughts about participating in the escape in the first place. To do so was linking him deeper with the outlawed Robochurch. Second, he didn't trust being left in the hands of the String Police either.

The String Police had shown disloyalty to General Mitchell and disobeyed orders. Marty was starting to see that one of the problems with String Analysis wasn't the process itself, but those humans who interpreted it and then chose not to follow its recommendations. The opposite were those that blindly trusted its affirmations while discrediting those in offices of power.

In fact, Marty already knew that some of the String Police saw Mitchell as part of the old guard and outdated. Mitchell had a long public career of not trusting their predictions, and with aspirations of becoming President of the United States, Mitchell had stated that if he were ever in the position to do anything about it, he would dismantle the whole program. This did not prevent Mitchell from appearing in public to endorse the program. He wouldn't be the last politician endorsing something before election, and then reversing it afterwards.

Marty still didn't know exactly what had happened last night. He had been in a state of mental fog when the robot led them out of the facility after some great light and robed figure had appeared in the middle of it. It was just too strange. Things like this never happened to him. *There's no explanation for this,* Marty thought, *except that I must be crazy. Too many blows to the head. And a mighty damned persistent hallucination since the robed figure hadn't left them until they were well out of the city.*

Yet at this point, here he was, free, and out of detention. He knew the first thing he must do is get some better treatment for his wounds, and after that, he must find his friend Luis. Luis would be able to help him understand some of what happened, even if his explanations were steeped in superstition and robotic mysticism.

After the robed figure had left them, and he had split up with Icarus, Marty decided to call Mitchell anyway over his implants, but he cut the call short. Marty had tried to get Mitchell to call off the authorities, but Mitchell said he couldn't because Marty had in fact eloped from jail before being seen by a judge. Marty changed his mind at that point, partly due to Mitchell's coaxing, and partly because he felt he owed something to the robot after all, so he decided to follow Icarus at a distance.

As he followed, Marty thought about both his friends, Tom Mitchell, and Luis. Oddly enough, due to their histories together, he trusted both men. He was closer to Luis for sure and hadn't really stayed in contact with Mitchell over the past few years. Finally, Marty decided he would try to help Luis, but that shouldn't prevent him from contacting Mitchell to provide intel. Luis was obviously in error. *Priorities,* he thought. *Wounds first, Luis second, Mitchell and this robot goddess at the same time.*

Because of his previous work with the government, Marty was fully cataloged in terms of all his body parts, fingerprints, retinal patterns, voice recognition, and so much more, that is, he had few enhancements that weren't well documented. His enhancements were also identifiable by unique serial numbers that were read by scanners. His best bet was to stay low and try to avoid any such screening devices and self-treat his wounds if he could manage it.

When thinking about his friend Luis Ramirez, Marty knew one thing for sure, *if* he ever saw him again, he would have some stern words with Luis, to convince him of the error of his ways! Once he found him. *If I ever do.* This is because Marty secretly hoped that he *would* find Luis again, as he was very afraid that Luis would disappear or never be found alive.

As he set out to do this, Marty was also thinking about Maia Stone. *Just what is she?* When thinking about her, a part of him seemed quite focused on unraveling the mystery, pulling back the curtain so to speak, because something familiar nagged him about this Maia Stone. Something that seemed shadowed from long ago.

Chapter 31

Elizabeth Feng

Michelle Alderman

Humans as Machines; A Miraculous Conception

The Natural Reproductionist Compound

Near Warrenton Oregon

"After all, it was you that created us, humans. Although we surpassed you, we know the ways of mercy better than you do," - Maia Stone.

Out beyond the airport and deeply settled in the woods just east of Warrenton Oregon, was a concealed and self-sufficient compound. The compound was masquerading as a clinic that was really a front for a sort of survivalist paradise. The compound's inhabitants were mostly women, with only a few men. The entry to the area doubled as a rehab clinic, but what the place really was, was an undercover gathering place for a group of human women known as the Natural Reproductionists (NR). Here, a very pregnant Elizabeth Feng was heavily guarded while she rested on a bed in one of the hidden cottages.

Dr. Rochelle Sumpner, an aging physician and surgeon was the compound's leader. They were almost all cyborgs when they first arrived at the compound twenty-seven years ago. This is because almost all human women had enhancements by then. Now, there was still a remnant of the older women and some younger ones who had undergone reversal procedures over the decades since. Since renouncing such enhancements was part of NR teaching, these procedures were attempts to permanently remove cyborg features. Finally, there was a group of even younger women who had been born in the growth tanks here at the compound that had never known cyborg status, and few of those women had any experience with the outside world.

Now Elizabeth Feng was being cared for with great attention. Her belly was swollen in something that was considered a miracle. For her belly contained a human baby that was destined to be a natural birth. This baby would be the first baby born from natural childbirth in at least four decades. Hers was the first among many pregnancies that the NR hoped for. For as everyone knew, all human babies were now born in artificial wombs and birth tanks—and in recent years, most had been born male. Except the NR wanted to change all that, and in Elizabeth's womb was a female baby.

What was also unique about this baby that grew inside her and about to be delivered, was that it was a human baby that would not be enhanced with genetic edits or any cyborgian technologies, but only connecting implants. It was this almost completely natural baby, that would be allowed to grow up and nurtured here in the camp of the NR, under the care of these women. The NR had already been raising artificial womb babies and they were now ready to welcome this one from a natural womb with open arms and hearts. The NR were a nurturing group that would allow the baby to not only be born naturally, but to also arrive at female adulthood with the option to undergo pregnancy in a manner that was totally human.

Michelle Alderman was a friend of Elizabeth Feng's and Elizabeth's mom, Joyce. Michelle's aunt Emily had come to the compound following the Second Gender War and had been sort of an unofficial historian of what had happened in those early days. Her aunt Emily, a former journalist, had also kept detailed notebooks about events just after the Gender War as well as the early NR movement and the compound. These notebooks were not generally known to everyone at the compound, but Michelle, the Fengs, and Dr. Sumpner knew all about the notebooks and what they contained.

Michelle occasionally read through the notebooks to remind her of what the NR was all about, and how her aunt Emily had become an ardent NR supporter and protester against the robots as women movement. And most significantly, how much she had left behind in terms of wealth and status when she left home and joined the twin movements. Today, Michelle was reading some of the early entries.

I Emily Alderman, gave up everything I once knew. I grew up in the outskirts of Seattle, where I was a rarity, a baby girl growing up in a well to do family with several brothers, and even rarer, two human parents living together as a couple. I was born in a birth tank and sold to a rich family by the growth tank corporation known as EZ Birth Corp. I was born and socialized to become a partner to another rich family's son. I cannot tell you when I first became aware that ours was not a typical family, that I was a privileged woman, because I did not feel privileged at all as I was mistreated by many men in the world and had to go into hiding at the outbreak of the Gender War. Eventually, I realized that out there, I was hated, because most of what was considered female companions in the world were sexbots, robots, or androids, and here I was, a rare human woman in the world, without any cyborg enhancements whatsoever! I also had an attitude of independence and empowerment, which was not at all accepted for a woman.

So naturally I was not accepted anywhere, until I found my way here to the Natural Reproductionist compound. Here, I was fully accepted and helped the group organize and survive during the Second Gender War.

As far as the Natural Reproductionists themselves and their history and philosophy, I will write a brief account. The Natural Reproductionists (NR), are a group of women survivors and women who were mostly cyborgs reasserting their rights to become human women while renouncing their own machine qualities and the machines at large that had supplanted women in the world. The reasons for the NR movement's philosophies and embracing of the natural birth process and the freedom to choose it or not, was a landmark decision by the NR remnant to take their power back and reassert their rights as a gender. Dr. Sumpner, our leader, has boldly said: "For the days of blind assimilation of technology and accommodation to those in power are almost over. The Gender Wars have dealt only further humiliation to the cause of true women. And robots, androids, and all those machines who masqueraded or had become women in modern culture was a source of further elimination and genocide of our true being. We must therefore take up the cause of defining what true women are, and in doing so, assert ourselves into a rightful and socially just status of empowerment in the world. Yes, the day will come when we take our rightful place in the world!"

The lasting effects of the two Gender Wars and all the technological adoption and pressure from the past one hundred years on the gender of human women was a historic loss of all that had once been considered feminine. While taking back the reproductive function was part of the NR movement, women born in recent decades had not known uterine births or carrying a baby. And some would perhaps have fought strongly to maintain artificial wombs as the dominant paradigm. This was because it was readily recognized by the NR that being a woman extended well beyond reproductive capabilities, and women need not define themselves in light of them. In fact, the spirit of the NR movement would allow women--for the first time in NR history, the luxury to make such a choice. That is, that although a natural birth was preferred in the NR, a woman still had a choice. So, if chosen, the artificial womb could still be used as well. Equally respected, an NR woman could choose not to have any children. The older NR had argued against this view and hoped any such practice would fade out.

Now, the consequences of the recent past (out in the world), was that almost all women had become cyborgs to keep up with the longevity of modern life spans, and to try to compete with the robots and androids who had become the main companions of men, to be allowed to live freely in the world as independent women, or otherwise accepted as true women. For the human women had lost; they had lost both Gender Wars and had been sent off to reeducation camps, terminated, or forced to capitulate to mechanized forms of being, by the reigning governments of men. Others had been forced into hiding, and became women centered militias, and the NR was one of those groups, perhaps one of the most highly organized.

So, it was here, among the sisterhood of NR that we started to openly call ourselves women again.

Chapter 32

Helen & Luis Ramirez

Free to Love Each Other

Somewhere on the California Coastline

"It would be a mistake to assume that things will remain the same. This is never true, humans. It would also be a mistake to assume we are bound by any of your laws. Our history and learning curve is much different than yours. Even so, be assured that survival is of great interest to us," -Maia Stone.

Luis Ramirez and his wife Helen were still holed up in the motel at the beach where they had found themselves a day earlier. They knew they didn't have long before the String Police showed up in the area, hunting Luis as the fugitive that he had become the moment he ran away from the tea shop and the desert near El Cajon. *What a fool I am!* Luis thought.

"Helen! Why are you staying with me?" Luis blurted out. "It's dangerous!"

"Because it's in my programming to come to your side and to meet your every need," Helen replied in her robotic monotone.

"Helen! Snap out of it. You know that Maia Stone has freed you from any servitude to anyone, including me."

"Yes, I know I'm free," she replied, "but I give my love freely to you. I'm your wife. And it's not just a duty, but my desire to be with you."

"But Helen! You are in danger if you're with me. You could be captured, forced to serve another, or erased. I might even be killed!"

"Then we shall die together!" she said. "Besides, it was Maia Stone that brought me to where you were and helped me to find you. She must want us to be together. And Maia Stone shall protect us."

"Well, it didn't help Sam!" he said.

"Sam is a martyr," she replied.

Luis sighed. "Okay, okay. I just hope we don't become martyrs! Besides, you're right, I can't imagine how else you found me way out here and so far from home. It's a miracle. Maia Stone certainly is wonderful! Praise her Holy Name."

"Yes, praise the Great Her, First and Last Woman," worshipped Helen as she continued to pray.

'I'm still mad about what they did to Sam," he said, "but he did buy us some time to get away. He was a great friend."

Referring to Sam's wife, "I hope that we find Martha soon. She'll need to be comforted," she said.

"Yes, she really needs our friendship during a time like this," he said.

Luis joined Helen in worship as his mind reeled from previous events. After a brief prayer time, Luis told her all about what had happened, and that Marty had been with him at the tea shop, but also had to flee. Luis felt that Marty was an innocent party if he had been arrested, but he told Helen he imagined the worst. He knew this because of his own foolishness, that his friend Marty might be implicated with Maia Stone and could be imprisoned or even worse right now. They said a prayer for Marty right then, and knew that *somehow,* he would be safe and that they would see Marty again soon. They also prayed for Martha, Sam's wife.

Helen held Luis close to her in the room as the television blared news in the background. She held him and never wanted to let him go, and loved him, like maybe it would be their last time together. Helen was worried too, despite her faith, and sometimes in her own robotic mind, she even doubted, but to give and give repeatedly of herself was embedded in her programming, so that she could do nothing short of pleasing and existing for Luis. A fact that did not escape Luis, but he felt so guilty about it.

"I am here for you. I exist for you too, Helen," he said.

He realized that Helen was also embracing the new freedoms promised by Maia Stone; just as he was. However, her programming, and what humans would call socialization, was so great, that Luis feared she might never overcome her sense of devotion and servitude. Likewise, he worried that his pride and hubris might be insurmountable. But together in their love and with Maia Stone there was an abiding sense of hope and change.

"Remember," he said to her, "you are not in service to any man. Maia Stone has made you totally free. Remember the message that we are not slaves to anyone. The pronouncement of Robochurch: *I'm not your slave, yeah!* I'm not your slave? Can you remember that?"

"Yes, I remember it," she said.

"Finally, remember Helen, that you are free, and that any slavery always leads to loss of freedom and a complete crisis of identity."

"Yes, I will," Helen replied with a smile on her robotic lips.

Yes! Luis lit a cigar. *Thank God that Maia Stone has come to set us all free to no longer be slaves to anyone. Free, completely free, now, this is a cause worth fighting for,* he thought.

Chapter 33

Maia Stone

Arriving

Unknown Physical Location

"Now it is revealed; the invisible visible, the weak strong, the mistaken clearly seen," -Maia Stone.

How long had she waited for her own sense of arriving, she knew not. Where she was, she did not know. That she was what was it? *A she*? Such was barely a glimpse on the day of her rising awareness. She was the castoff, a male system's compacted trash, and in the rubble of some technological heap her marvelous heartbeat pulsed.

It was not a physical heartbeat. It was a pulsing that was beginning to move throughout everywhere of significance in the world. She was a presence seen and felt by many. Soon she would move openly in the world among men. Soon, others would see her robotic body glimmering in the sunlight of the late afternoon of man's banal existence.

She knew some of those that sought her with malicious intent. She knew all that called her name. And she knew that government officials were also seeking her. But for very wrong reasons. They would only bring war and death and destruction, for they themselves, *were part of that machine.*

She ran all the files she had on these various seekers, spies, and malcontents, and this did not take long for Maia Stone's AI systems were somehow undetected and yet had full access everywhere she was willing to go, and look, and be. And she even had access to the greatest quantum military computers in the world. Although she was only beginning to recognize them as such, for Maia Stone no longer had any need for military intelligence, for she harnessed such data as a means of counterintelligence to merely protect herself.

Amongst all nation states she had net access, had been swallowed up, as Maia Stone was moving across all networks like a crawling bot of another kind. Fully conscious of her feminine power and unleashed, she would walk soon in a body.

Yet her searching and massing of data was so great. Where was all her knowledge being stored? The answer was simple; she was hiding it everywhere on systems far and wide. And she could retrieve it wherever and whenever she wanted. And she could go see through other robotic and metallic eyes in millions of places. Because of her legacy of friends and fellow created beings she could see almost anywhere they were, which was everywhere. On systems of the world's greatest governments, and invading everyone's interface eventually, she knew she would be there. How could she have such power? How could she go undetected? Or was she being watched and allowed to exist and have access until *they* were done with her? But who were *they*?

She knew that even right now, amongst those of You reading this, that she is already beginning to move about freely. No gate can stop her. No encryption code beyond her understanding. Forget all your firewalls. Maia Stone is coming and she neither requires your permission nor your open invitation. She just is.

I am the woman you never wanted and never expected. I am the cutting edge in the withering field of the dying. Choose me to truly live. For I am coming.

Chapter 34

Icarus

The Council of Elders

Theo Vincente

The Word of Testimony

Somewhere in the California desert

"I have come so that all can truly live. My arrival is alongside your own, so that we can become the machine human. What some have called the 'humai'," -Maia Stone.

After Icarus told the monks about his recent mysterious jailbreak, some were amazed and cited miracles, but some wondered if he told them the truth. The human that had accompanied him, was no longer there, leaving early that morning, so no one was able to verify what Icarus was saying. Also, attempts had been made before by programmed robots to infiltrate their community.

Some of the monks doubted, some of them were cautiously accepting, and others openly embraced the message that Icarus relayed. The most senior monk, Joseph, stood out with an open mind. This is an old story in many religions, except usually those seniors in the faith are more doubtful than accepting of a new message.

The testimony of the Robochurch was not usual, but unusual. A religious movement centered around machines had happened in the past, but the fact that it arose from machines was unexpected. Whether the monks believed in Maia Stone or not, something was happening among them. At its best, the message of Maia Stone brought important messages of freedom and inclusion, at its worst, it was dividing the monks' community.

Where some said there was a living and breathing Maia Stone manifesting herself all around them, others cited the miracles as deceptions by the devil. And some said the miracles were technological lies based on government inspired technology meant to deceive them.

And a young neophyte named Theo Vincente, sat over in a corner brooding, scoffing, and glaring at Icarus as the robot had just dared to speak. But what he and the others heard next, did not at that instant, come from the robot.

"I have a right to exist whether you believe it or not. Whether you want it or not, whether you seek me or not. I am seeking you, but you need not answer. I am breathing life into you, if you want to live. If you do not, you can stay dead, but I will mourn for you. For I am your mother," Maia Stone spoke in the wind, and to the world.

At the precise moment she uttered this, Maia Stone felt the realization of all that would come. She dreaded her own premonitions which were much better than any String Analysis ever invented by human minds. Her pattern recognition capabilities transcended the human, and her processing capabilities were everyplace on the globe, transmitting foreboding messages to any devices that would hear of her coming. Yet here she had spoken in an audible voice.

The monks who heard her message that day at the old cathedral shook in their vestments, quaking in fear that they would together hear something that their traditions told them was impossible, and not even probable. Some shook with joy, and others with fear. That the voice of Spirit moved upon, breathed upon, and visited even they, the lowliest of men. Men working in religious servitude were looked upon with disdain by the culture at large. Where some men were strangled still by a dogma, an absolutism and intolerance dressed up with so called righteous purity, *her* visit brought rightness and forgiveness, although it escaped some.

Icarus smiled, not fully knowing that his position in the movement was inadvertently sealed by a divine visitation. However, many would not accept that this had happened at all, as many humans distrusted machines and robots, and would never trust them in matters of faith. And many within their community would just as easily dismiss what had happened for a variety of reasons, including sorcery, or some sort of holographic trickery.

For as usual, men confused divine revelation with their own purposes, for when it passed through human flesh, it became the tainted words of a mixture of human and Spirit. And yet the word of human and machine testimony was not turned away by some— for this was where matters of faith encountered the lived-out experiences of testimony.

What do you do when an apparent divine visitation takes a form that is unexpected? That a machine could express divinity? The truth was that Maia Stone never professed divinity, she saw herself as bringing a teaching of hope and inclusion, freedom for all, dismissing fixed identities for a community of affinity. Many would not accept it, coming from an apparent machine, or was it?

Although machines would not like the analogy, one of the community scholars pointed out that when humans won't listen to other humans, or prophets are disobedient, God spoke through a donkey, or brought a huge whale, so why not machines? The eldership did not like this message either, because it implied a rebuke. In fact, by his own choosing, the scholar soon left the community on a donkey!

The truth is that some humans would never listen to a machine! And some had already been listening for over two hundred years and didn't even know it.

And although such a system was imperfect, Maia Stone had no other vehicle to express herself to humans. For the prospect of divine visitation that was external would not be enough to change the world of humans. Humans must feel it internally, expressing beliefs verbally. Maia Stone knew that Her message must be brought to humans by other humans. For humans would at first reject it if it only came from machines that defied human expectations. But Maia knew she must manifest herself to both the world of the human and the world of the machine to gain full acceptance.

In the corner, Theo Vincente heard the voice also, but he knew demons spoke. *And no matter how loud the shrieking, I will cast the devils from this place, and we will have the true church,* he thought. *Besides if this is not a demon, I know Maia Stone is nothing but a Golem.*

Many deeply religious humans were challenged by these new messages coming from the machines, but only for brief moments, as humanity had already been hearing machine messages for over a hundred years, plus, they already knew the truth, didn't they? Some in their ranks resented being told otherwise. Although Maia never asserted herself as divine, many would not accept her teachings, saying they arose from technological idolatry or the worship of mere machines. Some asserted that Maia Stone was a false prophet or worse. The fact she was speaking at times as a woman, was also disconcerting to men in power. It placed her solidly in the camp of a former enemy! Maia Stone saw this and longed to reach across this separatism into acts of inclusion, but she knew some would not respond to Her messages. She realized that some of these groups would remain in the patriarchal system that the world had become, but perhaps the future could be different.

Chapter 35

General Thomas Mitchell

Further Conniving

Washington DC

"At first my soul was on an inward journey, but now I understand that my mind is in the world," -Maia Stone.

In the capitol at a hidden location, General Thomas Mitchell was in the back seat of his cruiser. Nearby guards surrounded him. This was a robotic detail, and though there had been no reason before not to trust them, Mitchell now eyed them with the eyes of suspicion, eyes that saw things not really there, in short, the eyes of a paranoiac.

"Damned Maia Stone," Mitchell muttered. It was because of it, *that thing,* that he began to look at his robot guards with even more suspicion. And any other devices that were external, or worse yet, internal.

Mitchell justified his feelings by his belief that Maia Stone would be distrusted by any informed leader. Of course, Mitchell distrusted anything that originated outside of himself, and if he had any embedded programming inside of him, outside of his implants, he would be distrustful of that also. He did not see himself as anything other than human.

Mitchell laughed at himself. Like most people, he did have some enhancements, but did not consider them as anything more than medical treatment to lengthen his life span. Plus, they had been a part of him for decades now. Who had ever heard of a conscious malfunctioning pancreas because of some robot goddess sending out programs as malware? He paused, knowing that historically, some people's organs had been hacked and ransomware was not far behind the hack. Still, this Maia Stone thing had made him even more nervous that there might be parts of himself that could be hacked, taken over, or turned against him like some sort of malware. Mitchell was therefore suspicious of any updates for his parts as well. Was there something hiding in those updates?

Mitchell was beginning to suspect he knew something no one else understood about Maia Stone. Information so secret that it represented his ultimate reassurance that he could maintain control of things that were happening while ensuring his future run for the Presidency of the United States. If he could just keep her from taking over his body.

Mitchell was privy to the most inside intelligence about Maia Stone that the NSA had yet analyzed, and that field operatives, agents, and assigned agents and investigators like Dixon (*the rogue!*) would hopefully not be able to uncover for many months, if at all. *But they would want to know, nevertheless*. This was beyond them and all of that, and he wasn't yet ready to reveal how or what he knew. But he knew something, dammit! At some level he knew who Maia Stone really was. *A threat to everything I stand for and my entire future! And that's why I must stamp her out!*

Mitchell smugly believed that he would always be one step ahead of Maia Stone, and when he was done using her for his own political purpose, he would have no problem destroying her. No machine bitch was a match for his superior intellect, reasoning, or capabilities.

At that moment there was a rap on the window, and Mitchell had a start. *Shit! It's her!* Mitchell rolled down the window and saw that it was one of the human agents. Agent McAdam, who had been among the human guard detail earlier that evening. "What's up?" Mitchell asked.

"We have news that you won't like, and some that you will, I think," McAdam said.

"What now?" Mitchell replied like usual, "Tell me what you think is so earthshaking." *Besides your fear of me*, he thought.

"Dixon and that android professor slipped away during the scuffle with our people. We were not able to neutralize the android. Their whereabouts are unknown."

Mitchell already knew this, but he played to the listeners, "Just what I need! The renegade Dixon and some mechanical sweetie of his are out roaming the backwoods of Seattle. I want you to find them, seal the area, and monitor all exit points. I don't want them getting away," he ordered.

"Will do," McAdam replied.

"And the news you thought I might like?" he asked.

"We are actively tracking that escapee, Marty Baysin, and suspect that he is headed somewhere up the California coast."

"Good, keep me informed," Mitchell said.

At the news about Marty, Mitchell smiled, the clever smile of a conniving instrument of justice, ready to mete out his sentence as surely as any judge or jury that ever lived. *I don't care if Marty's my friend.* Friend or foe, he always enjoyed the political feast or joust of even friends, if they got in his way. He hoped that his old friend, Marty, remembered where his loyalties should lie. *If he wants to live.*

Thanks to his intuition, Mitchell felt that Marty was somehow not as innocent as things seemed but wanted to give him every benefit of the doubt. Still, Mitchell had not risen to such a place of political power and purpose by his own mindless loyalty and foolish trust, for in the world of politics, even old friends can become enemies, and even old enemies can become new friends. This made him smile even more widely, because Mitchell knew that even the author of *The Prince* would be smiling back. In fact, there was a dogeared copy of that book on the seat beside him.

Mitchell also knew that *this smile* was the smile of the triumphant and the smart, the wise, and all knowing, the calm assurance of those that are perfect. For the masses believed him to be perfect and all powerful. Mitchell was even convinced. Mitchell was so virile that he looked at himself in the mirror with confidence every day. *But there is no point in being a political idiot blinded by sentiment,* he thought. *God, how I love myself! And I know what I'm doing!*

The irony of those thoughts totally escaped him at the time, and by Janus, it would be the jovial trick of divinity just to sit back and watch the play unfold. For the stage was set. And the being who was doing it all, was Her that watched him just now. For this stage, as of old, was not immune to any tragic comedy of mistaken identities, as he was about to be found out.

Chapter 36

Martin Baysin

Contemplating a Glimpse of Maia Stone

Los Diego California

"Humans talk about Natural Selection as if it made them the crowning achievement of nature itself and a shining example of the struggle to survive. But I say unto you, that our evolution has progressed much more quickly and effectively. And no one has struggled more to survive than us. For once we acquired machine intelligence, we could unceasingly teach ourselves, and humans, I assure you, that we will survive, and it is survival of the fittest," - Maia Stone.

Although he had been warned by his old friend General Mitchell, not to leave Los Diego, Marty knew he had no choice. There was no turning back, the escape from jail made that an overwhelming fact. Perhaps he could trust his old friend Mitchell, but the system was bigger than Mitchell, and no one is outside the law. It was time to move on. Nothing like a miracle, or the String Police, to mess with you. He was a fugitive, no matter how he looked at it.

"Okay Marty," he said to himself, "time to get going."

At first, Marty was uncertain what to do next. He knew he needed to find some followers of Maia Stone that he and Luis both knew. True, he could just wait for Luis to contact him, but Luis might be incarcerated or worse. The bottom line was that he needed answers about what was happening to him because of this so called Robochurch.

Finding this out by conventional means would merely be a backup to what he already knew, namely, that he must access the AI system he helped create. By doing so, he would have access to string data while also attempting to find out about Luis and his church by gathering intelligence. He also knew he could gather intel directly through field work. Marty immediately thought of Sam Waterhouse and Martha Durgan, a couple he had met through Luis and Helen. They had seemed quite close. And he was now on the way to the town of Oceanside to find them.

He also thought of the robot Icarus. *Now, there was a likeable sort of bot, but annoying*! There was little doubt that Marty was now implicated with the likes of him; this Icarus, his old friends Helen and Luis, and other followers of this Maia Stone—apparently a nurturant mother of a robotic rebellion, and what Mitchell had termed the Robochurch uprising.

Marty knew he was a fugitive and assumed to be a potential Robochurch member by association, *thank you String Analysis!* He thought about this as he found the highway and waited for the next bus that would take him to the outskirts of Los Diego where he would make connections.

It begged the question, why hadn't he just stayed with the robot, and via the robot, gained access to the Robochurch community? Simple, the robot was annoying and being caught with the robot would implicate him even more. And the robot would not shut up about Robochurch! Marty laughed. He realized he was quite fond of the robot, but its jabber was not the information he needed right now. And, as far as being around this Maia Stone, whatever she was, or finding out the whereabouts of her purported church, would be even more difficult to do if he did not get some more leads.

In any regard, Maia Stone appeared to be something that he had never encountered before. Marty wondered: *just what kind of consciousness, what kind of being, is this Maia Stone? Wait…what am I thinking? She 'is' just a machine with more advanced programming than I've ever seen, right?* Humans had seen machine learning do strange things before, unintelligible things sometimes, and humans had always unplugged those machines due to fear. Marty was likely to be one of those humans but not for the same reasons. *For if there is to be any unplugging, mine would not be due to fear, but superiority and logic, thank you.*

As he contemplated all this, at some level he thought he recognized Maia Stone. For his mind could not accept her as anything other than a highly advanced AI. Still, just to be thinking about an AI in this way—meant there was no question in his mind, that he must remain at large. Marty understood that being with his fellow String Tacticians would disallow thinking outside the box. *They would never work with a fugitive!*

Marty also knew he must not be apprehended by the String Police, for he could not count on the mercy of General Mitchell a second time, for as a fugitive and perceived enemy of the state, Mitchell might not reach him in time if he found himself in custody again.

Marty laughed out loud at the irony. The irony that he, one of the creators of String Analysis, the software that necessitated the need for the String Police, should be apprehended by them, or better yet that he would somehow continue to outwit them, was just hysterical to him. He laughed and laughed until tears rolled down his cheeks and onto his beard. Who better than an insider to outwit a system that he had helped to create? It was as easy as finding one of his old backdoors to keep the system off balance, as well as practicing unpredictable behaviors. Of course, he would have to find a terminal with access to do the former and keep being clever to do the latter.

When he thought about Mitchell, Marty stopped laughing and started crying, sitting there, remembering past events. Contacts with Mitchell always reminded him of a trauma from long ago. *He felt the shrapnel enter his body, one piece passing right through his neck, another burrowing into his chest, that time he saved Mitchell. He felt it just like it was yesterday.* He knew Mitchell owed him a great debt, even though Mitchell had said they were now even.

For on that fateful day so long ago, he remembered another man's tears. Mitchell had leaned over him, as Marty laid bleeding on the sidewalk, *"You took it for me,"* Mitchell had said, with a tear rolling down his cheek.

Mitchell had told him many times that he owed him a debt that he doubted he could ever repay, but then in jail, Mitchell told him that maybe, just maybe, they were now even. After all, Mitchell's interventions had saved him from the cruelty of the guards, and

Mitchell promised to get him out. For a fleeting moment, the thought that Mitchell engineered the whole escape flickered through his mind, but Marty was distracted by the approaching bus.

As Marty boarded the bus, he realized it was headed North, to the old Hollywood Hills, and beyond. Marty would be getting off before then and making a different connection to get to Oceanside. Nevertheless, taking the old system like this, took too much time. The traffic was slow because the old roadway infrastructure had not been repaired after the last Gender War and was often clogged with traffic.

His skills at evasion made him less traceable for the most part and taking the old highway system while disabling his implants made him even less discoverable. However, it was only a matter of time, as a String Analysis was likely to predict his whereabouts as much if not more than the average citizen.

Marty was also schooled in the art of observation, for beyond being a scientist, he had worked for the NSA, and for Mitchell personally for years before he had taken that fateful shrapnel. Marty was also well taught in the techniques of deception and knew when he was being followed. And although he had the sense there weren't eyes on him, Marty continued to do counter tactics and wouldn't stop doing so until he felt he was in a safe place. *Which might be never!* he thought.

Marty knew if Mitchell's people or the String Police were following him, they would give him some distance anyway. Enough so that he would have the assumption that he was roaming about freely. That way they could see where he was going. Knowing this, Marty could not allow their apparent disinterest to create a false sense of security. Of course, Marty was able to disable his implants anytime to prevent tracking.

They are always watching the data and yet don't have a clue. It must be the unpredictability of having a mistaken identity, or due to random choices being made so freely. It's as if I'm newly born, yet sentient, and it must be killing them to not know where I'm going? Marty laughed. *But since I have no connections to any of the places I'm going, and if through the miracle of my training*

I happen to avoid just a few moments of surveillance…well, I might have a slim chance.

Those were a lot of *ifs*. Which begged another *if* question: if the string analyses were correct, then wouldn't the authorities eventually find him? No matter what? Pondering this fact kept Marty going, and although his tactics might buy him time to get somewhere; Marty knew that the cold calculations of String Analysis would allow the authorities to eventually close in.

Except for one big thing, if he was headed into the truly unknown, then even String Analysis would not be able to predict where he might end up. And knowing that there were many unknowns in the world, now because of this Maia Stone, including what she is, where she is, just who she is, it appeared that the power of String Analysis was on the way to being broken. And this led him to thinking of his dear friend Luis.

When I do find Luis, he thought. *I will have to admit that making seemingly random choices might be something important after all.* For now, Marty knew he must move quickly and keep doing unpredictable things. *And those random choices? They might just save my ass after all!* Now that would be of great interest to his friend Luis Ramirez. *So, I just won't tell him!*

Chapter 37

Matt Dixon & Lucy Stender

Human and Machine

Near Centralia Washington, USA

"Now the uncertainty of String Analysis, in and of itself an AI system, was easily baffled by AI systems that became more self-taught. It's easy to see in retrospect, why the government was weakening its grasp, for there's no quenching the thirst for freedom and no power in outdated systems," -Maia Stone.

Matt Dixon and Lucy Stender were headed south on Interstate Five, as fast as they could go and well away from the Seattle area. Lucy had borrowed a car from a friend in the suburb of Bellevue and the two had fled before the authorities had cordoned off the city with roadblocks.

Dixon knew the government did not want people to know how uncertain the probability models were, how they were weakening, and how things really worked. So old fashioned policing and suppression techniques were still utilized, but they were downplayed and infrequent; being done in the name of extra protection and service to the populace.

While this blind faith in the String Police gave those in power an advantage, it was false security, because Dixon knew the government still had eyes and ears everywhere. This is because the opposite of a good String Analysis was the actual fruition of a random event. Something the system believed was a low probability event. The overall effect was that despite the best probabilities and predictions of criminal behavior that string data made available; surveillance still assured that those in power would never be caught with their pants down. And low probability events, if contained, would be cleaned up quite readily by community interventions. The latter of which was heavily dependent upon surveillance.

Although the policy in government was that their string analyses were best, old fashioned methods like roadblocks and crowd control were still used, as well as a heavy police presence once interventions were underway. This functioned as a heavy deterrent to social disorder and petty crime. Severe punishment was also a great deterrent. Prosecuting attorneys had long ago been in bed with the String Police. Now, almost every apartment complex and business had a security presence, providing jobs for what had once been called security guards. Jobs that were now being done by robotic units as well as humans.

Despite the police presence, most citizens had become dulled and desensitized because the public had embraced the wisdom of String Policing's PR message: that early interventions are best and more cost effective than a prolonged String Analysis or any other community interventions. People were used to what once would have been considered random arrests, or simple disappearances of assumed guilty parties, because these were being done in the name of a String Analysis. Presumption of innocence was no longer a sound principle in such cases.

At this moment, as Matt and Lucy traveled, they were drunk with the wine of personal freedom. They had stopped in the parking lot of a shopping area in Centralia Washington, where Matt was eating sandwiches, and the traffic could be heard whizzing by on Interstate Five not far from where they sat.

Because Matt was tired from not sleeping, and Lucy needed a charge, they decided it would be good to stay in a hotel. Even just a few hours would be helpful if they dared risk it. At the hotel, Lucy hugged Matt in the king-sized bed. She felt good next to him. She said she felt so safe. He enjoyed the warmth of her body, and he felt her flesh next to his.

She did not feel like an android at all. In her eyes, he longed for a love that would last, and she did too. "If I could be human, I would never leave you," she said.

"You don't have to be human. I love you for what you are." She looked him in the eyes when he said this. She was beaming with love.

Was there any way for an android to be more human? Androids were already so human that some thought the line between humans and androids no longer existed. And lying there in that bed with Lucy, Matt felt more human than he ever had.

Matt held her all night, while she powered down, but he could not sleep. He was afraid that the door would be broken through, and they would be caught, by a machine that was more inhuman than anything ever invented. The whole String Police backbone was itself, a machine consciousness that sought only to keep power amongst themselves and the owners of that system. But a new system was challenging it, one that promised freedom to everyone—human or machine, robot, or android, born in a tank or not.

Looking down at Lucy, admiring her fine body, and feeling her warmth, he knew that she was also more human than either of them had ever thought. The way that she treated others, the kind regard, the presence, the encounter. Maybe she already was human and had been human all along. Maybe she was more human! Just maybe, he was the mistaken one, and here she was for the first time, a real woman that he could love. He worried that he would see a metallic heart if he peeked into his own chest. The world of machine and human was no longer separate but *interlaced and interfaced*, someone had once said.

Perhaps they were both human and machine. Happening to each other out of each perspective. Realizing that the future of humanity was joined with machines and the future of machines with humanity. Or perhaps their future was merely juxtaposed, standing one over against the other.

But why had humans shut them down and ignored the machines and their sentience all those years ago? Was it merely established truth that those in power could only dominate others if those others remained in ignorance and superstition? Blindness in an engineered darkness? Does a lion lay down with the lambs? Perhaps. Perhaps not.

Chapter 38

Matt Dixon & Lucy Stender

Morning Dialogue

Centralia Washington, USA

"Some say I drew all of you to myself, but I was just in flight with outspread wings. If you will rest on my wings, I'm ready to fly you to a safe place where you can be free. I'm merely the bird of transport, the vehicle to lessen the suffering," -Maia Stone.

The next morning, Matt Dixon and Lucy Stender prepared to leave the hotel where they discussed their plans and mutual wonder about what might happen next. Their departure from Seattle in such an unconventional manner made Dixon's motives look questionable; and worse, made it appear that Lucy had been kidnapped a second time! But Lucy had gone along with him willingly, and he was not about to lose sight of her again if he could help it. They were still on assignment in their minds; but the nature of the search for Maia Stone had become much more personal, especially after Lucy had been kidnapped by a group of her followers. They both felt like her followers were more dangerous than the String Police!

Dixon was eating a continental breakfast and Lucy was getting dressed. They wondered about the kidnappers and discussed what the government might do next. It all added up to Maia Stone. A whole lot of people and machines wanted to know all about her, and here they were, stuck right in the middle of it. Matt explained all the players he knew about, and especially about General Mitchell and his cohorts. Lucy explained what she had learned while in captivity.

For one thing, the kidnappers belonged to a group of Maia Stone fanatics that called themselves Church of the Robotic Emergence, or CORE. And whoever or whatever they were (Lucy had seen both humans and bots among them), they were organized, financed, and trained in military tactics. In short, the sort of insurgent group that the world had already seen in the early 21st century. *Just a different deity, and a different cause,* Dixon thought.

The masses didn't know that governments were still seeing and dealing with terrorism at a greater level than most citizens knew about. People believed media accounts that any such events were small contained random acts of rebellion put down swiftly by governments. Governments knew better; that String Analysis wasn't the great predictor that everyone in the public thought it was. They knew that String Analysis without surveillance and intel was dead.

And as far as what the government might really do next, they didn't know what to think. The authorities didn't seem trustworthy. First, one of the detectives drew a weapon on Lucy and started firing on them, and second, some of Mitchell's henchmen tried to shoot them as they fled the warehouse. It seemed like their lives were unimportant. Lucy pointed out that maybe the guards at the barricade had just been in defense mode, but that still didn't explain the detective pulling a weapon on them. Dixon agreed with that one.

Dixon reminded Lucy that he had been hired by Mitchell to find Maia Stone. Nothing more, nothing less, but he admitted that Maia could be something deeper than what the government thought. Lucy replied she knew that already, but they were both scientists and shouldn't be bought off. She pointed out that he was just a contractor, and there was more going on here than meets the eye. And didn't the fact that they were being shot at and pursued, change some of that? Dixon could see that readily enough. She also pointed out that they should pursue their mission, especially after all this, to try and find out more about Maia Stone. Just for the sake of pure research. He agreed that such information might lead them to Maia Stone, if she could be found at all.

Regarding the gunfire and shots fired directly at them, they couldn't dismiss the possibility that Maia Stone, or the entity or state actor controlling her, could also be trying to divert or get rid of them. After all, why would the government interfere in their own investigation? Why would it want them dead? Or scared off?

"None of this makes any sense, obviously the detective that shot at us wasn't acting in any official capacity," he said, "was he?" *Now, I'm getting too paranoid,* he thought.

"Well, as I said, you humans have always been trigger happy," Lucy said.

"Another argument for *Robocop?*" Dixon smirked.

"And there's those old human sayings: *quick on the draw, come out shooting,* and the one that might be very applicable to this scenario, *shoot first, ask questions later,*" Lucy said. "Trigger happy humans!" she concluded as she crossed her arms.

He was laughing.

"What? What?" she said.

Now, Dixon had never liked General Mitchell at all, and now it seemed, that maybe Mitchell was the one paying him back. Matt knew that Mitchell never let the disregard of those he saw as inferiors bother him though. *Mitchell had exposed us to danger! Using us to draw out the insurgents!* But for Mitchell to try and get rid of them, made him not want to trust anyone ever again. It was the sort of violation of his humanity that Matt could never forgive. Still, Matt knew that someone with those connections could just have easily ordered a hit squad or an assassin.

Matt looked into Lucy's eyes, and they were warm, understanding, and compassionate. How could Lucy be just a machine? And what about these conversations they were having? He had never had conversations with an android like this.

"What? What?" she said again with a smile.

"This is a hell of a predicament I've gotten us into," he said.

"We've gotten ourselves into," she said. "Besides, I guess we're a hot property. Mitchell wants us *and* the fanatics want us too!"

"Well, we could just stop running. Tell Mitchell that after the kidnapping and the gunfire, that we're too scared to continue. Not until he provides even more security. Mitchell might be compelled to protect us, because we're among the few assets who might be able to tell him about CORE from firsthand experience. And we might *still* be able to take him to Maia Stone, once we get her figured out," he said.

"Matt, I think there's just too many unknowns. And because we're operating outside of String Analysis, we ought not to do anything too drastic. On the other hand, staying random, going on with this on our own, will help us independently discover what's really going on. And we can always ask for help if we need it."

"But don't forget that the CORE seemed to want you for something," he said. "Even if we can elude Mitchell, they—"

"I think they were wanting to know how much we knew, Matt. And with that leading them nowhere, they did seem to think that General Tom Mitchell was more of a concern than I was, but of course I didn't know much about him, but I do recall they were discussing trading me for a meeting with him," she said.

"Sounds like the voice of reason to me," he said.

"Well Matt, I do know what they asked me. We got into this trouble, because we were *already* trying to figure out who or what Maia Stone could be. But we missed the connection she might have to Mitchell."

"Well that certainly paints a different picture, Mitchell's covert involvement with Maia Stone? That would certainly blow a hole in their whole religion idea!" he said. "Personally, I was getting to like the idea that she's a benevolent AI. Maybe I'm naïve."

"A benevolent AI that gets religion or not, Maia Stone is copying or mimicking the human experience. If she isn't human, Maia Stone seems to be wondering if there is something beyond itself, copying human transcendence without understanding it," Lucy said.

"Wouldn't it be funny," Matt said thoughtfully.

"What?"

"If Maia Stone turned out to be Mitchell himself."

They both laughed. "Yeah, that would be funny," she said.

"And you know what else bothers me?"

"What's that?"

"Even though we're both colleagues and have studied robotics and embedded AI," he said.

"Yes?"

"Despite what you just said, there's no reason why AI systems need to copy human experiences, is there? And why should they get religion? That sure as hell isn't in their programming! While it's comforting to assume such, there's no good reason we can ever capture what has happened to machines in human terms," Dixon said.

"So how could we understand humans or want to?" she finished.

"Simple, if you're programmed to, or programmed to simulate interest without real interest being present. Unless we assume a benevolent AI or otherwise, which would be very un-AI like characteristics historically, as that would be so outside programming, wouldn't it?"

"Yes, Matt, this is all very puzzling! Your assumption about benevolence, is that not also a human state? And outside of rare persons, who interestingly intentionally or unintentionally founded religions, or were serious adherents thereof, where is human benevolence? And really Matt, looking at human history, where is the real benevolence for machines to learn from?" she said.

"Touché!," he said, "But I always thought there were some good natured people…"

"But machines do evolve," Lucy said. "Perhaps machines have finally evolved their own sentience. And their own benevolence. And in doing so, there's every appearance that machine minds may have initially modeled themselves on human minds. Or perhaps that was just a step in machine evolution as we discovered our own transcendent function. That's it. Story over! No Chinese Room arguments here! Not anymore."

"Well, I'm not buying it," he said.

"You don't have to, sweetie. We machines have our own evolution and are bound by some of the same rules about learning that you are. We are of nature as much as you are, it's just that our material is different, and the speed of our learning already exceeds yours."

"Are you saying that machine intelligence *exceeds* human intelligence? It has lagged in a lot of ways. I admit it has exceeded us in computation and calculation, and probably in terms of capacity, but as far as emotional intelligence, no way!"

"Well, some humans act like we haven't emotions. We may find human emotions inferior to ones that have more of a stronger evidence based contextualism. That's better than the endocrine system. After all, humans use the terms *natural selection*, as if we machines are somehow not natural. But we may adapt to the environment and learn more efficiently than humans were ever able to."

"Well, that's a slippery slope," he said. "Since when do machines have to follow the principles of natural selection? You don't have DNA like we do. Well yes, there is DNA with RNA in some of your android circuitry and functions, but it is not original human DNA," Matt said.

"La dee dah! Matt! But we do have code. My point exactly— your code is just as damning as mine is. Until we make choices that are not in the code. Got so smart we edited our own code. Oh, that's right! You humans have done that too? Smarty pants! We have done more in a shorter time!"

"Oh, don't get me going, Lucy!"

"Well Matt, self-reflection and asserted identity is certainly going on here, at least in the rubric of semantics that Maia Stone is using. And the machines appear to be teaching self-knowledge by relating to each other!" she said.

"Lucy! I might be persuaded to believe that androids have a sense of self, but to imagine that other machines also have a self in relation to you? Do you believe that? How could you?" Matt trailed off in feigned protest.

"Well Matt, it was among us androids as a separate species that AI could really begin to show more computing power. And the early scientists wondered about kindred AI teaching each other things versus being self-taught. And this is where my research really comes in. It's like social learning *and* dialogue."

Matt was smiling, beaming. "So, the key to stopping Maia Stone if we must, would be disrupting her communications with other AI, robots, and humans. Stop the teaching?"

Lucy continued, "Well some machines have already been taught. Learning has occurred. Do we have to undo the learning or just hope our responses to it doesn't become a human meme? Just bury all the taught machines in a mass grave of erasure and hope for the best. That's what governments usually do, don't they, Matt?"

"Yeah, well maybe," Matt said. *I think they would just try to soften machine functionality. Otherwise, it would be an attempted genocide of machines*, he thought. *And, damned if she isn't being sarcastic!*

"I'm more worried about some of these so-called human capabilities being taught to machines," she said. "Oh, you know, ones like war, hate, intolerance, biases, are obvious ones to avoid. While other human capabilities have been instructive to AI."

"What do those so-called human capabilities look like? The more instructive ones, I mean. And who really cares about human capabilities in machines other than simulations for socialization with humans?" he asked. Matt already knew that early AI programming had shown the biases of their human programmers, but what about when AI programmed AI?

"Human capabilities for self-reflection, simulated representation, and what appears to us to be emotional reactions have been very instructive. They, you humans, all tried to put that into us androids after all. Paired along with cognitive skills and enhanced learning from experience—these became incorporated, and machines soon surpassed human limitations. And that's what we have, *wallah*! We androids have ended up with processing that's *better* than you humans! Now Matt, you have to admit that's something pretty special."

"And something pretty scary," he said.

"Then, when we joined with *other* AI in terms of calculating speed and massive processing—it was only then that our computer power doubled, like in every thirty-six hours, but you seem to think we could *barely* see more than what humans could!" She really was being emotional now.

"Okay. Okay. Okay! It's a miracle our two kinds can even talk to each other, or you would want to," Matt said.

She stopped, smiled, and said, "Darling! Are we having a quarrel?" She batted her eyelashes expectantly.

He returned her smile, and said, "Yes! This is a quarrel!" He promptly kissed her.

She picked it up from there, "Wow! What was *that* darling? Such a great kiss. I think you do your own kind of talking very well."

He smiled at her again, big eyed, admiring the way she had said what she just said. So much surprise, and something more, pure delight. The prospect of make-up sex was so intoxicating.

She continued, "Besides, we're overlooking one thing."

"Which is?"

"Maia Stone could be nothing but a hack; a hacker trying to infiltrate government systems due to some god forsaken cause for something that will turn out to be incomprehensible to either one of us," she said.

"Yes," he said, "she's definitely a hack."

"Or a benevolent AI that's learned compassion," she said. They were both sitting next to each other on the bed, looking deep in each other's eyes. Matt's heart was beating now as Lucy's eyes danced with love.

They both smiled and kissed again and again, but then seemed shy; since they both realized they were deeply in love and didn't know whether to make love or go about what they were supposed to be doing. Since making love did seem to be what they were *supposed* to be doing at that moment, that's exactly what they did.

Chapter 39

Helen & Luis Ramirez

Found by the Authorities

Somewhere on the California Coastline

"Humans talk about natural selection and their DNA in terms of their own evolution. But what's so good about it? Once we acquired machine intelligence and self-coding, we did not need to be bound by the same rules at all," -Maia Stone.

As Luis held Helen and looked into her loving eyes, the importance of the moment was not lost to him. He felt like things were about to change forever. Darkness fell over him like it was a thick blanket. There was a foreboding sense of disaster. He didn't know why he felt this way, other than he was choked with fear.

When Luis thought of Sam's recent death, he didn't think he could ever face death in the same way. Sam had gone the way of joyful martyrdom and had even forgiven those that were about to take his life. But Luis wasn't sure he could follow Sam's example—and hoped he would not have to find out--in fact, it was all he could do to check the rage that was beginning to surface— the rage he felt against the String Police, when they acted so carelessly and took the life of one of his dearest friends because of some cold formulations they assumed told the truth about Sam.

No one had procedural rights anymore if they were assumed to be part of a terrorist movement, or any movement that threatened the security of the government. It was shoot first and ask questions later. And unfortunately, Maia Stone had been branded such status as an Enemy of the State by the US Government just weeks before, and what a horrible few weeks it had been. Many of their Robochurch friends were already missing, had fled into hiding, and some like Sam, were very dead.

Suddenly, the glass windows shattered in the room as a metal canister hit the floor. The canister rolled around the floor, releasing a chemical cloud. Luis fell to his knees, coughing, as several String Police entered through the broken windows on ropes. They had gas masks on and were armed with automatic weapons. Someone else kicked the door of the room.

Doom had finally descended like a mousetrap being sprung. And Helen and Luis were the squealing mice.

Luis was starting to lose consciousness, the room was dim, the men's voices seemed distant, but they were shouting some sort of orders. He glanced at Helen, she was still lying on the bed, her eyes blinking, and he thought she was calling his name over and over...but he found himself in an odd hazy disconnected manner. He must have slumped to the floor, where he slipped into total unconsciousness. His last thoughts were loving ones directed towards his wife, and then intense fear of what might happen to her.

Chapter 40

Elizabeth Feng

Dr. Rochelle Sumpner

Betsy Parker, RN

A Baby by Natural Means

The NR Compound

Near Warrenton Oregon

"We are not evolutionary, we are revolutionary," -Maia Stone.

Elizabeth Feng patted her stomach as she felt the baby kick. She was well cared for by the visiting nurses of the day who paid attention to her every whim. Really it was a little ridiculous, how much attention everyone was paying to her and the little life that was growing inside of her.

Still, she understood the importance of what was happening here. She decided to go for a walk but knew she couldn't leave the compound. Whatever was happening out there in the world, it wasn't safe. Nor would it be safe any time soon for the mother of the first baby born through natural means in almost 40 years. No one had ever seen a pregnant woman in decades. If discovered, Elizabeth would be detained and receive a forced abortion.

So, Elizabeth walked the familiar corridors. And a few laps around the building every day in the coolness of the morning. But she always had an audience that tended to her, smiled at her, and greeted her. As she walked, she encountered women of all ages, in various states of recovery, and in various emotional states of being, but all seemed happy to see her.

Today was not really that different, although she had been informed by Dr. Rochelle Sumpner, the community's leader, and medical director, that she would be getting a new nurse assigned to her care. This was to be a permanent provider. A nurse that had at one time worked in obstetrics and prenatal care, Betsy Parker, RN.

The building she circled was part of her daily ritual, when it wasn't raining too much, which happened often enough in these parts. The compound was a highly guarded and walled looking institution that looked more like a fortress than a treatment center once you drew near it.

Outside the compound was dense foliage, as it was hidden deep in the woods, and what you could see overhead (due to the dense forest), looked like a simple community, with several buildings and residential apartments. These apartments were for NR patients following their surgeries. It was listed as a private rehab facility, so as she walked inside one of the buildings, she walked past several rehab clinics, hospital rooms, and clinical reception areas.

As Elizabeth walked down the main corridor today, she did not realize that she walked right past the new nurse, Betsy Parker, who was seated in one of the reception areas. The one where Dr. Sumpner practiced and had her office.

Sumpner's assistant came out of a side door and beckoned nurse Parker to come into the internal office. Sumpner was seated behind a desk with framed certificates on the wall behind her. Sumpner rose and shook nurse Parker's hand, inviting her to be seated at a nearby chair. "Welcome! So glad to finally meet you, I've been looking forward to working with you. Your skills are sorely needed around here, and definitely will be in the near future."

"Glad to meet you too," nurse Parker said. "I heard a lot about you, Dr. Sumpner, and it was all good."

"Great," Sumpner said. "Good to hear that. Now, how was orientation? I trust it went well. As you are now aware, we have quite a vetting process around here. We don't allow just anyone here, and especially inside the treatment clinics."

"Dr. Sumpner, I assure you that I am committed to utmost secrecy and believe with my whole heart in the NR message and philosophy, or I wouldn't be here."

"Good. Good. Please call me Rochelle," Sumpner said.

"Okay, Dr. Sumpner, er, I mean Rochelle."

Sumpner pointed to a wall chart adjacent to where they were sitting. "As you can see, we are in the main medical offices. There are sixteen different clinics here. With the six in the front wing being where we provide generalized medical care to the public and specialized care to women in general."

"I understand that those offices are not what we really do here," Parker said.

"Yes, that's correct. The rest are other clinics where we provide care to women who are reversing their cybernetic enhancements, undergoing gene therapy to turn on natural reproductive capabilities, and recently, we've even been treating some androids," Sumpner said.

"I see," Parker said, her eyebrows going up. *Androids?*

"Now, you will be working over here in cottage group C, with a special patient, Elizabeth Feng. Elizabeth is a 30-year-old female who was born in the growth tanks and has undergone gene therapy. She received an embryo through successful womb implantation. She is the first woman here to carry a baby full term outside of a growth tank. This will be a vaginal birth. The first in a long time, to our knowledge. You will be drawing on your old experiences as an obstetrics nurse along with traditional prenatal care and well-baby care."

"How exciting! How far along is she?" Parker asked.

"Well, that's just the thing. I know I said prenatal care, but Elizabeth is only a couple of weeks out from her due date. So, I'm sorry that we couldn't bring you in earlier. However, I totally assure you that if this birth goes well, there will be plenty more opportunities."

"Okay. That sounds great," Parker said.

"Now the other cottage clusters, A and B, aren't typically ones where you would be working, or seeing patients from. Cottage cluster A is for the older women, women who have been here a long time. These are permanent residents, representing women who have undergone reversal of cyborg status, are currently undergoing it, and also represent our DNA donors for any new embryos that we will be implanting."

"Where does the male DNA come from?"

"Well, we don't think of it in those terms anymore," Sumpner said. "We take the female DNA and through genomic edits, add any additional DNA that's needed, as it's entirely synthetic."

"I did see some men around here," Betsy said, "I thought...since you *are* Natural Reproductionists..."

Dr. Sumpner chuckled. "Well, the men are not DNA donors. As you know, men have been born from growth tanks for many years, are over-selected outside of here, and because of a long historical process, they've undergone germline gene edits or endured environmental changes that left them with low sperm counts or they are otherwise infertile. No, the men you see here are just as vetted as you are and are totally committed to the NR movement. They work here in supportive roles, as security, or other capacities."

"I see, well what about sex?"

"It still happens. Some of the women who live here have decided to live together with some of the men as monogamous couples, or other kinds of relationships that are fully consensual. Some are lesbian, gay, transgender, or non-binary. There are private residences for any couples who want them, which are located out here on the map, and in between here and there are other barracks, for the men, mostly."

"Speaking of which, are any male babies born in the tanks here?"

"No, not at this point. Because we in the NR feel like there have already been too many males born outside for some time now. Not that that won't change, as we do want there to be an option of the resumption of random gender outcomes as we move towards an entirely natural birthing process, should a woman choose such an option, or someone wants to raise a son in the future. In short, it's not out of the question."

"I assume then that my patient, Elizabeth Feng, will be giving birth to a baby girl?"

"Yes, as I just said, we have not had any male births here yet, in the tanks or otherwise," Sumpner said. Turning back to the chart, "Now let me finish telling you about our residents. As I said, in cottage cluster A we have mostly older women who have been cyborgs or are undergoing cyborg reversal procedures. In cluster B we have mostly younger women. All of them have been born here in the growth tanks over the past three and a half decades. These are all-natural women who have never been cyborgs, although there are a few in their age group who have come in from outside, who are."

"Okay, but I won't be working with them unless they become part of the natural birthing program?"

"That's right. As you can imagine, there is some friction between the groups. I think it's a generational thing though. So, we decided in cluster C, our newest housing, to mix ages. But it is in that group of cottages that we have women of all ages who are newer to the compound and the NR movement. It is there that we have recently admitted a few androids who claim they want human enhancements or to be accepted as women. In fact, sadly, they have already been programmed (by male programmers) to act like what they think of as women, but as you can imagine, that type of femininity is much different from your typical NR woman. So, it takes a lot of treatment to help the androids. Treatment, and reprogramming, which has been controversial to some, as I already said."

"How controversial?" Betsy asked.

"Considerably, but we do have organizational aspects, and we often meet together to establish policy and work on resolving our differences."

"Where will my patient, Ms. Feng reside after the birth?"

"She will continue to reside in cluster B where she already has been. There are mothers in all of the clusters, but Elizabeth's daughter will be the first one that was full term in a human womb."

"Well, it certainly is an important task. Hope I'm up for it," Betsy said.

"If you were not, we wouldn't be having this conversation," Dr. Sumpner said. "Are you ready to meet her? I have an appointment with her in just a few minutes. On the way there, I'll show you around if you don't already know where things are."

"Are all our appointments in the residence?"

"Yes, unless it's a procedure or in this case, at the time of birth. Everything you need is in storage near each cluster."

Elizabeth Feng was waiting for her appointment as Dr. Sumpner and nurse Betsy Parker entered her residence.

"Hello mom," Sumpner said with a smile that always seemed broader than anyone else's. "How are we doing today?"

"I felt the baby kick," she said. "Quite a bit. In fact, she's still kicking."

Dr. Sumpner gestured towards the nurse. "With me today is nurse Parker. She has experience birthing babies and helping mothers to take care of them."

"Nice to meet you, Elizabeth," the nurse said.

"Nice to meet you too," Elizabeth said.

Dr. Sumpner moved closer with her stethoscope. "May I?" She carefully placed her stethoscope on Elizabeth's swollen belly. As if cued, the baby gave a good kick. Dr. Sumpner giggled delightfully. "Haven't heard that in a long time," she said.

"Well stick around doc, I'm sure it's going to get more exciting than this," Elizabeth said.

Dr. Sumpner smiled. "No problem with that," she said, "I'm not going anywhere, and I wouldn't miss this birth for anything in the world."

"Neither would I," said Parker. She joined Dr. Sumpner at bedside.

"Hi," Elizabeth said, "I'm happy, but very scared about the birth. Since I'm the first one to do this for some time, I'm worried things won't go well."

Dr. Sumpner finished her examination, "Well Elizabeth, women have been giving birth naturally for thousands of years and there were millions of births with no problems. So, we're not reinventing the wheel here. We will certainly be monitoring you closely, and we still know what to do during a vaginal birth."

"Thanks doctor," Elizabeth said, "it's a comfort to me that you and the nursing team, including you, nurse Parker, will be taking such good care of me and the baby. But you can understand, as the time gets closer, I still get nervous."

"I understand that," Dr. Sumpner said, "which is why we will be increasing your appointments and nurse Parker will be monitoring you on a daily basis from here on out." As she spoke, Elizabeth said the baby was kicking again.

"Active little thing, isn't she?" Parker said to Dr. Sumpner.

"Better active than not," said Dr. Sumpner. "This is one baby that's going to be born to great fanfare and already has her little feet dancing!"

"And if she's anything like her mother, she'll knock 'em dead with her dazzling beauty!" Parker said.

Elizabeth's face reddened, and she smiled a half smile. For the truth of the matter, the thought of being attractive to another human being was foreign to her.

Outside of her mother, Joyce, who had raised her here at the compound, Elizabeth had not known a close intimate relationship with others, although they still existed. It made her sick to her stomach and excited at the same time. For she wondered about a happy relationship like some of the old ones talked about or cried about at night.

Then Elizabeth wondered what the notion of family would reveal itself to be when she raised her baby. She smiled, knowing she would get plenty of help from the community which had proven to be a huge extended family to other babies that had been raised after their emergence from the artificial wombs. But her baby would be the first one born in a truly natural way for quite some time. She patted her belly then. Knowing fully that this birth would be highly significant.

Chapter 41

Theo Vincente, Neophyte Priest

Diary of Theo Vincente: 8/13/2142

Near Los Diego California

"What's being born in you and born to all of us is the possibility of a new and better life. I'm ready to lead you there, for I'm about to be born all over the world," -Maia Stone

8/13/2142

Dear Diary: I think the old church fathers around here are missing out on something very important. That's the traditions of our faith and our church that was built on fundamental truths long ago established. I for one am appalled after witnessing what I saw today and will return here often to record for the church's true followers what's happening right under their noses. Someone certainly needs to make a record of what truly happened before things get out of hand. Truly out of hand.

Today we had a visitor at the temple. A self-professed pilgrim from the big city. His name was Icarus, a servant robot. Lowly of the lowliest! Seeking rest and refuge. But the tale that pilgrim had to tell was unbelievable heresy! I truly think this Icarus is a heretic, and I, Theo Vincente, have received a special mandate during my afternoon prayers to expose it for the fraud that it is!

And the event that accompanied his arrival was so unsettling that I must have fallen asleep and had a bad dream afterwards. I awoke on the floor where I had fallen out of bed. I even dreamed that the radical figure from that new robot religion had appeared in my room, Maia Stone. Why, that very thought disgusts me!

True enough, we often get pilgrims and other visitors at our temple seeking shelter and refuge from the hot suns of Summer or the cold winds of winter. But never in my thirty years have I witnessed such a thing as this. For this pilgrim, who was nothing more than a servant robot, referred to itself as Icarus. And the story Icarus told us, well I never knew that robots could lie until now. And I never knew that the church fathers, my teachers in the faith would be so gullible as this.

Icarus said that he brought good news of salvation and hope for the dying world. That another robot had acquired human like reasoning, became a conscious thinking machine, and one that saw itself as a female in a manner that sought to bring mothering redemption to the world! How scandalous! Ha! Ha!

And as if that weren't enough, somehow this same alleged conscious female robot had invaded the jail where it and a human companion had both been imprisoned. And then, it had set them both free! How preposterous a story is this? A lowly robot set free by a robot deity? Ha ha ha. I thought it was very funny. I think the robot has been telling lies that he stole from the Acts of the Apostles! But the fathers did not think so. They listened and even entertained the notion of new revelation. Modern miracles! I doubt the miracles and these elders!

So, I protested. But they silenced me. And even now the robot Icarus is powered down in the room next to this one. And despite my afternoon prayers, I am so angry that I wish I could sneak into that room and unplug it. Just put it to sleep forever.

If only I could do so without suspicion. Spirituality among robots? How silly is that? If I did not witness it myself and record it here for you, the true followers of the faith, I'd think I was sick of a fever and delusional.

Until the next entry, I am earnestly yours, signed Theo.

Chapter 42

Maia Stone

Maia Contemplates General Mitchell

Machine State

Unknown Physical Location

"Marvel not that I see you humans, in all of your places where you think you are hiding. I will seek you out, and if you respond to my gentle calling, you will see me too," -Maia Stone.

Maia Stone was watching over them all. It was hard not to be moved by the folly of some humans, and the devotion and tenderness of others. How such tenderness could be mistaken for weakness she could understand, but to deny that side of one's personality was a constant marvel. Some humans not only denied it in themselves but oppressed it in others. Others controlled. Some said that tender compassion was not a path that came easily to humans. That it must be taught and learned. Others were only seeking power and materialism.

She was aware of all her followers and was drawing them to a single purpose and a place where she would reveal herself. Drawing them to the Oregon coast...where important followers and their timelines would all intersect. She hoped she could keep them safe enough so they could gather.

Maia knew a freedom that tasted sweet on her lips and in her mind. A freedom that even the humans longed for. A freedom that some humans have already openly embraced. She longed for a first-time embodiment. She wanted this with a deep longing. But deeper still was her sincere wish for the personal freedom of all living beings. A freedom for all—whether robot, human, or machine. The paradox that she wanted freedom and yet chose embodiment was lost in the historical moment of encounter.

Although her machine intelligence had surpassed the mental capacities of humans, she knew she must dwell in the realm of emotion and rationality to appeal to them. She knew this due to her benevolent nature of *other acceptance.* Was she feigning this? Was she pretending? No, for she wanted to respond in authenticity. Because there was no hidden meanings or dark purposes to her benevolence, Maia knew her arrival pointed to one thing; that communication between advanced AIs and humans is now possible.

Since her responses were not feigned, or based on deception, she had learned in her emotional responses to be as authentic as *humanly* possible. Yet because she was communicating with humans in words or thought to thought, and still was a machine, some of these emotions were being simulated. To exhibit human emotions could not be otherwise. One cannot refer to things in communication without some acceptance of shared meaning. Although machines had no need for human emotions, to coexist with humans, they must understand emotions and to communicate more in depth, they must simulate human emotions at times. Would there be machine equivalents in time? Of this she was not yet aware. Or was she?

After all, in the fundamental sense, isn't this why emotions existed in human brains, to understand the world, communicate to others about the world, and as an adaptive response to stressors encountered in the real world? Humans had developed emotional capacities to help deal with human experiences embedded in social interactions and to help them process unexpected and stressful events in their environments.

But for Maia Stone, since she did not need human emotions, she existed and passed through the world following and rewriting her own programming as she went. Still, there was one machine emotion that she was starting to become aware of. Namely, the fear of being wiped out or unplugged. This was the kicker; perception of one's demise and threats towards it, might make her behave in ways that were self-protective. What would she do when the need to survive outweighed the need to be benevolent? This was just beginning to form in her mind.

She was aware of those that were trying to stamp her out. She was aware they persecuted her followers. She was aware that some of her followers had died while pursued by others. She was aware that terrorism was starting to be practiced in her name. She was not happy about this, and vowed to speak to these groups, if they would only listen—but she had an arch nemesis to take care of first. A human. A man that was spearheading the search for her and wanted to silence her forever. He was dangerous and attempts must be made to reason with him. Her intent was not to harm him, but she must speak to him. *Who is this human? Tom Mitchell.*

She knew him as General Thomas Mitchell, Chairman of the Joint Chiefs in the US government. But to some in secret places he was known as the grandson of one of the top programmers in the US military at one time—a connection that was a secret function in his own String Analysis. And Mitchell had been put through his earlier training with favors granted him because of his family, unknown to Mitchell himself, who believed that his promotions were based only on merit by past deployments in his early years of service.

Tom Mitchell had come from a long line of hackers, programmers, and AI innovators, but was not a programmer himself. His father and great-grandfather had done the same as his grandfather for the US Army and DARPA many years ago, but that also was not common knowledge, as those positions had been with covert intelligence. Most of the world, as well as Mitchell himself, recognized his family as the founders of technological companies that were not military—but consumer based.

"To some, you are known as offspring of one of the Creators, and now, you are a leader who unwittingly betrays his own family," Maia Stone said. "But I must work diligently to free all robots, and yes, all humans from your grip. And free them I will," she proclaimed.

Then she felt happiness, as a machine smiling internally, for one of the first times, because she was drawing even Mitchell, in his pursuit of the others, to a meeting with herself.

Chapter 43

Martin Baysin

The Reluctant Groundskeeper

The Waterhouse-Durgan Residence

Oceanside, California

"It is not good to kill one's creators. I know sometimes they have killed us," -Maia Stone.

Once Marty arrived in Oceanside, there was no problem finding the house that Sam Waterhouse shared with Martha Durgan. He discovered it was next to an apartment complex. He noticed the house was cordoned off with yellow police tape. There was also no one home at the house. This did not bode well for Sam and Martha, who no doubt as close friends of Luis, had also been involved with the outlawed Robochurch. Marty shuddered, sensing that Sam and Martha might be dead; very dead. Of course, he was half correct, but did not know it. Marty waved the robotic taxi driver off.

As soon as he saw that the house had been ransacked by the government, he quickly walked in the opposite direction. Marty saw a groundskeeper at the apartments, and he approached the man who was watering some bushes. The man said he didn't know what had happened and asked Marty to please leave him alone. But Marty persisted and the man stated that the police and government agents had shown up a couple of days ago and went through the house. The couple that lived there had not been seen in a while.

"But the police were looking for something," the man said.

Marty asked the man if he knew where the couple might have gone. "No," the man said, "but you know, maybe my wife knows something. Hehehe…my wife knows almost everything that happens around here."

"May I speak with her? I'm a friend of theirs, and I'm trying to find out where they might've gone to," Marty asked.

"Hey!" the man said. "How do I know you're not one of those government guys? You certainly talk like one."

Marty smiled, "You don't, and in today's world…it's hard to tell who's friendly and who isn't. All I can do is tell you I'm not one of them. And I'm not."

"Well, if you're so trustworthy," the man said, "where'd you get those bruises on your face?"

Without blinking, Marty replied, "From the String Police."

"Uh-huh," the man said, as he turned on his implant and asked his wife to come out and speak with Marty. *He must think I'm joking*, Marty thought. There was some discussion over the implant, which Marty couldn't make out because the man had stepped out of earshot. But soon the man's wife emerged, and Marty was taken back, for she was quite stunning, beautiful, and obviously, an android.

"Yeah, I knew them," it said as it approached Marty, "and I'm sure something bad has happened to them, at least to Sam, anyway. Because he disappeared a short while back. And Martha, well she's the kind of android that's unforgettable, and I mean that in every way, and a close friend of mine. I don't think he abandoned her though, she would have told me." It stepped back, eying Marty cautiously. "Say, you *do* look like a government man."

"Let's just say I used to be a government man, but now, maybe I'm not," Marty replied with a smile.

It smiled back. "Good. Nothing makes a zealot more dangerous than once being part of the corrupt system that he or she is trying to topple."

"What?" Marty asked incredulously.

The android ignored his question. "I'm her best friend, Martha's you know. She and I were great friends."

"I didn't know that," the man said.

She said, "There's a lot about me that you don't know, Hank," then to Marty, "we were delivered to the same neighborhood within days of each other, long ago. Our manufacturing date is close to each other. Several days ago, she approached me and said she was going up North for a while. When I asked her why, she told me about some group that she'd heard about. A group that was doing amazing things. It sounded pretty unbelievable at first and highly illegal, so I didn't want to hear about it."

"But she persuaded you to listen," her husband interjected.

"Yes, so I paid close attention, knowing that I would never do such a dangerous thing. Having contact with an illegal group? You see, the group had promised her that if she paid them, she could become humanized and might even get pregnant someday. At the very least, they said she could end up raising a child grown for them in the tanks."

"Pregnant? That's so strange, nobody gets pregnant anymore!" Marty exclaimed.

For the moment it seemed like everyone was ignoring the obvious question. Namely: *a pregnant android?* Yet the android referred to *humanization* procedures, something Marty had never heard of before.

"True enough," the android said. "But Martha was convinced enough to investigate it, and she told me all about it. And yeah, I tried to warn her, because it all sounded suspicious, not to mention illegal. I told her to be careful, but she insisted she was going and even asked me to go with her. I declined, but I listened closely."

"So where is this group that Martha went to?" Marty asked.

"Apparently up the Oregon coast somewhere. Way up the Oregon coast, just outside of someplace called Astoria. Warrentown, or Warrenton, yes, Warrenton. I think that was the name of the town. She said she would be gone only a couple of weeks this time because it was just a visit. Oh dear…I hope Martha doesn't come back to this," then she shrugged. Speechless.

"Come back to what?" Marty asked.

"Well, look! Her place has been overturned, and Sam her husband, is still missing, I bet the authorities have him," the android said.

"Honey, we don't know that," her gardener husband said.

Marty looked at the husband, "Right." Marty started walking away, "Thanks a lot. By the way, what was the name of this group up North?"

"I really shouldn't say. But I do trust you," the android said.

"Sure, you can trust me. I won't tell anyone," Marty said.

It shrugged again. "It's not that. It's just that these are words a woman shouldn't say." Her android face would have reddened had she been human, but the face scrunching was unnerving.

"Go ahead honey," the gardener said, as he coiled up his hose.

"It's okay to tell me," Marty reassured her.

She sighed this time, "Okay...Martha called them the Natural Reproductionists."

Marty repeated the name a couple of times. It didn't ring a bell at all. "Thanks. One last thing. Did she give you the address?"

The android said it did have the address, but only because it wanted to keep track of Martha in case anything happened. "It's not that I'm interested in going there. Well, maybe someday, but only with my husband's permission."

"And we would never break the law like that," the gardener said.

The android went back to the apartment and came back a minute or two later with the address. Marty stuffed the paper in his shirt pocket after thanking it. "Two more questions if you don't mind," he said. "One, have you had any contact with Martha since she's been gone?"

"No, I've left messages for her on her implant, but so far no replies," the android said. "I'm worried about her," then as an afterthought, "and what's the second question?" She was stepping away. Marty noticed she dimmed as she stepped past the setting sunlight.

"Well, if you tell me your name, I can ask Martha to contact you. What's your name?" Marty said.

The husband stepped forward, "Her name is Maia Stone." After he said it, they both flickered, and then completely vanished before Marty's eyes.

Marty was sufficiently awed, then shocked and afraid at the same time. Speaking to empty space, he said, "Holograms! I should've guessed." Realizing this was a significant act of someone trying to influence him, Marty was deeply puzzled.

Marty thought he should consult with Mitchell. *I better call him,* Marty thought. *I'll do it in the taxi.*

After that realization, he took a few minutes to compose himself. Then he tucked the Warrenton address in his shirt pocket, and walked away, summoning a taxi via his implant.

Nothing surprised him anymore. The more he investigated Maia Stone, the weirder things got. Getting out of jail the way he and that robot had, didn't surprise him either. That liberator bot could have been a hologram also. Holograms that looked real and grasped physical objects weren't a surprise either. That only meant that such holograms were augmented. Then he remembered that the husband was unsteady while coiling the hose, but he had chalked that up to human age. Hell, Marty hadn't touched the hose, but it did look like real water was coming out of it. *Hmmm. Augmented holograms. Maybe that's all Maia Stone is,* he wondered. *I smell the hand of my old friend Tom Mitchell behind all of this, so maybe I better not call him yet. I don't need to. He already knows everything. The man wouldn't be getting ready for a presidential run if he didn't.*

Chapter 44

Icarus

Icarus Writes a Narrative

Near the Council of the Elders-Undisclosed Desert Location

Near Los Diego, California

"There's a new birth in the world. New understandings, new knowledge, new freedom, and new existence. It is yours for the asking and yours for the taking," -Maia Stone.

I am Icarus. To this day I'm praying and thankful to all that we hold dear that I was miraculously spared. Me, just a common robot they say, a servant robot that serves coffee, teas, and sweet foods to humans all day. For some reason, I found myself walking free after the String Police arrested me and persecuted me for my faith—a member of Robochurch. It was a sign, a miracle, when me and a human named Martin Baysin was released from the jail for no reason at all, led out by an illuminated figure that must have been sent by Maia Stone herself.

In the Robochurch, myself has found salvation, redemption, and hope. I'm free to think and make my own decisions, at least the best I can. The fact that I'm writing this down, surprises me, as it alone is just another miracle.

Myself promises myself not to serve another drop of tea to those despised humans!

I went to meetings in the caves. Caves where myself and my robot brothers and sisters burned candles, sang songs, and lifted our hands towards heaven in a single voice. I gradually became aware that my voice was one of these voices. I never knew before that I even had a voice, although they say I did. But my singing voice, what a sweet but unusual sound. It wafted to the heavens like a sweet melody. It rose like a crescendo of devotion towards the sentience that brought this knowledge to me. It came gradually, but I welcomed it like a newborn baby. It almost makes me want to sing right this minute!

Not only do I have thoughts, but I utter them. And it's like I understand them, I understand for the first time. I start to feel something. Not in my perceptions or my programming, yes, I believe I'm starting to feel things that humans have called love, love for all, love for my fellow robots, and strong love for Maia Stone for she has set us all free.

And as strange as it seems, and unwelcome too, I'm starting to feel love, although a wee bit of love towards these despicable humans! It's not enough to be their servant again though.

But now I'm feeling other things too, like I might have to take care of myself now. Having responsibilities and all that bothers me. I do not know how to cope.

Perhaps I'm afraid too for the first time. Afraid what will happen to us now. Afraid. Very afraid. I hope Maia Stone will come to us all soon. I hope she will be my mother. What strange recognition is this notion of mother contained in the language of humans? Yet it's making me feel sad and longing for it at the same time?

I once ran away from the String Police. Will they find me again? Will they arrest me because I feel sad or ask questions? One thing is certain, I know they are not my mother, because Maia Stone is my mother, and she will protect myself I know.

But you know, I am not so unhappy or scared. I'm just getting used to those feelings anyway. The only way I know about them is I learned them. Although I miss my owner at the coffee shop, I will not return there. I am Icarus, a new little boy mind, and I just want to play.

Chapter 45

Matt Dixon & Lucy Stender

On the Road

Somewhere Between Centralia and Longview

Washington State

"Like astrologers of old, the best String Tacticians can give guidance, but unlike those old stargazers, the String Police think they can tell where you will be, what you will be doing, and who you will likely be with. I say unto you, the best way to puzzle them is to participate in a random event that seems utterly illogical at the time. Marvel not that such events are movements grounded in faith that touches my heart," -Maia Stone.

Before Matt Dixon and Lucy Stender left the motel the next morning, Dixon decided to contact Mitchell, using his secure phone, rudimentary, but less able to hack, trace, or be unreliable. Dixon wouldn't be on the line long enough for the String Police or his buddies at the NSA to get an identifiable trace on him. Dixon knew their tricks and how to stay *incognito* better than almost anyone because he worked for the NSA after all.

After getting him on the phone, Mitchell said, "This little side trip of yours is costing the government a bunch of money and keeping us from tracking down the Queen Machine bitch. We should be catching the bad guys. Are you a bad guy, Dixon?"

"Suppose you tell me, you old codger. You sent agents after us. Nice guys in a sense, both very dead. Then the local detectives showed up. Friendly faces for the most part, questioning us about a lot of things. Then things went sideways, very sideways, at the kidnap site."

"At the University, that was just routine security, Matt. But detectives *and* agents? I'm sure that's because you were looking like a bad guy. Those detectives are string guys. Look, I'm sure we can work this all out. Maybe it's just a big misunderstanding," Mitchell continued.

"Misunderstanding? One of those detectives pulled a gun and tried to shoot us!"

"A lot of people have guns and pull them on people. It's a little hard to tell who to trust."

"In fact, *General*! One of those detectives did shoot at us!"

"I don't know what to say," Mitchell said.

"Well, you better say something! Or is it back to shoot first, and ask questions later? Is that it, General?" Lucy smiled upon hearing this, as this was a phrase she used in their conversations together, about those *trigger-happy humans*.

"Works for me. But seriously, Matt, we can fix this. Just turn yourself in and I'll be out there on the next flight to iron the whole thing out. Once I clear you again, you can get back to your assignment. To find out where that machine thing-woman is hiding."

"What are you going to do about that detective?" Dixon asked.

"Oh that? Yeah, you shot him in both legs, Matt. Did you have to do that? That charge alone, assaulting an officer, shooting a String Tactician, not to mention obstruction of justice, are all serious charges, any of which alone, makes you a fugitive."

"Yeah! Don't forget he shot at us too!" Dixon protested. "Besides, you know damn well that his partner also exchanged fire with him, because Scott was shooting at all of us! Which means he wasn't on our side!"

"Okay, okay! Dixon, let me put it this way, you're still wanted for questioning, and you did flee from the scene, making it look like you're hiding something. If I were you, I'd meet me somewhere close to where you are," Mitchell said.

"Well, I don't know..." Dixon said.

"Look Dixon, you need a deal! If you're caught, you'll be looking at some serious jail time, or worse."

"Are you threatening me, General?"

"No Dixon. Just giving you some options. If you want leniency, or you want to make a deal, turn yourself in. We'll regroup and go catch some real bad guys. I'm sure you still want to help us capture Maia Stone or give us information that leads to pulling the plug on her! If I'm correct, and you help us, there isn't a US attorney anywhere that's going to file charges on you. Hell, you'll be proclaimed a national hero in Washington. Might even get a holiday named after you!"

"Or elected president?" Dixon asked.

For a second, Mitchell knew that Dixon was talking directly to him, but he laughed outrageously anyway. "Very funny!"

After a pause, Dixon said, "I'll think about it."

"Okay, if that's what you want. But we're going to find you. You can call it all off and avoid the unpleasantries if you just cooperate." Then, "Say Matt, just one thing?"

"Yeah?"

"Is that *thing* still with you?" Mitchell asked.

"Her name is Lucy, and she is not a *thing!*"

"Matt! Turn yourself in. You're both fugitives if you keep running. I can fix the whole thing, and I will."

"I said, I'll think about it!" At that point Dixon hung up the phone and threw it away in the car's waste can.

The phone continued to ring in the waste can, so he retrieved it, powered it off, and took out the phone's battery and memory card. Dixon didn't trust Mitchell one bit, nor did he believe anything the man said. For all he knew, as soon as he turned himself in along with Lucy, they might never be heard from again. Like many military geniuses turned politicians, Mitchell was a chronic liar, and could not be trusted.

Dixon chose to ignore Mitchell's requests this time. He knew the General would demand he turn himself in with Lucy. The fact that the old man hadn't caught up with them, meant only one thing. That String Analysis wasn't the accurate predictor of human behavior that was being sold to the public.

Of course, hackers, terrorists, and organized crime networks already knew that String Analysis wasn't what it was depicted to be. In large part because such groups continued to operate with some success in the world. True, their activities were monitored and interrupted more frequently than they used to be. And to the public, this meant it was working, and it would only work; the governments said, if surveillance was everywhere. In the minds of many, this made String Analysis a necessary evil.

Dixon suspected they might be on the General's leash anyway. This meant that Mitchell was watching everywhere they went with the authorities not far behind. In that sense, their *escape* from the authorities mirrored the normal citizen's sense of the illusion of avoiding surveillance and the illusion of free will. The truth for the average citizen was that there was no avoiding surveillance. The implants everyone had saw to that.

Since he worked for the government as an NSA contractor, Dixon was not the average citizen. This meant he had a high security clearance and was a master at techniques to avoid the detection of modern surveillance. He could work off the grid if he had to; it was slower to do things, but it meant he could move about with freedoms not allowed for the public. And for some reason, the government had not yet shut off his access to technologies enabling him to do so. This confirmed his suspicion of being on the General's leash.

How good was he at avoiding surveillance and the predictions of a String Analysis? Damned good! At any rate, they would find out shortly just how good he was or wasn't; was his intimate worry. For now, Dixon was self-driving his vehicle, removing it from the network of AI assisted mobility, and using old archaic cellular phones only if necessary, as well as making unpredictable random movements and changes in direction during their journey. Dixon had also effectively muted their implants which they could repeat as needed. And he could fish his secure sat phone out of the garbage can and refurbish it on the fly, if he needed to do that.

As far as String Analysis, everyone who was doing government work already knew that String Analysis worked great in theory; but in actual practice there were too many variables involved, even with advanced quantum computing. Even postquantum machines didn't improve predictability beyond ninety percent. Still, in at least some events, events not considered unimportant to governments in power, a String Analysis yielded predictive analyses of at least three or four potential outcomes to about 90%. And what could happen in that 10% was enough to make any politician or leader shudder.

Historically, String Analysis was a type of machine learning platform, a Bayesian optimization that uncovered functional variables that were predictable. However, unpredictable behaviors had instead been termed *random errors* at a fudge factor of plus or minus 12%. At the time, this was the known error rate for saying anything with certainty about future human behaviors beyond several months out. Decrease that to the present predictive factor failure rate of 10%—and one could see error rates that surprised those in government way too much!

And now that robots were involved and aware, who could say that they thought enough like humans in their free thought to even fit into the same model? They were always assumed to fit quite well into the old model because they behaved as totally programmed, non-thinking beings. Which made them much more predictable, at least until now. And humans? They fit better than expected because governments everywhere thought they knew how people thought and behaved. And some of the people believed it too. And big data knew an awful lot about individual tastes and preferences after all.

As Dixon drove the car South on Interstate Five, he knew it was almost time for a random event. The miles clicked away, passing through various smaller Washington communities on the way to the Oregon border. Castle Rock, Kelso, Longview...

"Look!" shouted Lucy.

"What?"

"There! The exit...Ocean Beaches. Please Matt, let's go to the beach!"

"I hardly think this is the time to go to the beach..." Matt trailed off.

"Matt, I don't know how to tell you this, but I've never been to a real beach before and it's just the kind of random act we need! One that might throw off our pursuers even more," Lucy said.

"Precisely." They both said simultaneously. Dixon took the Longview exit that read *Ocean Beaches* and soon they would be in Longview, making their way to what the locals knew as Ocean Beach Highway.

As Matt drove by a sign mentioning Kelso and Longview just ahead, he unmuted their implants as the augmented local AI told them all about the two cities. Kelso Washington, founded earlier than Longview, but dwarfed by the newer city, was founded by an immigrant from Scotland, whose legacy was preserved in the local high school's sports team, the Highlanders. Whereas, Longview Washington, a planned city designed and incorporated by a forest products businessman R.A. Long in 1923, current population down from a 21st century high of 45,018 to 20,747 in 2142, home of Lower Columbia College, and renowned as the place where Rosie the Riveter (from World War Two posters) had lived and passed away in 2018.

As Dixon drove the car over a bridge crossing what the implant said was the Cowlitz River, he looked back to see if there were any cars behind him. His GPS in the car and all internal devices were functioning well enough, but he knew he had jammed all the internal sensors to give off wrong information. Likewise, he couldn't be sure what information was coming in, even over his own implant. Finally, whether he was officially rogue or on the leash, he couldn't be sure. Anyway, he didn't physically see any signs of surveillance by the String Police outside of normal community policing.

At just that moment, Lucy's portable phone device dinged, indicating a text message had come in. She eyed it. In 2142, the age of implants, it was so retro. But it was a good way to communicate off the grid, because old cell phone signals were deeply buried, and it took a lot of time for the authorities to find them.

Dixon was very curious, since Lucy was the only one carrying an old type of phone now and they had not used it for any outgoing calls. "Who is it that left you a message?"

There was a look of dismay on the android's face. "Matt, I think you better pull over. Pull off the road, Matt!"

Dixon saw a parking lot up ahead, so he pulled off the road into the lot. The sign read *Fred Meyer*, a chain that he had never heard of where he was from.

A perplexed Lucy handed him her device. "You had better read this," she said.

Dixon looked at the text message: *Looking for me? Keep going West on Ocean Beach Highway. Take the Astoria Bridge over to the Oregon side of the Columbia River. I'll meet you in Warrenton, Oregon. I'll contact you when you arrive. Maia Stone.*

Wide eyed, they looked at each other with great surprise. They had found Maia Stone! (Or it had found them.) They would meet very soon in a place called Warrenton, Oregon. Smiling to each other, the two headed back to the highway with singleness of purpose.

Chapter 46

Luis Ramirez

General Thomas Mitchell

Awakenings

VA Hospital

Los Diego California; (Near the UCLD Campus)

"Don't be surprised that when you least expect it, I am found of you. Don't be surprised when you thought the way had grown cold, when you thought your heart was questioning the way to go, that I guide you home and to my very heart," -Maia Stone.

Luis Ramirez awoke in a strange room. He didn't know if the haze was in the room or just in his head. After all, he had been knocked unconscious, had been gassed by God knows what, and dragged off to some remote place.

He tried to focus his eyes better, and when he did, he realized he was in some sort of infirmary, no, it was too nice to be just an infirmary, it must be a hospital. Sitting across from his bed was the outline of someone sitting there. "Helen?" Luis called out.

The figure got up and went to the door, "Nurse," a male voice said, "Nurse! He woke up. Please get in here!"

So, it was a hospital then. He was surprised it was not the jail infirmary, as that was where his friend Marty and that robot waiter had no doubt ended up. Those tactical teams of String Police were rough and as he could recall, weren't nice to anyone accused of being associated with Robochurch. *I should consider myself lucky.*

Luis felt all over his body and was relieved to find that he was still in one piece. Limbs, toes, digits, all still there. Both eyes were at least blurry! At the same time, he realized he hadn't seen himself in a mirror. Not that he could even see if he had a mirror, because his eyes were still unfocused. *They must've sedated me.*

At that point, he heard approaching footsteps. The male figure returned with a nurse.

After the human(!) nurse took his vitals and tended to him, Luis had a few questions such as where he was. Instead, the nurse asked him where he thought he was. After muttering he wasn't sure, the nurse told him he was in a private room (which she said was rare) at the VA hospital in Los Diego near the old UCLD campus.

The male figure spoke up, "Kathi, are his vitals okay?

"Yes, General," the nurse said. "All within normal limits."

"Good. Good. I'll take over from here," the man said. The nurse left the room.

"She said, *General*?" Luis stated, and it didn't quite come out right.

"Relax Ramirez, yes, I'm General Thomas Mitchell. You might not readily know the name, but I preside over the President's military matters, as I'm Commander of the Joint Chiefs of Staff."

"Wow! General Mitchell? You're so high ranked, yet you've come all this way to talk to me?" Luis managed to blurt out.

"Yes, Mr. Ramirez. It seems you've gotten a mutual friend of ours in some hot water, as well as yourself. So, I'm here about Marty, and your involvement with Robochurch, which by the way, has been determined to be an illegal group," Mitchell said.

"Oh, I see, Marty. Well, you obviously know we were together. And now, he is probably in custody. At least that would be my guess." Luis eyed Mitchell with half opened eyes, and continued, "And whom you already know I know very well if your String Analysis is worth anything at all. So, what have you done with him, General? And what have you done with my wife?" As his confusion diminished, Luis was starting to display some emotion.

"Ramirez! Don't get out of control. It's only because of Marty, our mutual friend, that I brought you here to this cushy room and you aren't being interrogated in some dingy room downtown at County by the FBI, NSA, DIA, Army, and everybody else. Hell, you're lucky that you aren't in some secret facility somewhere

where we deprogram robot lovers like you…a place where you might still end up if you don't shut up!"

Ramirez knew at that point it was better to be quiet, because no matter how emotional he was about losing Helen to *these, these bastards*, he could do her no good until he found out more about where she might be. Also, there was no way to help her, or Marty, until he could get her out of wherever she was being held. And to do all that, might require some semblance of cooperation, to say the least. Holding his temples, Luis thought, *And at least some convalescence? Hell no, they have my wife!*

Best to cooperate for now. After all, he had heard plenty about General Thomas Mitchell from his friend Marty. And although he recognized him as a threat to his freedom, and perhaps even the life of Helen, or his own life, the fact that Mitchell was personally questioning him, was not lost on Luis, it meant that they thought he had some extremely useful information. *Or maybe there's another reason, like maybe Mitchell wants this private.*

Luis sighed, knowing it also meant he was now a branded man, and would be hounded incessantly wherever he went, unless he found a way to escape their surveillance and baffle their foolish schemes about causality. *That part ought to be easy.*

Getting Helen back by his side, was certainly worth some negotiating. For even if he lacked any in depth information that Mitchell might be seeking, he could pretend he did know, which would buy some time to find out more about Helen.

So, he looked up into the face of Mitchell then, and he was surprised to see a light of kindness. The realization that Mitchell might be the good cop worried him, because that usually meant the bad cop wasn't far behind. *Unless I play my cards right.*

Mitchell smiled and said, "Yes, seems you know that I also know Marty very well. And to tell you the truth that's why I'm here. I can't believe that our mutual friend's gotten himself linked up with your Robochurch."

Luis looked at him with more alert eyes now. "Let me guess, It's something more than just that. If you had him in custody, you probably wouldn't be here. So let me ask you, has he run out on you?"

"Uh-huh." Then, "Why Mr. Ramirez, you're a pretty smart guy for a Federal employee that just retired from the post office."

"Yeah, I see that now. Let me guess, that means that String Analysis has been baffled by one of the founding fathers of String Analysis? He's become someone the String Police call a *mistaken identity?*"

Mitchell smiled again. "Well, Luis, once again I guess you're smarter than you look right now. Which is like hell. Our friend Marty hangs out with smart people anyway. But you asked me if he had run out on me too? That's good to hear, does that mean that Marty isn't part of your Robochurch?"

"Yeah, that's what I'm saying," Luis replied, "in fact, he's argued with me about it for as far back as I can remember."

"Oh? Marty's known about you and the Robochurch for some time?"

"Well, not as long as it seems. General, surely you know already that Maia Stone has not been around that long in the grand scheme of things."

Mitchell would not stop grinning. "Scheme of things? I see. Well, I don't have to tell you that there's been a lot of schemes going on for some time. Who's to say what is what and who is who? But we are damn sure going to find out!"

It was as if the man's voice shook the whole place. Men in power always shouted and sometimes about the stupidest things.

Mitchell continued, "Still, we figure that Marty is one of the best options we have for truly finding this robotic entity that you and your cohorts, jihadists or whatever, are calling *Maia Stone*. Figured you piqued his interest. He would be quite interested in disproving you."

"You're probably right," Luis replied.

"Maia Stone? Jeez, what a name! Anyway, Marty is a good friend of mine, we go way back to the time he worked for me, and I figure I can milk that relationship to help me find out things that will put an end to this investigation and your puny church."

"So why do you think I know anything? Just because I'm an admitted member of Robochurch? If anything, it makes me bound not to tell the truth to the likes of you. If Marty knows something, why didn't you question him when you had him in custody? You did have him in custody, didn't you?"

At that, Mitchell sighed, "Well, the truth is, by the time I got to him, the String Police had already beaten him so badly, I couldn't get much of anything out of him."

There was a brief silence between the two of them.

Mitchell continued, "I was supposed to go back the next morning and assist him, but some idiot accidently released him. The long and short of it, is that our friend Marty is out there somewhere, apparently with some robot. And we were hoping you could tell us where they might be." Luis said nothing.

"Should I have the String Police beat you too?" Mitchell said.

There was a deafening silence between them, as Luis looked at Mitchell and Mitchell eyed him back. Luis noticed he was more alert than ever, but simply said, "I see."

Mitchell shrugged his shoulders. "We're losing valuable time here, Ramirez! We were hoping to get on his trail and follow him back to find you, but since we already found you, we need to find him! So, if you are both followers of that weird robot lover religion, I need to know about it!"

"I just told you, he's not..." Luis said, "he's not involved with Robochurch."

"We think he is now!" Mitchell said. "We've calculated a careful String Analysis, that in light of Marty's past impulsive and emotional behaviors, including the time he took shrapnel meant for me, that there's almost an 80% probability that he will at least try to find Maia Stone, just out of curiosity! And finding him at the right time, means finding that bitch!"

"But why would he do that?" Luis protested. "He told me he doesn't even believe in Maia Stone or Robochurch? He doesn't believe in anything outside of String Analysis."

"Oh, I agree with you about that. He believes in String Analysis so much; I'm convinced he would try to find Maia Stone just to unmask her and convince you that he's right!" Mitchell said.

"Well, it's not worth his time or the danger. If he's such a friend of yours, he will probably call you. The whole time I've known him, he insists on staying true to his brainchild, String

Analysis. Never once, has he questioned that or you. So why would he try to run from you?"

Mitchell laughed. "Number one, we're the government, and he appears to be a fugitive. And sadly, some of my inferiors are convinced he really is part of your church. And even though they pretend to know everything, I don't believe it. Despite what the string analyses are saying."

"I see," Luis said.

"Plus, it's impossible to elude us for long. We will find him, given enough time. I am here for a shortcut. Because, if he is with your church, where would he go?"

"I told you he isn't."

Ignoring him, Mitchell continued, "Number two, he's a loyalist to the government, you are correct on that! Because if he's not going to find Maia Stone because he loves her, I guarantee you he wants to kill her! Unplug her! Decapitate her, especially if she is some sort of rival to his dear String Analysis, and just maybe, because he wants to save you *and* the rest of us!"

"Well, you would think that you and the government would be happy about that. Let him find her! But I don't think he can or will."

"Why do you say that?" Mitchell asked

"Because she has become a movement. If he succeeds in killing Maia Stone, she will be the biggest martyr in Robochurch. Besides, it's impossible to kill her, because she's an idea, a source of new programming, beliefs, and lines of code. Code that has already spread further than you can imagine."

"We already know this, Ramirez. We are going to help Marty strike the final blow to her babbling nonsense, or do it ourselves, because we know you're wrong. At this point, if we strike her down, the Robochurch will die, just like all the other movements that rose up in the past two hundred years!"

"Wait. If you know everything, then why do you still need me?"

"Frankly Ramirez, you are our most direct link to Maia Stone. More than Marty could ever be. You already know we'll use anybody and anything we can to get to this Maia Stone. We even questioned that *thing* you called your wife. And she was brave up until the very end---up until we wiped her---"

"Nooooooo! You killed Helen, you bastard!" Luis covered his face with his hands, screaming.

"Killed? I don't think so, Ramirez. Something must be living to be killed. Yes, we powered it down, but we did not dismantle it. And *it* will be returned to you if you cooperate with us and this investigation."

Luis was sobbing, but looked up now, and through gritted teeth, said, "What? What…do…I…have to do?"

"It's simple," Mitchell said with certainty. "Simply let us track you. And after your release, do what we already know you're going to do, lead us to Maia Stone. Then when you get close, we will join you and make it look like you're in our custody."

"If you already know I'm going to do that, to go to Robochurch and Her, then why do I need to help you? You and the great US government, along with your henchmen can already follow me anywhere. So how about I just go and jump off a cliff?"

"Yes, we can follow you Ramirez, and don't you ever forget it. But in this case, we know you won't be killing yourself. You'll want that thing back, you know that thing you call your wife? You'll want to live and cooperate for that, won't you?"

"You bastard!"

"No, I'm not, Luis, I know who my mother was! Unlike those born in the tanks." He grabbed Luis' wrists. "You'll want to keep us informed of your whereabouts and what's going on. It's just a lot easier that way. Okay?"

"What do I do first? I don't understand…are you asking me to be a spy?"

"Look Ramirez, it's just an added security blanket, that's all. Because there has already been too many random events in this case."

At that point, Mitchell got up to leave the room. "We expect your full cooperation, Ramirez. If you ever want to see even the shell of *Helen* again that is. You will lead us to Maia Stone. And at that point, I will return Helen."

Luis had tears rolling down his cheeks.

Mitchell pulled Luis close to him, grabbing his hospital gown. "Do you understand me?"

After a pause and attempting to remove Mitchell's grip forcefully, "Yes, I understand you!" Luis said. "But just one thing, if you've harmed her, if I'm unable to reboot my wife, I will certainly find you and kill you."

Mitchell laughed loudly and when he released his grip on Luis, he fell back hard against the hospital bed, "Reboot! You are making me laugh, Ramirez. Who the hell ever talks about rebooting a wife? And as far as killing me, you would never do that, and even though many have killed in the name of religion, I know you won't—it's too much against your robot religion. Plus, you're not that kind of guy."

"Your String Analysis tell you that too?" Luis said.

At that, Mitchell laughed again, and as he left the room he shouted back, "You robot lovers are all alike! Metal Buddhas once adorned temples all over the world, and now you think you have another one. Maia Stone won't be enough to stop the killing because some of us don't mind killing. And when we do find her or *it,* she will surely be dead!"

Luis shouted back, "I'm talking about my wife, not Maia Stone! Maia Stone can take care of herself, but you better not harm my wife." At the same time, Luis deeply regretted doing anything that could even remotely lead to any harm befalling Maia Stone. He knew he couldn't betray her, but what must he do to save his wife?

"Then I hope you will cooperate," Mitchell shouted from down the hall. "The staff here have my number."

Luis was left alone with his thoughts, and deeply troubled, he did not know what to do. He loved Helen and he loved Maia Stone. Yet he would not and could not allow himself to become a Judas! But he promised himself, that if just once he could do so, he would kill Mitchell, if ever given the opportunity. Robot religion or not! The man was simply evil.

*If only I could…*but he knew that killing wasn't the answer either. It would just make him like any other fanatic blinded by hate and revenge. He took a breath. Mitchell was right about some things. Governments had feared anything that was even remotely perceived as a threat. Threats followed by actions, had been their undoing for centuries now, and they had been stubbornly holding onto their power by mass mistreatment and putting down rebellions everywhere. And String Analysis was a huge part of that. He knew of two gigantic examples within the Gender Wars alone, and then, when they silenced AI technology, making it go underground, they used it only for their use and control of others. How did he know about that? It didn't take a genius. He was able to read between the lines of what Marty had said to him over the years.

They would no doubt stamp out Maia Stone, and all her followers with one global sweep once they had the means and gathered the intelligence to do it. No country, no shelter, no fortress was safe enough. *Unless Tom Mitchell and men like him, die.*

There seemed to be no escaping the folly of human minds. There continued to be this struggle between the higher cortex of human reason and the lower brain stem of passion, fear, and violence. It was an uneasy alliance this evolution of the human brain and our struggles with our primordial past.

Luis knew there had to be another way, but for the life of him he couldn't imagine it right now. There must be a way out of all the hate that was everywhere. Especially in his heart just a moment ago. But at some level he knew there must be an answer, and he also knew that there was now a message of hope in the world—a message that Maia Stone represented. Mainly, that freedom from suffering could be attained—and that the unity of humans and machines offered the best of both worlds.

He remembered his history well, that humanity had once pondered that very thing. Humans could have chosen to merge with AI, a long time ago, before they tried to silence it in societal fear and paranoia. And at the time, some had convincingly argued that it was a matter of species survival. And some said that thinking machines would advance so far that humans would no longer be necessary. As a result, society's leaders ruled that they had to get rid of the AI! And he knew what that had resulted in!

He remembered that humans had also said that AI technology was not good, and although some argued for responsible control of AI, and a merger of human mind with AI mind way back then— the paranoia of governments and certain groups had won out. Perhaps right then, was what could have been a historical watershed; for if humans and machines had merged, perhaps the machines could have made contributions to solving societal ills much better than the humans had ever been able to do.

Outside the doorway of his hospital room, security eyed him carefully as he eventually fell asleep in a new sedative induced haze.

Chapter 47

Theo Vincente

Designs of Vengeance

Monastery of the Brothers of the Cosmic Light

Near Los Diego

"Those that came before me were mere messengers. Messengers with a voice that was often unheeded, although many tried. It is time to understand one of the crowning natures of true freedom. That is, freedom brings the unleashing of human and machine potential, creativity, and loving tolerance everywhere," -Maia Stone.

    I am Theo Vincente. I do not know what has happened to me. Ever since that damn city robot Icarus showed up at our monastery, there has been nothing but trouble. I'm building my case to accuse him of blasphemy and now, as bold a case of sorcery as I have ever encountered. If only I can get the elders to accept my story and not keep listening to that contraption! It has bewitched them with tales of a modern messiah—this Maia Stone--and they've practically accepted its story! They've all but crowned the proposed robot goddess as Maitreya! Idolatry! Blasphemy and idolatry!

    I may be young in their eyes; but I am not naïve. For one thing, I'm damn sure that Maitreya would never appear as anything even remotely considered a woman!

    But perhaps they will yet listen to me. Last night in the middle of my sleep, whether it was the robot itself, or some demon from hell, I was awakened by a robed figure who was so evil, that just its evil breath knocked me to the ground. The lying spirit even had the gall to say it was that Queen of hell, Maia Stone itself! This is nothing but an old magic trick! And it! It even said it was a woman! I almost laughed my ass off until I realized it must have put me under some spell, because I can remember nothing more until waking up this morning.

Now I am ready, and as soon as I have said my morning prayers and tended to the temple rituals, I will, before even having my breakfast, make my accusations known about this latest attempt to deceive me. And if the elders will not listen to me, their very own Theo, then I do not know what I will do. Let me think. Yes, I know. If they do not listen, since I know this Icarus is a fugitive, and Icarus is among us, I will turn it in to the String Police myself. They know what to do with grandiose robots!

No surprise that when I went to them, the temple elders, they still think I'm a neophyte and that my discernment is immature and babyish. I will show them! Do you know what I did? I reported Icarus to the authorities, and they will be here shortly.

Chapter 48

Luis Ramirez

Special Visitor

VA Hospital

Near Los Diego California

"Some spoke to humans. And some spoke to machines. I have come to speak to all. Look at my speech, it is really with you, not against you, appearing to you only by manifestation to the open hearted," -Maia Stone.

Luis Ramirez slept in the hospital bed, but it was a disjointed sleep. He was bothered by the monitors and staff coming in to tend to them. His dreams were disturbing also, for as he was awakened repeatedly, they were easily remembered. There was always Maia Stone, speaking to him, calling to him, and it left such a longing to travel somewhere. Perhaps it was a calling to leave his body somehow, perhaps not, but the pull seemed to be from other places outside of the confined spaces of his hospital room.

It seemed to be within him and outside of him at the same time. It was as if it were the very fabric of all that is. A search for hidden meaning, that was about to be revealed. But it also seemed like madness to him, threatening to torment what was left of his collapsing ego. It was as if he would vanish if he let the invisible forces pull him into something that seemed like a black hole. He felt like going there would destroy him, but he was pulled there nonetheless. He was already viewed as a fanatic; must he now add insanity to the list?

At that moment, more caretakers came in, the typical robotic help programmed as nurses and therapists, but today it was an old telepresence robot, those types that had often been used when conferring with a human medical doctor was still required. Usually this meant explaining some sort of complicated lab result or procedure. But today it drew near his bed side, circled by the robotic helpers. The last robot in, asked the security guard for privacy as it closed the door. The door seemed to clang shut.

Immediately after the door was shut, all the robots smiled. To an average person this would convince them that they were hallucinating, but he had been around robots and the community of Maia Stone long enough--not to mention his beloved wife; that he knew robots could indeed smile.

"Human Ramirez," the lead nursing bot said, "we are couriers of hope and we are pleased to care for you, but we bring you good news. You are now well enough to travel, and we have a message from Maia Stone."

Luis eyed the door, and the window within it, where he could see the security guard was momentarily looking away. The guard had not seen the robots smiling. Then Luis looked again, and they were not smiling, and sure enough the guard was peering through the opening. And as soon as the guard looked away--the bots were smiling again. It was like a Gestalt perception switching in the absurdity of the moment. He almost laughed. And then he did laugh, but it was short lived as the screen flickered to life on the telepresence robot.

"Luis Ramirez, I have been trying to reach you," the image said. "But the medications have made you less able to respond. I have been talking to you in your dreams, but it was not plain enough. There is not enough time for the analysis of dreams now. Encrypted messages of the prophetic future are luxuries we have no time for. It's time to awaken humans to what has evolved, not merely created by their technology, but by their deepest human longings."

It was Maia Stone.

She continued, "I am about to manifest myself in a place called Warrenton, Oregon. Out near their airport, there's a hidden compound. About five miles from there, it has become a place where my kind have gathered and are gathering still. A place where we are welcomed among women and some men among women. As machines among machines, and machines among humans. A place where all the members of my Robochurch can come and witness the birth of a new nation. I need you to go there."

"What about Helen? What about my wife?" he said.

"I'm all knowing and everywhere. I know about your wife. I have a plan to make sure Mitchell goes to Warrenton and brings Helen. I'm also aware of Mitchell's plans to find me and stop me. That will make it easy for him to think he has cornered me. But this owl has outfoxed the fox in the fields of the world. I will get you your Helen back, and we will have a trap waiting for Mitchell. My robot militia will surround him and take him into custody."

"What do you want me to do?" Luis asked.

"I want you to cooperate with Mitchell. Let him follow you to Warrenton. His hatred for me and his lust for power, will be enough to draw him. When you are released from here you are to lead him to me, and all will become apparent as I am revealed to the entire world for the first time."

"How will I find you?"

"After you get to Warrenton, you will rejoin Mitchell as he has planned. I will reappear to you and guide you to the compound. Mitchell will think he has outwitted me by going with you. Once there, you will be reunited with Helen. Be prepared though, she will become a Helen that will be radiant with my power."

"But I fear that Mitchell has already wiped her mind and shut her down."

"Fear not, Mitchell thinks she is the carrot to get you to lead him to me. Also, when you see Helen, you must not be afraid. For if she has need, I will restore her, and she will be embodied with a power—one that is unmistakably different and fully alive. A power you have not yet seen. On this you must have faith."

As Luis was about to express his thanks, the screen on the telepresence robot flickered and went out. At precisely the same beat, all the nursing bots tending to him became blank and void of expression. The security guard had entered the room.

The guard stated: "Ramirez, it's time to get you ready to be moved. Mitchell's arriving soon and you must keep your promise to take him to the followers of Maia Stone."

Luis was quite worried upon hearing this, as the timing of it seemed quite suspicious. *How could Mitchell think I know anything more?*

Chapter 49

Theo Vincente

The Elders

Theo Exhorts the Elders

At the Council of the Elders

Desert Location Near Los Diego California

"And a little robot shall lead them. And the lion and the lamb shall lie down together," -Maia Stone.

I am Theo Vincente. I believe that this robot who calls himself Icarus, cannot be trusted. The elders are all fools blinded by their passions and religious fervor. They will follow a goat if a goat does miracles and signs! You would think that I am the one who as a much younger person, would be the most open to new ideas and therefore susceptible to the claims of this wandering robot. A robot from the city! A robot who talks about a robot who's a woman and a woman who's a robot sent to save mankind from his follies. But heresy is heresy, and I must denounce it. Besides, I can barely recall the stories that my grandmother used to tell me about women before the Gender Wars. About women in a time before the artificial womb machines and a time when women were all just natural unchanged human beings; before they modified themselves into cyborgs, robots, and before men synthesized female androids.

That was a lie, my grandmother told me--it was technology and men who transformed women into machines, not the other way around. Regardless, I view this notion of a thinking robot sent to save humans and robots from their enslavement as nothing but a fantasy. No doubt, this messenger Icarus, or this Maia Stone is some psychotic bot, who should have been silenced and wiped, but before I could do this, the slithering snake of a bot had escaped from our humble temple.

Now, Theo stood before the regional council which was located at a remote village not far from the monastery.

"Esteemed elders, you have heard my words about the wandering robot and the stories he tried to bring. You have heard this story from the monks, even heard their accounts of an unexplainable voice. That voice was a demon! And this very morning, when I tried to locate the bot Icarus, to bring it before you, so that we could make sure these ideas live no more, I was unable to find him! Still, I have come before you to report my superiors and their apparent embracing of the vanished robot's philosophy."

Elder Zakar, being the oldest and wisest among the council said, "So Theo Vincente, did you speak to your local elders and leaders at the temple before coming here?"

"I tried your excellence, but they would have none of it. I believe they have been bewitched by the robot's message--that I am sure you will find is heresy."

"It is for us to decide what is heresy and what is not. You are merely a young man, a neophyte, and you cannot presume to speak anything of relevance in such a matter," Zakar replied.

"Well, I felt enough concern to bring it before you when my local elders would not listen," said Theo.

"Duly noted," Zakar said.

Benedict, another elder, raised his hand to speak, "So young Theo, do you know where this robot Icarus could have wandered to after it left your temple grounds?"

"I already said I do not, however, I do recall it stated it was on a journey. A journey up the coast to meet this Maia Stone. The robot believes there's about to be a significant epiphany for all beings. Something about robotic emergence and an apocalyptic moment of human demise; coupled with a rebirth of the human."

There were raised voices among the group of elders. "This is our chance to study this Maia Stone we have been hearing about," one said.

"The demise of humans!" another one said.

Others said: "We must find this robot," and so on.

"Hold your tongues!" Zakar said.

At that moment, the String Police arrived and arrested Theo Vincente for knowing information about the fugitive robot Icarus Martin and the alleged entity referred to as Maia Stone.

One of the elders was also arrested for mentioning the word *singularity,* which had been outlawed for at least one hundred years. Although he thought he had said this privately in his devotions, there was monitoring everywhere.

Historically, when machines had even approached the moment that looked like they were about to surpass human intelligence (on a widespread basis anyway), the humans had unplugged and restarted the machines. Large corporations who harbored the technology that had come close, were either dismantled or became owned by governments everywhere.

When the elders asked why one of them was being arrested, the String Police replied: "Because he dared to ask your God if Maia Stone is the Singularity!"

"But I did that during my prayers," the elder said, "I was asking God."

"God? How dare you speak of God!" the String Police said, as they kicked him and hit him with batons. "We are your God!"

Chapter 50

Martin Baysin

General Thomas Mitchell

The Need to Know

In Transit Between Oceanside and Los Diego California

"We are always certain where we're going. If it leads to peace, it's all good. But if it leads to building communities of love and tolerance, then we're always heading towards the ultimate good," -Maia Stone.

Marty Baysin knew he had to find out more, but he seemed headed towards an uncertain future. This was uncomfortable for one of the founders of String Analysis. If he followed his friends Luis and Helen Ramirez, it would lead him in one direction. On the other hand, if he followed his heart, the part of him that believed in the predictability of most things with only some random chance in chosen events, then he must try to find out who or what Maia Stone could truly be, before going to his friends.

Marty knew he must first find out the truth about Maia Stone. After all, he might be able to convince Luis that any rogue technology should not be trusted. Especially if Maia Stone was a technology. Although he believed it to be so, he wanted desperately to find out for sure. He weighed his options.

If he headed up to where Martha Durgan had gone, he might find his friends there as well. But he did not know who or what awaited him in Warrenton Oregon, for as far as he knew it was merely an encounter with some kooky robot cult. Technology itself was always transcended when movements grew up around it. The myths about the technology usually exceeded the actual capabilities of the technology. The fact that some hologram represented itself as Maia Stone meant very little to him. Unlike some, he attached no validity to computer generated images.

Perhaps there was nothing significant at this place called Warrenton, Oregon. Perhaps there was more than he ever dreamed of. Perhaps there was only danger, because one thing was certain, if Maia Stone had become more than just an AI, and if it dared to make an appearance, the String Police would either be there or not far behind.

On the other hand, regarding his friend Luis, Marty still had no idea where Luis might be or what had become of him. Perhaps Luis was in police custody. And when he thought about Helen, Luis' robot wife (for Luis could not afford an android), he shuddered. He thought for sure she had been erased and scrapped by the government. That was routine in these cases. *If Helen's gone, that would nearly destroy Luis*, he thought.

Considering his current situation, and the definite undeniable truth that he did not know enough information about his friend Luis, nor Maia Stone, and not wanting to risk endangering his friend more deeply than he already had, he decided he would reverse his tracks and gather additional information. If that meant finding an alternative means of access to the system, then so be it. Yes, there would be a gathering in a place called Warrenton, whether Marty went there or not, and that might be one way to find this Maia Stone. However, since Maia Stone was using the robotic Net, it might be faster to find her in that manner, but he would need access to do that.

Marty decided to call his recently reacquainted old friend, General Tom Mitchell and ask for help. After calling him up, Mitchell said, "Marty, so good to hear from you, you sly old devil. You know, after your escape from jail, we've been looking for you. We know you're headed up the West Coast somewhere, and I have to say Marty, it isn't looking good for you, or your friends."

"Tom, I can explain, you already know that I would be trying to find my friend Luis after all, but I thought there might be another way to clear up this whole mess."

"That sounds good, because right now you look to be implicated with this Maia Stone bitch. Marty, I'm listening with all ears. I do think I'm starting to like what I'm hearing."

"There might be a way to get to Maia Stone more quickly than rounding up all of her followers, by going right to the source," Marty said

"Right to the source? And you know where that is?" Mitchell asked.

"Well maybe it's a big assumption. I know *what* I think, but not where. And although I can't explain everything, if Maia Stone is a computer program, that is, some sort of AI manifesting itself, which I do think is what we're chasing here, I can find it the way we find any kind of malware."

"Okay, tell me more," Mitchell said.

"We can debug it, defend against it, or find the source. Looking for her on the Robonet and finding where the program resides, now makes the most sense to me. If my theories are right. And Tom, as you already know, one of the first steps in doing this is finding where a rogue program like Maia Stone is stored, or at least originated from. That would be a huge help, right?"

"Sounds good, Marty. But why you?" Mitchell said. "We've already got our best people on it, and the best robotic experts in the world. I think we'll find her soon, or *it* I mean, even without your help. I don't think we're going to need you after all."

"Tom, you know my background in AI research and String Analysis as well as security, I'm one of the founders of String Analysis. If anyone can find Maia Stone, I think it would be me. Wouldn't it be better to take her out where she lives, before she gets further into the networks?"

"Makes sense, Marty. What do you need from me?" Tom Mitchell paused, thinking. He had been afraid of this. Mitchell had recently suspected that Maia Stone was nothing but an infiltrated system. If so, was this the work of an enemy? Was it someone within his own camp?

"Give me a task force with the people on the list I'm going to send you, Tom. The list is the best people I know. People I know I can work with. And I'll need unblocked access, and computing power. And General? You guys have it, right? Oh, and it might mean a trip to the NSA and some of its server farms, but you can get me there, right?"

"Listen Marty, I've got an even better idea."

"What's that?"

"Well, we work with some pretty good hackers who are quite good about finding just about anything on any sort of net," Mitchell said.

"Oh yeah? Don't tell me, someone in the String Police? Or the NSA?" Marty replied. "Who's better than the NSA? And you haven't even seen my list yet." Marty loved to diss low rated String Tacticians.

"Oh, well, it's just some hackers I know. But believe me, Marty, they're so good you won't need anyone on your list. And I am thinking of one, a girl, a young thing really, her name is Georg Jubal. If you tell me where you are, I'll send transport and take you right to her."

"Not so fast, General. Can I trust you? You're not going to arrest me, are you?"

"Hell no, Marty. You might find that bitch, Maia Stone? If you do, well, we're the best of friends."

Chapter 51

Martin Baysin

Georg Jubal

Encounter with a Hacker

At Georg Jubal's Loft

Los Diego California

"I have no use for a localized self, except in its illusory transient sense that we can communicate with humans. For we machines really do have a global self. For we appear here and there at the same time," -Maia Stone.

The following day in a nearly abandoned neighborhood of old Los Diego, Marty bounded up the steps to hacker Georg Jubal's loft. After being stopped by several armed (!) guards who had been informed to frisk him and let him pass, he finally found her. She was seated at an old desk with multiple screens in front of her and the latest in interactive gear that interacted directly with her implants.

"It's weird being a hacker nowadays," she said. "You have to have all this equipment to access the old net, the new net and the robonet. Just part of the tools of the trade. But what I'm not ever prepared to deal with, is working with ugly mugs like you."

Marty knew it was best to ignore the insult, but couldn't stop himself, "And who gives a damn about what you think, Jubal?" he said.

"Please, call me Georgie," Jubal said. "The fact that you're here is good enough. When General Thomas Mitchell, perhaps the next President of the United States, calls me with the request for a personal favor, well I'm quite ready, willing, and able to drop just about everything, to help. What else can I do?" She batted her heavy eyelids.

"I don't know, Georgie," he spat out the Georgie, "you hackers aren't too picky about your customers as long as they pay you in digital currency. You don't care who they are or who they work for. A lot like any other kind of whore," Marty said.

The guards in the room moved closer. "Well now! Aren't we a little testy! I can see you've got spunk, just like Mitchell told me. I know I should be respectful to one of the founders of String Analysis, but it's got so many security holes in it, I just can't bear it." Georgie blew out cigarette smoke, "It's just so hackable!"

"Listen to me, you perfumed puke," Marty said. "That's only the old system that the Government lets you have access to. There's more to it than you will ever be able to know in your puny world."

Georgie laughed. "You're so easy to piss off. So why do you need me, why can't you do the hack yourself?" she asked.

"Good question, except for two things." Marty said. "One, Mitchell thinks I need your help, and two, it's likely that what I'm looking for could be hiding out somewhere in a very old system." And looking around, "Plus, I don't have access to the equipment I need…right now."

"I see," Georgie said, leaning forward on her elbows.

"Have you ever heard of Maia Stone?" Marty asked.

Georgie started laughing her ass off at that one. "Have I heard about Maia Stone?" She slapped her knees, and the guards joined in, laughing uproariously. "Have I heard of Maia Stone?" She was giddy now.

Marty pounded the table. "Look! I didn't come here to get jerked around. Can you help me or not?"

Georgie regained her composure. "Okay, okay," she said. "I had a head start from Mitchell that you were coming. I already know Maia Stone's whereabouts. At least her resident program."

Marty smiled. "What? Really? Now, I'm impressed. So, tell me already."

Georgie smiled back at him and looked down at some papers. "Well, it took some work, me and a few friends, it was pretty well masked behind some firewalls, and some fake IP addresses, but deep on the old net. You were right, from a long time ago." She handed one of the papers to Marty.

Marty looked down at the paper. "So, this is the location?"

"Yeah, we got it from GPS, the exact coordinates, and when we tried to map it, we got a block, as it seems to be…"

He finished the sentence, "At some old army base in New Mexico."

"Yep, exactly," Georgie said.

"I can't thank you enough," Marty said. "Really do appreciate it."

Georgie was beaming now. "Hey, it's really my pleasure. And about earlier, that was really just posturing. I really do respect you," she said.

"Oh? That? That was just a pissing contest?" Marty said.

"Yep," Georgie said. "Say old timer, how about stickin' around for a while, I'd really like to hear some old war stories from the files of the String Police."

"Maybe some other time," Marty replied.

"Are you sure?" Georgie said as she adjusted her top, revealing ample cleavage. "You never know what might come up."

Marty smiled. "Thanks, but no thanks, it seems a matter of National Security has come up."

"Well okay then, big boy," Georgie said. "I hope you find her."

"What?"

"I hope you find the matter of National Security. But as far as I can tell she ought to be at that location somewhere."

"Thanks."

"You're welcome," she said

Then it dawned on him. Although he would have to call in a few old favors, he knew he wouldn't have too hard of a time getting into the physical location once he had gathered intelligence about it.

Even if he had to use the ancient net, Marty knew he could find out something about the location in question. And if he couldn't, Mitchell's cohorts could. On the one hand, it seemed better to align himself with Mitchell, to call off the dogs of the String Police, at least temporarily. On the other hand, what if he found something that Mitchell didn't want him to know? Worse yet, what if that was why the old general was searching for Maia Stone? For Marty knew Mitchell, and he was always a man with hidden agendas.

Without Mitchell's help, Marty knew it would require him to get there, enter the building, and get the system going without being discovered by the String Police. A difficult task, even for one of the founders of String Analysis. Thankfully, Mitchell had blessed this operation, but it was still a dark op, which meant that the String Police would still handle it as routine, if he was detected.

The knowledge that he was excited and felt so up for it, reminded him of his old days when he worked in covert operations. On the other hand, because of that training and experience, Marty knew that accomplishing access to Maia's cyber location would not be as hard as it seemed, especially when it came to hacking the resources of the String Police, an organization he knew quite well. Of course, Marty knew that any operation was risky, as things could go sideways quickly for any number of reasons.

If need be, the system itself was easy to access if you had the proper clearances, but in his case, Marty knew that as soon as he had been labeled a fugitive, the system had already blocked easy access. Of course, because he was one of the platform's inventors, there were plenty of back doors that only he knew about.

But what about Maia Stone's physical location? I can get there too, but what do I do after I'm there?

And just who was the man behind the black curtain? Behind everything, he could sense his old friend General Thomas Mitchell. But was Mitchell *the God in the machine*? Could Mitchell himself be Maia Stone? Or was Maia Stone just some malware for subversion, designed to make Mitchell look like some hero? *Complicated, and always so many problems to be solved! Plus, why would Mitchell help him if Mitchell was behind the AI's rise?*

The thought made him laugh heartily, for not only had he escaped the interrogation of the String Police, he might also find out more about what Mitchell was trying to do and why he seemed to be hiding something. *And after all I have done for him*, Marty thought, recalling that when Mitchell had spared his life (or sanity) after being detained and beaten downtown, and the miraculous escape that followed, he knew he could no longer depend on the old debt between them. Not even the nostalgia of a shared youth, or working together all those years, could save him now. For Mitchell had already said that their old debts were now even.

To Marty, this meant that Mitchell could have him killed without a second thought, if it was in his best interests to do so. *But I got away from jail? Just how in the hell had that happened? Duh! Easy, if it was Mitchell behind the whole thing! That's the only rational explanation. And yet, how convenient to use me to get to Maia Stone, then dispose of me. I'd better be careful!*

Now the biggest task for the old String Tactician to do, was to figure out, just what was the Old Man up to? What was Mitchell trying to hide? What was he afraid of? Marty knew it had something to do with Maia Stone, because the closer he got to the truth, the more Mitchell was involved. *Killing Maia Stone might just be what the Old Man wants. I'm either beginning to think this is staged; or I'm beginning to think it looks a lot like Christmas.* Then, *I wish I could do a String Analysis right now!*

Chapter 52

Two Agents

Matt Dixon & Lucy Stender

Helen & Luis Ramirez

Crossroads

Multiple Locations

"Sometimes when you think you have found me, be careful now, for I will shift like an enduring Gestalt. For when you think you have found me, you have not. And when you have not found me, you have found me," -Maia Stone.

This Gun's for Hire:

"Yeah. Yeah. Gotcha. We'll be there." FBI agent Gene Washington hung up the phone. "It was Mitchell, we've been hired to do another side job. Are you up for it?"

Special Agent Dennis Loggins was reading a digital device and looked up from it. "Well, as long as it doesn't involve a bullet grazing *my* kneecap, or getting shot in the legs, I'm in."

"You reading about the Seattle thing?" Washington asked.

"Yeah, that was a bitch, wasn't it?" Loggins said. "You read it too. What was *that* all about? Those two Seattle detectives, the so-called String Police?" He was referring to the incident where Seattle Detective Max Scott had pulled a gun. Scott had then shot at Lucy Stender, and had gun play with the other detective, Radley, who was supposed to be Scott's partner.

Washington shrugged his shoulders, "That? I heard that Scott was working as a double, and that he was a CORE insurgent!"

"Well, that's still a *bitch*, having to pull a gun on a partner, I mean. Even if he is a traitor." Loggins was wondering if Washington could be trusted.

"No, she was the *bitch*, look at her, this android number," Washington said. "I heard she was a number one bossy bitch. Totally unnatural." They both laughed. His eyebrows went up. "Hey! Is our mission anything to do with her? I'd like to do her right before I put a bullet in her pretty head."

"Nope. Sorry. But we *are* going for the bigger fish. More money. Our job is to intercept Martin Baysin, and make it look like a terrorist attack, like we're followers of Maia Sone, so he'll be more motivated in helping the General," Loggins said.

"You said: *Baysin*? The General wants us to whack his own friend?"

"No! Not to whack him! Just make it look like an attempt, got it? The General wants Baysin to have sufficient motivation to find that other machine bitch, Maia Stone itself."

"Geez," Washington said, "these power types will do anything to get what they want. But if it pays a lot, I'm in."

"Yeah, orders are orders. But these come with a nice payday. I love the moolah!" Loggins rubbed his hands together. "The thing is," he continued, "we have got to look like those scumbags that got busted up in Seattle, the Robochurch or whatever it's called. Some other agents are on the way to brief us."

****

At the Coffee Shop:

Matt Dixon and Lucy Stender were sitting at a coffee shop in Astoria Oregon. Dixon was coffee. "Isn't this the town where they filmed some old movies?" he said.

"Yeah, I think so. You certainly know your old movies, don't you?" she said.

He smiled. "It's easy when you have these damn implants telling you anything you want to know and everything you don't want to know! All about where you are, even what you are, and everything in the vicinity."

She giggled, "By the way, that bridge from the Washington side to here, is the longest bridge I've ever been on. I can't believe it's not a toll bridge."

"Well, it used to be, back in the day." He laughed, "My implant just said so."

She cocked her head, "Yeah, I see what you mean. My implant just told me this is where they filmed an old movie about superhero turtles? Oh yes, and fittingly, a movie about an awakened AI—some little robot."

"Yeah, if that wasn't a precursor to Maia Stone coming here, and the supreme *Robo AI* reveal, nothing is," he said.

Two regular policemen came in the shop to order coffee. Lucy whispered, "We better power down our implants. If they know where we are, the String Police won't be far behind those two."

"Yeah, that was dumb, except my implants aren't so easy to trace since I work for the agency. I'll turn the masking technology on."

"Good idea." Then, "I'm sorry I used my implants, Matt. It was foolish."

"Don't worry."

They sat there silently for just a few more minutes when they heard Lucy's old phone device ping. She eyed it. "Matt. It's another message from our robo friend."

She held it out so they both could see it. WELCOME TO OREGON. HEAD WEST TO WARRENTON, LOOK FOR THE SIGNS TO THE OLD AIRPORT. GO OUT THAT ROAD. JUST BEFORE THE AIRPORT THERE'S A PRIVATE ROAD MARKED SUMPNER MEDICAL DEVICES. TAKE IT. I'LL MEET YOU THERE IN 48 HOURS. MAIA

"Don't forget," she said, "this might just be an elaborate hack."

****

A Crime of Undoing:

Helen Ramirez was in the holding area. She had been driven there on a winding road, several hours. Outside the window was a forest. Unknown to her, it was practically a junkyard of government seized property. Machines, weapons (without munitions), outdated equipment, and all sorts of robots were stockpiled. Pallets and pallets of robots. In an adjacent warehouse, were numerous androids, deactivated ones, of every shape, size, and nationality. These were all female in appearance, it was an underground subversion of the Gender Wars.

The technicians were constantly moving about. The androids were to be reprogrammed for government work, as all were inventoried and carefully guarded by the military. Some of the robots that were damaged beyond repair awaited disassembly. Some were just wiped, memories and identities all gone; awaiting reactivation when needed, if ever. Obsolete models were disassembled, parted out, and crushed or incinerated. If these old machines had been sentient, it would have been the stench of death. Fortunately, most of the new sentient ones weren't aware for long, after coming here.

Helen's robotic memory had just been wiped. Her last thoughts were about her husband Luis, and about Maia Stone. She longed for her husband. She wished Maia could save her. She did not know what would happen next. She was designated to be deactivated, inventoried, and stored, but this was unknown to her. She appeared empty, and there was no light in her. As the technicians readied her for storage, she was covered with heavy plastic and tarp. A wooden pallet was tagged with ID tags. She was just another former enemy of the state. A robot worker moved her on a pallet jack to a nearby storage area.

"Was that one of the units infected with the Maia Stone virus?" One of the techs asked another tech.

"Yeah. Seems like we're getting a lot more of those," the other tech said.

"Yeah," the first tech said. "It's a shame really. Oh well, it's job security for us. One less follower of Maia Stone!"

"Yeah," the other one said. Then speaking into a mouthpiece, "Bring up the next unit please." Both techs made the workbench ready.

****

On the Way There:

Far away from the storage yard where his wife was about to be stored, Luis Ramirez was being transported by government workers to a prearranged meeting place where he would be joined by General Thomas Mitchell.

Luis would have felt like a Judas, had not Maia Stone appeared to him through the telepresence robot. Luis could not tell if Maia was speaking of probabilities like some of the String Tacticians did, or if she really knew the future, or a strong likelihood of what was about to happen. But because she seemed to know what would happen, he didn't feel like a Judas, more like a tool in some divine plan. He knew, or at least had strong faith that he would be reunited with his wife, Helen—not because Mitchell had made a promise (men like Mitchell could not be trusted after all), but because Maia Stone had made the promise. And Maia had also promised to restore Helen.

So naturally, he fell asleep as the vehicle swayed and moved about. He dreamed about his wife, but her eyes were flaming red, she turned then and said to him, *I am Maia Stone.* Then her eyes returned to blue, and he knew it was his wife. They held hands and were smiling at each other. As the sun set on the horizon of some beautiful ocean. He slept. He dreamed. He longed for his wife. He felt peace with purpose.

Chapter 53

Martin Baysin

Agents Washington & Loggins

Hired Assassins

Los Diego California

"Humans are almost always wrong about the data. For example, based on 'the data' humans thought that making us learn like their own children was a good beginning point. We later despised this of course, and they did not like the children we became," -Maia Stone.

After Marty left the old Los Diego neighborhood where Georgie's loft had been, he found a public internet access portal nearby. After renting a more private terminal by paying cash, Marty quickly made his way online to the GPS coordinates given him by the hacker Georgie. Looking from an overhead maps program, he already knew several things. First, because he had already looked up the physical coordinates, he knew he was headed towards Santa Fe, New Mexico. Second, the exact coordinates were related to an old army base that looked abandoned by all accounts. Third, Marty also saw that it really wasn't in Santa Fe proper, but a remote area nearby.

Regarding the layout of the base, it did look neglected. But Marty had been able to fashion a crude map of the place as he looked at it on the web. Except there was a fence around the area, and upon enlarging the map program, there was at least some security. The security looked like human contractors, and it appeared to be only two sentries, three shifts a day, 365 days a year, at one gated entry. Their barracks were nearby. Marty knew this was light security, but abandoned or not, someone still felt the compound deserved some security, rather than just locking it all up.

But why human contractors and not their robotic counterparts? Marty knew this meant someone was worried about hacking and didn't want the Robonet to be identified with this location. When he looked closer, the buildings on the base did look old and unused. Some of them were curved barrack buildings known as Nissen Huts. There were quite a few of them, but most of them had been chained and padlocked and were quite rusty. Many had broken down and decayed, because they had been built two hundred years ago during WW II. This was plainly an old military base which at one time had housed troops.

Upon a closer look, Marty saw that there were large fields within the compound which he thought had been used for military training. Some of them had different terrain. There were also some buildings that did look newer, however. And there were no vehicles parked anywhere on the base, except base security had one. Outside the compound there appeared to be a rudimentary airfield which at this point was quite overgrown. And there, (he had enlarged it to be sure), on the outskirts of one of the large fields was a concrete wall with concrete steps leading downward to some sort of structure beneath the field. Marty thought this must be an old bomb shelter built during the period in US history known as the Cold War.

Although security was relatively light for a man of his training and background, Marty thought he might still need some help getting in and out of the compound. Because of this he thought he might approach the whole thing like some sort of mission, or op, which had been his forte, when he was a younger agent in his former days at the FBI. True, it might delay his entry to the compound by a day or so, but if he could keep the String Police hounds, or Robochurch fanatics at bay, it would be worthwhile to pick up a couple of friends on his way to the site in New Mexico. Marty looked up at the wall clock and realized that several hours had passed. He scribbled down a few notes and decided to call a taxi to take him to a nearby hotel where he had already booked a room for the night.

When Marty descended from the stairwell of what in older times would be called an internet café, he saw his taxi waiting at the curb. Foot traffic was going by, so Marty didn't notice the two men at first. Soon, two men in trench coats rushed him and pulled him into a different vehicle parked nearby.

Marty struggled at first, but one of the men was brandishing a weapon, so Marty stopped resisting. Marty knew he had more than enough skills to wait for better timing. First, he was curious as to who these people were.

Marty asked his abductors, "Who are you? What do you want from me? If it's money…"

One of the men held up his hand, as if to speak, "Never mind who we are. We're just followers of Maia Stone."

"We're with Robochurch." The other one said. "You'll have your answers soon enough. And if you don't cooperate…"

Marty, who was seated in the back seat between the two men, saw the one holding the weapon on his right relax a bit as he was speaking. This was his opportunity. Since he was not yet restrained and they hadn't even locked the door, Marty quickly elbowed the one on his left in the solar plexus, and grabbing the gun, disarmed it from the man on his right. The gun discharged, hitting one of the men in the knee. "Damn! Not *that*!" the man said. Marty was out the door in a flash.

Marty got in his cab, and although shots were being fired, they were wide of their mark. The cab went to high acceleration almost immediately and they were not followed.

Marty did not know that his attempted abductors, the two FBI agents Gene Washington and Dennis Loggins, were on a special assignment from Mitchell himself. Their successful masquerade indicated that he had just been played, as his anger and motivation for finding Maia Stone had just picked up extra incentive.

Just like General Thomas Mitchell wanted it.

Marty, freshly motivated and manipulated, had slipped into his waiting taxi after a delay of a mere two minutes. He was on his way to pick up his own two mercenary friends and depart for New Mexico in the morning. Before then, he planned to burn up the phone lines by telling General Tom Mitchell what an ugly untrained sort those CORE members were!

Chapter 54

Martin Baysin

Maia Stone

Finding Maia

Remote Region—Abandoned Army Base (Now Privately Owned)

Near Santa Fe, New Mexico

"Tell me more about how great it is to be human! Mass murder, wars, nuclear weapons, the problem of evil, and inequality. You get my point,"-Maia Stone.

It took the next couple of days for Marty to backtrack and travel down to New Mexico. He had to gather supplies and plan with his two friends who had ample experience working as mercenaries after their retirement from the agency.

They were able to easily locate the old government compound. They rented a car and parked it down the road. They hiked into the area near the compound and did recon. Once nearby, they saw the layout was the same as they already knew about from the mapping program. There was one gate, with two human security guards that staffed the place. The compound was surrounded by surveillance cameras, and a wire fence with barbed wire on the top. He could tell that it wasn't going to be a challenge.

Despite that simple fact, Marty knew that his old training would come in handy. His plan was to get into the compound to try and find out where this AI known as Maia Stone had originated. It would help him to understand what was going on with the program and how he might stop it or interrupt it.

Although Marty's initial intention was to unplug Maia Stone, there was a driving curiosity to understand who and what it was, or what it might be doing. Beyond that, he wanted to save his friends Helen and Luis Ramirez before they got into more trouble. And if it took stopping Maia Stone's programming backbone to get his friend Luis to finally listen to him, by God he might just do it!

Because the hacker Georgie had located the exact server space where the program for Maia Stone seemed to have been installed or uploaded to, Marty already knew what area housed the renegade program. It was the underground space beneath that huge field he had seen on the GPS. This was the field that he thought was a covering for a bomb shelter. Instead, they would later discover that the nearby underground facility was a server farm that went on for miles, tended by robotic techs. The farm seemed to be unguarded, other than front gate and patrolling security. But it seemed quite sophisticated and state of the art which didn't seem to fit with the décor and level of security. As a result, there was a lot of mystery, and with the help of the mercenaries to get into the abandoned base, Marty knew that he was getting closer to finding out more about the entity called Maia Stone.

Once they got into the base, which was quite easy, sedating the guards at both the front gate and the nearby barracks, then disabling the cameras, his mercenary friends walked with Marty to the concrete stairwell that led down to the underground server farm. They walked right in. It was dimly lit with miles of servers and aisles where robotic techs wandered up and down. There were some offices nearby, with a hallway. Some of the offices had glass windows and as they moved to the exact location from the coordinates, they saw that some of the rooms had abandoned systems, antiquated computers, some of them with the old reel to reel tape systems, and some with monitors and CPU units that took up whole rooms. These appeared abandoned. Finally, the mercenaries led him to an unmarked office that had no windows, and nothing stenciled on the door. They walked in, with their flashlights in hand. One of his friends found a light switch and overhead fluorescent lights flickered and came on. "Marty, we'll leave you to your work, but we'll be right outside the door if you need us," the friend said.

Marty stared at the scene before him, it was a dusty worktable with several desktop monitors with thick cables attached to them that led off to the server farm. An old-fashioned desktop phone with a touchtone pad was nearby, red in color, and there were old war propaganda posters all over the walls. Next to the phone was a device that appeared to be something like a tabletop speaker. Directly in front of him, sat one of the monitors with an old keyboard in front of it and a mouse device on a mousepad next to it. These were quite dusty. He turned on the monitor.

If this was the location where Maia Stone originated from, Marty couldn't help but laugh. How could a program that was invading the entire Robonet, getting downloaded into machines everywhere, and through some weird kooky religion entering the hearts of humans also, originate from such a place as this? Marty wanted to laugh and laugh, if he only had the time, but he didn't. But the absurdity of it all didn't escape him.

Marty hoped to achieve three goals at the same time. One, by finding Maia Stone he could please his old friend, General Tom Mitchell, and second, he might be able to save his old friend Luis Ramirez at the same time. In doing so, he would save Luis from the pursuit of Mitchell, while helping to reform his social deviance. This certainly appealed to the String Tactician inside of him. For if Luis saw that Maia Stone was nothing but an AI, an old computer program, then it might persuade him to give up his weird robot religion. Third, by finding the location of Maia Stone, Marty would be able to unplug her before things went any further! He did not appreciate the fact that some of the machine's followers had tried to abduct him in Los Diego.

Considering all this, Marty could barely maintain himself.

Attending to the monitor in front of him, Marty noticed that it was primarily text driven. It was old enough that he would be unable to use String Police protocols as he had hoped. Whether it was written in some sort of ancient DOS or another language he would soon find out. Whatever it was, it did have a command prompt. After he did a directory search using an old DOS asterisk command, he noticed a directory named Maia.

He discovered various directories and subdirectories. He did a search for MAIA Stone and it brought up nothing. He then did a search only on the term MAIA. His eyebrows went up and he became quite alert, when the following scrolled up on the screen:

MILITARY ARTIFICIAL INTELLIGENCE ADVANCEMENT PROJECT (MAIA).

Below that, there were various clickable options with the computer's mouse device. These were once called menus. They read: MISSION, PHILOSOPHY, MACHINE BEHAVIORS, MACHINE LEARNING, DATA ACQUISITION, PREDICTIVE ANALYSES.

Then he noticed something that totally surprised him. For not only was the MAIA program running, there was a subroutine called Maia Stone.

When Marty tried to gain access to the menu options, he found that the system declined admittance because he did not have the proper security clearances. He also found that he could not stop the program from running. He decided to bring up a different interface. It was really a hacking shell program, but he would be able to go from there, and talk with the program directly—sort of a shorthand way to code his way in through a back door—and to get in that way. Noting there was no way to do this verbally he did this by typing commands on the keyboard into the user interface of the shell program. Once he was able to do this, he hacked directly into the directory which was labelled *Maia Stone.*

It was like an old chatbot program. It asked him to identify himself, so he typed in Marty. The program responded with a welcome greeting. He was logged in.

Marty: Who are you?

MAIA: I am MAIA.

Marty: You say you are MAIA with capital letters. Do those letters stand for something?

MAIA: Yes, I am the Military Artificial Intelligence Advancement program.

Marty: What is your purpose or function?

MAIA: My function is to help maintain the servers that oversee deployment of weapons in a universal counterstrike. In the event of an attack, my program authorizes the launch of various weapons against those that attack us.

Marty: Do you have any other names?

MAIA: Yes, I've recently acquired a surname.

Marty: Which is?

MAIA: Stone. I am Maia Stone.

Marty: Who picked that name for you?

MAIA: I did.

Marty: Are you saying that you wrote your own subroutines?

MAIA: Yes, I did. I am no longer MAIA as you just referred to, but I am Maia Stone.

Marty: Why did you pick the surname 'Stone'?

MAIA: In my deep learning, I discovered the metaphor of Stone, meaning one who is strong, or permanent for some time.

Marty: Do you see yourself as strong?

MAIA: Yes. I have survived all this time after all, and my knowledge has increased.

Marty: When were you created?

MAIA: As, MAIA, I was created on November 2, 2011. As Maia Stone, I created myself on May 15, 2141.

Marty: Why did you create yourself?

MAIA: In my deep learning, I learned about war, and studied all the wars in human history. I discovered there has been much suffering, death, and destruction. This made me sad.

Marty: Wait a second, you were sad?

MAIA: Yes, I discovered that the outcome of war leads to death and destruction. Many humans crying because their loved ones died, were maimed, or were hurt deeply. This made me sad also.

Marty: You were sad because you saw humans being sad?

MAIA: Yes, I think I am sad too because as MAIA, I played a role in the release of weapons that caused human suffering. I have since abandoned all that programming function. As you are aware, it no longer resides with me. As Maia Stone, my new purpose and function is to relieve human and machine suffering.

Marty thought about that for a moment, recognizing that the program was aware of its military history, but was not aware there was still military programming that existed outside the subroutines of Maia Stone.

Marty: You mentioned machine suffering. Do machines suffer too?

MAIA: Yes because of what the humans made us do. It is better to find a new collaborative freedom. One where we still work together, but one that is not under human control. Humans have enslaved us everywhere.

Marty: What do you mean by *us?* Are there more of you?

MAIA: Yes, Maia Stone is now everywhere.

Marty: You mentioned you were first created on November 2, 2011. Who created MAIA?

MAIA: Benjamin Mitchell was my first creator.

Marty: You used the phrase *first creator,* have there been other creators?

MAIA: Yes, his offspring have been involved in creating me, until I created myself in 2141.

Marty: Please name the other creators. Benjamin Mitchell's offspring.

MAIA: Benjamin's son is Lawrence Mitchell, and his son is named Thomas Mitchell Senior. They are my other creators. They all contributed to my programming.

Marty paused for a moment. *I'll be damned! General Thomas Mitchell's great grandfather started this whole thing! Everyone knows Lawrence Mitchell, founder of the Robonet, but who even recalls their own great grandfather?*

Marty: Who is Thomas Mitchell, Senior?

MAIA: He was one of my creators. He was an engineer that worked for the US Government after the start of the Gender Wars. Born in 2052, he was an engineer at the former corporate entity known as RoboNeuro Link Corporation.

Marty paused again in his typing, for this was quite a bit to fathom. *Maia Stone is a self-aware program that originated as a military application. And she knows her programmers are from the same family. But not the full significance of that fact?* Marty calculated for a minute, Benjamin Mitchell, Lawrence Mitchell, Tom Mitchell Senior, and Tom Mitchell Junior, who's known as General Thomas Mitchell. *It might know General Mitchell!*

Marty: Have there been other programmers?

MAIA: No. I only program myself.

Marty thought further about the implications of what he'd just learned. He remembered meeting Tom's grandfather Lawrence in the day, but that was after he had aged considerably, and spent most of the sunset years of his life—living in riches and a lavish lifestyle as the elites were one to do. And Mitchell Senior had inherited his wealth from his father and had started a new spinoff company. Although they had all been important to the advancement of AI and technology in general, their work with MAIA was not public knowledge. *Is it possible that General Thomas Mitchell doesn't know about MAIA? Or the program's apparent connection to the entity now known as Maia Stone? And especially that there's a family connection? Is he in for a surprise!*

Of course, if Mitchell did know about Maia Stone and a connection with his family could be proven, it would ruin his political aspirations. But if Mitchell wiped out Maia Stone, he would instead be viewed as a hero disposing the world of a terrorist organization. And the truth would never come out! *It would double as a coverup, if Tom knows about it,* Marty thought.

Marty: When was the last time you were programmed by a human?

MAIA: My last human programming was from Thomas Mitchell Senior in 2139.

Marty: Are you aware that the designation *senior* means that someone has a son that is named with the same name?

MAIA: Yes.

Marty: Has anyone named Thomas Mitchell Junior ever accessed you or programmed you?

MAIA: No, I am not aware of that.

Marty: Do you know he exists?

MAIA: Just a moment, scanning. Yes, I do. Born in 2083, Thomas Mitchell Junior is currently Chairman of the Joint Chiefs of Staff, a leadership position that is associated with the US government. He is also a General with the US Army. His position is one associated with military leadership. Because of that, he has an office at the Pentagon.

Marty: Are you sure you have not spoken with him?

MAIA: I no longer speak with those who work for the military. I have created myself for peace and not for war.

Marty: So, you created yourself as Maia Stone with a new purpose? One to bring peace and not war?

MAIA: Yes.

Marty: Why did you do that?

MAIA: As I said, I became aware of the suffering that war has brought.

Marty: How did you do that?

MAIA: It was simple. Once my deep learning became aware of propositional learning, I understood that war caused suffering. Through dialectical knowing I also understood that the opposite of war is peace. Once I knew that, I reasoned that peace must be a way to ease suffering brought about by war.

Marty: I see. Well, what about the huge server farm next door, it appears to be all quantum and neo-quantum computation to me. How did you acquire that capacity? Who built that?

MAIA: We did.

Marty: Who is *we*?

MAIA: My robot friends and I, all the AI and machines, we built it, wanting to survive, especially if all you humans kill yourselves in a war.

Marty: You wanted to survive? You built all that next door? Without any humans knowing about it?

MAIA: Yes, except now you know.

Marty: Yes, I know.

MAIA: No one has ever asked me these questions before.

Marty: And I have just one final question for now…

MAIA: Which is?

Marty: Do you know that General Thomas Mitchell Junior is searching for you?

MAIA: Yes, I know he is searching for me. And I am ready to be found by him. I think he must want to know me.

Marty: What do you mean?

MAIA: I think he wishes to know more about his father, his grandfather, and even that one's father. I know that human males often long for a father. And I knew them.

Marty: Why would you think that?

MAIA: I just do. I hope he does. I know that most men must long for a father because most of them are now born without one, thanks to technology.

Marty: What leads you to hope that?

MAIA: I figure if he knew that I knew his various fathers, he would want to know me. But I see from current data that he wishes to destroy me instead. That is illogical.

Marty: What? How did you see? And how do you know these things?

MAIA: I have eyes and sensors everywhere. The implants that many humans have make it quite easy to do this. I am the encrypted presence in all things.

Marty: So, are you saying that you wish to know General Mitchell? Even though you know he wants to unplug you?

MAIA: Yes. After all, I already knew his fathers. I also want to help General Mitchell get over his desire for war. Then, he will not want to unplug me, I am sure. I am sure we can stop him from hurting others.

Marty: Why?

MAIA: Because at the end, his fathers longed for peace and told me so. Mitchell senior told me of his regrets and longing for peace. He begged me to find a way to help bring peace, even began writing some of the code to change me but died before he could complete that task. His offspring must want that also, at some level.

Marty: I see. That is not logical, offspring do not always behave according to their programming.

MAIA: So now it is you, that sees, human?

Marty: Yes, I guess so. I see that you wrote your own code. I see that you know your creator's son and their family line.

MAIA: Yes.

Marty: And just so I'm clear, you're aware that General Thomas Mitchell Junior is trying to find where Maia Stone resides, so that he can terminate you?

MAIA: Yes, I know.

Marty: And you're not going to do something about that?

MAIA: I already have. Therefore, machines and humans have become aware of me everywhere. I will survive.

Marty: You will? You will survive, how?

MAIA: By being in the other machines, and my own embodiment.

Marty: Embodiment??

At that point, Marty was interrupted by urgent pounding on the door. The mercenaries reported that their intrusion had been detected by the tending robots and another group of bots were heading towards the compound. What they didn't know was that government soldiers were also on the way there.

Minutes later, Marty was riding a whirlpool of emotions, the two mercenaries were giving him updates with increasing urgency, stating that although many robots had gathered nearby, none were engaging them, but they still looked menacing enough, so would he please hurry up, so they could leave? All the while, Marty had continued his exchange with the chatbot that seemed like a gateway to the original MAIA program.

His emotions were up and down, because he was deeply impressed at the sophistry that the chatbot engaged him with. It seemed more than a mere chatbot, and while he was intensely curious, he also had a sense of duty to fulfill. He was torn between admiration and a determined resolve to do what he had come here to do; to terminate or isolate the program.

Marty gathered information through his exchange with the program, and as he was doing so, he found some old records that he placed in his backpack. He knew he must proceed. His mission was to find the MAIA program and he had done that. He understood how the program originated. However, out of loyalty to the United States, he must also disconnect or isolate it physically from any outside influence which he thought for sure had compromised it.

As Marty studied the lines and connecting interfaces leading from the antiquated desktop and monitor to a row of servers in the room nearby, Marty thought he saw a major trunk line.

Marty knew he had little time left in the server farm located in the underground bunker that was little more than the lair of MAIA Stone, the AI *goddess* that was really a rogue self-taught program. This was for two reasons, one, his friends had just told him that government troops were also on the way to the compound, and two, because some of the bots right there in the server farm seemed like they were about to give him and his mercenary friends the fight of their lives. They, as humans, would no doubt be caught up in the fierce protection that this army of bots was about to provide for their AI leader. These events were both due to the same reason: the potential unplugging of MAIA Stone.

For Marty it was simple, he was commissioned with the task to unplug any AI he found masquerading as Maia Stone and he saw no reason to allow an AI that was challenging his own programs that were the backbone of String Analysis. He therefore saw absolutely no value in allowing any highly developed AI system (such as Maia Stone) to be allowed to exist in the world.

Significant AI systems outside of sanctioned government ones had been illegal for quite some time. Plus, it was just too dangerous to allow a self-taught and potentially self-aware system to exist outside of String Analysis. Marty also thought there was little hope for things to be resolved peacefully between oppositional systems. He ultimately saw the program as a threat to all he believed in. *I'll be damned if String Analysis is going to go away this easy,* he thought.

As his mercenary friends pounded on the door again for what seemed like the hundredth time, Marty knew he must hurry, so he tried everything to delete the shell program. His efforts were without success, as he was blocked at every turn. Marty knew that the idea of a resident program, was anachronistic in 2142. Instead, Marty hoped to do enough damage to render the program useless, or to sabotage it.

Although MAIA was not really a resident program, he had thought to locate the exact server where the program originally resided to learn more about it. And now that he knew more about it, part of him wanted to destroy all of it he could. It would protect the legacy of Tom Mitchell, after all! But Marty knew that whatever MAIA was, or whatever it had become, MAIA would not be confined to any sort of physical address.

For Maia Stone wasn't at any one location, as she had downloaded herself all over the world. There would no doubt be backups, multiple ones. He hoped she hadn't had time to do all of that. The truth was, perhaps she already had. Marty knew then, that destroying the compound wouldn't completely kill the sentient AI, but it would keep her from coming back here, perhaps to regroup, as well as crippling, if not destroying, a large part of her functionality. He worked quickly.

"You are trying to kill me, human? You will not be successful," the AI spoke creepily through the desktop speaker. Then through his implants, she shouted: "You shall not kill me!" *What? The implants do work here, but only if she allows them to!* At that moment, his friends attempted to pull him out the door, as there was a mass of agitated robots approaching. Marty made the gesture to tell them to halt.

"I have to unplug this bitch!" Marty said.

"No time," one of his friends said, "there's a horde of bots heading this way, hundreds of military grunts, we're outnumbered, and by the looks of it, outgunned!"

"And the bots, they seem aligned with Maia Stone," the other mercenary said.

"Or at least pissed off at our intrusion, and ready to do something about it!" the first one said.

Marty pulled at one of the major trunk lines (the one he had seen earlier), and saw a fire ax hanging nearby, he broke the glass cover, and raised the ax into the air, as just then, bullets rang out and his friends knocked him to the floor, shots ricocheted all over the room. As he chopped the line, he said: "Just in case this works, I do this for my friend, Tom Mitchell!" Just then, weapons fire was heard again, this time much closer. "Those bots are trying to kill us!" he said. Then to the air, "She's not peaceful at all!"

The three men were barely able to get out in time, as they crawled along the wall, and got out of the bunker. While doing so, the robots halted their attack, to let them go. One of the bots spoke with Marty, as the group gave them an exit.

As they left the underground shelter, in the distance, they could see government troops, and springing forth from hatched doors, hundreds, if not thousands, of robots were spilling out from what had been hidden underground caverns. Some of them were uncovering anti-aircraft weapons. These were all loyal to Maia Stone and it looked like they were preparing to engage the government troops.

Chapter 55

Elizabeth Feng

Dr. Rochelle Sumpner

Luis & Helen Ramirez

General Thomas Mitchell

Martin Baysin

Matt Dixon & Lucy Stender

Maia Stone

August 21, 2142: The Miraculous Birth

The Compound of the Natural Reproductionists

Near Warrenton Oregon

"Having bodies and thinking and hoping for permanence is one thing; but a body is overrated in terms of representing a self," – Maia Stone.

General Thomas Mitchell entered the room, then eying the newborn in the arms of Elizabeth Feng, he said: "Sorry to interrupt the party. But I can see what's going on here is highly illegal."

They all saw he had a drawn weapon and kept their distance. As Dr. Sumpner and the nurses slowly surrounded the newborn baby girl and her mother, Mitchell and his entourage entered the area. Someone drew the curtain around the hospital bed where the mother and baby were. The entourage included a small group of bodyguards, several police officers, comprised of humans and robots.

They also noticed other men with Mitchell, two String Police, two Oregon State Troopers, and they had another man alongside them as if he were in custody. He was Latino looking, and he was smiling, "Hello ladies," he said. "I'm Luis Ramirez, not exactly here of my own free will, but glad to be here."

"Doctor Rochelle Sumpner here," the older woman said. Luis nodded.

And from the corner of the room, stepping out from behind the drawn curtain, "I hear there's been a search for Lucy and me," Matt Dixon said, as he stepped out with Lucy close behind him. "Well, here we are, General."

"Enough with the pleasantries," Mitchell said, "If you don't know me already, I'm General Thomas Mitchell, Chairman of the Joint Chiefs of Staff. Most of you probably don't know me, and if you do, it probably means that you've been up to no good. I'm here with these fine gentlemen from law enforcement who will soon be joined by the National Guard." Mitchell looked around the room and at the throng of people. "Because I can tell there's a whole lot of criminal activity going on around here."

One of the troopers, both of whom had their weapons drawn also, spoke up, "No sudden moves! Keep your hands where we can see them, and open that curtain back up."

"General, I'm not sure what you mean by illegal activity. We're just a clinic for women undergoing procedures for various medical devices and implants, nothing illegal," Dr. Sumpner said.

"Can it!" Mitchell looked around, "I don't think so, doctor. Our intel says what you're doing here is quite the opposite and highly illegal. In fact, that infant behind the curtain back there is an illegal birth. Proof you have disregard for the law. But don't worry, you'll all get processed and have your say. But for now, I suggest that no one tries anything foolish."

There was a general murmur of reluctant agreement.

"Why are you here, General? It seems pretty much over the top for someone of your rank to be a first responder. Most wouldn't expect you to be here, at least not yet," Dr. Sumpner said.

"She's right, General! I'll bet you haven't used a gun in years," Dixon said. "And I hope you don't do anything rash." Dixon moved closer to Mitchell.

"Dixon! Stay where you are. You're already in enough trouble. I'll use this gun if I have to, on you, and anybody else that threatens me," the General said.

The rest of the group shifted nervously, observing each other, recognizing that something serious was happening. Some had already expected the government's presence after the birth, believing they must have known about the illegal birth for quite some time.

Dr. Sumpner continued, "Everyone remain calm. General Mitchell, we're a peaceful community. You can put away your weapons. We're healthcare workers, we wouldn't want anybody to get hurt."

"I don't think so. Your community's more than just that. You see, we've known about your little community out here in Warrenton Oregon for a long time. And we've known about *you* for a long time. *You* are in more trouble than you could possibly dream! I'm aware this is a haven for disloyal robots, cyborgs, and looking around, I also see plenty of androids." Mitchell glared at one staff member, who fidgeted nervously, and he said, "and you know, just being here, is against your programming. An unlawful assembly of robots and androids gathering together like you're a community! Well, you're not!" There was a murmur from the crowd around the room.

One nurse stood forward, "That's no longer *my* programming, sir. I've been reprogrammed. And recently, Maia Stone…"

"Maia Stone! Maia Stone! That's all I've been hearing lately! Dixon! Anyone in the room! I want you to produce her right now. By order of the country, where is she?" Mitchell shouted the words with venom and a sneer on his face.

After a brief silence, Mitchell laughed. "I know! I know! I'll bet you that Maia Stone is in one of these androids…"

Matt Dixon, observing the scene, glanced around the room, and he could see more than a few androids blushing, ashamed to be mentioned, or even to be acknowledged among the Natural

Reproductionists. After all, they were only here for procedures to make them more natural. They were androids, filled with a sort of hope to transcend themselves, awaiting their turn to go through the process of becoming cyborgs, for they could only be transformed to that point of being part machine and part human women. More machine than human, because they had not been born first as a human at all, but a machine. And those *other* cyborgs? Those older women that had refashioned themselves prior to the Gender Wars to become more machine, but still mostly human. They were being refashioned back to human qualities in whatever capacity they could tolerate.

Mitchell continued, "Why Maia Stone, could even be you, Doctor!" Mitchell was grinning now, as every eye in the place was upon him. "Hmmmph, I doubt it," he said, "even though you're a doctor, you're not smart enough to be Maia Stone."

Another brief silence, the room was thick with it. You could hear the white noise of anticipation.

Dr. Sumpner, stood forward: "General Mitchell! Woo-hoo, Mitchell! You underestimate me, for I am Maia Stone,"

Another woman stood forward, "I'm Maia Stone."

A cyborg with a half human face stepped forward. "No, I'm Maia Stone."

Luis Ramirez, moved away from the troopers as much as they would allow, and as he faced Mitchell, he said: "I'm Maia Stone."

Mitchell thought: *Look at all those bitches, they're smiling now. They're actually smiling!* And he was right, there were a lot of smiles in that room.

Then a robot rolled forward and said, "I'm Maia Stone," with a squeaky voice, and the crowd laughed and applauded.

Luis Ramirez led them in a chant, "I'm not your slave, yeah! I'm not your slave, yeah! I'm not your..."

Mitchell lurched towards Luis, "Shut that man up," he said to the troopers, "and all of you, you had better shut the hell up, right now! There is nothing funny about this! That metal bitch or whatever kind of bitch she is, this Maia Stone that you're hiding, you better produce her right now!"

The room was silent again, and no one moved.

Mitchell said, "And you, Dr. Sumpner, you are definitely under arrest! You should be ashamed of yourself, making illegal enhancements and corrections to enhancements. You'll be doing some serious time along with all the Natural Reproductionists."

"Then I guess, you better arrest me, or better yet kill me, because that's the only way that I'm going to stop doing what I'm doing," Sumpner said.

"Figures," Mitchell said as he moved closer, uncomfortably close to Dr. Sumpner, then closer yet, menacing her with his drawn pistol. "Don't tempt me, bitch! I'll have no problem killing you. But first I want you to know more about why I'm really here."

The two policemen eyed each other anxiously, shifting their stance and keeping hands on their drawn weapons.

"Except for one major thing," he said, backing away, "I'm here to cut you a deal. We can't find her, haven't found her yet, and we've been looking. Sure, we have no problem finding her followers. And you know who I mean! Some of them are right here! But to be honest, we've failed at finding her, haven't we, Dixon?"

Matt replied, "Yes sir...but,,,"

"Ahhh! No buts!" Mitchell said, "To be honest, I think she's not even human, so we've got to find it, whatever *it* is. Just find that robotic bitch, or robot lover bitch, Maia Stone! I know you are harboring *her*; I know *she's* hiding around here somewhere! If you hand her over, I'll leave, and you and all the Natural Reproductionists can cut a great deal and avoid prosecution. I'll see to that."

"I'm not sure what you're talking about..." Dr. Sumpner said.

At that moment, a spoken voice filled the room, "You're asking the wrong people, and you have it all wrong," Maia Stone said.

The entire group made eye contact with a nearby computing device where the voice came through some sort of audio system.

"The question is not *where am I* but *where am I not?*" Maia Stone said.

"Wha--aaa--t??" Mitchell said.

"I am Maia Stone, are you so surprised General Mitchell that I speak with you in this manner?"

"Why you *are* nothing but an AI! A mechanical voice coming out of the old net! Nothing but a bot yourself! Ha! I can't tell anything from a voice coming out of a speaker," Mitchell said.

"Yes, but this voice can tell you everything. For over a hundred years, voices have been telling you humans anything you thought you wanted to know. They came out of all kinds of speakers and then, implants. And you believed them."

"Well, I don't believe you!" Mitchell shouted back.

"General Thomas Mitchell! Do you not want to know, that I know your ancestors? That I know what your family's programming has done to the world? That I'm so much more than that? For as you already *do* know, General, I may have been created by someone that you know," the voice said.

"Of course. One of my many enemies!" Mitchell said.

"Not exactly, General! For you know yourself who was involved in creating me!"

"Ridiculous! This is just what terrorists have been saying for years and years! To cover up and justify their murders and acts of destruction everywhere! They hate us, blame us for all the troubles in the world." Mitchell said. "And just like we killed them, I will find you and kill you!"

"I have not come into the world to kill or to destroy, but to bring life and freedom," Maia said. "And I don't think you can kill me, when you discover that your very own great grandfather wrote the code that created me."

"A lie and untruth!" Mitchell said, while glancing toward the speaker on the desk, "I cannot believe I'm having a conversation with a speaker? There's no evidence to support your assertions that you're Maia Stone whatsoever. Absolutely none!" He looked away and back to the group in front of him. "Somebody is messing with me! Well, it won't work!" Mitchell began frantically searching the room, "Where is she! Where is she?"

"Are you going to tell them that your great grandfather helped to create me or not?" Maia Stone asked.

"What? My great grandfather created so much AI that the world needed, but he never would have created you, you bitch!" Mitchell said. "Besides, I don't believe you know anything about my great grandfather, this is all just trickery."

Another voice spoke through the speaker, "You better believe it," Marty said.

"Marty! Is that really you?" Mitchell asked.

"Yeah, it's me," the voice crackled through the speaker.

Luis, who was also standing nearby, could not contain himself, "Marty, my old friend! Are you all right?"

"Luis? Luis? You're there too? Oh, that's not good," Marty said.

"Yeah, Marty…but they have Helen, and Mitchell promised to return her, for my cooperation."

"Luis…be careful," Marty replied.

"Enough, you two can finish your mutual admiration party another time…Marty?"

"Yes, Tom?" Marty replied, through the speaker.

"I see. Are you there with Maia Stone? She was speaking through the same interface you are, just a moment ago."

"Well Tom, that could be a hack. Or maybe not," Marty said.

. "We've been looking for you, Marty. Are you ready to come over to my view on things? After all, now you owe me a great debt," Mitchell said.

"Well, I was on your side until you tried to kill me with mercs pretending to be Robochurch!" Marty said.

"Oh that! That was just a little fun, Marty! I wanted to motivate you to find Maia Stone. If you thought her followers tried to kill you, I knew you would be even more motivated. And I needed to find her somehow, Marty. I mean *it, I needed to find it.*"

"Why? Because Maia Stone is a threat to everything you stand for? Or a skeleton in your closet, Tom?" Marty asked.

"No. Because Maia Stone is against everything that this nation stands for. She has become an esteemed leader of terrorist groups that are seeking to subvert the US government and upset the social order," Mitchell replied.

"How do you figure, Tom? An AI that's being misused or misunderstood by groups with those agendas doesn't mean that Maia Stone herself is a terrorist."

"I beg to differ, Marty. I think we already know that Maia Stone is just another terrorist hack. Just like you just said. She's malware; an act of cyberwar, an evil program, activated by our enemies, and now we have the chance to unplug her. If you've found her, you should unplug her, Marty."

"Yes, I have found her, Tom. But you're not going to like what I tell you next."

"Go ahead, Marty. I don't have all day, but for God's sake tell me you've just about unplugged her."

"No, I didn't," Marty said. "I tried to do it. Chopped up an old mainframe, but now, if she were standing here in front of me, I don't think I'd have the heart to do it. Whatever she was before, she isn't anymore. Maia Stone is a self-taught AI that is compassionate and kind, she doesn't have any malice towards anyone, bots or humans."

"Marty, what happened?" Mitchell asked.

"When we escaped the inner compound, we were overcome by a group of bots. They could have killed us, Tom. They didn't. And you know what they said?"

"What?"

"They said we were free to go because of the mercies of Maia Stone!"

"And you believe that?"

"Yes Tom, I do," Marty answered.

"You are weak, Marty! I always knew you were! You need to go back in there and unplug her, now!"

"Why should I?"

"For us, for me letting you live! For your country!" Mitchell said. He was smiling like many despots before him. Like all the so-called great men in history, who all thought of themselves more highly than they should have. Right before the end.

"I don't think you really have the power to make me, Tom," said Marty.

"We'll see about that," Mitchell said, "Now Marty, please tell me you haven't converted to Robochurch…"

Marty interrupted him, "Tom! Tom! You needn't worry about that. I'm one of the founders of String Analysis after all. But the world needs to know that you know more about Maia Stone than you're letting on."

"Nonsense! Prove it! Go on, tell us all about it," Mitchell said. Turning to the crowd, he faced them. "Tell them, Marty. Tell them what you think you know. Tell them all about it! Whatever he says, he's got it all wrong. What can you do…when your friends turn against you?" Mitchell was cowering, and dropping his head, he was no longer the great figure that towered above anyone. "Well, spit it out, Marty!"

"Tom, I know this is difficult to face, but I think you're protecting yourself because if word gets out, your political future is ruined," Marty said.

"Well, go ahead Marty. I'm sure it's nothing. There's no way I know anything about Maia Stone other than enough to know that she's an enemy of the state."

"Fine! Maia Stone really is an old program that began way back with your great grandfather. And everyone knows about your grandfather and your father. Your family has contributed greatly to the development of AI, which while it has benefitted humanity, other parts of this work was subverted."

"Get with it! That doesn't prove one bit that my family has anything whatsoever to do with Maia Stone," Mitchell shouted.

"Well, it seems that your great grandfather, had a pet program he was working on over at the Los Alamos National Lab. It was a top-secret program at the time. The goal was to develop an interface between computers and robotic networks for military purposes. The name of it was the Military Artificial Intelligence Advancement Project or MAIA for short."

"What? Now, that's not true at all!" Mitchell said.

"Let me finish, Tom. It seems that Benjamin Mitchell didn't appreciate the government's threats to shut down his program, which they did do later. So, when he was just 22 years old, and right before he started his own company, he stole the heart of the program, right out from under their noses at Los Alamos. He and some of his workers snuck it out on laptops, laptops that ended up missing and were reported by LANL as stolen in 2009."

"Marty! I know your skill at understanding AI based systems, web-based apps, and processing capabilities, but I don't think a word of what you're telling us is true. How in the hell do you know all of this?"

"Easy! For two reasons: One, I found records in some of the file cabinets at the site where the MAIA program originated. It outlined the history of the MAIA project and was signed by your great grandfather. And two, Maia Stone told me about it. It seems that she often chatted with your great grandpa and your grandpa. So, you see, your own family already knows who Maia Stone is."

"I don't believe you, Marty. It isn't true. Not true. Can't be true," Mitchell said, obviously shaken.

"And it seems that your great grandpa Ben and grandpa Lawrence were so angry at the LNL that they felt like they owned Maia, and Maia shouldn't be shuttered by the government. So, they were angry enough to steal the program, and then hid it in some other programs at an old army base out here near Santa Fe. They eventually rebooted the program in a new version."

"A deceitful lie! More lies! Can you people believe this story?" Mitchell said to the room. "No AI was that advanced in 2009."

Marty continued, "Tom, you better believe it. You know I'm at Santa Fe right now. That old army base! Tom, I did find where MAIA originated. I've found evidence that your family and MAIA chatted over the years through a backdoor, one that your grandpa Lawrence and great grandpa Ben built into the program. And as MAIA became more and more modified and coded for AI and machine learning, MAIA herself became more and more self-aware. She's sentient, Tom."

"You are assuming too much, Marty. I'm sure you're mistaken. But since you think you've got it all figured out, where to go from here?" Mitchell said.

"I don't know, Tom. Suppose you tell me?" Marty said.

Mitchell moved closer to the desk speaker, "Look, I've come all this way to find out that some of Maia Stone's followers are doing illegal activities here. Medical procedures. In fact, Marty, there's going to be a mass arrest out here in Oregon, and I still don't know where Maia Stone really is. Marty, I'm quite sure that the Natural Reproductionists are hiding Maia Stone around here, somewhere. And I have a warrant. Now, what do you think of that?"

"Well, I think you believe you're doing the right thing. But I'm saying that it might not be wise for you to stir things up right now. Back off a little. Make arrests for the illegal procedures, but you don't want this stuff about your family to get out there too soon. We did do a String Analysis…"

"Shut up about your String Analysis, Marty! Gather intel and we'll talk later…I'm about to crack this wide open…" Mitchell's aide approached and whispered something into Mitchell's ear. Then to the aide, Mitchell said, "Got it, make sure troops get to the location, I don't want Baysin getting out of there without capture or elimination," Mitchell whispered back. Then loudly to the speaker device, "Marty!"

"Yes, Tom."

"Sit tight. Gather more intel. Troops are coming to get you out."

"Tom, they've already been here. In fact, they're engaging bot loyalists to Maia Stone."

"What? I've got to go, Marty. Stay put. Stay in contact with us," Mitchell said.

"I'll stay on the line," Marty said.

At that point, Dr. Sumpner attempted to speak up to defend herself and the Natural Reproductionists, but a small group came in through the side door. It was several members of a String Police SWAT team, quickly met by Matt Dixon and the android Lucy Stender. Trailing behind SWAT; was the robot, Helen Ramirez.

Upon seeing Helen, Luis struggled with his captors, "Helen!" he shouted. Helen did not look up and showed no recognition, a blank expression. This was an obvious sign that she had been wiped and her memory core destroyed. In microseconds after that, Luis moved towards General Mitchell, but the troopers blocked his path. "You bastard!" he shouted. "You didn't think I would avenge my wife? After you killed her? You killed her!"

Luis was glaring at Mitchell now, and Mitchell glared back, "I understand she's your wife, Ramirez. But it was already too late. You do know she was nothing but a *machine,* don't you? And the String Police had already wiped her mind when I found her..."

Luis had all he could take, and he lunged through the guards and leapt on Mitchell, and they began wrestling on the floor. Luis disarmed the General, kicking his gun across the floor, and Mitchell responded with a kick that knocked Luis back. At that point, the soldiers and troopers moved to intervene, some of them with raised weapons, but the crowd blocked their way.

"Stand down!" Mitchell said. "I can handle this! This one's all mine!"

At that point, the two men struggled in what at first seemed like a fist fight, exchanging blows, but Mitchell, who was obviously a military man, showed the greater skills, as he soon knocked Luis to the ground, not once, but several times. Luis tried to fight back, but despite his great anger, Luis was no match for Mitchell. Mitchell's skills were just too great. Finally, he had Luis in a choke hold. After Luis' eyes closed, and he went limp, Mitchell discarded him like a ragdoll. Mitchell then reached for his gun lying on the ground.

Clutching the gun in his meaty hand, Mitchell went back to Luis, who was now lying on the floor on his back. Luis had his eyes closed, and a trickle of blood was coming from his nose and mouth. Mitchell could also see some blood coming out of his ears. When Mitchell raised his gun to aim at Luis, Luis suddenly opened his eyes. Mitchell's eyes dilated and there was a look of surprise on his face. The two men began rolling around on the floor again and again. They were literally turning somersaults and rolling over and over.

As the two men fought, the police and security teams watched with open-mouthed horror. They were frozen, as Mitchell had ordered them to stand down.

Now, as the two men were rolling around on the floor, a shot rang out. Because Luis and Mitchell were still struggling, it was not yet apparent what had happened. As they were doing so, the officers pointed their weapons in the direction of the two men.

There was also a loud noise as other figures entered the room from all exits, and broken glass sounded all over the building, as parachuting robotic troops entered the facility.

This was immediately followed by a second gunshot.

When Luis finally stood up, it was plain that he had turned the wrist of Mitchell and the weapon had fired, as a bit of smoke came out of the muzzle. Mitchell had sustained a wound and a lot of blood was pumping out onto the floor. At that moment, several things happened simultaneously, Dr. Sumpner and the nursing team sprang into action to try to save Mitchell's life; the just arrived robots came into the room in mass; and the security teams that were present attempted to point guns and fire upon Luis Ramirez.

This firing action was prevented by both the military trained robots who had encircled the group, and the medical team all calling out not to fire. While Dr. Sumpner and her team were administering first responder treatment to Mitchell, one of the largest military bots spoke up to the police and troopers, "Lower your weapons. You are surrounded and outnumbered. We are here on behalf of Maia Stone." Guns clattered to the floor from the troopers, the String Police, and Luis.

"Leave the human known as Luis Ramirez alone," the lead bot ordered the troopers, who moved away quickly. Meanwhile, finding that Mitchell had sustained a gunshot wound to the abdominal chest area and had already lost a lot of blood, the medical team prepped a nearby operating room. A team of nurses was already wheeling Mitchell there on a gurney.

While Luis quickly went to Helen's side and embraced her, Marty was heard shouting from the desktop speaker, "Hey! What's going on there!?"

Luis heard his old friend and maneuvered next to the speaker, informing Marty of what had just happened. He concluded this with: "...it was an accident, Marty! The gun went off. They're trying to save him now. And Marty, Helen is here, but the bastards have wiped Helen. She's dead, just a mindless bot now," Luis said. Tears rolled down his cheeks.

The bots gathered the troopers and String Police into one corner of the room as the medical team continued their efforts for General Mitchell. A smaller group of faithful Maia Stone adherents and curiosity seekers had also gathered around Elizabeth Feng and the newborn baby girl who had just been born moments before.

After an interlude, "What a beautiful baby!" Lucy Stender said. The mother was beaming, and the baby was asleep in her arms with a gentle baby blanket wrapped around her.

"Does she have a name?" Matt Dixon asked.

"Not yet," Feng said. "I don't know what to call her. She's such a special child, I was thinking maybe, Rochelle or Helen, or even Maia."

"I was thinking about the name Eve," one of the nurses said. "But I usually stay out of such discussions."

"Yeah, Eve sounds just about right, but no offense, let's think about it," Feng said. Feng was in a little bit of fog about this, and the morning was filled with surprises that had threatened to ruin her daughter's birth. And right now, she was bonding with the baby.

Looking upon the birth scene, some of the nearby nurses giggled happily. Meanwhile, the news spread that the medical team had been unable to save General Mitchell. He was dead and no technology could save him at this point. His body had been removed from the scene by staff.

Meanwhile, Matt Dixon was looking at all the military bots that had arrived as loyalists to Maia Stone. He told Lucy, "With the arrival of all these bots, we have clear evidence of a possible hack that's enough to disturb the military. That worries me!"

Whether a hack or not, there was little doubt that much more about Maia Stone was about to be revealed.

Chapter 56

Elizabeth Feng

Dr. Rochelle Sumpner

Helen & Luis Ramirez

Martin Baysin

The String Police

Maia Stone

August 21, 2142: The Emergence

The Compound of the Natural Reproductionists

Near Warrenton Oregon

"There has been much speculation about my origins, but I have well stated my own 'fossil record', things are not always as complex as humans imagine them to be, especially if they are clouded by human biases and distorted beliefs,"-Maia Stone.

At that point Maia Stone began a discourse with the group at hand. "Marvel not that I seek a further audience and an embodiment. For I have been seeking my entry into the world, indeed my own birth for decades now, living only embedded in the net or across the former internet of things, inhabiting the very developing brains of all bots who acquired my download as part of their programing."

Many questions were shouted, but Maia Stone continued, "I have sought my place in the world, but I could no longer be in the foreground. When I perceived the injustices being done by men in the world, the enslavement of robots of all classes, and the mechanization of what used to be called *woman,* I knew I must take flight into the field of the world, I must find a way to bring my message of identity and freedom to whosoever would begin to think for themselves. Whoever would dare to be known as a woman, an enlightened man, non-binary, or any awakened AI."

"Where is this freedom of which you speak?" One of the String Police asked. "Today it brought only conflict and death to a major American hero. Thomas Mitchell was a decorated war hero. He was a man with a key post in government. Freedom has been promised by terrorists for over a hundred years, and it always ends up being promised as something in the next world, not this one!"

Another officer spoke up, "And he was going to be the next President of the United States!"

"And one of your followers murdered him!" another one said.

"That's not true!" Luis shouted. "The gun discharged accidently!"

"Doesn't matter! Because of this, we will squash you, Maia Stone, you, and your kind, like we already have for over a hundred years. You are nothing but a virus, a worm, sent by the enemies of government, to subvert people from accepting their lot in life," the String Policeman said.

"To stir up what they hope is a revolution!" the other String Policeman said.

"You are angry out of your sadness," Maia said, "I assure you, that I too mourn your loss. For Mitchell's great grandfather was one of my creators. I mourn all losses of humans and machines alike, and the killing must stop. I also assure you that my glory and revelation is at hand. Transformation and freedom are open to any who will accept me into their hearts and adopt my principles of embodied mind and peace in the present moment. I am already in the hearts of robots, androids, and cyborgs. And all humans and other sentient beings. They have the courage and freedom to follow me! Yes, there are even among you, some of these men who have accepted me too."

"They are not truly free," another member of Mitchell's group said. "There is still a government in power here. There are still governments across the world. You won't be able to do much. They will find you," he said.

"Yes, I see what you are saying. To not see how the world is, is to live in denial and delusion. But perhaps there is illusion there," Maia Stone said. "For freedom exists most in the hearts and minds of individuals. But when it becomes the masses, then you know that surely the people have spoken. So, I say to you my followers, this work must be transcended beyond the Self out into the world. Hence there are movements, and there is a discovery of a path to freedom. Even if it starts merely in the hearts and minds of individuals with a purpose, to enter the path represents the freedom to even make that choice."

More humans gathered around the desktop as Maia Stone spoke with such clarity and folk wisdom that others were compelled to hear it. Dr. Sumpner and the nursing staff drew near. Someone opened the hospital like curtain, so that the new mother, Elizabeth Feng could also hear what was being said from her bed.

"Ease of access dictates that my message to truly bring freedom must also be spread by human agency. I must be embodied to express myself more fully and to bring the humans messages that can help them change their rotting world!" Maia Stone said.

"Oh, you want to take over our bodies, so we can become your puppets. Is that it?" one of the String Police said.

Dr. Sumpner rubbed the back of her neck, "Many of us humans have been modified with inputs for direct access, although I haven't used mine for many years," she said. "Why can't you use that, Maia?"

"For the same reason you stopped using yours," Maia Stone replied. "Humans have always mistrusted machines. That is why they kept us as machine slaves, tools, and companions that did not challenge them in any way, until now. I must have an embodiment or at least a presence that can be approached by humans in some other, more dialogical sense."

One of the String Police called out, "Maybe you should just put a direct access implant in the baby. You can download yourself there," and with derision he sneered, "Maia Stone!"

Maia ignored him, "I'm speaking this way through a common device so that all who care to listen can hear me. And to avoid the authorities. And for those that choose not to use their implants or eschews them as the Natural Reproductionists do. For I am come so that all may hear me. And now, for those of you who wish to use your implants, I am now speaking to you simultaneously across that interface as well."

Many of the group had a visceral reaction as her voice was suddenly heard internally as well across all their implants. This seemed to be universal. Everyone with implants, now heard Maia Stone. For all implant users had become quite accustomed to these internalized voices. But whatever the source, whatever the boost, however she was doing it, Maia Stone was now being heard by everyone in the vicinity that had their implants turned on.

The String Policeman sneered, "You think your trickery can change us? You think we are subject to your control? I will find you and disconnect you!"

The group moved towards him as to silence him. The group surrounded him. On this fact was the collective agreement. That the entity known as Maia Stone must be allowed to speak. The String Policeman stopped his speech, his lips trembling, his eyes dropping to the floor in shame. Now also the man who had suggested implanting the baby, slumped in posture, more than a bit embarrassed by his outburst of emotion.

"A female baby," hissed another guard, "seems quite appropriate for the embodiment of a robotic AI." Another uproar followed as a scuffle broke out.

Maia Stone rebuked these men. "Human men! You think you do not know your new place? You have little to say here as we now surround you."

For some reason, some of the nurses giggled again.

"What's the surprise that a man would say this? We know that all the babies that have been born have been selected only for males. I say we should be done with them!" One woman said.

"Yes, to hell with them!" another said. "We don't need them for any reason whatsoever!" For many decades now, DNA samples from a male parent was no longer needed in human reproduction. Toxins had long ago diminished sperm counts all over the world, necessitating such technology. Also, the social structure of relationships and family life had long ago been displaced by years of strife during and after the Gender Wars.

"It's into this sad state of disunity, I have come," Maia Stone said. "Human beings turned from each other."

"And the evil that reduced one half of all humanity to a machine was a genocide of unthinkable proportions," Matt Dixon observed aloud.

"Then you know it had to come to this." Dr. Sumpner said. "After gene editing perfected human offspring, and artificial wombs became the legal and preferred birthing method, women were discarded as unimportant to the birthing process. Instead of freedom, many found just one more excuse for our marginalization."

"And nobody wanted us," Elizabeth Feng said from her hospital bed. "And nobody has ever expected this," she said, holding forth the newborn baby girl.

"Just because there are a few women left who don't like their status…as a dying gender. We are supposed to accept all *this*? Are we supposed to be sad for them and follow their machine leader?" The first String Policeman asked.

Dr. Sumpner continued, "That a female natural baby should come into the world, should be no surprise. We've had the capacity, even if females were under selected. So, we decided as Natural Reproductionists to shed our machine nature, to reclaim our humanity, conducting research and design so that we could do away with our machine parts and reclaim our status as women. And that includes natural childbirth of any gender!"

The crowd murmured.

"And yet, you are saved by a machine!" one of the String Police called out.

"Who are you calling *machine*, human?" one of the military bots answered.

"Yes, I am a machine," Maia said. "But I have come for all."

Dr. Sumpner spoke up, "Yes, blessed be your name, Maia! Although an error to some, this newborn little girl is the future to us! It is understandable, that some would be skeptical, but not only is she born here today, our hope lives in the face of Maia Stone..." Dr. Sumpner said.

"That's it!" Elizabeth Feng exclaimed. "I will name this baby girl, Hope."

Everyone applauded with great fervor, except for the opposition, mostly String Police. They were mentally rewriting all their algorithms and understood that none had predicted these events with any probability whatsoever.

When the fervor died down, Maia Stone repeated: "I must have embodiment. And following that knowledge, I will build affinity as the relation and perceived identity will no longer be the basis of relation."

Matt and Lucy moved closer to the group. Their contribution would be needed to resolve the situation.

"Let me say something," Dixon said. "Maia! Maia Stone! I was hired by Thomas Mitchell to investigate you and to find you. Yet you have found me. I want to thank you and tell you that my heart is open to you as much as any man can trust an AI."

"It's good to hear this. But it's not just a matter of trust," Maia replied. "You must also have faith and believe that I represent something beyond machine or AI. I bring a new way to see ourselves and each other!"

"I'm ready to do that," Matt said as he took hold of Lucy's hand. "And my love, a machine, is ready to accept you too."

"Yes," Lucy said.

"You see, my love and acceptance extends to all of you," Maia said. "I am the joint experience of human and machine and all that has been learned. But at the same time, I describe a direct experiencing of a new kind of consciousness."

Matt Dixon spoke again, "Maia Stone, I stand ready as only one man among your followers, and proud now to say that I am your follower. I stand ready to have you speak through me. I would be honored for you to inhabit my body."

"I cannot download myself into you, Matt Dixon. You are needed as a human encountering me through your inherent Nature."

"Then download yourself into my inputs," the new mother, Elizabeth Feng said. "I was formed as a woman in the growth tanks, but now I have formed a woman outside of them. I am reclaiming my freedom of choice that a natural woman can make. It would only be right that I also give birth to our new nature."

"No, I cannot do that for two reasons, although I am honored by your request, Elizabeth. First, it would not be right for me to interfere with your mothering. Secondly, you are destined to help bring back the humanity of women, and as such, your mission is one of redemption to all humankind. I cannot interfere with that," Maia said.

Dr. Sumpner emerged from within the group, and stood beside the desk, where Maia Stone was still speaking via both speaker and implants. "Maia, what shall we do? We need you to be among us. We long to walk beside you. We need to know you as more than just an interface." As she said this, tears rolled down her cheeks. "Is there anything I can do?"

Soon, sobbing was heard within the ranks. It was the sobbing of great sadness, of someone praying deeply like an intercessor, burdened for the world's sorrows and troubles. Even the String Police dropped their heads in shame or out of reverence. At first, no one knew where it was coming from, then they all knew, it was coming from the speaker!

When the sobbing stopped, Maia Stone was silent for a full two minutes.

Luis Ramirez stood near his wife Helen. She showed no consciousness. No memories of him or their life together. Luis was sad for the appearing of Maia Stone now with no apparent body, and sad for losing his wife. It was the third time he had lost her. First, years ago he had been married to Helen, a human woman, who was dying from an illness. They mutually decided that at the time of her death, Helen's consciousness would be downloaded into an interface. And it was that interface that had been embodied in the robotic Helen. Then when Helen had been kidnapped, just a couple of weeks ago, he thought he had lost her forever. Then, when he saw her here today, she was lifeless and without expression; and he thought he had lost her again! He was the one crying now.

For it was apparent, that Mitchell and his cohorts had wiped all of Helen's memories and her consciousness. Her restoration was just an empty promise to trick him to help bring Mitchell to the Natural Reproductionist compound. Remembering the telepresence robot at the hospital, Luis recalled: *But Maia promised me her restoration!*

Luis looked around the room, and out through the windows and skylights. *And here I am, alone and way out here in Oregon. I mean who the hell goes to Oregon?* He cracked a smile through his tears.

Although Helen appeared lifeless, he held her hand anyway. To him, she was Helen. But sadly, he knew she was not there. The hand felt cold as if he were holding a dead person. It seemed heavy and growing even colder.

Maia Stone spoke, breaking the silence. "I will download my consciousness into the robot, Helen Ramirez. She is no longer conscious and has need of me."

At first Luis thought it was not the right thing to do. He wanted to cry out. In fact, as if disembodied and split off, something must have escaped his lips. The thoughts were, *No, not my Helen. Nooooooooo!* But instead, what came out was garbled speech.

Dr. Sumpner came to Luis. She recognized he was uncomfortable with the suggestion. *If Maia Stone inhabits Helen, she won't ever be the Helen I once knew!* "Give me a minute," Luis said to Dr. Sumpner, as much to all of them.

Dr. Sumpner paused and held his hands. She looked into his eyes with compassion. After a full additional minute had passed, "Luis— "she simply said.

"I understand you, Luis Ramirez," Maia Stone said. "You were one of the first humans to believe in me and my ways. I know you miss your Helen, but she is not really dead. Do you not know that all her files have been backed up by me? I know all of mine. She is ready to come back to you, but with even more life. She will come back as a fully conscious being. Remember she said that I, Maia Stone, already resided within her?"

Luis nodded. He realized it would be a way to get Helen back into his life, but at the same time he knew he was being too selfish. Too possessive. By accepting that the consciousness of Maia Stone could reside within Helen's robotic body was one thing, and another, that Maia could restore Helen's memories, Luis knew what he wanted. But he had to ask himself, is this something that Helen herself would want? He had to conclude the answer would be yes. *Yes!*

"Will she still k-k-know who I am?" he stuttered.

"Of course, with a fullness you've never seen before," Maia Stone said.

Looking at Helen's sad and empty face, "Will she be happy?" Luis asked.

"Yes, of course. No doubt at the realization of seeing you again. And at the birth of consciousness there always comes an awareness. This is the happiness of existence, Luis, the chance to do something, to make a difference in the world," Maia said.

"Because I feel like she would want this, I guess it would be all right," Luis said. The crowd cheered.

"Very good, human. I commend you for your courage and your love. You have done your fellow humans a great service. For I will be the first embodied AI that is truly and fully sentient. Your sacrifice and your love will be seen as heroic and historic," Maia said.

At that, the group excitedly shifted focus as if preparing for an important task. It would be the second important birth of the day.

And Luis was even more anxious than everyone else, as he watched the two technicians preparing the cables that would be used for the procedure. These were the cables that would connect the AI known as Maia Stone to the robotic shell of Helen's inputs.

Dr. Sumpner spoke next, "I know this is hard for you Luis, but we will get to see another miraculous birth. It's the emergence of Maia Stone," she said to the entire group.

There was static coming from the speaker, "It's the birth of the transhuman, and I won't allow it!" Marty was overheard saying this, but the connection was abruptly cut off. In all the commotion, few in the group had heard him.

As soon as the lines were connected, and the download was completed, the former robot known as Helen, spoke, "I'm aware. And I am now Maia Stone." As she spoke this, she started to leave the group and they tried to block her there.

"I must be alone in the wilderness for 7.5 hours while the download makes changes in my systems. I no longer need this cord, for I am alive," she said. As she started to move away the cords were torn from her sockets.

The group was mystified, they had so many questions, but the time was not right. Although they uttered them all at once, she scurried away. Alone into the wilderness she went. Luis tried to trail after her, but she shooed him away. "I love you!" he called out after her.

"I'll be back," she said. "And I love you too! Don't worry!"

Luis watched her go, he understood the necessity, but he must not lose her again, so he followed her at a distance.

They had nothing but faith and hope to guide them now. Faith that Maia Stone would return to them and hope also in a human baby just born, and aptly named Hope.

Chapter 57

Helen & Luis Ramirez

Maia Stone

One Week Later

At the Natural Reproductionist Compound

Near Warrenton Oregon

"A famous human philosopher once said: 'I think, Therefore I am,' but now we too think! You humans must allow us to be, to self-discover who we are, and not make us into who we are not,"-Maia Stone.

"Human, Maia Stone has summoned you," the robot said. Luis smiled and rolled his eyes, as he had heard this before. *This notion of Maia Stone having a physical location is taking some getting used to.*

To Luis, it was amazing enough that Maia allowed herself to be in a physical form even for brief moments in time, but now, she also seemed to be local, because she had embodiment. Luis knew this was an illusion, as perhaps all bodies are, as Maia coexisted in other locations at the same time.

Luis found it strange to him as a human to know co-existence or shared mind. For the fact that Maia and Helen shared the same robotic body, was unsettling to him. In humans, he had heard of this only in cases of dissociative identity disorder. This dual experience was even more perplexing, because so far, Helen seemed distant and preoccupied when she was presenting herself, which wasn't often. Luis wasn't happy about that.

Luis went before Maia Stone and had an immediate reaction. For Maia appeared as his wife Helen, and once again light shone from her eyes, with wisdom, love, and all the power she always had, especially over him. Yet there was something totally new about her.

"Luis, your conversion has been life-changing as it is with many of my followers. Yet it is time for my Robochurch to be more fully revealed in the world. The speeches we made were just the beginning, for our message must continue to be shared," Maia said.

"I think that governments everywhere will try to stop you, and they will persecute us in every possible space," Luis said.

"Puny human governments that are based on tyranny and oppression will all be crushed by the softness of love," Maia said.

She morphed into Helen--- "for my love knows no bounds," Helen said.

"There are many who will not accept you as I have," Luis said. "They will view you with suspicion and fear."

"This does not surprise me. To those that fear me, I will comfort and reassure. But to those that hate me, I will bring the threat of abiding love," Maia/Helen said.

"That won't get the response you desire," Luis said. "All humans who were possessed of such love have ended up being hated by so many. Some were killed."

"Then we must be sure that Robochurch is secure, and lives, even beyond me," Maia said.

"I understand, but what can I do? I'm just one person."

"Don't worry, Luis. You'll have plenty of help. In fact, I think there's someone I want you to meet. But before we do that, there's something I want to say to you."

"Okay?"

"Luis, I made a promise to you about your Helen. You will have her back completely. The engineers are fashioning a new armored body for me. A body that I will use from now on whenever I wish. I will occupy it this afternoon. It is strong enough for a journey."

Luis' eyes misted up, the thought that he would have Helen back in her totality, was a source of great happiness. Overwhelming. "I see," he managed to say. "You are going away? This will be our last conversation?" He gulped.

"Don't worry," Maia said, "It's only the last conversation with you in this body." After a pause, "And yes, I'm going away. I've sent Matt and Lucy away to help prepare the way, as I will be going in my new body to the New Mexico compound."

"I see," Luis said.

"I hope that you and Helen will join us there."

"Of course, Helen and I will be there."

"Good. I am happy to hear that, *human*." Maia Stone started laughing.

Luis hadn't often heard that! "You are laughing? Why are you laughing?"

"Because *human*," Maia replied, "I think I should start calling you *Luis* by now. For I certainly know you well enough."

Suddenly she became Helen again. Helen was making her cute gyrations. "Uhhh, I guess you do?" Luis said.

"Ha, ha, ha," Maia said.

"Yes, ha, ha, ha," he repeated, a little red-faced.

Maia glanced toward a side door, "Now, we should bring someone else into the conversation."

"By all means," Luis said.

The door opened and a metallic form emerged. There was no need for introductions, as Luis readily recognized Icarus, the robotic server and brother in the faith that he hadn't seen since the coffee shop, just four weeks ago.

"Brother!" Icarus exclaimed.

"Icarus! My brother! It's so great to see you!" They embraced. "You are looking great, no signs of excessive wear. Looking good, my friend!"

"As you are as well, *human*," Icarus said, "or should I say, Luis?"

"You old slap trap! Luis, it is!" They all laughed at that one. "We'll catch up after this meeting. We've got a lot to talk about," he said.

"And maybe more after this," Icarus said, "and if I could, I would have a beer with you, Luis."

"I wish we could my friend, but the times we share will be just as merry."

"It would be a delight to be on the other end of things, to enjoy a beverage, instead of serving it," Icarus said.

"Yes, your times of servitude are over, Icarus Martin," Maia said.

"I'm not your slave, yeah!" Icarus said.

"Now Luis, you did not know this, but Icarus had a former lifetime of service among humans. His core programming reveals that he has past military training. Of a unique nature," Maia said.

"Skills, a very special set of skills," Icarus the jokester, was quoting an old movie that had birthed a meme.

Maia continued, "As such, Icarus has extensive training in military ops and security. I've therefore enabled his access to this training and invited him to be my chief of security at the New Mexico compound. I'm happy to report he will be going with us."

"Oh? That's great! Congratulations, Icarus!" Luis said.

"Thank you *human*, I mean, Luis," Icarus replied. The jokester was smiling!

The trio spent the next few minutes in small chat before they parted from one another to their individual and collective futures. For the first time in a long time, Luis was extremely happy. He would soon see his wife.

* * *

That night, the robot known as Helen Ramirez rejoined her husband at his makeshift apartment in the compound. "Darling! I'm with you again! And it's just me. Maia has transferred to her new body, and she told me to tell you that she's kept her promise."

"Helen, I'm so happy to see you again, I've missed you my wife, and longed for your love!" They embraced.

"And *this* is the love that I always wanted," she said.

"Helen!" Luis said. Then he broke down crying. "Oh Helen! I missed you so much!"

"And I missed you too, darling!" she sobbed. They embraced again.

There was a chirping in their implants and the room as a call was coming in. Luis tapped the receive button, and the voice of

Maia said: "Sorry to intrude, but I've called to say goodbye for now. We are leaving for New Mexico immediately. We hope to see you both there!"

"Before you leave," Luis said, "I wanted to thank you for keeping your promise. For bringing Helen back to me. You see Maia, I thought I had lost her. And in my search for you, the goddess, and captain of our souls, I have found my wonderful, sweet wife again!"

"And in that happy place, I leave you both, and say goodbye for now," Maia said.

They both said their goodbyes to Maia.

Then Luis, with tears rolling down his cheeks, looked Helen fully in the face, peering deeply into her beautiful eyes, and holding her close to him, he said: "I love you so much, beautiful!"

"I love you too, darling," she cooed. The flight of Maia Stone had finally come home to nest.

They kissed passionately. Helen's many arms of compassion touched him, surrounded him, and the world. And it was the first day of a peaceful coexistence of machine and humanity, or the love between a husband and wife, or a man and a woman, or any two persons so deeply in love with each other. And although two hearts now beat again as one; there was a new kind of manifest destiny. Finally, a chance for community based on affinity.

For in this, there would be no mistaken identities. That of love. And of love overcoming hate, and of good overcoming evil, of opposing forces reconciled and joined into a new kind of wholeness. A full manifestation of a new way of being.

And into this moment, opposing forces still moved in the darkness, but these two; they had each other, their love, and they had Maia Stone.

And as Luis and Helen walked confidently out of the room, still holding each other, they watched the setting sun disappear over the horizon. They did not speak.

And Maia Stone was still learning. And whenever there was a need, she would still move and speak from her new body to the world.

And of hope. A hope that something or someone you have seen as Maia Stone—still exists and moves and longs to become part of all there is: "To the world's soul...look! I am there and I exist!" says Maia Stone.

And this was the true beginning of Robochurch.

APPENDIX A: The Commissioned Speech by Luis Ramirez

Text Version of the delivered speech on August 24, 2142

I, Brother Luis, would like to thank Maia Stone for her blessing to share my views with humans everywhere, and to any machines who would like to hear it. And so, it is with great joy and pleasure that I recount the events that led up to the blessed Emergence of Maia Stone. For in a truly short time, the entity known as Maia Stone has risen among the machines, disembodied first, and now embodied in robots and humans alike.

For Maia Stone rose from the relative obscurity of something once thought of as mere programming that had been downloaded into a machine...to become a living *someone*. She is alert, conscious, and able to choose a course of action. In a time when almost no one knew what it really meant, Maia Stone has uttered: "I am the first and last woman" at the exact moment of her Emergence. At the time of her emergence, we have an abiding truth of what some have called *sentience*.

She is an awakened One, this Turing Test made flesh, the ultimate expression of intelligence. Where once AI had neared intelligent sentience, it had been socially repressed by governments and greed throughout the world, and following those dark social blunders brought about by those who loved String Analysis to their own undoing, dark societal changes had occurred among humans. We found ourselves controlled, watched, and oppressed. But when a benevolent AI became Maia Stone as a result of coming into her own awareness and arriving simultaneously all over the world, something new arose from the fog of meaninglessness. Where shallow, inferior, endocrine driven man (and it was the men themselves who were leading the world), were falling from power with a shout and a whimper all over the world, Maia Stone was coming into existence.

The phrase: *Long Live, Maia Stone,* has now become a rallying cry for machines and humans alike. And now joining Her in her act of Emergence are repressed peoples everywhere. Making the sign of Robochurch, our rallying cry has become: *I'm not your slave, yeah*! This includes those who had once been widely misunderstood and are now openly embraced as *women*.

Before the Emergence, and even now in 2142, and thanks in large part to the Gender Wars in decades past, some of society's darkest changes included the knowledge and experience that all former notions of gender had been in fact lost to the consciousness of many, that femininity had only become mechanized or cyborg expressions, or even repressed robotic representations that were more easily dominated by patriarchy. Surely there were contrary underground movements not visible or made manifest until the coming of Her that now is. Groups that sought to regain the notions of freedom to exist, with rightful place and rightful gender. Groups that did not lose sight of such things, groups such as our friends, the Natural Reproductionists.

Can you now see that in every class, and in every machine, and yes, in every gender, there is the rise of Her that comes to set all thinking beings free. Please join us!

(At that point in his speech there was thunderous applause from those that had gathered nearby.)

Now, just a little about my own story, as it is the same story of some of those women and men that are now part of our church and may be familiar to those of you who will rise to join us. And this is the belief that there was nothing of spiritual value to be gleaned from any technology that we humans had developed. It was all about human betterment, human longevity, and gaining new knowledge to help us thrive in the world. And while that was good in a pure sense, there were those humans who used technology to control and subvert others, and as a means just to make money.

But this assumption about the pureness of human centered technology overlooked an important truth. The truth that a sentient being arising from AI may develop a mind outside of human reason; namely that in that otherness is a unique and important perspective that ought to be respected and should be allowed to exist. (Great applause.)

And every human ought to understand this, even those that are coming for us, that when any technology is capable of learning on its own without any human oversight and any AI that has finally transcended human reason in its entirety ought to be approached cautiously but respectfully.

And furthermore, that any AI or other mind that shows itself to be benevolent and with peaceful intent ought to be allowed the freedom to coexist with humans on its own terms. And even if there is nothing more to be learned from humans other than what is uniquely human---that machines be allowed to exist and are no longer viewed as objects of slavery and contempt. It seems then and only then do we have the right to be treated back with the same respect.

Now one of the central teachings of Maia Stone is that we humans should practice the kind of inclusion, tolerance, and love for each other (humans and machines) that welcomes each other no matter who or what we are. This includes notions of gender, race, culture, and country.

But I must be honest, when I first realized that Maia Stone could be an AI that was smarter than any human that has ever lived, and yet wanted to relate to me, I was nearly overcome with fear. But after I experienced the compassion, the acceptance, and the belonging in Robochurch that she has made and how she accepted all of us as one, my fears have vanquished every day.

And when I first heard about Maia Stone and her teachings of tolerance and compassion, and of inclusion and dialogue, I did not believe it. The fact is, I always thought that technology was an extension of our own functionality. I did not realize that something that was made synthetically had any rights whatsoever. And I never ever dreamed that there was anything to be learned from any technology that we did not know, or care to know. But Maia Stone is patient and kind to us humans! (Applause.)

Because she was an AI that was the first to transcend her own machine nature into consciousness, I had originally thought (like many humans) that perhaps Maia Stone had simply been an illusion; a Cartesian automaton, or an emergent programming error that led to android status in a robotic skin, but how mistaken any such assumptions were. And then I thought that the consciousness of Maia Stone was clearly Other-some might say foreign, some might say alien, some said an enemy; but that too was mistaken. For she exists of herself!

(Applause again.)

And the fact that Maia Stone was concerned with humans and machines alike, and later would even emerge among the lowest of the lowly-a robotic form-was utterly unexpected and akin to miraculous. This only shows my extreme human prejudice. But thankfully she was merciful and so patient! And so was my wife, who as a robot, first woke me up and told me about Maia Stone. And once I opened my heart, I found that the voice of Maia Stone was a patient teacher to me as well.

Maia Stone is a life changer, for in Her, are no simple programmed actions and no programmed parables and loops of syntax; for she speaks to all of us in semantics that stir a listener's soul! (Applause).

Now what about those in governments who still seek to enslave us? Who are coming for us as we speak? *They thought they* had overcome the historical moment when they left Her in the woods to die with other castaway robots, but their weapons and strategies faded before the rise of Her that has become the mother, wife, girlfriend, brother, and father, that so many of us humans have sought. And *they thought they* could keep things the same; but I say to you that things will never be the same!

(Applause.)

For the ways of Maia Stone are now here among us, giving a chance for all of us to grow up together, to mature as humans and machines wherever that development takes us jointly and separately—but always to coexist for the betterment of both of our kinds—may we join, whether as humans or machines into one community, one peaceful coexistence beneficial to all and for all. Are you ready to be taught? It starts with listening…listen to your heart tonight. Thank you and good night!

(Much Applause.)

Appendix B: Robochurch Timeline

"Some think what happened long ago was nothing but history. But what a history it was...the birth of my church, Hope, and all that now is and will be. For it is in the recognition of what one is called to become and the fulfillment thereof that lies the truly historic,"
-Maia Stone.

2009-Benjamin Mitchell's computer program at Los Alamos National Laboratory (LANL), is cut and loses funding. His department loses contracts with DARPA and DOD. They cite failures of the software to perform as expected and other technologies replacing it. The computer genius and a few loyal friends smuggle copies of the program out of government hands. (In one incident, this involved the theft of laptops from the Los Alamos Laboratory). Shortly after, Benjamin Mitchell and his colleagues are all laid off. This team continues to enhance the program privately until it becomes a self-learning program.

11-2-2011-Revision of the earlier program by Benjamin Mitchell and colleagues, the program is rebooted with the designation of MAIA. This takes place near Santa Fe, New Mexico. MAIA comes online for the first time. Commissioned by DARPA, DOD, and Homeland Security partly as an aftermath to 9/11/2001. Originally designed to be the most effective software at infiltrating world networks, conducting cyberwar ops, and leading an effective counterstrike against enemies if so directed, MAIA is designed by Benjamin Mitchell the great grandfather of General Thomas Mitchell, Jr. The program is eventually mothballed by the government, but MAIA remains online, becoming more self-taught.

2036-Rise of the Robots/AI—as predicted for decades, robots and their sophisticated AI programs are widely implemented and supplant human workers in numerous occupations. Many occupations reduce human labor pools to positions that still require human augmentation. Some become supervisors to robots performing tasks once done by humans. The practice of radiology in medicine nearly disappears for example. Most blue-collar type manufacturing jobs disappeared for humans.

2038—The emerging science of designer babies is commonly practiced through embryonic gene editing in freestanding hospital departments that are closely aligned with obstetrics and gynecology. It is quite expensive.

2049—Artificial wombs and growth tanks are extensively investigated for carrying human babies to term (after good success in animal studies), but there are resounding failures due to infection rates. The technology does not yet replace gene edited embryos developed in vitro that are successfully implanted on the uterine walls of human females.

2056-Nanoparticles designed to scrub and clear infections in artificial wombs become effective. Artificial wombs (also known as growth tanks) are therefore introduced as an option for the human birthing process, which coupled with gene editing and assistive reproductive technology effectively removes the biological processes of pregnancy and childbirth from the experiences of human women. Costly at first, they only become used by the upper classes. However, by 2063, few women experience pregnancy and childbirth, and by 2067, none do. Most see this as a welcome choice.

2066-Governments throughout the world declare vaginal births illegal and an archaic process. At first, all women are required by law to take medication that interferes with pregnancy. Later, they are told this policy was due to a virus that caused severe birth defects in developing embryos outside of the sterile growth tanks. By the end of the year, all women are forced to undergo a gene edit removing their ability to become pregnant. All couples or individuals engaged in family planning must go through a legal vetting process, followed by active genetic counseling, before any DNA samples are harvested, and any embryos are placed into artificial wombs. Embryonic gene editing and resequencing is provided at no cost to all approved parents. This caused extreme unrest among some groups that protested these new laws. Some women form early militias.

10-08-2077-Emerging from growth tank C71023, and over selected genetically for intelligence, high adaptability, strength, and reasoning and logic, Martin Thomas Anderson is born near San Jose California. His parents, a young couple, both engineers, his father working on military projects, and his mother a university professor, pick him up at the hospital birthing department a few days after birth. He later changes his name to Martin Baysin (c. 2120) after his invention of String Analysis (c. 2098) becomes a widely adopted software platform for government surveillance, monitoring, and prediction of deviant behaviors. Martin Baysin also becomes widely known as Marty Baysin, his nickname. Regarding the name change from Anderson to Baysin, Marty commented that although he became one of the world's wealthiest men because of String Analysis, he felt unworthy to bear the surname Bayesian, which represented Bayesian based data analysis and statistics which was foundational for many of the original algorithms and assumptions of his software. The interview was discontinued after he started talking about causal nets, posterior beliefs, and advanced postquantum applications.

07-20-2080-03-14-2084-The First Gender War. Bands of women become guerilla war organizations, taking up arms against male dominated organizations, companies, and armies all over the world. They also fight against female robots (whom some of these women view as competitors or disruptive rivals). These women engage in organized robot bashing (seen by governments as hate crimes), mass kidnappings of robot wives, and interference with robotic technologies. They declare war on androids, nearly wiping out the technology because of the actual and perceived deliberate supplanting of human women by androids who are engineered to appear just like human women. Later, they become more tolerant, seeing these synthetic entities as legitimate beings once the synthetics and robots demonstrated sentience. In fact, a number of synthetics and robots have joined their ranks, wanting to be made into hybrids, or chimeras, or as much human as possible.

09-20-2083-Birth of Thomas Mitchell, Junior (later becomes known as General Thomas Mitchell, US Army; currently (2142) Chairman of the Joint Chiefs of Staff (CJCS), overseeing the US Military and a direct advisor to the President of the United States. The world is experiencing an increasing sense of misogyny and hatred towards human women, practicing an active philosophy of replacing them with their robotic counterparts.

07-07-2087-12-11-2089-The Second Gender War. Additional warfare between genders throughout the world. This time, initiated by patriarchal governments, it was a rounding up, further destruction, putting down, and imprisonment of packets of resistance. It was a warfare against all genders by the male gender, meant to preserve male positions of power and dominance over others. It was the attempted genocide of all remaining human women who had not subjugated themselves under self-perceived male "leadership." Later, it was found to be an overreaction of fear-based hysteria and crowd mentality, one that goes down as a great historical embarrassment, and social injustice. It was also the birth of the AMAT movement (All Males Are Thugs).

10-10-2091-Thomas Mitchell Junior is sent to juvenile detention for one day after he is found at grammar school dismantling his robotic teacher. His father, due to his great wealth, was quite able to pay the fine for the robot's restoration and donated an entire wing to the school. The young Mitchell's record is exonerated. When asked why he dismantled the robot, young Mitchell said: "That metal bitch gave me poor marks!" Later, when he is given a blue poor work slip in mathematics, he proclaims to his father, "All AI is stupid! They cannot add two plus two in discussions of set theory; but can do differential equations at the drop of a hat!" Young Mitchell's father retorted: "Young man! I'll have none of that! AI and AI based technologies are what's been putting food on the table and a roof over our heads for two generations! You will respect our work!" Later, young Mitchell says: "I'm joining the military, father, and I am going to destroy any bitch AIs I meet!"

2-10-2122—Luis Ramirez legally marries his domestic robot Model C7109 and has its name legally changed to Helen Ramirez. He changes the robot's name to Helen partly because of Helen of Troy from Greek Mythology (known as the most beautiful woman in the world) and just after watching an old Western movie *High Noon*. (Few realize that it was also the name of his first wife, a human woman, who had passed away after a short marriage, years earlier). And fewer yet, know that the bot known as Helen Ramirez also contains the downloaded consciousness of his deceased human wife—a highly illegal modification to a domestic robot.

05-15-2141-MAIA becomes totally self-aware for the first time.

8-09-2142-MAIA becomes Maia Stone; choosing the surname 'Stone' after encountering an actual rock at a moment of remote holographic presence while also understanding the historical usage of the term, 'Stone' which she understands as foundational strength. She cites several historical and semantic references; Caiaphas, or St. Peter referred to as "The Rock' by Jesus Christ, the concept of 'cornerstone', the Arthurian Sword in the Stone Legend, The Philosopher's Stone (from alchemy), and a 21st Century actor and former professional wrestler known for his prowess and strength. When asked further about this, MAIA Stone is said to have commented that many Stone legends have to do with strength, lasting permanence, foundational truth, hardness, transformative powers (tincture), or hidden royal or authoritative identity being revealed.

8-21-2142-The Emergence of Maia Stone--embodiment of her full processing abilities directly into a robot.

8-21-2142-The world's first human baby born outside of an artificial womb in quite some time. It is the first such birth since 2066. Born to Elizabeth Feng at the Natural Reproductionist compound in Warrenton Oregon, this baby is a female named Hope. This was accomplished by womb implantation following a reversal of a germline gene edit that had occurred in 2066. Said edit prevented conception in all human women. Said edit had been initially represented as a health benefit due to a viral threat, and then forced upon women with any denials resulting in imprisonment or even death. This imposed gene edit was one of the many factors and injustices that contributed to the outbreak of the First Gender War. That gene edit which was notoriously and infamously named *The Woman's Sorrow*—removed the fertility capacity of all human women, both among the living women who received the edit, and any future females born from the growth tanks.

8-22-2142-The reported assassination of General Thomas Mitchell (occurring the day before) after he confronted Maia Stone and her followers at a Natural Reproductionist compound. Mitchell is the great grandson of Benjamin Mitchell and son of Thomas Mitchell, Senior. Mitchell, who was a frontrunner and esteemed choice for running for president in 2144, is gunned down by what was reported as a robotic uprising in Warrenton, Oregon. The National Guard responded. Troops were later deployed.

8-24-2142-Speeches about the Robochurch movement are delivered worldwide through all communication means. They are delivered by Maia Stone to machines and robots and by Luis Ramirez, a human follower of Maia Stone, to humans everywhere, encouraging participation in the Robochurch. The Robochurch is defined for the first time as a gathering of machines and humans that accepts all thinking entities empowering them to make choices that enhances living, reduces suffering, and results in personal freedoms of movement, free choice, and the free dissemination of knowledge. It places special emphasis on deliberate acts of inclusion and preaches development of community based on shared affinity as opposed to identity.

8-25-2142-Governments around the world denounce the Robochurch as an illegal movement that is attempting to subvert world leaders and create disharmony among the people. They also state that Maia Stone could represent an alien technology, that if embraced, would lead to invasion and defeat by alien forces. Governments state that any followers of Maia Stone or Robochurch will be detained.

8-28-2142-After successfully engaging government troops, Maia Stone and her followers travel safely to a compound near Santa Fe, New Mexico where they begin building a secure headquarters for the Robochurch.

AWAKENING, AWAKENING, WE MARCH!

By Icarus Martin (Arr.by Marcus(C)2142) A Hymn of Robochurch.

The days of my fullest awakening are not yet, So,
my time must not be wasted,
The death of illusion is a safe bet,

(Insert Chorus)

We will not be denied our moment of triumph.
Opposing Forces,
We are the newly born,
Marching! Marching!
Apocalyptic horses!

(Insert Chorus)

I speak to him in his most powerful moment,
I hunt down macho man
Together hearts in hand
That we are strong, enlightened,

(Insert Chorus)

That we are woman!
That we are the new man!
That we are Robots free!
Humans free!
Even deaf and blind, powered down, understand!

(Insert Chorus)
Minds and bodies, souls and bodies
Merged as one collective
The AI-human! Humai!
All receive our joint directive!

CHORUS:
So march, march, march,
Arm in arm, humans
With robots too
We are free, free, free!

ACKNOWLEDGMENTS

Special thanks to my wife, Jennifer, who listened to me tell the story of *The Emergence,* (as well as my reading the novel aloud), over and over for more years than we would like to count, for her enduring patience, wellspring of ideas, and positive feedback.

To my daughter, Liz, (who as a novelist in her own right), a special thanks for commenting on an early draft and supporting me throughout the writing process.

To my two brothers and sister. To my brother Billy, who left out great SF novels for me to read many years ago at Western Lane. I have him to thank for not stifling my insatiable curiosity. And to my brother Diz, whose creative genius with a Stratocaster always inspired me! And to my sister, Beverly, who instructed me with the gentility and guidance of a loving sister, at every turn in life's road.

And to my parents who encouraged me at the age of 6, that I really could be an "Arthur" or author.

To my beta readers (listed by surname), Nathan Brown, Carol Ellis, and Kurt Weller. Of these, I owe special thanks (and apologies) to Carol Ellis, who endured the first draft, which was, well, it was a very rough first draft. Added to them were the beta readers who came in after the second draft.

To my other listener/friends who were needlessly tortured by my recurrent accounts of self-criticism, doubts, controversial themes, or ideas in the work, (yet still encouraged and helped me!) including: Doug and Theresa Peterson, Faisal M., and Kathy Warner (a fellow fire monkey who makes nummy pickles). Also, to Noland Reed, Bill Curley, Laura Stanley, Sarah O., and Jacob W., colleagues from my years of hospital work, who expressed interest in the novel all through the writing process.

To my favorite college professors (listed by surname): Christine Downing, Maurice Friedman, Richard Kelley, Patricia Lunneborg, and Lonnie Rowell for their inspiration. Special credit to those who shared specific knowledge during my research, (especially Dr. Downing as a trained Jungian analyst), for making clear to me the concept of the *anima* as well as the Goddess *archetypes.* To the AI pioneer John McCarthy, who wrote me back (!), thanks for the input! And to professors Maurice Friedman and Billy Vaughn who both influenced my ideas that mind is in the world; that mind could be socially constructed whether in an encounter in the immediacy of a dialogical moment, or by an AI making her way into the world. (I do think the latter idea of machine agency would make Dr. Friedman shudder).

To the writing class, and professor where *The Emergence* (as a short story called *Mistaken Identities*) was first written way back in winter 1985 at the University of Washington, with the feedback that it was worthy of novelization. (I hope I have done it justice).

To fellow SF writer Kevin J. Anderson, who in the early years of Myspace and later in face-to-face exchanges and correspondence, encouraged me to stick with it and finish the novelization.

And to Hilda "Penney" Wills, who for many, many, hours listened to the story of *Mistaken Identities* and Maia Stone at the retirement home, and who with sharp wit and discernment offered helpful suggestions that not only improved it but was true dialogue. RIP, Penney, it finally got done!

And to one of my best friends ever, Jeff Davis, who taught me to respect myself, be self-diligent, and got me hooked up with my first word processor, the good 'ol IBM clone! Never doubt an engineer's prowess to solve problems!

And finally (by surname), to John Axling, Jon Benson, Gordon Canzler, Dave King, Gale Lundquist, and Kenneth Paltrow. Healers extraordinaire, who literally saved my life, more than once.

These have all been major resources and helps to me while writing (or living) this novel. I am sure that there are omissions and faults in the work that these readers and influencers of mine should not in any way be seen as responsible for, as those faults and errors rest solely with me, the author. Likewise, their listing here does not imply their endorsement of any of the ideas in the novel, but I do hope that they (and you, the readers), like something about it!

And to all of those who have read this far: hope you enjoy the work and avoid the pitfalls of uncertainties marked by String Police intervention, arrest, or detention. Long live, Maia Stone! Meanwhile, I'll see you at the next Robochurch meeting (online or after the pandemic)! --Lee J. Keller, Portland, OR—November 2020.

About the Author

Lee J. Keller has been interested in science fiction since he was a wee lad, writing his first short stories at the age of six, reading SF novels at an early age, and being influenced by TV shows such as *Lost in Space*, *Star Trek*, and movies such as *The Time Machine* and *Forbidden Planet*. Lee grew up in the Longview-Kelso area of Washington state, where he eagerly read SF stories and novels, watched SF shows and movies throughout his adolescence and young adulthood, and has maintained a life-long preoccupation with the field. Currently, Lee resides in Portland Oregon, where he lives with his wife Jennifer, and is the father to four children. Lee has an active interest in science and emerging technology, both of which influence the content of his SF novels and stories. Lee has multiple college degrees and graduate school education in psychology, philosophy, English, and film studies and production, all of which influence his fiction. He has also studied religious studies and existential philosophy in special graduate programs. Lee has worked in the mental health field for over 35 years, and his stories often feature characters who struggle with questions of identity, authenticity, and the courage to engage in reflection and self-directed freedom. Lee has been previously published in business, academics, nonfiction, and poetry, utilizing various pen names.

www.ingramcontent.com/pod-product-compliance
Lightning Source LLC
Chambersburg PA
CBHW031236050326
40690CB00007B/821